T G Trouper lives with his wife in Essex, England. He has one son, who currently resides in America.

T G worked in live music production for many years, dealing with the technical requirements of some of the biggest artists in the world. Only after retiring to look after ailing parents did he find the time to take up writing, something he regrets not taking up sooner. He is also a singer and guitarist in a couple of bands.

With thanks to my wife, my good friend Gary and to Louise and Lucy.

T G Trouper

ASTRID-BOOK II

Good People do Bad Things

AUSTIN MACAULEY PUBLISHERS™

LONDON ★ CAMBRIDGE ★ NEW YORK ★ SHARJAH

A CIP catalogue record for this title is available from the British Library.

ISBN 9781528987080 (Paperback)
ISBN 9781528987097 (ePub e-book)

www.austinmacauley.com

First Published 2023
Austin Macauley Publishers Ltd®
1 Canada Square
Canary Wharf
London
E14 5AA

I wish to thank Austin Macauley for their faith in my work.

Prelude

"My granddad was a soldier."

The café was all but deserted; the young soldier sat staring into space, lost in his thoughts when the voice of the small child broke him out of his daydream. He turned to see a young girl, about eight years old, smiling up at him.

"What do you do in the army?" she asked, wide eyed.

He smiled down at her. "I shoot big guns; it's called art—"

"Artillery?" she interrupted.

"That's right, but how does a little girl like you know about artillery?" he said, raising the pitch of his voice slightly and exaggerating the intonation.

"My granddad told me."

"Was he in an artillery regiment?"

"No, he used to jump out of aeroplanes."

The girl's father appeared with a cup of coffee and a glass of orange juice and went to sit at another table. "Come on, let's sit over here and leave this young man to finish his coffee without you asking questions." He looked at the soldier. "She asks a lot of questions."

"I don't mind."

"But, Daddy, I want to know about the army."

"I really don't mind questions; children should be encouraged to ask questions." The soldier gestured to the seats opposite him. "You can sit here if you like."

The little girl eagerly shuffled along the bench seat and sat directly opposite the young man, while her father sat down beside her.

The soldier looked at the little girl. "So, your granddad jumped out of aeroplanes, did he?"

"Yes, he was a para shooter."

"You mean he was a paratrooper."

"Yes," she relied, an eager grin on her face.

The soldier turned to the father. "Was he your father?"

"Yes."

"Did you serve?"

"Sadly not, I wanted to, but failed the medical." He pointed to his chest and mouthed the words 'Bad heart, not good, it's serious'. He glanced down at his daughter who was transfixed, intently studying the camouflage pattern of the soldier's uniform. "She doesn't know".

The soldier nodded slightly, acknowledging the father's health issue, then turned to the little girl.

"My granddad got a medal. It's in a little box, it says…" She hesitated and looked up at her father. "What does it say, Daddy?"

"It says 'For Valour'." He turned to the soldier. "He was the first ever soldier to be presented with that medal by Grand Field Marshall Hallenberg," said the father, with unmistakeable pride.

The soldier's jaw dropped open a fraction. "Hold on. There have been very few 'For Valour' medals handed out. And you said your granddad was a paratrooper and received the medal from Hallenberg himself."

"Yes, but I didn't see that, it was before I was born. I've only seen photographs of him," said the little girl.

The soldier paused for a moment. "What is your name, little girl?"

"Brigit, Brigit Malaya."

"Was your granddad Sergeant Leon Malaya?"

"Yes," she said excitedly.

"How do you know his name?" said the father.

"Everyone knows about Sergeant Malaya and what he did to get that medal. I would love to meet him and shake his hand."

Brigit's face dropped and she looked sad. Her father put his arm around her and pulled her in close. "We lost him last year. Brigit got very upset; she spent a lot of time with him and it hit her hard."

"Daddy was in hospital for a long time and granddad took me out to the park when Mummy was at work. He always made me feel safe, and he taught me how to stand up to the big kids when they wouldn't let me play."

The young man thought for a moment, then smiled. "Well, as I can't shake his hand, I will do the next best thing and shake your hand, Brigit." He held out his hand and took Brigit's; it was tiny, and he felt a twinge of emotion as the soft warmth of the child's skin touched his.

"Now I can tell everyone that I have shaken the hand of Sergeant Leon Malaya's granddaughter."

Brigit's eyes opened even wider as her sadness dissolved.

"He never told us what he did to get the medal, though we always knew it had been something big," said Brigit's father. He stopped short. "Sorry, I'm being very rude, I haven't introduced myself, and father was always very keen on proper manners. My name is Alexander Malaya."

"Pleased to meet you, I'm Corporal Keefer." He held out his hand and shook Alexander's, then looked at Brigit. "And I can also tell everyone that I've shaken the hand of Sergeant Malaya's son."

Brigit fidgeted excitedly as she looked at her father then back at the corporal.

"The field reports from the day are part of a leadership training course. Do you want to know what he did?"

The father hesitated; Brigit looked up at him. "I want to know, Daddy."

The man smiled. "Okay, tell us."

The soldier shuffled in his seat for a moment, his face a mixture of amazement and admiration. "It was during the first war against the Northern Alliance, though they weren't called that then. It was just called the tribal war, a leader had emerged and managed to unite all of the northern tribes. A contingent of men was sent into the Vela Valley and were quickly surrounded. Your grandfather's parachute regiment was flown in to help them, but the map position was wrong, and they ended up deep in the tribal area. After the commanding officer was seriously wounded, your grandfather assumed command and led his men forward, reached the surrounded men, fought off a counter-attack, then carried the officer to safety. He ignored an order to stay put and went back and led all the men to safety."

While he had been talking, Brigit's eyes had grown ever wider.

"Your granddad was a very, very brave man, he saved a lot of lives and with the exception of the officer, none of his men got hurt."

He saw that Brigit had noticed a small scar on his face.

"Have you ever been hurt?" she said, slightly worried.

"Yes," he said solemnly, then paused and grinned. "But the other guy got hurt more."

Brigit beamed. "Why did you join the army?" she asked excitedly.

"To do what is right. To keep little girls like you safe, like your grandfather did when you were in the park. Sometimes there are bad people who want to take things that don't belong to them, and by having a strong army, they know they can't do it. Being strong keeps everyone safe."

11

"What are those two marks on your sleeve?"

"It's my mark of rank; I'm a corporal."

"My granddad was a sergeant, he had three marks on his sleeve. What did that mean?"

"It means that he was more important than me and I would have to do what he said."

"Why?"

"When you start in the army, you are a recruit and you have to do what anyone says. Then you become a private second class, then a private first class, but some regiments call them troopers, and you still have to do what anyone with a higher rank than you says. Then, if you are good, you get made a lance corporal, which is one mark. And if you continue to be good you get two marks, like me, and then you can tell troopers and lance corporals what to do."

"What do you have to do to be good?"

"When you are given an order, you have to carry it out straight away and do it right and you have to be able to make those ranks below you do it right as well."

The father looked down at Brigit and saw she was captivated by the young man. He gave an almost imperceptible nod to the soldier to carry on.

"Men like your granddad are so good at this that the men under their command do what they say because they want to, not because they have to."

Brigit turned to her father; her eyes wide open in wonderment. "Granddad was a good soldier, wasn't he, Daddy?"

"Yes, he was a very good soldier."

The father and the soldier looked at each other and both felt a little lump in their throats.

Brigit turned back to the soldier. "What is an officer?"

"Officers are very important men. They have to make a lot of very hard decisions and tell soldiers like me and your granddad where to go and when to fight. They are with you and if there's a problem, you have to go to them, and they tell you what to do."

"Granddad used to say that there were a lot of different sorts of officers, he said that some of them were idiots. What's an idiot, Daddy?"

"It's someone that's not very clever."

"Why are they in the army then?"

"I don't know, Brigit."

"Well, I think it's silly to have officers in the army that are idiots," said Brigit firmly.

The soldier coughed and felt himself blush. "Out of the mouths of babes…" he said quietly.

"How many different types of officer are there?"

"Do you want to know the full army rank structure?"

"Yes please," she said, as she fidgeted around in her seat, getting exited again.

"Well. In the army it goes recruit, private second class, trooper, lance corporal, corporal, sergeant—"

"Like Granddad," she interrupted.

"Yes, like your granddad. Then there's a sergeant major, then a warrant officer. Anyone can become any of these, but to be an officer, you need to have a good education." He glanced at the father. "Theoretically," he muttered. He turned back to Brigit. "Officer training is hard; it can make grown men cry."

"I never cry if things are hard. Granddad said that it's no good crying, you just have to grit your teeth and get on with it," said Brigit.

"She doesn't cry much, never has," said the father, the tone of his voice a mixture of pride and concern.

Nonplussed, the soldier didn't know how to respond, so decided to carry on with the rank structure. "For officers, it goes: second lieutenant, lieutenant, senior lieutenant, captain, major, lieutenant colonel, colonel. If you are good at following orders and giving them, you get all of these promotions, but to get any further and become a general, there is a really hard exam. Generals are very important, and their rank goes: general one star, general two star. General three star, then major general, and there's only one major general."

"A major general must be very important."

"Yes, they are. A major general can tell anybody what to do; they have to make a lot of very, very hard decisions. The only people who can tell them what to do are the army council and Grand Field Marshal Hallenberg."

"What's the army council?" said Brigit, transfixed by the young soldier.

"The army council is made up of five men, all of them having been major generals. They make the really big decisions and tell the major general what they want, and he has to work out how to do it."

"Who is Grand Field Marshall Hallenberg?"

"He's our leader, he decides everything that has to happen in the country."

"Is he a good man?"

After a slight pause, the soldier said, "Yes he is," but with slightly less enthusiasm in his voice as before. He looked at his watch. "I'm sorry, I have to go now."

"It's been great talking to you," said Alexander. "Hasn't it, Brigit?"

Brigit smiled even wider and nodded excitely.

"And thank you for telling us about my father."

All three got up to leave; Brigit skipped as they went to her car. Alex and the soldier chatted.

"She's a delightful little girl," said the soldier to Alex.

"How come you are so good with children?"

"I wanted to become a teacher, elementary school, you know, get them really young and put them on the right path."

"What stopped you?"

"There was an attack by the Northern Alliance on a bus full of school children. My sister and her kids were on it. They were unarmed, completely defenceless; the attack was so cowardly, and it made me want to join the army so maybe I could play my part to stop it from ever happening again."

"Were your sister and her kids all right?"

"Yes, but they were very lucky. They were at the back; the bus hit some sort of mine which blew the front off, then it was raked with machine gun fire." The soldier hung his head and sighed. "Other people weren't so lucky; fourteen dead and twenty-two severely injured."

"I remember that," said Alex.

"We never found out who did it though. We went after the tribes pretty hard after that – took out the leaders that we could identify. It slowed them down for a couple of years, but they regrouped eventually."

"But no more attacks on school busses."

"Fortunately."

The two men shook hands and went their separate ways.

****

Katriona Malaya bopped down in front of her daughter, straightening her tie.

"There, now don't you look smart in your new school uniform."

"I liked my old school uniform better," said Brigit.

"Yes, it was nice, but you can't wear that to your new school, can you?"

"Why do I have to go to this school now?"

"Sweety, we had to move because of your daddy's work." Katriona lied, the family needed to be nearer to the hospital that Alexander spent so much time at.

As a child, Alexander Malaya had contracted a streptococcal throat infection while his father was away on an extended tour of duty. That had developed into rheumatic fever, and one complication of the infection was that his heart valves were now slowly degenerating. The leftover effects of his body fighting the infection were now fighting his own tissues, with his autoimmune system seeing the cells in his heart tissue as pathogens.

A simple course of antibiotics could have prevented this, but his mother, Pachna Malaya, maybe through loneliness, or maybe through mental illness, had met, and was in thrall to a man in his late middle age, who called himself Brother Dagan Malin. He was a charismatic leader of a cult, though Brother Dagan always insisted that it was just a group of friends, nothing more. He preached a relentless gospel against medicine, convincing his followers, as they quickly became, that all doctors were frauds and all that was needed were his healing hands.

Years later, the reason for his hatred of the medical profession emerged. Brother Dagan Malin had been Doctor Stelin Malakin, and his license to practice medicine had been revoked when it was realised that he was performing unwarranted gynaecological examinations on fit and healthy young girls. His years of bitterness slowly morphed him into a semi-religious figure, attracting women whose husbands were away in the military. He revelled in their devotion to him, and none was more devoted than Pachna Malaya.

When the nine-year-old Alexander fell ill with a sore throat and fever, Pachna took him to Brother Dagan, who announced, "The child must stay in our meeting hall," which Pachna readily agreed to. Dagan also decreed that the pain and vomiting were good things. On day six of the infection, Dagan put his hand on Alexander's forehead and stated that the child would recover in three days.

Dagan had been a general practitioner for over twenty-five years and would have seen hundreds of streptococcal infections and would have been fully aware of the disease timeline. He used his knowledge to manipulate his followers, and in particular Pachna. After Alexander recovered, Dagan instructed everyone to call him Healer Dagan.

Alexander was in good health by the time his father came home, and his mother had forbidden him to say anything to his father about Dagan. The damage was only discovered on Alexander's fifteenth birthday when he tried to join the army and failed the medical. By the time he and his father had returned from the recruiting office, Pachna was missing but had left a note saying what had happened; Dagan was also missing. Alexander never saw his mother again. Leon divorced his wife after two years of desertion.

"But I don't know anybody here, I haven't got any friends."

"You'll make new friends, so don't worry about it."

A look of anxiety flashed across Brigit's face. "But I'll be the youngest in my year."

Alexander Malaya entered the room and smiled at his ten-year-old daughter. "Who's a big girl now, eh? Are you looking forward to your new school?"

"Not really, Daddy. I don't know anybody there."

"Have you thought about what we talked about the other day?"

"Yes Daddy."

"So, what do you want to do when you grow up?"

"I want to join the army."

Brigit's mother and father looked alarmed.

"Well, I suppose you could be and army nurse like my mummy was," said Katriona.

"No, Mummy, I want to be a soldier like Granddad was."

Katriona and Alexander looked at each other with slight worried looks on their faces. Her father bopped down. "Granddad fought in wars, and it's dangerous, plus, in wars you sometimes have to kill people; you don't want to do that, do you?"

"But Granddad always said that his time in the army were the best days of his life."

"It's not a life for girls, sweety," said her mother.

"Why not?"

"It's a hard life, and like Daddy said, it's dangerous, really dangerous."

"But it's what I want to do, I've made up my mind."

Alexander thought for a moment, then bopped down so he was at eye level with her; he took hold of her hands and smiled. "You can be whatever you want to be. We will always support you." He glanced up at Katriona, she nodded. He tapped Brigit on the head.

"What you have in here, your brain, that will get you to where you want to be. So use it." He took hold of her wrists and held her hands up, rolling her fingers to make fists. "And these, your fists, are for anyone who gets in your way – anyone. So use them."

In his youth, Alexander had been a fighter, but as his disease progressed and the hospital visits became more frequent, his ability to fight diminished. All of this was kept from Brigit and for her sake he maintained the tough guy attitude.

He turned serious. "You will have to fight for what you want, and fight those who want to stop you, so I'll give you the same advice that Granddad gave me. Don't start fights, but if anyone picks on you, you punch them on the nose as hard as you can. Then you punch them again, then you punch them again. Got that?"

"Yes, Daddy."

"Never let anyone see that you are afraid, and if you are ever surrounded by a gang, don't wait; see who the biggest one is, they're usually the leader, then hit them first, but look out for the little one behind you, they may have a weapon. Don't be afraid to take them out as well. Then go back to the biggest and hit them again, get them on the ground and make sure they don't get up again. I'll deal with any problems later."

He held up his hand, his palm facing her. "Now, show me the combination that Granddad taught you."

In just a couple of seconds, Brigit threw a right, left, right onto her father's hand. He was shocked at how fast she was, and how much it hurt, and he noticed the look of angry determination on her face. Granddad had taught her well; she had shifted her stance and put all of her weight behind every punch. He rubbed his hand and smiled. "Yeah, that should do the trick."

"Just remember what Daddy said, sweety. Don't start any fights," said Katriona slightly nervously.

Her father stood up and frowned. "You can do anything, Brigit, don't let anybody stop you from getting where you want to go or being what you want to be. Study hard, use your brain and learn all that you can. And always remember, you are a Malaya, we don't start fights, but we sure as hell finish them. And also, always remember that us Malayas don't take any shit from anybody."

"Language, Alex," snapped Katriona.

****

Brigit stood outside the school gate; a touch of anxiety fluttered in her stomach. She was starting halfway through the year; she would probably be the youngest in her year and she was from a different part of Correla. She knew that all of this would make her a target for someone. But she thought of her father's words as she pushed the gate open, and a smile broke on her face as she strode into the playground.

Slowly, children stopped playing and looked at her. She quickly scanned the faces that were staring at her.

How many of these will I have to put on the ground? she thought to herself as she held her head high.

****

"BRIGIT MALAYA!" shouted the art teacher. "Why have you drawn a tank? Why are you always drawing military things? Why can't you draw a flower like a normal girl?"

"Because I want to join the army, miss."

"Do you want to be an army nurse?"

"No, miss, I want to be a soldier."

"Oh, don't be so stupid. Girls don't become soldiers."

"But I want to be a soldier."

"Now, you listen to me," said the teacher, getting cross. "You are ten years old; no child knows what they want to do at that age."

"But that's what I want to do. I'm going to be a major general."

The teacher scoffed. "You really are a stupid, stupid little girl, aren't you?" She turned to face the class. "Did you hear that boys and girls? Malaya here says she is going to be a major general."

Some other children in the class started to snigger. Brigit turned and glared at them, then her father's words rang in her brain. *"You will have to fight for what you want…don't let anybody stop you from getting where you want to go or being what you want to be…"*

She turned back to the teacher. "I am not stupid, I am going to join the army, I am going to be a soldier, and one day I *am* going to be a major general."

"No, you're not," snarled the teacher.

"Yes, I am," snapped Brigit.

"How dare you talk to me like that? Get out of my class and go and see the headmaster."

****

"You again," said Mr Strafford, the headmaster. "Let me guess, this is about your idiotic notion that you can join the army as a soldier, and you've been disrespectful to one of the teachers when they pointed out that you were being stupid." He folded his arms and sat back in his chair, looking smug. "I'm right, aren't I?"

"I am going to join the army."

"I am going to join the army, what!" he said, frowning.

"I am going to join the army, sir."

"No, you are not, you silly little girl. But I have to give you some sort of punishment for your insolence, so you will do some research and provide me the names of all female combat soldiers that have ever been in the army."

"That is pointless, sir. There has never been a female combat soldier in the Correlan Army. I will be the first."

Strafford sighed. "Detention tonight. One hundred lines 'I am a stupid girl, and I will not join the army'. Now get out."

****

Brigit turned the corner to see Celine Novak and her gang at the other end of the corridor. She didn't hesitate and kept walking towards them. Celine stepped forward and blocked Brigit's path. Rather than trying to push past – because she knew that was what Celine wanted – she stopped, ignored the others in the gang and looked her in the eye.

"You're going to make me late for my lesson."

Celine scoffed. "That's the point." She looked around at her sycophantic mates, who sniggered.

Brigit glanced around at the other members of Celine's gang, there were four of them.

"I don't like you," sneered Celine.

"So what?"

19

"I said, I don't like you." Celine was slightly irritated that Brigit wasn't intimidated by her. "I don't like your hair."

"Again, so what?" said Brigit, fixing her gaze on Celine, who was not used to people defying her.

She glared at Brigit, then produced a pair of scissors from her pocket. "I'm gonna cut your hair."

Brigit stood her ground. "No, you're not." There was a pause, Brigit looked directly into Celine's eyes but could see in her peripheral vision that a couple of the gang had taken a small step backwards.

"The reason I said you are going to make me late for my lesson is this."

Brigit landed three heavy punches on Celine's face. Celine staggered backwards, then fell to the floor. Remembering her father's words, Brigit turned to see the smallest member of the gang moving to grab her. She didn't punch the young girl; a hard slap across the face was all that was needed.

"Back off," she shouted to the shocked gang, then turned and fell on Celine, landing two more punches while Celine cringed trying to protect herself.

She sat on Celine. "So, you were going to cut my hair, were you?" she said menacingly, as she picked up the scissors and waved them menacingly at Celine, whose eyes were open wide in fear.

"Were you going to cut it like this?" She grabbed a lock of Celine's hair and cut it off almost level with her scalp. Celine opened her mouth to cry out; Brigit shoved the lock of hair in it, then stood up while Celine coughed and spluttered trying to remove the strands.

"Stay away from me, Celine, or next time I will really hurt you."

She walked away, smiling to herself and looking at the slight redness of her knuckles. "It was good advice, Dad," she said to herself.

****

Brigit sat at the desk in the detention hall, calmly writing 'I am a bad pupil' over and over on a piece of paper. A teacher sat silently at one end of the hall marking some classwork; it was Miss Melnyk, young and new to the school and one of the few teachers that Brigit had any respect for.

"Finished, miss," said Brigit as she handed the paper to the teacher. "One hundred lines as required."

The teacher took the paper and counted the lines; there were one hundred, all neat and even. She sighed and looked at Brigit.

"Why did you do it, Brigit, why did you attack Celine Novak? I have spoken to her, she said you attacked her for no reason."

"She is a liar, miss."

"Her friends have corroborated her story."

"They are also liars."

The teacher sighed and softened her tone of voice. "Brigit, you must understand that we can't have physical violence in a school. Beating someone, it has no place here, and it achieves nothing."

"Celine is a bully, she got what she deserved."

Miss Melnyk said nothing, and Brigit knew that this meant that she agreed with her. The teacher handed back the paper.

"You must go to Headmaster Strafford's office now, he wants to speak to you."

****

Brigit stood in front of the headmaster's desk and handed him the lines. Strafford took the paper, didn't bother to read it, screwed it up and threw it in a bin.

"Remain standing," he snapped. "Your assault on Celine Novak is as unacceptable as it was unprovoked."

"It was not unprovoked, she—"

"Silence girl." Strafford shouted. "You speak when I tell you to and you will start your sentences with 'Sir'." He jabbed an angry finger at her. "Your attack *was* unprovoked," Strafford said firmly. "What do you say to that, girl?"

"Sir, she threatened to cut my hair."

"She did not."

"Yes sir, she did."

"I have spoken to witnesses, they say that you approached Celine, swore at her then attacked her for no reason."

"They are liars," she said, deliberately missing off the 'sir'.

He held up a letter and waved it angrily at her. "This is from Hiam Novak, Celine's father; it's from his lawyer. It is notice of intent to take legal action against the school. He will sue us, and he will certainly win." He put the letter down and glared at Brigit. "Celine's father is a very important man in this town."

"Is that why you suck up to him…sir."

"What! How dare you."

She glanced at a test paper on his desk; even upside down, it was obvious that it was Celine's and a 'D' had been rubbed out and a 'B+' written in. Strafford hurriedly covered the paper and scowled at her.

"Or does he pay you to change Celine's exam results…sir," she said defiantly.

"Your lack of respect will not go unpunished," snarled Strafford through anger and embarrassment. "I will deal with you tomorrow morning. Now get out."

****

Strafford stood on the stage in the school assembly hall. It was early in the school day and before any classes had started. All the pupils and teachers sat waiting for him to speak. Everyone was there, even the ancillary staff: cleaners, cooks, ground keepers; all were there. Strafford had decreed that all should be present. A few of the adults exchanged curious and worried looks, puzzled as they were at this unusual request. The pupils chatted quietly to each other.

Strafford eventually cleared his throat and the hall fell silent. "I want to speak to you all today about discipline and the importance of maintaining respect for authority." He cleared his throat again and took a sip of water. "In this world, there have to be rules and there has to be a chain of command, and that chain of command must be respected or anarchy will ensue. Figures of authority, whether they be elected or appointed, make decisions, and subordinates must abide by those decisions. And it is not for the subordinate to question those decisions."

A couple of the teachers exchanged looks of bewilderment; Strafford had never addressed the whole school in this manner before.

"For once the decisions are questioned by subordinates, or suggestions made by subordinates that contradict those orders, respect will be lost, discipline will be lost and then the whole system will start to break down."

He paused for effect.

"There is one pupil here who has shown a great deal of disrespect, both to a fellow pupil by attacking her and to me by being verbally disrespectful. That pupil is Brigit Malaya and now she will see that there are always consequences to every action."

He pointed directly at her. "Get up here now, girl."

Brigit stood up and calmly walked up the steps and onto the stage. She could see Celine in the front row, smirking.

"You are going to regret the way you spoke to me yesterday, girl," he said quietly, so that only she could hear. "Hold out your right hand."

Brigit knew what was coming, she fixed her gaze at him and held out her hand, turning it so her palm was facing up. Stafford picked up a cane, flexed it then turned to address the hall again.

"As I said before, there are always consequences to every action."

He turned to face Brigit, raised the cane high above his head then struck the palm of her hand with as much force as he could. Brigit cried out in pain and doubled over, holding her hand. There was an audible gasp from the teachers. She glanced at Celine and saw her laugh.

Strafford sneered at her. "Maybe you'll think twice next time you're disrespectful, now get off the stage."

Brigit stayed put, slowly straightened up, wiped the tears from her face, then slowly and deliberately held out her hand again. An excited murmur ran through the hall. Strafford glared at her, he said nothing and raised the cane again. Brigit cried out as the cane struck, and again she stayed where she was and held her hand out.

"How dare you challenge me," he said as he struck her again. Again, she cried out, again she held her hand out, again he struck her.

Miss Melnyk turned to one of the other teachers. "This is wrong."

Apart from her cries of pain, Brigit said nothing and just stared into Strafford's eyes.

The fourth strike had split the end of the cane, and the fifth strike cut Brigit's hand; a small pool of blood collected in her palm. There was a stunned gasp from the whole hall as the sixth strike sprayed blood up and onto his face, flecks landing on his glasses. He froze with the cane raised high above his head.

Miss Melnyk ran onto the stage. "Mr Strafford, that's enough," she shouted, and positioned herself between the headmaster and Brigit. "Mr Strafford, put the cane down." He seemed in shock and slowly lowered the cane to his side, his face blank and his mouth hanging open. She reached over and took the cane from him. "I think you should go now, Mr Strafford."

He turned to look at her. "What?" he said feebly.

"You should go now, just go."

He turned to face the hall and saw the shock on the faces of the pupils and the contempt on the faces of the teachers. Brigit looked at Celine, she was crying.

Brigit moved towards him, he looked down at her, a pathetic look on his face.

She looked up at him. "There are always consequences to every action. One day you'll be old…" She held up her hand, showing the cut and the blood. "…then I'll come for you and you will pay for this."

His shoulders dropped and he left the stage, walking slowly through the mass of pupils that parted as he made his way. He didn't look at them, just kept his eyes on the floor, but felt their visceral contempt and the disgust from the teachers.

The school nurse ran onto the stage and put a bandage on Brigit's hand, then lifted her arm above her head.

"Keep your hand above your head, let's get you to the medical room."

A couple of the cleaners went on stage and cleaned up the splashes of Brigit's blood as the nurse led her away.

****

Brigit winced as the nurse wiped the cut.

"I'm sorry, I know it stings but I must clean it."

Brigit nodded and gritted her teeth.

"Now it's clean, I can see that there's a sliver of cane in your hand; I have to get that out or it will become infected." The nurse took a pair of tweezers. She looked at Brigit.

"It's in quite deep. You're not going to like me after this; it's going to hurt a lot, I'm sorry."

Miss Melnyk moved close to Brigit, put her arm around her shoulder and held her hand.

"Just be quick," whispered Brigit.

She flinched as she felt the nurse get hold of the splinter, then cried out as the nurse pulled it from her hand. Miss Melnyk squeezed her hand tight and stroked her hair as Brigit's emotions finally took over and she started to cry.

The teacher looked at the nurse. "Do you think any bones are broken in Brigit's hand?"

The nurse gently moved Brigit's fingers up and down, making her gasp.

"No, I'm certain that there aren't any." She turned to Brigit. "Sorry again, but this is going to sting."

She picked up a bottle of antiseptic and tipped some directly onto the cut. Brigit closed her eyes tight and winced but didn't make a sound as the liquid did its job. Miss Melnyk wiped the tears from Brigit's face as the nurse bandaged her hand.

"Why did you do that, Brigit? Why did you hold out your hand so many times; he could have hurt you really badly."

"I wanted him to see that I was not afraid of him, or of anything he could do to me."

"Why? What purpose did that serve? You know, life isn't a game of chicken, Brigit. What you did was silly."

"When I join the army, I will not be able to show any fear."

"Oh Brigit, not that again. You are thirteen years old, no girl your age knows what they want to do when they grow up."

"I do."

"Look, soon you'll start getting interested in boys if you aren't already; eventually, you'll meet a boy and get married and have children."

"No, I'm not interested in boys," Brigit said firmly. "I'm going to join the army and become a soldier; I want to fight," she said with a determination beyond her years.

Miss Melnyk looked at Brigit for a while, wondering what she really meant when she said she wasn't interested in boys.

The nurse finished bandaging Brigit's hand. "I want you to come and see me this afternoon and then every morning and afternoon for the next week so I can change the bandage and check for infection. You can go now."

****

The next morning, Brigit was walking towards the medical room when she saw Celine at the end of the corridor; she was on her own. She kept walking and made no eye contact with her. As she got close, Celine stepped aside to let her pass. She had taken a few paces when Celine spoke.

"I'm sorry, Brigit."

Brigit stopped, paused and slowly turned to face her. Celine looked at the bandage on Brigit's hand; tears welled in her eyes. "I am so sorry, Brigit, what I did was wrong. Seeing you on the stage with Strafford made me realise what a coward I have been. I've changed, and I've told my father everything; he's not going to sue the school." She hung her head in shame, then looked back up, tears rolling down her face. "Please forgive me."

Brigit nodded slightly, accepting Celine's heartfelt apology, then turned and went to see the nurse.

****

One evening, Brigit was sitting alone on a bench in the school sports field, revising for an exam when Miss Melnyk approached and sat beside her.

"Brigit, are you really sure you want to join the army?"

"Yes, Miss Melnyk, it's all I've ever wanted to do."

"Right then. I've spoken to my cousin; he's a lieutenant in the army. He said that girls usually go into logistics or the army medical core. But I told him that you said that you want to be a combat soldier. He was surprised and didn't believe me at first, but I told him how determined you are. He said that girls are not conscripted and have to volunteer as a general recruit, but it was best for you not to do that as they'll stick you wherever they want. He said the best thing for you is to volunteer for an officer position, then you can choose a combat role. To do that though, you'll need a university degree; it doesn't matter what the subject is, but they do need a pass of at least a B1."

The teacher studied Brigit for a while, then reached into her bag for a packet of Cavana cigarettes and took two out. She lit one, took one drag then used it to light the other cigarette and handed the first one to Brigit. "I know you've started smoking; I can smell it on your clothes."

Brigit took the cigarette. "What course do you think I should do?" she said, as she blew out smoke.

"Correlan literature. It's a short course, only two and a half years, and to be completely honest, it's not very hard; study well and you'll easily get an A1. And if you want any help, you can always call me." She paused and looked at Brigit with an expression that the girl found hard to read. "I'll always help you, Brigit," she said softly, then took a deep drag on her cigarette and leant back casually on the arm of the bench. There was a moment of silence as she studied the young girl.

Brigit finished her cigarette, stubbed it out on the back of a metal ruler then put the butt in a tissue. She thought for a few moments. "I'll need an application form for university."

"I'll sort that out for you, there's plenty of time." She frowned a little and sat forward, moving closer to Brigit. "There is something that I've been meaning to talk to you about. Since the incident with Strafford, you've gained a lot of respect from pretty much all the girls in the school. And it has to be said that the school is a happier place now that he's left and his deputy, Miss Korhonen, has taken over, but you don't seem to have any friends. Why is that, Brigit?"

"I'm too busy, Miss Melnyk, I—"

"Call me Sophia," she interrupted.

"I know that I have to study hard…Sophia."

"The girls here all respect you – even Celine Novak speaks highly of you! Your class work is excellent; the teachers can't say enough good things about you. You play well in sports and are a good team player, but they say that away from team activities that you are a bit distant, a bit aloof. Is there a reason for that?"

"My dad always says that you have to work hard to get what you want and not let yourself get distracted. I study all the time, it's just my way."

"Are you sure that's the only reason, Brigit?"

The young girl looked at the teacher for a few moments. "Yes," she said unconvincingly.

Sophia leant forward and took hold of Brigit's hand. "I know what it's like to be different, Brigit. I know how it feels when you are not like other girls. If you are ever confused about anything, if there are aspects of your life that you are trying to understand, talk to me. I want to help you."

Brigit sat, unsure of what Sophia meant, and just nodded.

"If you are uncomfortable talking to me at school, you can call me, call me at any time, or you can come to my house. I don't normally do this, so it is best that others don't know, otherwise I'll be flooded with girls wanting advice."

Sophia took a piece of paper and wrote her phone number and address. She handed it to Brigit, then stood to leave. "You do understand though, that you should only call me Sophia when we are alone."

"I understand, Sophia."

Miss Melnyk walked away, leaving Brigit wondering what she meant and if she should ever go to Sophia's home, but deep down, something told her that she wanted to.

****

Brigit sat outside a coffee shop, textbook in one hand, pen in the other, scribbling notes in a workbook. Her head was down as she re-read a passage from a classic novel from the last century by a famous Correlan author.

"Brigit?" came a voice that sounded familiar. "Brigit Malaya, it is you?"

Brigit looked up to see a girl from her old school, someone she hadn't seen since she left.

"Leila Rhodes, oh you look fabulous. The two girls looked at each other for a moment. "Have you got time for a coffee?" said Brigit gesturing to a seat.

"I've always got time for a coffee, particularly with you," said Leila as she sat down opposite. A waiter came over and took an order for two cappuccinos.

"What are you up to?" said Brigit.

"Just been to the gym after work, and you?"

"Just doing a bit of homework, I'm at university now. I'm doing a course in Correlan literature, I should pass; God knows why I'm doing this course though, it's not going to help me at all, but it's dead easy and I need a degree if I'm going to sign up for officer training."

"So, you're still going into the army, wow."

"Yes, it's what I've always wanted to do."

"That got you into a lot of trouble at school, didn't it?"

"You could put it that way."

"Strafford was horrible to you, how's the hand? I was certain that he had broken your bones, the bastard."

"No broken bones, though I did think there were some at the time."

"You were so brave; I could see how much it hurt you, we all could."

"The cane had a little split in the end, it cut me quite deep and there's a little scar, look."

She held out her hand; Leila took it and studied the mark where the cane had struck, stroking Brigit's palm and holding on for maybe a little longer than was really necessary.

"Six times he hit me, and I think he knew he'd lost all respect from the teachers and the kids after number five."

"I heard he had a nervous breakdown, and rumour has it that he sweeps floors in a factory now."

There was a pause and Brigit looked into Leila's eyes. "I've got my own place now, it's not much, just the usual two-room student digs. Do you want to come back? I'll fix us something to eat."

"Yeah okay, that'll be cool."

"Well, when I say 'fix us something to eat' what I mean is I'll bung a ready-meal in the microwave. But I do have a bottle of red wine. It's a bit rough though."

"Is it alcoholic?"

"Yeah."

"That'll do," laughed Leila.

****

The two young women chatted over the crusty over-cooked lasagne, leaving the scalding crispy edges 'till last and eating the centre, which was only just hot enough. They finished eating, then emptied the last of the wine into their glasses, sat on a couch and carried on chatting. Eventually Leila looked at her watch.

"Oh my God, I'm going to miss the last bus home; well actually, I think I have."

"Well, why don't you stay the night then? The couch pulls out into a bed and I can find some blankets."

"I suppose I could do. Yeah, why not, thanks."

"I could do with some female company; I don't get to talk to many women."

"You were always really quiet at school; you didn't talk to many of the girls."

"You know, there was a reason for that." Brigit moved a little closer. "Look at me," she whispered, then as Leila turned to face her, she leant forward and kissed her on the lips.

Leila pulled back a fraction and looked quizzically at Brigit. "What did you do that for?"

"Because you're beautiful and because I wanted to." She suddenly sat back, and her face dropped. "Oh, I'm so sorry, I've offended you, haven't I?"

"No, I'm not offended at all, but if you're going to kiss me, kiss me like you mean it."

"Okay then." Brigit put her arms around Leila and held her tight, kissing Leila on the lips, but lingering this time. She heard Leila sigh, then pull away.

"That's not a kiss," laughed Leila. "This is a kiss." She took Brigit in her arms, laid her on her back then leant over her and kissed her passionately. She pulled back and looked deep into Brigit's eyes. "Have you ever done it with a girl?" she whispered.

"No."

"Do you want to?"

"Yeah, it's all I've ever wanted to do," replied Brigit breathlessly.

"Let's have a shower together, then I'll show you what you've been missing; are you ready for it?"

"I've always been ready."

"Okay pretty girl, prepare to have your world rocked."

****

Leila rolled onto her back, grabbed a towel and wiped the sweat from her brow.

"That was unbelievable," gasped Brigit still panting from her last orgasm. The two women lay side by side on Brigit's bed, both staring up at the ceiling.

Leila frowned. "Are you sure you've never had sex with a girl?"

"No, never."

"My God, what you did deserves a medal. My orgasm was so intense when I came, I thought I was going to faint."

"I had two orgasms," said Brigit proudly.

Leila laughed. "Yeah, I know, I heard."

Brigit blushed, then smirked.

Leila pulled back the covers and looked at Brigit's body. "Oh God, you're beautiful."

Brigit pulled the covers off Leila then propped herself up on one elbow and spent a few moments silently looking her up and down. "I have a confession to make," she said, as she ran her hand across Leila's breast.

"Oh, okay, let's hear it."

"We were in different classes when we were at school, but we always had sport lessons at the same time on the same day. I used to watch you in the showers afterwards. I thought you were just the most perfect girl I had ever seen; I used to get a funny feeling inside whenever I saw you. I mean, you were naked, and by then I already knew that I wanted girls. Then one day I saw another girl washing your back, and I was so jealous."

"Really!" Leila propped herself up on one arm, so she was facing Brigit. She leant forward and kissed her. "Well, if it's confession time, you'd better hear mine."

"Okay."

"I used to watch you."

Brigit's eyes opened wide. "Did you?"

"Yep. I used to see you, and of course, you too were naked, and I thought, how do I get this gorgeous young woman to notice me. Her with her pretty face, perfect breasts, perfect bottom and nice wispy little muff…" She lifted the sheet again and studied Brigit's crotch. "…Which I'm glad you still have." She flopped down onto her back. "I had the real hots for you, but every time I tried to catch your eye, you turned away!" She laughed. "It was so annoying. The other girls said that you were stuck up, but I just thought you looked lonely and I wanted to be your friend and obviously I wanted to have sex with you as well, my, did I want to have sex with you! But I didn't know if you were gay, because we all have to hide it, don't we!"

"Oh, I wish I'd have known, I'd have been over there in a shot to wash you." She smirked. "You'd have had the world's cleanest tits!"

"Just my tits?" said Leila, raising one eyebrow.

"Oh, don't worry, I'd have washed everywhere else, I would have been very thorough. I'd have been able to eat my dinner off you."

"You can do that later if you want. I'll put some honey on my nipples and you can lick it off."

"I haven't got any honey, so we'll just have to pretend there's some on you, won't we?"

Leila sighed. "You know, when we met earlier today, I wasn't sure if you were gay. I was kind of really hoping you were, because all those feelings that I had about you came flooding back. But I didn't want to make the first move, just in case. Then we came back here, you kissed me, and I was not disappointed."

Brigit smiled and felt a contentment that she had never felt before.

31

Leila looked at her curiously. "You say you've never had sex with a girl before, but have you had any sort of relationship with a girl."

"Well, not really, though do you remember the teacher, Sophia Melnyk?"

"Miss Melnyk, she was the one that stopped Strafford. How do you know her first name?"

"Well, I was staying behind after school one evening doing a bit of revision, and she came up and spoke to me, just a sort of friendly chat and said I could call her Sophia, provided there was no one else around. She asked me why I didn't have any friends and said that she knew what it was like to feel different to other girls. She even gave me a cigarette! I wasn't sure if she was coming on to me or not."

"Oh yeah, she was," laughed Leila.

"Yeah, well, I found that out later. She said that if I was curious about anything that I could go to her house and talk about it. She wasn't that much older than me; she was twenty and I was fourteen by then and yeah, I was curious. I'd known for a couple of years that I wanted girls, so I went around to see her. I didn't really know what was going to happen though."

"What did happen?"

"Well, not a lot really, we had a couple of a drinks and chatted for a while about different feelings. We cuddled and kissed a bit, but then all of a sudden, we were both hit with the whole teacher/pupil/my age/her giving me alcohol thing, and it all got a bit awkward. I went home; I never went around to see her again, and I avoided her at school."

"So, she got you got all revved up then slammed you into reverse. That must have been really tough."

"Revved up? Yeah, you could put it like that!" Brigit laughed. "But you know what though?"

"What?"

"All the time I was there, I was wishing it was you, not her."

Leila bit her bottom lip then held Brigit close, nuzzling into her neck. She pulled back and Brigit stroked her hair, guiding a lock behind her ear. "Sleep with me tonight, Leila, let's catch up on lost time."

Leila got a bit sleazy. "Do you want to do it again right now?"

"I thought you were never going to ask," said Brigit as she slid down under the covers.

****

A pigeon coo-ing at the window woke Brigit; she was surprised to see Leila sitting on the edge of the bed with her head in her hands.

"What's wrong, Leila?"

Leila sighed. "That was a mistake. We shouldn't have done it."

"Why not?"

"Well, for one, it's illegal."

"But nobody's going to know. I'm not going to tell anyone," said Brigit anxiously.

"That's not the point."

"What is the point?"

Leila turned to Brigit; tears were in her eyes. "The point is, I want to see you more and we can't do that, we can't take the risk."

"And I want to see you again. We could keep it quiet."

"No, someone will see us and report us, and we just can't take the risk."

"But—"

"Brigit! They put girls like us in prison," Leila interrupted. "And do you know what they do in prison? They try to 'cure' us. Do you know how they do it?" she had desperation in her voice.

"No."

"They withhold food, the only way a girl can get any is to agree to have regular sex with the male guards." Leila burst into tears. "It's so fucking disgusting." She wiped tears away with the back of her hand. "I can't go to prison, I'm so sorry; I shouldn't have put you in this position."

Brigit put her head in her hands. "I started it," she said wearily.

"Believe me, coming home to you, seeing you every day, sharing your bed, making love to you, it would be just the most incredible thing. But I think it's best if we never see each other again," said Leila, tears welling in her eyes. "I'm so sorry."

Brigit hung her head and sighed. "It's all or nothing for us, isn't it?" she said as she handed Leila a tissue. "What will you do?"

Leila shrugged with an air of resignation as she wiped her eyes and sniffed back the tears. "I'll get myself a cover. I've had a couple of boyfriends, so I know what I'm letting myself in for." She shuddered with revulsion and sneered bitterly. "I suppose I'll have to go back to sucking cocks. I've done that before, just because I thought I had to, and I wanted them to be happy; puked my guts up every time afterwards though. So maybe I'll have a kid, women often lose interest in sex after childbirth, so he'll go off and have an affair. I'll pretend I don't know, and he won't pester me for sex. Maybe it'll be a girl and I'll have one less dick to deal with."

Brigit began to cry. "I love you, I always have," her voice descending into a whisper. She looked up at the ceiling. "What am I going to do?"

"I love you too, but forget me, it's the only thing you can do. Forget everything I've said and done, forget all about me. Harden your heart, Brigit, harden it. Put it in an iron safe and throw away the key so no one can ever hurt you the way I have." The two women embraced, both sobbing.

"It pains me to see you so upset, Brigit, it physically hurts me to know what I've done to you. But for you and me." Leila sighed. "There's no place in this country for girls like us. Hide your love away."

****

It was during her first week of her second year at university that Brigit got the call. A female administrator entered the lecture hall.

"Brigit Malaya," she called out. "There's an urgent call for you, please come with me."

The lecturer gestured for her to leave and she got up and went with the administrator.

Brigit picked up the handset and heard her mother's voice. Katriona was breathless and hesitant. "It's your dad."

A shudder ran through Brigit's body and she suddenly felt cold. "What is it, Mum?"

"He's…" Her mother's voice cracked with emotion. "He's had a heart attack; he's being taken to hospital right now."

Brigit slowly sank down into a chair.

"You have to come home, Brigit, it's serious." Brigit listened as she heard her mother start to cry.

"I'm leaving now, Mum. I'll meet you at the hospital. I'll be there as soon as I can." She put down the phone and turned to the administrator. "I've got to go right now, don't know when I'll be back."

The woman nodded, and although she had only heard part of the conversation, realised that it was important. "Okay, I'll let your tutors know."

****

The nurse directed Brigit to a side ward. There was no smile or cheery greeting; Brigit knew what had happened. She could hear her mother crying as she approached the door. She stopped outside and took a few deep breaths, then entered.

Her mother immediately got up and threw her arms around her, holding her tighter than she had ever done. She buried her head into Brigit's shoulder and sobbed.

"He's dead, Brigit, he died an hour ago. He knew you were coming; he tried to hang on, but he just couldn't."

Brigit looked down at her father. The staff had already removed all the tubes and monitoring equipment and had straightened the bed sheets. His expression was neutral, his eyes were closed and his mouth shut. He just looked like he was asleep, and for a moment Brigit imagined he was going to wake up and make one of his silly jokes.

She let go of her mother and went to him. She sighed. "Goodbye, Dad," she whispered as she bent down and kissed his forehead, fighting the feeling of revulsion as her lips touched his already cold skin and trying not to let the shock of that show.

There was a gentle knock on the door and a nurse, and two medical orderlies entered.

"We have to take him down to the mortuary," she said as the orderlies clicked the brakes off the bed.

"Can't we stay with him a little longer?" cried Brigit's mother.

"I'm sorry," said the nurse, firmly, but with compassion. "We need this room, there's another critically ill patient, and all the other rooms are occupied."

Brigit and her mother followed the bed as it was wheeled along a corridor. They approached a set of doors. The nurse turned to them.

"This is as far as you can go; I'm sorry, but you can't come in here."

They watched as the doors opened and the bed was wheeled in and the doors slowly close. Katriona's legs buckled; Brigit grabbed her and led her to a chair.

****

Brigit looked down at the casket, sighed then dropped a handful of soil, scattering it along the length. She had been the last in line and stood watching, as in keeping with Correlan burial custom, the gravediggers immediately started to shovel in soil. She watched as the casket slowly disappeared from view.

She turned and looked at her distraught mother. "I can't cry, Mum, why can't I cry? Dad meant the world to me."

****

The phone rang, Brigit knew who it would be and what the conversation would be; it would be the same as earlier in the day. The same as yesterday and the day before. The calls had started six months ago; at first it was once a week then once every two days, then once a day. Now it was several times a day. She frowned and picked up the handset.

"It's your mum," came Katriona's slurred, pitiful, disembodied voice.

"I know it's you, Mum," sighed Brigit.

"I'm so lonely. I just wanted to hear your voice."

"This is the third time today that you've called. Mum, I told you, I have to study."

"When can you come home?"

Brigit ignored the question. "Have you been drinking?" she said crossly.

"No."

"Mum, don't lie to me, I can hear it in your voice."

"I have to do something, I'm so lonely."

"Mum," snapped Brigit, "I know that you have neighbours coming in to see you every day. I know that you go out every day. I know that you go to the social club three times a week."

"I know, dear, but it's not the same without your father."

"Mum, it's been nearly a year now. I know it's been hard on you, and it's been hard on me too, but you have to move on."

"I know, dear, but it's so hard, what am I going to do, what am I going to do?"

"I have to go now, Mum. Goodbye." Brigit put the handset down before her mother could reply.

The chirp of the phone woke Brigit; she had selected the sound of a crow's call to her mother's number so she knew what she would hear. She sighed and looked at her alarm clock; it was three twenty in the morning.

"Come home, Brigit," Katriona's voice was more slurred than usual.

"Mum! You're drunk."

"Just come home. Why won't you come home?"

"Mum, I can't, you know it's finals week. I have to present my dissertation in six hours' time; if I don't, I'll fail my degree. I'll never be able to join the army."

"But I need you here," Katriona's voice was pitiful. Brigit had lost all sympathy months ago and now always found herself getting irritated at her mother's pathetic tone.

"I can't be there, you know that. I'll call you after my exams are over," she snapped.

There was a long silence, Brigit could hear her mother crying. She eventually spoke. "What is the point of anything?"

"Mother! Pull yourself together. Getting all maudlin is not going to help."

Katriona seemed not to have heard and just kept repeating, "What is the point of anything," over and over.

Brigit felt her anger rising. "If I fail my exams because of this, I will never forgive you – never." She put down the phone and pulled the cord from the wall socket. She checked he clock; it was nearly half past three.

"I'm not going to get any more sleep now – thanks to you, Mother," she said aloud. She made herself a coffee and opened her revision notes. "Might as well do some last-minute cramming."

****

Brigit stood in the entrance hall of her university, eagerly scanning up the list of exam passes. Her heart pounded as she got ever higher; she knew she had done well and was pretty sure she had passed, but she was nearly at the top now and hadn't seen her name.

Then there it was, third from the top: Malaya, Brigit, ninety-eight-point-three percent, next to that in bold letters was 'A1+'.

"Yes," she shouted, pumping her fist.

A hand landed on her shoulder; she turned to see her tutor smiling at her.

"Well done, Brigit, I never had any doubts about you," he said, not even trying to conceal the pride he had in her.

She turned to leave; a feeling of euphoria filling her as never before. As she got outside, she saw Elise, her mother's neighbour; her face hard and stony.

"Brigit, it's your mother; she's dead. She took her own life," Elise scowled. "How could you? I always knew you were a daddy's girl, but how could you leave your mother to grieve on her own. What sort of daughter are you?"

Stunned by the news of her mother's death and the vehemence and audacity of the woman, Brigit took a small step backwards.

Elise sneered. "I found her, I called the doctor, I called the funeral directors to collect the body, but you're going to have to make all the arrangements. That's the least you can do; you clearly couldn't be bothered to do anything else. She'd taken pills, but what do you care?"

The shock of her mother's suicide quickly evaporated and feint red mist started to form in Brigit's eyes as the woman berated her.

"Katriona told me what you had said to her; it was disgraceful. And all because for some reason you think you can join the army, you stupid little girl." Elise paused and sneered, looking Brigit up and down disdainfully. "I mean you, who the hell do you think you are, joining the army, what a load of nonsense. I always thought there was something wrong with you. Maybe if you had got yourself a normal boyfriend and had a normal life, you'd be a normal girl and would have looked after your poor mother, like a normal daughter is supposed to," she jeered.

Suddenly, Brigit stepped forward, grabbed Elise by the throat and slammed her up against a wall. She raised her fist and fixed her gaze deep into the woman's eyes.

"Fuck you. You know nothing about my relationship with my mother and if you ever talk to me like that again, I will put you in hospital. Do you understand me?"

"Yes, please don't hurt me," said the now terrified woman.

"I will make all the arrangements. Stay away, and if I ever see you again, I will hurt you." She released her grip and shoved the woman away. "Now get out of my sight."

Off to one side, and unbeknown to Brigit, there was an army officer. He was in civilian clothes; her army pre-application had flagged up that the exam results were due today and he had been sent to check them. He had seen the altercation with Elise. He took out a notebook and wrote: 'Brigit Malaya, very aggressive, great potential if trained well' then smiled to himself and put a tick beside her name.

****

Eleven months after her altercation with Elise, Brigit was enrolled in the army and was based at an officer's training camp. There were other women there, but no other women were in the combat training section.

Brigit was in one of the reading rooms on the base. She selected a textbook on artillery and was interested in how calculations for range were made. She was about to sit and start studying when some recruits came in and surrounded her.

One moved in close. "I heard about your antics with Chapelle. So you think you can fight, do you, Malaya?"

She looked around and saw she was surrounded by a group of male officer recruits. Standing in front of her was Alondra, he was taller and physically much bigger than her. He sneered at her. "We don't like girls in the army; they're a liability, too weak to be of any use."

She looked him in the eye and noticed a few of the other men smirking. "I'm prepared to disappoint you."

Alondra scowled at her. "You need to be taught a lesson, and after that, maybe you'll request a transfer to the quartermaster store where you can do something more suited to a woman, like ironing."

"Who is going to teach me a lesson, you?"

"Yeah."

"Is that why you need these guys for backup." She gestured over her shoulder but kept eye contact with him."

Irritated that she wasn't intimidated by him, he leant forward bearing his teeth. "They're just going to watch." He looked at them. "This is between me and her, so stand back and enjoy the show."

Her first punch caught him on the chin, her second uppercut to his jaw knocked his head back. Dazed and shocked, he swung wildly at her, she dodged to the side and as he turned, caught him with a kidney punch. He cried out. She kicked behind his knee and he collapsed to the ground. She fell on top of him, grabbed his head and was about to slam into the floor when they heard the voice of the base commander.

"What is going on here?" he demanded.

Malaya and Alondra stood up and everyone stood to attention. There was a moment of silence, then Alondra spoke. "I tripped over, sir, and I banged my head; Officer Recruit Malaya was just checking to see if I was all right, sir."

The commander looked at Malaya. "Is this true, Officer Recruit Malaya?"

"Yes, sir."

"Malaya, show me the backs of your hands."

She held out her hands. He looked at them and frowned deeply. "Your knuckles are quite red; do you have an explanation for that, Malaya?"

"It's a rash, sir; I will go to the base doctor to have it checked, sir."

The commander thought for a moment. "That is a good idea, because anything that damages the hands may reduce the ability to handle a weapon." He turned to Alondra. "Your face is also quite red, so you must have hit the ground quite hard."

"I did, sir."

"Well, it is fortunate for you that Malaya was here, isn't it?"

"Yes, sir, very fortunate."

The commander paced around the room, looking at every one in turn. "Looking after your comrades is a vital part of your training. You must learn to rely on each other and build trust..." He paused and looked at Malaya and Alondra. "...regardless of your personal feelings. Your life may one day depend on it."

He paced back and forth studying all the recruits then stopped and looked at Alondra. "Try to be more careful in future. Tripping over was surprisingly clumsy of you."

"Yes, sir, I will be more careful in future, sir."

The commander turned to Malaya. "Go and see the doctor and get your 'rash' checked out, because I do not want to see it ever again on your hands – do I make myself absolutely clear, Officer Recruit Malaya?"

"Yes, sir."

He turned to address them all. "Always remember who the actual enemy is."

"Yes, sir," came the unison response.

****

Rumours of the incident spread quickly throughout the recruits along with reports of the growing respect she was earning. Far away in another training camp, Officer Recruit Lothar Valerian listened to a couple of recruits discussing her.

"A woman in combat training?" he asked incredulously.

"Yeah, volunteered for front line training, going to go into the infantry – apparently."

"And are you telling me that this Alondra chap let a woman get the better of him."

"Yeah."

"Well, she'd better never meet me then; I'll put her in her place, because the day that we have women on the front line is the day we lose."

****

There was an extra dimension to life in the Correlan military that interested Brigit. She had finished training, was in a regiment and had recently been promoted to captain; she now had access to the government's population database and could look up any name and address that she wanted. It was late in the evening; she sat at her desk in her quarters and poured herself a large brandy, a drink that she had recently found a taste for. She lit a cigarette, then turned on her computer and typed in a name of a man from her past. It turned out to be a fairly common name, with thousands of entries. She never knew this man's forename and sat for a while wondering how to refine the search.

"Age," she said aloud. "He's got to be in his late sixties by now." She selected the age criteria box and entered '65 plus', then entered 'Male' in the gender section. Immediately the list dropped to three hundred and eighteen, all spread across the country.

"Hmm," she grunted. "Never going to be able to check all of them." She poured herself another brandy, stubbed out her cigarette and immediately lit another one. She highlighted these names then typed 'Occupation' into the search box. Two hundred and ninety-three returned various menial jobs, the trivial kind that old men did to keep themselves busy and feel useful. The rest returned 'Retired'. She thought for a moment, then highlighted the results, clicked in the search box, and typed 'Former occupation'. One name jumped out at her.

"Yes, got him," she shouted. The address showed the man as living in a non-descript town just outside Balssen.

****

Brigit recognised the old man shuffling down the street. He had the demeanour of a grumpy old man whose life had not gone how he wanted and was permanently angry. She watched as he went into a bar; she thought about going into the bar so she could watch him. She was so sure he would not recognise her that she even thought about going up and standing next to him at the bar and ordering a drink, but decided against it. She could wait, she'd waited long enough; a couple more hours were not going to make any difference. She lit a cigarette, turned on the car radio and tuned into a classical music station.

By the time he left the bar, it was late, and he was a bit worse for wear, obviously drunk. She got out of her car, then followed him into a deserted side road. She walked up behind him and tapped him on the shoulder.

He turned. "Who the fuck are you?" he grunted, his alcohol-laden breath carrying aggression that only partly covered his misery. She held up her right hand, showing him her palm.

"What are you doing that for, you stupid bitch?"

"Don't you remember me?" she said.

"No, now fuck off and leave me alone."

"You can't see the scar anymore."

"I told you to fuck off," he said, raising his voice.

"I am a captain in the Correlan Army."

He moved closer to her and leant forward. "Big fucking deal," he snarled. "Now piss off before I lose my shit. I ain't afraid to hit women," he shouted.

"I know," she calmly replied.

Her first punch to his nose wasn't too hard, not enough to make him fall over, just enough to make him put his hands up to his face. His right side was exposed, and her second punch was much harder. She picked her target well, hitting full force with a left hook between the sixth and seventh rib on his right side. She knew that the initial impact would not hurt him too much, but the impact of the ribs against his liver would cause a pain that would quickly build to excruciating levels. He gasped and his hands dropped from his face as he grabbed his side. A right hook to his chin snapped his head around and a follow up punch shattered his already damaged nose. He staggered back and collapsed to the ground.

She stood over him and held out her palm again. "Remember me now?"

He looked up, glaring at her angrily and shook his head as he wiped blood from his face with his sleeve.

"Mr Strafford, I am Captain Brigit Malaya."

His look of anger was swiftly replaced with shock and then fear.

"I told you that one day you'd be old and that I'd come for you, because there are always consequences for every action, aren't there?"

****

"So, those were a few scenes from my past, episodes, vignettes, snapshots, postcards even, call them what you will; just some of the shit I've had to put up with all my life; just some of the things that have made me who I am, along with the love that I am forever denied. But there are more – so many more issues that I have buried and tried to forget, but they are still there.

"Everyone was always telling me what I couldn't do, everyone saying that I was stupid, everyone telling me that I was a silly little girl, thinking I could join the army. Everyone always saying that I had to behave like a normal girl – whatever one of those is. They said girls are too weak to fight. But I should really thank those people, because all they did was make me more determined. I joined the army and I fought on the front line. I have fought and killed people with weapons, and I have killed people with my bare hands; I have ordered people to be killed. Do I sound weak to you? Well, do I? I was the first ever female colonel. I took and passed the general's test and became not only the first female general but the youngest ever general. And now I am Major General Brigit Malaya and I command the army."

Prologue

"So, here I am after ten years of war and apparently, I'm a hero, well to some people at least, not me though.

"I don't do so many of the assassinations any more, I mostly fight with regular troops; I get a short-term assignment to various regiments during critical missions. I am told that they look forward to me being posted to them. Captain Astrid Peterman, hero of the Arralan Republic – maybe I should wear a cape. Excuse my sarcasm, I'm exhausted.

"The Correlans know who I am now, they all have a picture of me, the one from The Silk River Restaurant, where I looked straight at a hidden security camera. God knows what horrible things they'll do to me when they catch me, because they also know what I've done. They'll want information from me, and they have particularly nasty ways of getting it, but it's not if they catch me, it's when they catch me.

"I've had ten years of fighting, ten years of killing. Ten years of risking my life every day and what has it achieved? Well, I'll tell you what it has achieved, nothing, a great big fat steaming pile of nothing.

"I became an assassin to shorten the war; so how many people have I killed I hear you ask; well, I honestly can't remember. So, too many then. And did I shorten the war, no of course not, the war goes on, the war always goes on.

"For ten years, I have lived only for the war, kidding myself that I was doing the right thing; my actions, as despicable as they really are, shortening the war and saving lives as a result. I have dedicated my life to the cause that I justified to myself as being the right one, but was it?

"And do you want to know what ten years of celibacy looks like? Well, you're looking at it.

"I am tired and I just want it to be over, and if I die, well, so be it."

Capture

Astrid leapt out at the young trooper, but at the last moment he saw her and sidestepped. She hit him side-on and both fell to the ground, his assault rifle falling a few metres away and out of his reach. Rising quickly to her feet, she pulled her combat knife and went for the man again as he lay on the ground. He kicked out at her, making her dodge to one side. Although young and fresh out of training, he was good, with faster reactions than other enemy soldiers that she had encountered.

He rolled to his feet, drawing his knife as he did so. She was between him and his firearm; his heart raced as he recognised her; he knew that she would not let him escape. He also knew that despite the order that she was to be taken alive, he would have no choice but to kill her, for if not, she would certainly kill him.

For a few moments, they stood still looking into each other's eyes. His mouth was dry, and his stomach churned. He had always assumed that his first kill would be with his gun at some sort of distance, without being able to see the face of the target as the bullet hit, nor hear the scream of pain or see the spray of blood. But this would be so much more personal. Now he would feel her death; he knew where to stab, the training had taught him that, but what would he do then? Would he just let her fall? Would he embrace her and lower her to the ground to die with some sort of dignity? Would there be some sort of respect for another soldier's life? Training had taught him how to kill but had not prepared him for these feelings. As he tried to swallow his fear, a series of thoughts flashed through his mind. What if she slashed him? What if he killed her, but she maimed him during the fight? What would it feel like? Would it hurt?

Astrid moved first, diving towards him, knife in her right hand. He knew that her aim was to grab his wrist and twist it to make him drop his knife and drive hers through his ribcage into his heart through the side of his body armour where there was no protection. This was standard, this was what he had been taught, so he was ready. But instead she dropped to the ground and kicked out, hitting just behind his knee, knocking him off balance.

He fell down hard, winding himself, the back of his hand hit a rock making him lose his grip on his knife which clattered away. Astrid seized the moment and jumped onto him, grabbing his jaw and pushing his head up. Sitting on his chest with her knife raised high, she was about to plunge the blade into his throat when she paused. He was completely vulnerable, his neck was exposed, and he was unable to fight back; it would be quick and easy, he would feel some pain, but it would not last long. She had killed people like this before, so what was different about this one?

"Please don't kill me," the terrified young man whispered.

A shot rang out and a bullet hit the ground beside her, throwing dirt up into her face.

"Halt," a voice shouted behind her as she heard the unmistakeable clicks of weapons being cocked. She looked around to see four troopers each with their assault rifles aimed at her. She knew their orders were to take her alive and unharmed, but they were nervous, and she couldn't risk panicking them. She tossed the knife to one side then raised her hands, slowly stood up and turned to face them. She looked the squad leader straight in the eye and nodded; he made a barely perceivable nod back, a recognition that she would not resist, and then she slowly turned around, crossed her hands behind her head and dropped to her knees.

It was over.

The General's Office

Astrid sat strapped by her wrists into a chair in the office of Major General Brigit Malaya, the commander of the vast Kandalan Base and the highest-ranking woman in the Correlan military. Astrid felt alone and vulnerable in way she had never felt before and had no strength for defiance, she knew it was all over for her now.

Malaya dismissed the two guards that were standing behind the chair that Astrid was strapped into, then sat back and flipped open a report folder.

"This is the preliminary report from Lieutenant Jackan on your capture."

The general blithely scanned through the document for sections that she had already read and had made a mental note of, grunting quietly and scoffing at the some of the passages, even laughing at others. She read them out, skipping through the padding and picking out the salient points of the report.

'*...I immediately recognised the enemy captain and realised that our comrade was in extreme peril...I knew that there was no time to lose...I decided to make the arrest myself...I decided that it was imperative that I leave my weapon behind as this might slow me down...and take the prisoner by hand...I ordered my men to stay where they were and sprang forth from my position...*'

Malaya lowered the report and looked at Astrid.

"Sprang forth?" she said incredulously. "Who the fuck writes 'sprang forth' in a combat report for God's sake."

She continued reading aloud, with a sarcastic and mocking tone to her voice.

'*...The enemy officer was clearly surprised at my speed and agility...it was obvious that she recognised my superior fighting skills and that it would be futile to engage me in unarmed combat...She immediately surrendered to me...the leadership and courage that I showed impressed my men...will serve me in good stead as I rise through the ranks.*'

"That wasn't how it happened," said Astrid softly, her head bowed down, cowed by her situation.

"I know." Malaya tossed the report onto her desk and snorted disdainfully. "I've already spoken to his men; they said that Jackan cried when he saw it was you, and he was so afraid that he pissed himself."

"His men were lined up behind me and I gave myself up." Astrid stared at the floor, wincing, and moving her wrists to try to ease the tension from the restraints.

"Yes," said Malaya. "He sent his men forward to get you and stayed well back out of danger. He'll rewrite this magnificent work of fiction over and over again to give himself even more glory. He's ordered his men to memorise this preliminary report, and that will be the version of events that they will have to give to the inevitable inquiry. It's just the sort of self-serving horseshit that the army council likes. The useless little fucker will get promoted for this, but I'll make sure he gets sent some place where he'll die within a couple of weeks. The army doesn't need people like him." She made no effort to hide her contempt for the man.

Malaya looked up at the clock. "Ah good, nine o'clock, and as I'm officially off duty now, I can have a drink."

On a small table in a corner of the office was an array of fine cut-glass decanters, most containing clear amber liquid of various shades. She went to the table, picked up one of the bottles, pulled the stopper and poured the liquid into an equally fine cut-glass tumbler. She swirled the glass and held it up to the light for a few moments, studying the rivulets of alcohol as they condensed on the sides and flowed down.

"This is one-hundred-year-old brandy; it costs nearly half a year's wages, apparently." She took a mouthful then shrugged her shoulders.

"It tastes like all the others to me. It was given to me by a major who either wanted promotion or wanted to fuck me." She checked herself and half laughed. "Fuck me? Well, that was never going to happen, but he wasn't to know." She looked wistfully out of the window for a few moments, and then turned to face Astrid.

"I told him to impress me, I told him to do something courageous. So, he volunteered to lead a mission to deal with some problems. We were having a bit of trouble in the northern tribal areas and off he went, got captured and the bastards skinned him alive. We know that because they took lots of pictures while they were doing it and sent them to us."

She looked down at the floor, shook her head slightly and sighed a little. "The poor bastard, no one deserves that."

She sighed again, remembering the images. She turned to Astrid again with a look of angry disbelief. "You know, there were women and children present and the images of them pointing and laughing as he suffered got to everyone who saw them. But they did it outside and from the topography in the background of the pictures, we were able to finally work out where their base was. It was in a valley with three routes in and steep hills either side of each of those routes. Helicopter gunships drove them all to the centre compound then a couple of waves of ground attack planes dropped napalm canisters, lots of napalm – we didn't have any more trouble after that."

Again, she held the glass up to the light, and fascinated with the meniscus, she swirled the liquid and studied it for a while. She seemed to snap out of the apparent daydream. "Oh, I'm sorry, and I am being very rude. Would you like some?"

"No thank you, but could I have some water please," said Astrid, her voice slightly hoarse from a dry throat.

"Of course."

Malaya grabbed a plastic bottle from a small fridge and cracked the top open. Then held it to Astrid's mouth and slowly tipped the bottle so she could take a sip. As she did so, she gently held the back of Astrid's head, steadying her.

"Thank you," said Astrid. She looked down at the straps holding her arms to the chair, then looked back up at Malaya and nodded towards the bottle in her hand.

"I could hold it myself, but it would be difficult like this," she said, looking down at the nylon zip ties and pulling at them. "These are not necessary; I'm in the office of the commander of the largest base in Correla, I'm surrounded by tens of thousands of soldiers. I'm not going to hurt you."

Malaya studied her for a few moments. "No, I don't think you are."

She took a pair of stout scissors and cut the straps – with a little wariness. She was well aware of Astrid's reputation but also trusted her for some reason that she couldn't quite understand.

As she released the restraints, Astrid touched the back of Malaya's hand, stoking it briefly. "Thank you," she said, looking up at her.

Malaya put her hand on Astrid's shoulder and squeezed gently. "You're welcome."

She sat back in her chair at the other side of the desk and watched as Astrid quickly downed a third of the bottle.

"Not too fast," she said. "It's cold and you'll get stomach cramps."

"I know, one hundred and fifty millilitres to start, then have a rest before drinking any more of it."

It was her first drink since being captured and she fought the urge to drink it all at once, but Malaya was right.

Malaya smiled. "Hmm, straight from our field manual, chapter one, basic survival."

"Straight from ours as well."

Astrid knew that this small talk was a ploy, a power play designed to keep her off guard, as was the story of the major. She'd used the same tactic herself prior to interrogating a prisoner. But even so, there was a curious, slightly soft edge to the major general.

Malaya picked up a packet of Cavana cigarettes and tapped one out. She put it in her mouth, then picked up an ornate lighter. She was just about to light the cigarette when she noticed Astrid was looking at the packet.

"Oh sorry, do you want one? I just assumed that you don't smoke."

"No thank you, and no, I don't smoke."

"Do you mind if I do?"

"Go ahead, I am hardly in a position to stop you," Astrid's voice was weary, and not just through tiredness.

Malaya smiled then went to light the cigarette, but stopped, put down the lighter, took the cigarette out of her mouth and rather awkwardly put it back in the packet. It was almost as if she couldn't or didn't want to smoke in front of Astrid.

"I used to smoke more than sixty a day, now I'm down to five a day, so I really should stop altogether, it's just a filthy habit," she said, avoiding eye contact as she screwed up the packet and chucked it in a bin. "Not to mention the fact that it's a really expensive way to commit suicide."

"So, no cigarettes are going to be stubbed out on the soles of my feet then?" said Astrid anxiously.

"No, at least not by me." Malaya gathered herself again. "There'll be plenty of others to do that."

"It won't be necessary."

"That's as maybe, but they'll do it anyway – even after you've told them everything."

There was a lack of menace as the major general spoke. There was something else, an inflection in her voice, it was subtle, but it was almost concern. She took off her jacket, sat back in her chair, removed her tie, undid the top four buttons of her blouse, and pulled it open a little bit more than necessary, exposing the tops of her breasts. She sat looking at Astrid. A few minutes of silence passed, eventually she spoke.

"You're not what I expected," said Malaya as she relaxed back into her chair.

"What did you expect?" Astrid's voice was quiet, subdued.

"Someone harder, someone toughened by combat, someone not so, well, feminine."

Again, Malaya sat and looked at Astrid for a while, she had a look of curiosity rather than dominance. She smiled. "You know, we only have one picture of you, and I must say, you are much prettier in real life."

Astrid smiled despite the awkwardness of her situation. "Nobody has ever said that to me before."

"Well, it's true."

It was Astrid's turn to study Malaya; she had broad shoulders and a lean but muscular body. Her hair was short, dark and shot through with grey. The set of her eyebrows and her dark-hazel eyes gave her a serious look, but when she smiled this made her attractive, almost playful. In anyone's eyes, she was a handsome female and the authority that the uniform gave her enhanced that.

"You are an attractive woman. And who doesn't love a girl in uniform," she paused and looked away. "I know I do," she said quietly.

"No one has ever said that to me either." Malaya felt herself blush a little but quickly regained her composure.

"Well, it's true," said Astrid, copying Malaya's words and looking directly into her eyes.

"Is there anyone back home for you?" Malaya's question was slightly more probing than casual.

"No, no one. It's difficult for me to form relationships. I work with men, but I don't have relationships with men."

Astrid looked away, unsure of what to say next or how it might be taken. She turned back to face Malaya, and with her head down slightly, she looked up at her. "I have different preferences, if you know what I mean."

"Yes," said Malaya thoughtfully. "Yes, I think I know what you mean."

"Is there a special man in your life?" asked Astrid.

"Oh no. I'm definitely not the marrying type." Malaya laughed and looked away. "My preferences certainly see to that."

Questions

There was silence for a few moments while both women thought about what the other had said and what they may have meant. Malaya leant forward and smiled reassuringly.

"Look, I have to ask you some questions, is that okay?" Malaya's voice was softer now. "I want you to relax, there are just some things I need to know."

"Okay."

"They tell me that you appeared to hesitate. That you had the man down, throat exposed and the knife in your hand, but you didn't strike. Why was that?"

"Why?" Astrid sounded exasperated, as if the answer was obvious. "Why kill this man? What purpose would it serve?"

"But he was your enemy."

Astrid sighed wearily. "Yes, he was, but he was only a boy. I looked in his eyes and he was frightened. I've seen that look before but never has it affected me. I have killed so many people, I have spilled so much blood and what has it achieved? It would have been over quickly for him, but what then? I would have taken another life but destroyed so many others in the process. His mother, father, brother, sister, girlfriend or wife, or maybe even children. Would it have shortened the war? No. And in that moment, I knew what I had to do, and six months of doubt were over for me."

"Six months?" The general was puzzled.

"Six months ago, there would have been six corpses, him, the troopers and Jackan."

"And there would have been your battle trademark, your signature, always a knife, never a gun. Why is that?"

"It's not always a knife, but I only ever use a gun on a sniper mission. In regular combat, it's bang, bang, bang, and everyone knows where you are. At night, bang and flash, even with a flash suppressor, they know where you are. You hit someone in the chest, and they go down, but you don't know if they're dead, they could be wearing body armour, then get up and come back at you. With a blade, I get up close and personal, one quick strike to the back of the neck and they're dead before they hit the ground. I get so close to some targets that they don't even realise that I'm there to kill them."

Malaya nodded thoughtfully. "Cold logic, but I can understand it."

She looked at Astrid with a slight wry smile. "And before that, there were the 'accidents', weren't there?"

Astrid hung her head and nodded ever so slightly, then shook her head in shame as she thought of all the families she had destroyed. She was a soldier and those had been her missions, but now it all seemed so pointless and cruel.

Malaya frowned a little. "They were clever, I'll give you that." She relaxed back into her chair. "So why six months ago? What is so different now?"

Astrid sighed again and paused, the general seemed okay with the pause as if she sensed that Astrid was going to unburden herself somehow.

"Six months ago, I was at a strategic planning meeting at central intelligence, reviewing the assessment for the war in the coming year—"

"Sorry to interrupt, but what was a captain doing at a planning meeting of such a high level?"

"I'm not a captain, I'm a major colonel. My rank is kept secret so that I can go on operations and report back on units that are under-performing."

Malaya's jaw dropped a fraction. "Well, that's something I wasn't expecting." She thought for a few seconds; the rank structure between the two armies is different, and Astrid's rank of major colonel was only two levels below her rank of major general. "We will get a lot of information from you."

"Yes, you will."

"Yes, we will, and make no mistake, it will not be easy for you." Again, there was a lack of menace in her voice.

Astrid paused for a moment, her head hung low. Conflicting loyalties did not tear at her heart, she knew what she had to do, and she knew that this was the right thing. She raised her head and looked at the general.

"We know your battle plans for the spring offensive."

"How?" the general asked, with a hint of disbelief in her voice.

"Some transmissions were intercepted, old codes that we had cracked had been used. Military intelligence filled in the gaps. Also, some of your officers did not use the correct security protocols, some were not even encoded."

The general thought for few moments wondering if she would ever be able to find out who had caused such a breach in security. "So, when we launch our main thrust, your wonder weapons with their multiple warheads will destroy our tanks and—"

"They don't work!" it was Astrid's turn to interrupt.

"What!" snapped the general, more in surprise than anything else.

"They don't work." A hint of desperation crept into Astrid's voice. "The guidance systems are too inaccurate and every time, they veer off course in the last few seconds. Most of them don't even have warheads. Your tanks and armoured personnel carriers will be quite safe."

"We obtained footage of the test firings; they show that each one was a direct hit resulting in total destruction of the target."

"The tests were faked." Astrid let out a hollow laugh, more of a contemptuous grunt. "We used your AT103 anti-tank missiles that were purchased on the black market, the films were deliberately leaked and we knew you'd see them. It's all part of a bullshit plan to misdirect your main thrust."

The general gasped. "This cannot be true."

"I have no reason to lie to you; I know you will use drugs to get the truth out of me, so why would I make this up now?"

"Hmmm…" The general looked Astrid straight in the eye for a moment, but then averted her gaze and fiddled with a piece of paper on her desk. "You are right about that; our methods to obtain information from captives can be modern sophisticated truth drugs or electric shocks and beatings, sometimes it gets a bit mediaeval. So yes, getting to the truth is only a matter of time and as such, I believe you when you say you are not lying."

She avoided eye contact and sounded almost embarrassed to admit to the brutal levels of abuse practiced by her people. "You'll be a mess by the time they've finished with you," she added with a slight tremble in her voice.

Astrid sighed again, but this time lifted her head and looked directly into the general's eyes, who took this as a sign that her prisoner was about to relieve herself further.

"As you know, Professor Sharn was our chief weapons designer—"

"Was?" again, the general interrupted.

"Yes, was, past tense. He was our chief designer, but he was killed in one of your air strikes on a residential compound two years ago."

"But we have seen pictures of him attending the missile tests."

"No, his twin brother has been seen attending the missile tests – more disinformation. Sadly, while the professor was a genius, he was in the habit of taking his work home with him, all of which was destroyed in the fire that followed the bombing that killed him. Also, he kept a lot of the finer points of the designs in his head. No one has been able to complete his work on the guidance systems and starting again from scratch would take too long, so it was decided to bluff and hope you fell for it."

"You said that some of the missiles don't have warheads, why is that? It makes no sense."

"Remember the fuss that was made when one of your airstrikes hit a food processing factory?"

"Yes. International condemnation of a strike against a supposedly civilian target. How could I forget it? We always said that it was a military installation."

"It was."

The general snorted and smiled wryly.

"The warheads needed a special explosive and the factory manufactured the precursor chemicals. We can't make enough now, so only one in ten has a warhead, not even the missile launcher crews know that."

"How have you managed to keep all of this from us?" the general's tone of voice had no sense of threat, instead it had become casual, more of a conversation than interrogation.

"The only thing that works efficiently in that country is the propaganda machine."

"That country?" the general quipped, picking up on Astrid's form of words. "You said 'that country' not 'my country', why is that?"

"I don't consider it my country any more. Whether it's this pointless war, or the brainwashed public or the stupid leaders. I don't know which, maybe it's all of it. All I know is that I just want it to end, I have no home and nothing to live for either."

Malaya sat back in her chair rapidly processing all the information and wondering how plans would have to be changed. Then she sat forward eager for even more information. "So, back to this meeting, what happened there that has caused a change in your attitude?"

"Put simply, the plan devised by high command is to meet your forces head on, then fall back and allow you to take the northern city of Manchia. When you start to move south from there, you will come within range of the missiles. They are gambling that you will believe the leaked information about the weapons and halt your advance, then we would sue for a negotiated peace. The border would be redrawn you could keep Manchia – a city of three million."

"That would be a reasonable plan if your weapons worked, but foolish if they don't, surely your high command knows that and—"

"We know we're going to lose! We know the bluff won't work!" Astrid interrupted, with desperation in her voice again. "Only the high command thinks we can have a peace treaty. The high command doesn't know about the missiles."

"I don't understand; how could they possibly not know?"

"Military intelligence believe that bluff is the only way to achieve peace and they have been feeding the same propaganda to the high command, their reasoning is that if the high command believes it, then they will make credible plans. The staff officers, the ones who know the truth – including myself, have been ordered to keep quiet."

"And the truth being that as soon as we realise that the weapons don't work, we will press on with the advance."

"Correct."

"I am shocked; how can your military intelligence do this?"

"They have been lying for so long I think they've started to believe their own bullshit, they are gambling with tens of thousands of lives, maybe hundreds of thousands."

"It's obvious to me that you let yourself be captured, so why did you do it? Why have you come to me, what do you hope to gain?"

Astrid sighed. "I just want to save as many lives as possible on both sides."

"How?"

"All forces opposing your first advance will be assembled on the northern border where the ground is flatter. Instead of going south, if you swing east, then head south, you will be largely unopposed. I know that the terrain is not ideal tank territory, but it will take too long for the defending forces to be redeployed. There will hardly be any fighting, you will hit the capital inside one, maybe two weeks and the war will be over. I will give you all the details."

"You are willing to give me this information and betray your country." The general was incredulous.

"If I gave up this information during interrogation, it might have been passed to lower ranking officers who would have just dismissed it as being made up by me to end whatever horrific things that they were doing to me, and you might never have got to know about it. But by coming to you, I know you will believe me." Astrid sighed deeply and shook her head. "This war has got to end; this is the only way," she said wearily.

"You can give us all the information, but that will not stop you from being executed," said the general with a slight shake in her voice.

"I know; I probably deserve it. I have killed so many people, I have so much blood on my hands. I don't know if I can live with myself anyway." Astrid wiped a tear from her eye.

"I will try to ensure that they are not too hard on you, but there are no guarantees, a lot of people want revenge."

Astrid let her head sink down onto her chest. "Thank you," she said weakly.

"How can I believe you when you say you know our battle plans?" Malaya's voice was much softer now, curious rather than questioning.

"I have a data stick, it's all on there, along with our plans."

"Where can I find this data stick?"

"It's in my pocket."

"In your pocket!" gasped the general in shock. "They didn't search you?"

"No, they seemed afraid of me, Jackan told them to put the ties on my wrists, nothing more. Then they put me on the truck, and they all sat on the other side just looking at me."

"Unbelievable," sighed Malaya. "What pocket is it in?"

"Top left pocket of my shirt."

Malaya moved behind Astrid and slipped her hand into the pocket. Astrid sighed a little as Malaya's hand brushed across her breast. She put her hand up to hold Malaya's. Malaya pulled back a little, but then let Astrid take her hand and put it back on her breast. A shiver ran through Astrid's body as she felt Malaya touch her.

"It's been a long time since a woman has touched me there," she said, closing her eyes.

Malaya pulled back for a moment, thinking of what to do and say next; she leant forward a little and spoke softly into Astrid's ear, "It's been a long time since I've touched a woman there."

She stroked Astrid's hair for a moment, then reached down, slipped her hand inside Astrid's shirt and gently fondled her.

Astrid turned and looked up at Malaya.

"I know what's in store for me, I have shed so much blood and I have sacrificed years of my life and for what? All I want is to just love someone, one last time."

"Call me Brigit. Come with me, let's get you showered; you're going to stay with me tonight."

"What about the guards, won't they be suspicious?" Astrid looked towards the door, uneasy that two were standing in the corridor only a short distance away.

"No need to worry about them, I have told them to wait outside. They won't move until I tell them to." Malaya gently stroked Astrid's hair with the back of her hand. "We won't be disturbed."

To one side of the office was Brigit's personal quarters, a small four-room furnished home. A living room, kitchen, bathroom and a bedroom. Brigit led Astrid through into the bathroom. She undressed first, she took her time and seemed to take pleasure in being watched. She stood in front of Astrid, naked but for her dog tags, they looked like jewellery against her perfect skin. She put her hands behind her head and moved her feet apart, level with her elbows, the way she had done with Anna at Don Bahlia, displaying the taut athletic body that regular exercise brings. Her body was beautifully proportioned, lean and muscular but not overly so. Astrid looked her up and down, admiring her physique.

Astrid took off her clothes then stepped forward, took Brigit in her arms and kissed her, shuddering slightly as their bodies touched.

"I want this," said Astrid breathlessly.

"I want you," whispered Brigit, her voice tremulous with desire. "I've always wanted you."

They kissed and caressed each other as they showered, then Brigit led Astrid through to the bedroom.

Malaya's Life Story

The sex had been passionate and energetic, both women giving vent to their pent-up feelings after so many years of enforced celibacy, and each had taken what had been so willingly given by the other. They lay silently on the bed for a few minutes, letting their bodies relax and drinking in the last of the waves of the intense pleasure that they had both experienced.

Brigit's nose had a slight bump in the bridge, and she saw that Astrid had noticed it. Brigit rubbed it with her finger, feeling for the little ridge where the bone had broken and had grown back unevenly.

Sensing Astrid's curiosity, she offered the explanation. "Boxing match in the first year at officer training college, we all had to do at least one bout in our time there; it was supposed to be good for morale. Three rounds, that was enough. We didn't get a choice over who we fought, and I was picked to fight against a girl who was bigger, older and clearly stronger than me. Lena Chapelle was her name. She'd had several matches and had a huge chip on her shoulder and fancied herself a bit; sort of 'look at me, I'm a champion, I'm gonna destroy you' attitude. That didn't work on me, but I was a bit confused as to why I'd been picked to fight her as all the other girls had been evenly matched. My God she could hit hard, and fortunately for me, I had received some good advice from a trainer at the gym about blocking, but towards the end of the second round, I let my guard down and she caught me and broke my nose. I went down, got up after a four count still dazed and vulnerable. I had blood all over my face, but then the bell went."

"Saved by the bell, huh?" said Astrid.

"Yeah, literally saved by the bell; if it hadn't been for that, she would have certainly beaten me. I'd got up too soon, but the bell gave me time to recover. Third and final round, she came steaming out obviously looking to finish it, but she was way over-confident. One of my seconds had told me that he had noticed that just before she threw a right, she raised her left arm a little and if I was quick, I could catch her. Sure enough, first thing she does is line up a right, she was so focussed on the punch that she didn't realise that her left side was exposed – my chance. I hit her as hard as I could with a right to the ribs just below her left armpit. Our gloves were quite thin with none of the thick padding that you usually get. I heard her gasp; it hurt her a lot. And just as the second had predicted, she expected me to follow up with my left to her head, and immediately went to defend her right, but I followed up with another right, straight to the side of her chin. Her head snapped around and her arms dropped.

"I got her with another left and right to the face as she went down – I was quick in those days. Then I followed her down and just laid into her while she was lying there, too stunned to defend herself, and we weren't supposed to do that. The ref' pulled me off but I still managed to give her a couple of kicks while she was on the canvas. I have this theory about fighting, you get them down and you keep them down. I had broken her jaw, three of her ribs and her face was a bit of a mess; she was crying and in a lot of pain. I was disqualified of course but it was a message to everyone who was watching – fuck with me and you will regret it, no matter how big you are or how tough you think you are.

"I got disciplined for it – no off-base permits for a month, big deal, but later I was taken to one side and told that the senior staff watching actually approved of my level of aggression. I was also told that I was the only person who had ever understood the purpose of the fights. They were not to see who was best at boxing, but to see who was ruthless enough to take someone all the way down – even a colleague, and that it showed I had enormous potential and I would be watched."

"That's why they put the two of you in the ring together, to see who really was the toughest."

"Yeah, I figured that out thirty seconds into the fight." Brigit rubbed her nose again and as she did, Astrid took hold of her hand and lightly ran her fingers over the back, studying the hardened skin.

"You've had a few fights, haven't you?" she said, looking at the scars on her knuckles.

"Yeah, back in the day, we sorted out personal issues the old way. No gloves; bare fists, it was unofficially approved of; it meant that it was over quicker, and you actually did less damage. The skull is harder than the bones in your hands, so you can't hit too hard or you'll break your fingers. But I really fucking laid in to some of them; needless to say, I always won."

"You assaulted a superior officer once, didn't you?"

"Senior officer, no way was he superior." Brigit checked herself and looked quizzically at Astrid. "You know about that?"

"Yes, err, sorry. Read it in a report a couple of years back, didn't have any details though."

"Hmm, been keeping tabs on me eh?"

"Yeah, the file is fairly big."

"Well, don't feel bad, our file on you is huge," Brigit said playfully.

"Anyway, I was under the command of this real dick of a major. How he ever got to that rank I will never know. I was a senior lieutenant by then and we were out on an operation in the east against a tribal warlord. Three days in, he got it into his head that we were going to get cut off. Yeah, there was the possibility of being out-flanked, but I pointed out two, maybe three strategies, and that we had plenty of food, water and ammunition, but he said the only thing to do to protect the troops was to surrender. I was incensed; I told him that if he didn't recant his proposal, I would be forced to relieve him of his command. He refused, so I punched him in the face and laid him out cold. The upshot of it all was that he was charged with cowardice and I got made up to major."

"Was he shot?"

"No, he went quite mad while waiting for his trial and ended up in an asylum. The prison guards found out that he had a fear of snakes, so they used to drop them into his cell when he was asleep. A few months of that was all it took, and he went completely gaga. Mind you, life in a Correlan asylum is a fate worse than death."

Astrid ran her finger underneath Brigit's dog tags, admiring them as if they were jewels on a fine necklace.

"These don't come off, do they?"

"No, once you enlist, they're put on you and clamped. The chain is too small to get over your head and it's made of a steel alloy and quite tough. So, if you want them you would have to find a pair of strong cutters." She paused and smiled. "Or you could always cut my head off."

Astrid dragged her finger lightly across Brigit's throat. "Hmmm…about there should do." She smirked and made gagging sound. Both women fell back on the bed laughing.

****

62

"Being a lesbian here is risky, especially for you, isn't it?" said Astrid, turning her head toward Brigit and frowning a little with concern.

"Oh God yeah, very risky," Brigit replied grimly; she rolled onto her back and stared up at the ceiling. "Being gay or lesbian here is a serious criminal offence, for it 'destroys the moral fibre of the country' apparently," her voice was sarcastic and contemptuous as she recited the line from the law. "For a woman, being gay is classed almost as treason as it is deemed in law that a lesbian is a woman who is unwilling to have children and therefore unwilling to support the country in its war efforts."

"That's so wrong and it's harsh."

Brigit seethed, and gave full vent to her frustration. "Not as harsh as the punishments. For a civilian, it's bad enough, you're arrested, tried, found guilty – no one is ever found innocent – and sentenced to life in solitary confinement. Homosexuality is classified as an incurable infectious disease of the mind, so no close contact with anyone ever again. Just a lifetime of verbal abuse from the prison guards, however long or short that may be. Most top themselves after six months or so, the loneliness gets to them more than the abuse. They're given the means – bed sheets that rip into strips easily, and they're given plenty of opportunity; they are left alone for hours on end. And so what if another queer or dyke is found hanging in their cell. No one will care, and if they have a family outside, they won't even be told." She made no effort to hide her anger.

"God, I knew it was hard, but I didn't know it was that bad, so what's it like for a military person like you then?"

"Arrest, some pretty serious interrogation as to who I've had relations with – I think you know what that means; the interrogators reserve a special level of viciousness for gays and lesbians – and if I confessed, I would be left alone in a room with a loaded gun and told to get on with it. If I didn't confess and it came to trial, I would be found guilty and my punishment would be that I would be transferred to infantry, busted down to the rank of private third class; that's a punishment rank that's lower than a raw recruit; I would be in the first assault in whatever the next battle was, and I would not be allowed a weapon or any means of defending myself. I'd be told that I would have to find a weapon, and if by some miracle I wasn't ripped apart by the first salvo against me and I survived the battle, I would be given the chance to do it all over again, and again and again until I was dead."

She paused and the indignation in her voice faded. "But you know what, as strange as it seems, that isn't the worst part for me. We all know, when we sign up for service, that a violent death is possible, probable even, but what they would also do is expunge my service record. It would just show that I enlisted; nothing would remain of my career and I would just be forgotten."

"And still you serve."

"Yes. Ridiculous, isn't it? But then I can't do anything else and maybe things will change one day."

"How do you cope?"

"I don't really; I have a morning routine of running, swimming and couple of hours in the gym, then I bury myself in work, as I always have done. Fourteen to sixteen hours a day and then I'm too tired to think about it. I used to drink a lot of brandy every night; that helped me forget – a bit. But only until I realised that I was well on the way to liver disease and cut down. I have had one or two encounters over the years, but you have to be so very careful, you have to get yourself a cover."

"Is that why you got engaged to be married, to get yourself a cover?"

Brigit pushed herself up on her elbows and looked down at Astrid with an expression of exasperation. "You know about that as well! Good grief can't a girl have any secrets?" she gasped.

"Yeah, err, sorry." Astrid looked a little sheepish. "Saw it in the file as well." She paused for a few seconds. "So tell me about it, I'm intrigued now, there wasn't any detail."

Brigit flopped back down and sighed, half smiling.

"Oh Karl, my darling fiancé, what a tragedy that was. You see, I knew from a very early age what my preferences were and still are. But I kept them in check because I also knew from an early age that they could get me in an awful lot of trouble. So, I went through school studying like mad, taking exam after exam and playing the total swot. I would tell anyone who asked that I had no time for boys or any of that nonsense and all the time, I secretly lusted after the other girls. Oh God, did I lust after them – all of them. I had to keep my distance though, so I got a reputation for being aloof, but if only they knew all the things that I wanted to do to them. I'd see them all naked in the shower; there were twenty or so gorgeous, fully developed young women. I'd be up one end, watching them out of the corner of my eye, and they'd be down the other end washing each other's backs and so on. It was a good job they didn't ask me to do it, who knows where my hands would have ended up! And I'm sure I saw some of them masturbating from time to time. Maybe they were, or maybe they were just having a very thorough wash, I don't know. One always seemed to be looking at me when she was doing it, I wondered if she was gay and whether I should approach her. But then I had this little voice of doubt inside me that kept saying, *You are only seeing what you want to see*, and I suppose I was."

"Okay, back to this Karl, tell me more about him."

"It came time to leave school; all the other girls had found boyfriends or got married and became stay-at-home mums. I knew what I was going to do, I was going to join the army, it's what I always wanted to do. I knew that I just couldn't do the domestic thing; that wasn't for me, and let's face it, me getting pregnant was totally out of the question, so I volunteered to become an officer in the army. I did pretty well to start with as an officer cadet and was told that I would climb the ranks quickly once I was commissioned and in a regiment. I left training as a second lieutenant and joined the fifth heavy infantry. There were quite a few girls in the regiment and every few months there would be a social event. But it was quickly made very plain to me that any girl not in a relationship was expected to make themselves 'available' for the male officers."

"What! Fuck that," exclaimed Astrid, genuinely surprised.

"Yes, fuck that indeed, there was no way I was going to do that, so I just didn't go. I stayed in barracks and read up on tactical theory, regimental history, anything that would help my career. And I saw the girls when they came back, some with the bruises on their bodies, some girls looking shocked, some girls crying. Some actually liked the danger of fucking married officers, and others thought it would be good for their careers, but those girls were so wrong.

"I'd been there a while and been passed over for promotion twice, so I went to the base commander and asked him why. He said that my exam results were excellent and that he had heard nothing but praise about me from the senior staff, but the army liked its officers to be in relationships, preferably married, he said it gave the officer something else to fight for."

"What a load of patronising crap!"

"Yeah, but I could hardly tell a two-star general that, so I had to come up with a plan. I went to one of the wretched social events and there was an older man there, a civilian, which was unusual. I made a few enquiries and found out that he was Karl Davat. He was the deputy minister for arms procurement, and he was there simply by chance because the regiment had just taken delivery of a thousand new assault rifles. He was a divorcee, and I thought to myself, *This is perfect, an older man – more than twice my age, and a civilian, he'll do*. I can have a long-distance relationship by phone and make sure that when he's around, I would have to be away on manoeuvres. I could easily track his movements around the country, and it was not beyond my abilities to find out his schedule for up to a month in advance. So, I watched what the other girls did and copied them by undoing the top few buttons of my blouse and showing a bit of cleavage. Men like that, apparently."

"Well, most men do," said Astrid, nodding knowingly.

"Yes, so I've heard," laughed Brigit. "But he must have liked it a lot. I went over to him and looked up with big doe eyes and all he could do was gawp down my top. We chatted; well, he talked, and I listened. I laughed at his pathetic jokes. He told me that he had been divorced for fifteen years; he said that one day the wife had just walked out on him without saying why, except for there wasn't another man, and he had no idea why she had left, and how he hadn't found anyone else to share his life with.

"I did that banal thing of running my finger around the top of my glass with my head down but looking up at him and said in the most alluring, innuendo laden voice I could manage. 'Well, that could change.' His eyes nearly popped out of their sockets; he nodded towards the stairs and said something like 'we could start a relationship tonight if you like'. I smiled sweetly and said I had to be going. Familiarisation exercises on the new weapon were scheduled for the next morning, but that it had been nice meeting him and hoped that maybe we could meet up again sometime. At least the bit about familiarisation exercises was true, the rest of it wasn't.

"A couple of days later, he called me, and we arranged to meet during the day – I was very keen on not seeing him at night – and we met, and we met a few times more over the next few months, same routine every time. He talked, I smiled, I listened; well, I pretended to listen, bored to tears, but it started to work quite quickly. Maybe it was because he was a minister in the government, maybe not, I don't know, but I got promoted to lieutenant after only a few weeks, and then I was told that I would be fast-tracked to senior lieutenant, which was what the plan was all about. But the mistake I made though was in thinking that he was an older man who had not had a regular partner for fifteen years because he wasn't interested in sex, and my God, was I wrong about that.

"As I was now a lieutenant, I qualified for quarters of my own, so I finally and very reluctantly, relented and invited him back to my room, and it wasn't long before he was asking when we could have sex; he went on about it all the time. I had to make some pretence at a relationship, so we kissed and cuddled for a bit; that wasn't very nice, particularly when he put his tongue in my mouth. Then he grabbed my breasts and squeezed them hard and hurt me. I told him not to do that and he just said, 'Why not?' I made up something about an accident during an exercise. Then I made up some bullshit about my strong moral principles and how I was going to be a virgin on my wedding night. So, he then blithely said, 'Well, if you want to remain a virgin, we can have anal sex.' I said 'no' maybe a little bit firmer than I meant, but for God's sake, why do men want to do that; it's disgusting."

"Yes, it is, it's disgusting and it's degrading," said Astrid with more than a hint of bitterness.

Brigit looked at her with a faint frown of concern. "Oh, you poor thing, did someone make you do that?"

"Yes, and trust me, you don't want to."

She paused for a moment, letting Astrid's comments sink in.

"Carry on, what happened then, I'm okay, really, I'm okay," said Astrid.

"Well, after that Karl got a bit cross, he said, 'Well, the least you can do is give me a blowjob then.' It was more of a demand than a request. I said that I thought the moment had gone and we should just watch a bit of TV. He stood up and said that a relationship without sex is no relationship; it was like a meal without wine. I tried to make a joke of it by saying that I'd had plenty of meals without wine and there was nothing wrong with them. He didn't see the funny side and stormed out.

"The truth is that actually I didn't really know what a blowjob was, I sort of had an idea what it was, but didn't know what to do, so I asked one of the girls in the regiment and when she told me, I nearly heaved. She said it was great and she loved doing it because it made her boyfriend come – and I only had a vague idea of what that was as well. We'd all had our obligatory one-hour sex education lesson in school but that was couched in flowery language and with pictures of rabbits to stop the teachers getting embarrassed, and remember, I'd never had a boyfriend before.

"She said that as it would be my first time, if I didn't want to go all the way, I could always finish him off by hand. I must have given her a blank look, because she made this gesture with her hand that was like shaking a can of spray paint. She said the most comfortable way for me give him a blowjob was to lay on my left side on a sofa with my head in his lap holding his dick with my right hand, but then he wouldn't see anything, so I might have to kneel in front of him, so he could look at my breasts. She said, 'You've got to let him see your tits; he'll like that, and it'll get him going quicker.' She said that maybe, I should have a strong drink beforehand, make sure he had a good wash first and expect to get a bit of jaw ache and that I should have all my clothes off and let him have a good long look at my crotch as that would get him really hard – but obviously, she didn't say crotch, she used that other 'C' word – which I've never liked. She kept on saying things like 'when you get used to it, you'll really like sucking him off' and she kept using that 'C' word; it was just horrid, just so coarse; she wasn't doing a very good job of convincing me.

"Another girl came in and joined in the conversation, 'If you're bothered about it, just let him come all over your face, like this…' She had some porn magazines that she had bought for her boyfriend and she showed me a couple of pictures; there was a naked woman on her knees, with five naked men standing over her, and her face was absolutely covered in semen; it was in her hair, in her eyes. It was ghastly, and my only thought was how can a woman possibly get any sort of pleasure from doing that. I knew that the girls were only trying to help, but even so…" Brigit grimaced and shuddered as she recalled the image.

"Well, it's not really about the woman, is it? I don't think she's supposed to get any pleasure from doing that."

"Why do it then? And why allow someone to take photographs of you? It is so degrading; I just don't get it."

"It's just men getting off on their power over women, and she probably had no real choice anyway, she was either threatened or needed some money."

Brigit paused and sneered her nose up a little as she thought back and remembered doing the deed. "I went back to my room and mulled it over, and I realised that as grim as it was, I'd have to give it a go, and Karl was my only option right then, so I had to keep him in tow, I had to think of the end result."

Brigit stopped, and both women laughed at her unintended pun. She laughed. "Apparently, all women give their husbands or boyfriends blowjobs, so I asked myself just how bad could it be? I thought about all the disgusting things I've had to put in my mouth during survival training. You know the score, you must have had to do it, eating worms, digging up beetle larvae, eating them and drinking your own urine to stay alive."

Astrid nodded. "Yep, the joy that is survival training."

"Yeah, survival training is gross, but it's what you had to do in that situation. We don't have backup rescue during survival training, so it's survive or die, and in my current situation, giving Karl a blowjob was what I had to do. But still, this was oral sex with a man, and there is a bit of a difference between that and not starving to death. Also, I thought he was getting a bit suspicious; there was something in his voice when we talked. So, I called him up and apologised for the way I reacted and said if he came over, I would do something special for him. He was around within the hour. I had already had a couple of brandies and was as nervous as fuck, which is unlike me. I asked him to have a wash – if it had been up to me, I would have poured boiling bleach over it and scrubbed it with a wire brush, but he was quite thorough. I think he knew it was my first time."

"He sat there and leered at me while I took all my clothes off; he made a circling gesture with his finger, which I took to mean 'turn around slowly while I study your naked body'. I really didn't like that – I didn't like that at all, but I thought, *Okay, this is what I've got to do*. Then he got *it* out; I didn't know whether it was big, small or what, I'd never seen one in the flesh before, so to speak. I sat beside him and held it like I'd seen in that wretched porn mag and it was rock hard and hot, really hot, which took me by surprise a bit. I really, really, really didn't want to do it, but I just couldn't put it off for any longer. I laid down with my head in his lap, opened my mouth as wide as I could, put it inside, closed my lips around it and bobbed my head up and down. I was just starting to think to myself that this wasn't too horrible when…" Brigit grimaced again.

"Oh, I think I know what happened next," said Astrid, sneering her nose up.

"…he put his hands on the back of my head so I couldn't move away and ejaculated in my mouth!"

"Oh yuk."

"He must have been desperate, it had only been a matter of seconds, and there was just so much of it. It took me by surprise, so much so that I inadvertently swallowed some."

Astrid put her hand over her mouth in shock. "Oh God no, what did you do?"

Brigit laughed. "Well, what do you think I did? I threw up, I threw up all over him. I can laugh about it now, but I couldn't at the time because I couldn't stop throwing up. Every time I thought about what had just happened, I heaved again – oh God, just thinking about it now is making my stomach churn. But by now I was on the floor, on all fours, naked, retching away. I must have looked like one of those hairless cats being sick."

"What did he do?"

"He did his nut. 'I knew you'd fucking ruin it,' he yelled. But by then I had been heaving so hard that I must have burst a blood vessel or something and I was bringing up little clots of blood. When he saw that, he pissed off straight away."

"He did nothing to help you?"

"Nope, just left me there."

"He was a right little charmer, your Karl."

"Well, I was able turn to it to my advantage. I called him up a couple of days later and said sorry. Can you believe it, I had to apologise to him for fuck's sake!"

"Oh, the things we do for love…err, careers, I mean," said Astrid mockingly.

"I told him some pile of crap about me being checked out by a doctor and had been told that I had a rare allergy and what I had was human seminal plasma protein hypersensitivity, and that meant I was actually allergic to semen."

"I have heard of that before."

"Oh yeah, SPH is a real medical condition, but I just didn't have it, at least I don't think so, let's face it, I'm never likely to find out now, am I? I looked it up, apparently; it's the cause of a lot of infertility. I had to make sure in case Karl checked up, even though I knew he wouldn't."

Brigit smiled and chuckled a bit gleefully.

"I said that the doctor had told me that being sick had saved my life, because the form I had was so acute that now if I had any more contact with semen, it would produce an even more violent, possibly fatal reaction, even if I just got it on my skin and definitely fatal if I ingested any. Just the smell of it could cause severe breathing difficulties."

"Well, it does stink."

"Oh God, it is foul, isn't it?" Both women screwed their noses up.

"I could tell he was getting grumpy so before he could say anything in response, I said that it was treatable with a course of drugs and that I would be cured by our wedding day. That perked him up and he said, 'So, six months then.' I said, 'No, it would be at least a year.' Then he got all shitty again and said that if I was allergic to semen, how they would know if I was cured; would I have to suck off the doctor at regular intervals? He was all sarcastic when he said it. I said no, and for him not to be silly, and that there was a hormone-based cream that they would put on my skin that mimicked the allergen. Then I put on this low sexy voice and said that once the course had finished, we could set a date for the wedding and to make sure the treatment had been successful. I would give him a blowjob and let him do what he did before, and that as I had been cured, I now wouldn't throw up. I was gagging as I said it, but at least I had bought myself some time. We announced the engagement and saw each other about every six weeks or so, sometimes I would be able to say that I was on my period, and then he would look at me as if I was a leper, but I couldn't use that too often as one day I saw him make a note of the date in his diary. So there had to be some sex every now and then."

"What was the sex?"

"The sex was me doing what he told me to do, which comprised of him leering at me while I got undressed, prancing naked around the room pretending I was enjoying it – which I didn't – then I would sit in a chair in one corner of the room with my legs open with my fingers stuck up my vagina, fondling my breasts with my other hand, trying to look like I was getting off on it – which I wasn't – and all the while he sat in the opposite corner, trousers down around his ankles, dick in hand, wanking. The only saving grace was that it didn't last long, thirty seconds tops and he would suddenly stand up, do it all over the carpet, get dressed then just fuck off."

"Leaving you to clear it all up."

"Yes, and there was always so much of it. It was disgusting, and it was starting to leave a stain." Brigit shuddered with revulsion. "It was gross, really gross, and all the time I had to make it look like I was pleased for him. But you know I had realised quite soon after I met him why his wife had left him and why he was still single."

"That he was an arrogant, obnoxious, self-centred chauvinistic bastard and that no woman in her right mind would want to be with a creep like him?"

"Correct."

"So, you said it was a tragedy, what happened to him?"

"Oh, err, he, erm, died," said Brigit a bit too nonchalantly, looking away, fiddling with the sheet and smirking.

"Oh really," said Astrid, over-exaggerating the feigned surprise for comic effect.

"Yes. As I said, he was deputy minister arms procurement. Then one day, the actual minister was about to make some crap-filled speech to parliament. He got up to the podium, opened his notes, suddenly grabbed his chest, keeled over and died of a heart attack, live on TV."

"All of which meant that your Karl would automatically become Minister Davat."

"Yes, though it wouldn't have been straight away, there would have been formalities to go through first. There would have to have been a transition period of a couple of weeks before he got promoted, picking his staff, sorting out his new office, getting briefed by aides and the civil servants, that sort of thing. But then once he got the promotion, he would have had a whole new level of security which meant that I would have no access to his schedule. He would be able to turn up on base unannounced and I would not be able to control the relationship."

"So how did Karl die?"

Brigit rolled over onto her front and propped herself up on her elbows, grinning like an imp.

"He was assassinated. Actually, it was the very day before he was officially promoted and would have got the extra security, such unfortunate timing. He was on his way to parliament to finish moving things into his ministerial office. The car pulled up right outside the main gate and as he got out, a woman stepped forward; he probably thought she wanted his autograph. He was vain enough to think things like that. But instead she pulled out a Nagler 5.2mm submachine gun on full auto and put the whole magazine, twenty-two rounds, into his chest in under a second before the driver/excuse for a bodyguard, could react. When he did respond, he wrestled her to the ground and then there was a big explosion. The report later said that she had an estimated 350 grams of military grade explosive in a dildo stuck up herself."

"Good grief! Was there anything left of her?"

"All they found of her and the driver that was recognisable were bits of his arms and legs and her hands and feet, the rest was just a mush of bones and blood, oh and his head, what was left of it, was found hanging in a tree about two hundred metres away which freaked out the civilians who saw it, unaccustomed as they are to what an explosion really does to a body."

Brigit was sarcastic, not hiding the distain she felt for those civilians who want to see heavy artillery being fired or big bombs exploding but who would recoil in horror and revulsion if they saw the effects of an explosion on a human being, and the fact that these same people are the ones that would be most vocal about the brutal futility of war. She sighed, irritated, but calmed herself.

"There was an investigation and the conclusion of the final report was that she had most likely been on her way to carry out a sabotage mission and that Karl was probably just a target of opportunity. He was just in the wrong place at the wrong time, and that the woman had been watched by her handler who detonated the explosive by radio link when it was obvious that she was about to be captured."

Astrid now rolled onto her front and also propped herself up on her elbows. She leant forward and gave Brigit a playful kiss on the cheek, then ran her hand down Brigit's back and onto her bottom making her shudder with pleasure.

"Now tell me," she asked wryly, "where were you when this all happened?"

"Oh, would you believe it, by an amazing coincidence, I was in the city that day; actually I wasn't that far away, I even heard the explosion," said Malaya with a slight smile.

"I asked for and was given permission to read the eulogy at his funeral. I wrote it myself, and I must say, I almost believed it. It was full of bullshit and meaningless epithets, like how he was such a good man and how much of a tragedy it was that the country would never know what a great man he clearly would have become. How I had seen the greatness in him that no one else had, blah, blah, blah, future leader blah, blah, how no other man could ever come close to what I had with Karl etc....And – and this was the crucial bit – that I could never, and would never be able to love another man, so strong was my love for him. The army was my husband now and a whole other bunch of crap like that.

"I even managed a tear or two. It's remarkable what a few drops of ammonia on a handkerchief will do. Then suddenly Grand Field Marshall Hallenberg got up and came over to the podium. I wasn't expecting that, and it made me a bit uneasy. He gestured for me to stand aside as he took the microphone. 'This woman has suffered as I have suffered,' he bellowed. 'She has lost a loved one, just as I lost a loved one, she has vowed never to marry and to give her life to the army, just as I vowed never to marry and to give my life to the army.' Then he made this big show of pulling off the black armband that he had worn since his wife died and handed it to me. 'Let this woman's solitude never be an impediment to her life and career in the army, for it is an honourable thing that she does.' As I took it and put it on, everyone stood up and started clapping. Now that really took me by surprise, and in that moment, I knew from then onward that all the old chauvinists would have to back off. I made a point of always wearing the armband to any social function and making sure that when I was photographed with any top brass, I always had it on show."

"So, with him setting the example of never marrying again, no one would ever dare refuse you a promotion."

"Correct." Brigit smiled triumphantly. "Neat huh?"

"How did his wife die?"

"Oh, she was the very first of our civilian casualties of the war. The stupid cow shouldn't have been where she was. She was visiting the front line – checking up on him probably – and stepped on an anti-personnel mine. It turned her inside out."

"It must have been one of ours, sorry about that," said Astrid, a bit apologetically.

"Oh, don't be, it's always been known that it was a Correlan mine. And besides, I never met her, but by all accounts, she was an absolute fucking bitch. Hallenberg was glad to be rid of her so he could carry on with all his mistresses – sorry, I mean his personal assistants. Mind you the assistance they give him could hardly be more personal, if you know what I mean." Brigit smiled, revelling in the rare little bit of gossip that she allowed herself.

There was a long silence as both women got lost in their own thoughts.

"There's one thing I am curious about Karl's assassination," said Astrid with a wry smile. "I've fired Nagler 5.2 submachine guns many times," she said thoughtfully. "To empty the entire magazine and get all twenty-two rounds in an area the size of a man's chest is hard to do, even at close range. The thing is breathtakingly fast and kicks up and to the right, you have to hold it very firmly. It takes a lot of practice and training, the kind of practice and training you only get in the army. And that military grade explosive, not easy to come by, even on the black market."

"You know these terrorists, they are very resourceful, and they get more skilled every day," Brigit's tone was a bit too matter-of-fact as she waved a deliberately exaggerated dismissive gesture with her hand.

Astrid pushed herself up on one elbow.

"Was she an army deserter that you found?" she said playfully.

Brigit pushed herself up on one elbow, turning to face Astrid. "She might have been," she smiled.

"And had she joined the Northern Alliance to fight against the government?"

"Possibly."

"And did you contact her and pose as a senior member of the Northern Alliance?"

Malaya beamed delightedly.

"Oh, meeting her was pure serendipity, I was up north on a fact-finding mission a month or so earlier and quite literally bumped into her; she didn't recognise me, but I have the faces of deserters burned into my memory. A few weeks earlier, we had captured some NA fighters and 'acquired' valuable intelligence of their command structure, so I knew the correct code words to use when meeting a possible NA contact. I had spent quite a bit of time in the northern territories in my youth and had been stationed there for a couple of years, so the voice was easy to put on, y' know like." She drawled out the words with the lazy accent of a Correlan northerner.

"She took it all at face value, so over the course of a week I met with her three times. My original plan was to use her as an unwitting double agent. She said that she had deserted after hearing that some government soldiers had raped her sister; she was disillusioned with the army anyway and when the military police wouldn't investigate, she went AWOL and joined the NA.

"I listened and showed all the sympathy I could and made all the right noises. She was adamant that she wanted to strike at the government, so that gave me an idea. I played her along, telling her all the things she wanted to hear. Eventually I told her about a sabotage mission, I told her to move to the capital where I would provide her with the necessary equipment and to wait for my signal. I also told her that the mission was ultra-top secret, and she was not to talk to any of the other NA commanders about it."

Astrid wagged her finger feigning disapproval. "That's terrible," she said.

"Well, look," Brigit said apologetically but defiantly at the same time. "The way I saw it was that I had a duty, as all officers have, to turn in deserters. If I had, she would have suffered horribly at the hands of the guards; they'd have tortured her for information, raped her to within an inch of her life and then she'd have been hung, also I had this problem which I had to do something about. So, after a couple of weeks, I contacted her and told her that the mission parameters had changed. It was still sabotage, but if on the way she saw the opportunity to assassinate a government minister, then that would become the priority – and I knew that was what she most wanted. I met up with her and gave her all the kit she needed and made sure that she would be in the right place at the right time.

"I was also quite up front about it, I said that it was extremely risky, with very low chance of survival, but she said she didn't care, she had sworn an oath to die for the NA and their struggle was worth more than her life. I knew when and where he would be, and it was just a question of putting her outside parliament as he arrived. So, I think that I did her a big favour, she went out on a blaze of glory, striking one up for the Northern Alliance, and I got my problem solved."

"Didn't that cause problems at the ministry, what with the minister dying of a heart attack and the successor being gunned down?"

"Good God no, all the work in government is done by the department. All the ministers do is rubber stamp the decisions, report to parliament and take all the credit. If there are any problems, then the department heads make sure that some junior takes the blame, because they all use the CYA principle."

"CYA?"

"Cover your arse. Rule number one, never take the blame. Rule number two, never take the blame and so on. I even heard it said that with the minister dead and my beloved Karl not taking up his position as minister that the department was far easier to deal with."

Astrid frowned. "I hate all that political crap, all those armchair warrior bastards up there in their ivory towers throwing orders around and never getting their hands dirty. They should come and work with us, and then they'd see what the real world is all about."

Astrid's Life Story

"It's not illegal in your country, being gay, isn't it?" said Brigit.

"No. It's not illegal, but it's not really legal either."

Brigit frowned slightly. "I don't understand."

Astrid sighed a weary sigh borne of years of frustration with a system. "There's no law against being lesbian or homosexual, but it is heavily frowned upon. If you are suspected of being gay you get arrested on some other charge – there's always something they can pick you up for – then you get a lifetime of harassment from the police. You have to keep moving home, you can never settle anywhere."

"I never knew that." Brigit sat up and was openly stunned.

"Yeah, well, not quite the free-thinking liberal democracy you thought it was, huh?" said Astrid bitterly.

Brigit sat with her mouth open in disbelief for a few seconds.

"I am genuinely shocked by that. We've always been led to believe…"

"Yeah, well, like I said before, the propaganda machine is the only thing that works properly in that country."

Astrid had a weary tone to her voice and spoke with an air of resignation. "There were these clubs though, they would put on ladies' nights once or twice a month. You could sort of get your rocks off there if you were lucky." She seemed to perk up at the memory.

"There would be four or five male strippers on each night and the place would usually be packed with frustrated housewives and unmarried women keen to see a stiff dick for the first time, God knows why, they'll soon get fed up with it once they're married. So the place was always full of women, no men other than the strippers.

"Even the bar staff on those nights were all girls. Gay girls would go but they would be right at the back pretending to be interested. What you would look out for was a certain make of wristwatch. It was a kind of flag if you were in the know. You'd ask the time. If they said, 'Quarter to,' it meant they were already with someone or weren't interested, if they said, 'Quarter past,' it meant they

77

were up for it. You'd wait for the guys to be doing their thing on stage, and while everyone else was looking the other way you could have a snog and get your tits felt and maybe a quick finger fuck." The frustration with the law made Astrid use language that was far coarser than she would normally do. "But it wasn't very satisfying, and you had to be really careful."

"Why did you have to be so careful?"

"The police!" She paused as anger flashed across her face. "They're all total fucking pigs," she snapped, then paused again, scowling.

"But my God, some of them are bastards, real bastards. They will arrest a girl, and then cut her a deal that she had no choice but to go along with. They will make sure she was left alone provided that she went to the clubs and gave them the names of other girls. If you asked the time and they said, 'Half past,' it meant they were informers and you felt really sorry for them because every now and then, they would be put under pressure from the cops and they would have to turn some poor girl in. After a while, you didn't need to ask the time, you could see the sadness in their eyes of what they were being forced to do and that they hated themselves for it. So you never knew what might be waiting for you outside when you left the club."

Brigit sat open mouthed in shock. "I don't know what to say, that is just horrible. Oh, why do we have to suffer so much?" A hint of anguish crept into her voice. "What is it that we do that is so bad that we have to get treated like this? Why can't we be left alone to love who we want to love?" Brigit stared at the ceiling taking in everything that Astrid had just said, trying to come to terms with the fact that everything she thought she knew was wrong.

Eventually she turned to Astrid. "So, what about you, what's your story. Have you always known?"

"I found out quite late." Astrid laid back down and stared up at the ceiling. "For the first ten years of my life, I was happy – you know that I was brought up here, don't you?"

"Yes, your parents worked here."

"We moved here when I was about six months old." She pushed herself up on her elbows and frowned a little, as if recalling something she didn't want to.

"I always thought that you had been born here."

"No, that would have made things very complicated when the problems started, I'd have legally been a Correlan national." Astrid sighed and laid back down.

"My parents decided to move back home; they saw the build-up, they heard the speeches, saw the harassment of foreigners, watched as the troops were mobilised. I didn't know anything, I was ten and a half, all I knew was that I had to leave all the friends that I had made and move back to a country that I didn't know anything about and didn't call home. I was brought up bi-lingual, fluent in both languages, and I thought that was normal, I thought everybody spoke two languages; in fact, at the time I didn't even realise it was two separate languages.

"I didn't know anyone, and all the kids at my new school teased me and said I was a spy, I didn't know what a spy was. Then my parents started rowing all the time. I only found out years later that they had both been having affairs and had to leave their lovers behind. They kept on saying that they came back to keep me safe, I didn't know what they meant, and so I thought that the rows were all about me and that somehow it was all my fault.

"I started missing school and began hanging out with some older kids, I guess they were a bad influence, but at the time I thought they were really cool. They smoked and drank and didn't go home for days at a time. I lost my virginity at thirteen, and that was just horrid. The girls in the group kept saying, 'You've got to do it, it's great, you'll love it,' and all that crap. So I finally did it with this eighteen-year-old guy who was rough, and he hurt me. I cried all night, but all the girls said that it was always like that the first time and that after a while, I would have an orgasm and it would be fantastic."

Brigit sensed that Astrid was starting to fight with her emotions. "Look, you don't have to tell me if you don't want to," she said, gently stroking Astrid's hair.

"No, it's okay, I want to, I've never told anyone else this before and it's cathartic," she wiped a tear from the corner of her eye.

"I left home when I'd just turned fifteen, I couldn't stand it any longer. They weren't rowing any more, they were just drunk all the time, too pissed to even notice whether I was there or not. Both of them sitting in silence in different rooms in the house that became filthier, more squalid every day, they were just avoiding each other. By that time, I was sponging off a couple of older guys that I knew. I moved in with one of them. They got sex, I got food and somewhere to stay; I would alternate between them, one for a couple of weeks, then the other.

"Yeah, I used them, but they used me. But one day, they both just disappeared; they had apparently decided to travel and hadn't bothered to tell me. The food in the shabby flat that one of them used ran out after a couple of days and I was starving. I had enough self-control not to steal, I wasn't going to risk an arrest – I knew what happened to young runaway girls like me in prison cells – and besides I still had just enough morals to know that stealing was wrong. I knew that some kids did drugs to keep the hunger at bay, but I also didn't do drugs. I saw what that did to the older girls and there was no way I was going down that road either."

Astrid struggled with words for a few minutes, starting sentences then stopping, her breath shortening. Tears welled in her eyes, her voice became hesitant. Eventually she spoke.

"Then one day, this guy came to talk to me; he said he was a priest, he gave me all these God-bothering pamphlets. He told me to read them and they would help me," her voice wavered as she forced the memories out.

"After a couple of days, he came back to me. He said he had been watching me for a while and that he would give me some money if I let him do something. He was in his late fifties, like, over forty years older than me. He told me what he wanted to do. I didn't like the idea, but I didn't really have a choice. I needed the money, I was so hungry. We went back to the flat, I stripped off and gave him a blowjob, then he pushed me onto this mattress, rolled me over onto my front and got on top of me. He got this cream which he said would make it easier; he squirted some on my backside and rubbed it in a bit and as he did that, he put his finger in my anus; that was vile, it didn't hurt as such, but it was so uncomfortable. He was masturbating with his other hand and after a minute or so, he got on top of me. Then he put 'it' in – around the back."

She closed her eyes tight but was unable to stop her tears from streaming down her face.

"He had to push so hard, and he kept saying 'just relax your muscles' but it hurt so much. I was crying and begging him to stop, but he just kept saying 'just a little bit longer' and he seemed to like that it hurt me. He went on for ages, eventually he came inside me which was just the most disgusting thing I have ever experienced, then he stood up and he completely changed.

"He was crying and kept asking me to forgive him. He said that he was a devout religious man, but his wife didn't understand him and that he was sorry and how ashamed he was. Then he suddenly changed again, he snarled at me. 'But you wanted it like that didn't you, you like it, you dirty little slut, I've met little whore scum like you before, tricking good men of faith like me for your own dirty pleasures. Well, here you are, this is what filth like you do it for.' He put down a whole bunch of money beside me and left. I laid there and cried for hours. I just couldn't understand why he had been so horrible."

Brigit wiped the tears from Astrid's cheek. "You poor, poor thing, I had no idea."

"I hated myself for years." Astrid spat out the words angrily. "All my self-esteem had gone; I was degraded and ashamed," she hissed through clenched teeth.

"I didn't even bother to try to get this elusive orgasm thing that was supposed to be so wonderful. I thought, *If that's what guys want, then that's what they want,* and I couldn't change that." She calmed down and wiped away the tears with the back of her hand.

"Eventually I hooked up with a couple of new guys and told them the deal. 'You fuck me, so you have to feed me.' So for a year or so, I went to a lot of parties, just me and a load of guys and I became the latest trick. I put on a really good floorshow. I did everything, oral, anal, two at a time, three at a time. You name it, I did it, but still I just felt empty, and the more I slept around, the less human I felt.

"In my heart of hearts, I knew it couldn't continue, so I decided to try something new. At seventeen, I left that group behind and enrolled as a student nurse at a hospital. I didn't have any relationships for a couple of years, I didn't want any. Of course, I saw girls naked in the communal showers, but I didn't feel anything, and despite everything I'd done, sex with a girl never actually crossed my mind." Astrid smiled again; the pain in her eyes disappeared, and she sighed, recalling a pleasant moment in time. "Then one day she arrived."

"The one?"

"Oh God yeah, was she ever the one." Astrid looked wistfully into the distance. "I didn't know it at the time, all I knew was that I couldn't take my eyes off her, I told myself not to be so silly, but whenever I saw her, I became breathless and I knew I was blushing. She would look at me and smile, and I was like some stupid teenage girl with a crush, which I suppose I was. But I just couldn't stop thinking about her. Then I was alone in the shower one day and she walked in. I can't begin to say what it was about her, because I just don't know what it was; she wasn't beautiful, but there was just, I don't know, there was just something about her, and when she took her clothes off and got in the shower next to me, I had shivers running down my spine.

81

"She smiled at me and asked me to wash her back, my hands were shaking; I felt so foolish. She turned around and moved my hands onto her breasts. Then she kissed me and said softly, 'Come on'. We went to my room, kissed and caressed each other. I was still shaking, but I wasn't nervous, I just wanted this so bad. We made love, she went down on me and it was just incredible; I couldn't believe how good it felt. I went down on her, I'd never even thought of doing that before, but it was just such a natural, gorgeous thing to do, and oh God, it was so good. She was so loving, so giving, and the orgasm that I had waited for so long was beautiful beyond words. She showed me who I really was, but in the morning, she was gone, and I never even knew her name. That was twelve years ago, she turned on my lights and I have been longing for that feeling ever since, I never thought that I would find it again until…" She held Malaya's hand up to her cheek then kissed it. "…Until today when I met you."

The two women embraced, holding each other tightly, kissing passionately, both crying, but not through sadness.

"I can't believe I've finally found someone who's my equal, someone that I could spend the rest of my life with, and it's you," said Brigit, emotion cracking in her voice as she nuzzled Astrid's neck.

Astrid dropped back, Brigit propped herself up on one elbow, looking down at Astrid, admiring her naked body. She slipped her hand between Astrid's thighs.

"If only there was somewhere, a place we could run away to," said Astrid longingly. She opened her legs a fraction, and took Brigit's hand, guiding it up her inner thigh, encouraging her. "Somewhere where we could put aside our differences and live the way we want to."

"And love the way we want to," said Brigit. "I would lick you so hard, you wouldn't be able to walk straight."

"A desert island, somewhere warm, somewhere we could grow old together."

"Just the two of us, catching our own food, no orders to follow, naked all the time. It would be so good."

Both women lay staring up at the ceiling for a few minutes, Brigit's hand on Astrid's crotch, her fingers moving ever so gently back and forth. But slowly the warm blanket of fantasy slipped away to be replaced by the cold air of reality.

"Too many people have seen you; if it was just that imbecile Jackan, I would put a bullet in his head without a second thought." There was a long pause. "I can't protect you." Emotion cracked Brigit's throat again.

"I know."

Brigit's voice turned to sadness. "I know what they're going to do to you, and I can't bear the thought of it." She gasped and held Astrid tight.

"I knew exactly what would happen to me when I let myself be captured," Astrid spoke softly to calm Brigit as she stroked her hair. "I am under no illusions."

"But I can't help you," said Brigit in anguish, as she pulled away a little, Astrid wiped the tears from her cheek.

"Actually, you can."

"How?" Brigit was puzzled.

"Tell me exactly what will happen tomorrow."

"Really?" Brigit was shocked that someone would choose to know what awaited them in a situation like this.

"Yes, please, it will help me."

Brigit sniffed back her tears and composed herself. This time it was she who struggled with the words, opening her mouth to speak, only to check herself and mentally rephrase what she would say. Finally, she was calm enough.

"They'll come for you at nine thirty. I—"

"No, no, no," said Astrid. "More detail, I need to know pretty much minute by minute from now on."

Brigit looked deep into Astrid's eyes. "Are you sure?"

"Yes, look, it really will help me to come to terms with it all. I know it will be hard for you, but please, I need to know."

Brigit sighed and lay back on the bed, staring up at the ceiling, breathing deeply. At last she spoke.

"Captain Krall, my aide, will drive from her quarters on the other side of the base, and at five thirty precisely, she will walk through the main entrance and ten minutes later will enter the shower; she likes to shower before anyone else, actually. I think she just considers the other women to be uncouth and doesn't want to be with them. At five past six, she'll leave the shower room and get a coffee, then at six twenty, she'll sit at her desk. Ten minutes early, always the same routine, it never varies."

"What's she like?"

"What's she like?" Brigit laughed but without humour. "She's the spitting image of you, you could be twins." She looked closely at Astrid's face. "Your eyes are a similar colour, and your hair is very close. The resemblance between you is uncanny, so much so that she's been arrested a few times and on a couple of occasions, she's been badly beaten up by the guards. The last time the beating was so severe, it nearly killed her. I didn't recognise her when I saw her in hospital. After that, I issued her with a special warrant card with my stamp on it. Any arguments she just shoves it in their faces. Needless to say, she is very hostile towards the guards, and to everyone else; come to think of it, she now has what they call a 'resting bitch face'."

"What about the two outside?"

"She just about tolerates them, she's really stroppy to the others though."

"What then, I'll still be here. Won't that look a bit odd?"

"I'll tell her that I had the guards bring you up from the cells early, she won't ask them about it, and they won't tell her."

Brigit paused, breathing deeply, aware of the enormity of the next part of the time line.

"At nine fifteen, a squad of military police will arrive and at nine thirty, they will enter my office. I will sign a piece of paper and they will take you. I won't see you again."

Astrid held Brigit, stroking her face and smiling to ease her troubled mind.

"It's okay," she whispered over and over. Slowly Brigit calmed and eventually a slight smile returned to her face. Astrid leaned over and gently brushed Brigit's hair back.

"Thank you, thank you so much. Now this is for you." Astrid said in a soft, reassuring voice as she slipped her hand between Brigit's thighs and leant down kissing her gently on the lips. Brigit put her hand on Astrid's thigh.

"No," said Astrid. "This is just for you, this is my parting gift to thank you for this night of love that I have longed for, for so many years. I want to give it to you, and I want you to take it from me."

Brigit relaxed as Astrid gently worked her fingers while kissing down around her neck then further down kissing her breasts. Brigit's breath eventually started to quicken. Astrid could hear, feel and see the woman's heart pounding. She kissed around her neck, gently licking the skin with the tip of her tongue, feeling the pulse in her neck. She kissed below her ears and breathed heavily into her hair. Brigit began to writhe slowly, holding her breath for a few moments before exhaling deeply. Astrid kissed her neck, gently running her teeth across the skin, teasing her. Brigit tensed, her neck tight as her back began to arch. She held her breath as the small of her back lifted off the sheet at the point of climax.

Suddenly Astrid moved, clamped her hand over Brigit's mouth, grabbed one hand and knelt on the other. Then bit down as hard as she could across Brigit's jugular vein; she wrenched her head back, tearing open the blood vessel. An arc of crimson sprayed out onto the wall, her hand stifling Brigit's scream.

"Did you really think I would let you live?" she snarled as Brigit bucked beneath her. "You organised the Kindala massacre, you organised the Dantu massacre; a thousand civilians, old men, women and children. You let a thousand prisoners of war starve to death rather than feeding them. And you…" Astrid was breathless with anger. "…You sent the assassin that killed the only man I ever loved. And I swore that one day I would rip out your throat and look into your eyes as you died."

Brigit bucked again, trying to throw Astrid off and screamed, trying to bite through her fingers. It took all of Astrid's strength to hold Brigit down, but already she was starting to weaken.

"Everything I said to you was a lie, but thank you, you have told me all I need to know to just walk out of here."

Astrid had watched enough people bleed to death to know that the woman only had a few seconds left and that she could release her grip. Brigit wouldn't even have the strength to even speak now. Brigit looked up at her, anguish mixed with anger in her eyes.

"I hate you," she mouthed. The blood flow had almost stopped.

"I lied about our weapons, they are all fully functional and very effective. There was one truth though, we do know your battle plans and your army will be annihilated. Think on that as you rot in hell. Now just die, you bitch, just die."

Brigit let out a long final breath, fluid gurgling in her throat, then her pupils dilated, her head rolled to one side and she was gone. Astrid looked down at her with contempt, she was shattered. Listening to Malaya's life story and making it look like she was interested, then ad-libbing her entire life story, making it convincing, eliciting sympathy, adding pathos and a little humour, keeping the continuity, being careful not to contradict herself and making it flow as if it was all being recalled from memory had been exhausting. It had all taken so much longer than she had planned. But now she was tired, hungry and thirsty, and covered in blood.

She looked again at Brigit's corpse and thought of her personal mantra of 'no red lines and nothing off limits' the mindset that she had decided on all those years ago and how it had brought her to this office and enabled her to fulfil the promise she had made to herself and kill Malaya. "I told you that I get up close and personal, I told you that my targets don't know that I am about to kill them. If you had listened, you'd still be alive." Astrid went into the bathroom, picked up a towel and wiped away blood from her face, then rinsed some blood out of her hair. Anger rose within her as she looked back at Malaya's body. "How dare you say that I was your equal?"

Astrid's life had been almost the complete opposite of the one she had described. From an early age, she had wanted to be an improvisational actress, but when war broke out, she had felt an overwhelming sense of duty and had given up all thoughts of acting to become a nurse, and it wasn't until much later that she discovered her fighting skills and thus her true calling. She had retained her acting skills and they had served her well today.

She looked back down at Malaya's corpse; she felt no pity and felt no remorse. Malaya's death was the mission, but a mission that she had almost let fail. And that bothered her.

She recalled the mission briefing; it was held four days ago in the office of intelligence command chief, Colonel DeSalva; she knew him well and respected him. He was a straight-talking man and would not ever seek to lessen the impact of unwelcome news or the prospects of a bad mission outcome. As usual, it was just the two of them, and his expression told her that this was a serious mission.

He took a file marked 'Eyes only IC Chief Colonel DeSalva' from his desk drawer and handed it to her. "Don't open it yet," his tone was business-like but friendly. "I need to talk to you first. Please, sit." Astrid pulled up a chair and sat directly opposite DeSalva.

"As you are aware, our strategy has always been to eliminate the enemy's senior commanders, and as our most efficient assassin, you are at the top of their most wanted list, of which you are also aware. We have received information regarding a change to the enemy's attitude towards you. The rule was always that you were to be summarily executed as soon as you were caught. We are not sure why, but this has changed recently, and a new rule has been issued that you are to be taken alive and as unharmed as possible, and to be transported immediately to the Kandalan Base and presented to the commander. We surmise that the base commander will want to interrogate you before the military police take you. This is just a guess, but it plays into our hands.

"Your mission is to allow yourself to be caught and then assassinate the base commander before making your escape. You will be dropped by helicopter inside enemy territory and you will have to make your way towards your target's base. How you achieve everything else is up to you, but I don't need to tell you that this is very high risk, and there is no way of lessening the impact of this mission for you; we estimate your chances of surviving are around five percent at best. But whatever the outcome, it is win-win for us. If you succeed, then another major player is taken out of their game. If you fail, it will still show that we can get an assassin into one of their bases and that will unnerve them."

The colonel paused uncharacteristically. "The only other person that knows about this mission is Field Marshall D'Frey. I chose you for this mission after discussing it with him." There was another pause, this was unusual. Astrid sensed something significant was coming. "We considered giving this assignment to someone else, but it will be a difficult mission and you are the best."

This had not been meant as flattery to boost Astrid's ego before the mission and she had not taken it as such. Her mission planning was always meticulous, but plans can only be made with the information at hand and with educated guesses as to how the enemy would react. Plans often fall apart, and that's when the ability to improvise makes the difference between success and failure. And her supreme ability to improvise is what makes her the best.

"We have to move fast on this one and I'm afraid you will only have two days to come up with a plan. Now, when you meet your target, you must not let your personal feelings get in the way, as that might cloud your judgement."

This was a strange thing for him to say to her; in previous operations, he had never even suggested that her personal feelings could allow her to compromise a mission.

"Sir?"

"All will become clear, the name of your target is on page one in the file, you may open the document now."

Astrid opened the file, and all did become clear very quickly, under the heading of 'Target' was the name Major General Brigit Malaya, beneath that was a photograph of her. Astrid's heart skipped a beat and she breathed out heavily upon reading the name – the name of a woman that she had sworn to kill all those years ago. Though trying hard not to show her emotions, she could not help but stiffen and the colonel noticed the change in body language.

"As I said, do not let your personal feelings get in the way, as you well know, she is utterly ruthless and vicious with it, and by the time you meet her, you will almost certainly be weaker than her. You must find her weakness and exploit it; the file contains her personal profile. It is extensive and has taken years to build up and analyse…" He looked down at the file, avoiding eye contact with Astrid. "…and we think there is a course of action which we feel shows promise, read the profile thoroughly and see what you think." He paused again. "We believe that she would be open to seduction and all that is entailed in that."

Astrid knew immediately what he meant. She had always considered herself heterosexual, and she enjoyed all aspects of sex with men, but if seducing Malaya was the course of action to take, it would almost certainly require her to perform oral sex on a woman. This is something that no heterosexual female would willingly do, but it paled into insignificance when put against going into combat, or killing people with her bare hands, or being captured and suffering relentless abuse and interrogation.

"Is there a problem?" DeSalva asked, unable to keep a faint hint of concern from his voice.
"There is no problem, sir." She looked back at Malaya's picture. "But why is time so short?"
"She personally ordered the change in the rules regarding your capture; this tells us that she would want to see you. She made the change without consulting the army council, and they had approved Kedara's original order for you to be shot on sight. They may not like her new order and overrule it, hence the urgency." He opened the file on the army council personnel. "First, a bit of background that may help you. On being promoted to major general and therefore the commander of the Kandalan Base, she had promoted her only rival for the post – General Lothar Valerian – to command a basic training camp in

the north. It was to get him out of the way. Training Camp North is used to take 15-year-olds and does little more than teach them how to march in a straight line. Valerian has changed the training regime; they are tougher, much tougher than they were before and now get weapons training. After Training Camp North, they move to Training Camp East where they used to do little more than teach the recruits what end of a gun to hold, now they have to give them more advanced weapons training. We have information that Malaya wrote to the commander of training camp east suggesting that they also incorporate training on tactics and the ability to think and act independently if their commander was killed in battle. And despite coming from a senior officer, this was flatly rejected. The commander said that he would only change the training regime once told to do so by the army council."

He turned back to the file on the army council and pointed to an individual.

"This guy is in his late eighties; intelligence says he is very ill and could die at any time. As a major general, Malaya is next in line to take his place. She will automatically get the promotion. She is obviously a favourite of Hallenberg – few women have ever got beyond the rank of captain before – so the army council will not be able to raise any objections. She would then be able to order the change in training, and that would be bad, very bad for us. They outnumber us ten to one. The only way we have been able to hold them back is because of the appalling quality of their troops. If they are better trained..." He shook his head. "We would expect to be over-run in less than a year."

"One last thing before you go: Field Marshal D'Frey wants Malaya's dog tags as proof of her death. He hasn't stated why, but I presume it is because she is so high ranking that the Correlans would try to conceal it."

Astrid was puzzled by this request, as her mission reports had never been questioned before and radio intercepts would easily confirm the killing. But he must have his reasons and her role as a soldier was to carry out orders and not question them. She dismissed the thoughts, stood, saluted and left.

She had spent the night reading the profile through several times, and she realised that DeSalva's analysts were correct, this was the only feasible way to carry out the mission. And if sex with Malaya is what the mission required, then that is what she would do.

She remembered DeSalva coming to see her as she left for the mission, he shook her hand and said goodbye. He had never done this before; he looked into her eyes and wished her luck. She understood exactly why he had come this time. She saluted then turned and left.

****

She had mixed feelings as she sat on the bed. There was no issue with homosexuality in her country; society there had long since accepted it as simply another lifestyle, no greater or less significant than any other form of human relationship. Being gay or lesbian was never an impediment in any aspect of life. In fact, differences were celebrated, for her country, Arralan, *is* a freethinking liberal democracy, one that she was proud of and one that she had sworn to herself that she was prepared to die defending.

Was this why she was so easily able to concoct the story of the anonymous lesbian nurse, or was there something deeper? She recalled the strange feeling she had inside as Brigit first touched her breasts while she was feeling for the data key in the pocket of her shirt when she was still in the chair. At the time, she had put that down to the natural anxiety of her situation, but deep down she knew it was more of a frisson, a feeling that she suddenly realised she wanted.

Her mind swung back to the activities of an hour ago. She had been surprised by how tender Brigit had been. She had expected her to be dominant and aggressive, cruel even, taking what she wanted and giving nothing, but the opposite was true. Her caresses had been gentle, with a lightness of touch that suggested she wanted more to give pleasure rather than receive it. The kissing was sensuous, the touching soft and slow and while Brigit led to start with, gently fondling Astrid's breasts, Astrid had found in herself an emotion that she hadn't experienced for years. Desire, deep, deep desire that was growing with every moment that went past. At first, she copied Brigit, kissing her, caressing her breasts and slipping her hand between her legs, but gradually she took the lead.

She remembered how her heart started to pound as she eagerly moved them both into position for mutual cunnilingus; she had never done it, but it was now the only thing she wanted, and she wanted it so much. She remembered the feeling of Brigit's tongue as it touched her. She remembered how her breathing quickened before moving close to Brigit and succumbing to the overwhelming urge to do the same to her. The pleasure sensation grew rapidly and the orgasm, when it came, was the most intense she had ever experienced, not just because of what Brigit's tongue was doing to her, but what her tongue was doing to Brigit.

A couple of seconds later, she heard Brigit gasp as she too achieved orgasm. As the feeling slowly subsided, she found herself in a dreamlike state.

Was she bisexual? Was this episode a one-off as a convenient vent for years of abstinence? Or was she far more deeply in character for the mission than she realised, but she knew the she hadn't imagined the feeling of lust that she had experienced.

Then she remembered the jolt that had suddenly shot through her. She had forgotten the mission! For the first time ever, she had allowed something else to take precedence in her mind. She had always assumed that she was heterosexual and would have to act the part of a lesbian, but she did not act; it was real, and the sexual desire within her that she had been oblivious to and that had surfaced so abruptly had put the mission in jeopardy. She would have to put this into her report, along with a request for an in-depth psychosexual analysis.

She remembered thinking quickly; changing position to move so that she could kiss Malaya on the lips. They exchanged satisfied smiles and laid side by side. Astrid quickly scanned Brigit's face and was pretty sure that there was still a degree of tension and making a move now would be foolish. More work would be needed before she could get Malaya into a position of total vulnerability and carry out the mission. This was going to take much longer than anticipated.

But that was an hour ago, the mission had been accomplished and there was still an awful lot to do.

Killing the Guards

She needed to get rid of the guards as she was still not convinced that they wouldn't come in at some point, but first she needed some energy and something to keep her awake. She had not eaten for nearly twelve hours and only had one bottle of water. Adrenaline was keeping her awake, but now that the primary mission had been accomplished, she didn't know how much longer that would last. She found some energy bars in the kitchen, the kind with dense, slow-release carbohydrate. She ate two; these would keep her going for a few hours, and she would take some with her when she left.

There was a coffee maker with pots of freshly ground Robusta coffee. She didn't like coffee, but she knew that caffeine would hit after about five minutes. She was also very tired and had to sharpen up her mind; it was imperative for her to be alert for the next couple of hours or she was certain to make mistakes. She decided to use a trick she had heard about but never tried; it was risky, but the following days would be full of risks. After looking through some drawers, she found a timer. She drank two mugs of strong coffee, set the timer for 20 minutes, then sat in a chair and fell asleep. The timer duly pinged; she woke instantly, and the caffeine was doing its job, she felt bright and fully awake.

While she had been led to Malaya's office, she had noticed that there were no surveillance cameras and that the office was positioned so that no one needed to walk past. The entrance was not in any line of sight, and she was confident that nobody would notice if the guards were not at their posts.

In one of the drawers, she found some long and thick nylon zip ties, the type that had been used to restrain her. She took out three and formed them into a loop about half a metre across.

She hoped that the guards were as obedient as Malaya claimed and would deal with the female guard first. On the way in, she had also noticed just how poor the audio was in the intercom system, and the distortion should be enough for her to fool the guards. She pressed the intercom button; lowering her voice, and affecting the eastern accent, spoke into the microphone. "Kaman, come in and shut the doors behind you, leave your weapon behind and wait in my office. Kobashi, wait outside. I will call you when I need you."

Quickly she moved into position. She heard the female guard enter the Krall's office, lay her carbine on Krall's desk, then enter the main office, both times dutifully shutting the doors behind her.

"Come into my quarters."

Though this was highly unusual, Kaman did as she was told. As she stepped through the door, Astrid dropped down behind her from a chair on the other side of the door. She slipped the loop of zip ties over Kaman's head and down around her neck, holding the latch and yanking hard on the loose ends.

The ligature snapped tight around the woman's throat, but Kaman instantly remembered her training and instead of reaching up to try to free herself, she dropped her hands to her sides and stepped forward. The natural reaction was to release the pressure first and try to free the garrotte. But this would waste too much time and would be futile, the training was to step sharply forward away from the assailant, reach down and grab a combat knife with one hand while drawing the sidearm with the other. Then the blade was quickly put behind the ear to avoid cutting the throat and slipped between skin and the garrotte to cut it, while turning and shooting the assailant. It was a move that took immense courage and presence of mind, and it was not uncommon for deaths to occur during training of this move.

But Astrid had received the same training and anticipated the move. She got there first, simultaneously pulling the knife from its sheath and the side arm from its holster. She cut the lanyard that attached the sidearm to the belt and threw both weapons to one side. Immediately the woman panicked and grabbed at the thick nylon strap. Astrid took hold of one of the loose ends and pulled it tighter. The woman staggered forward, as she did so, Astrid tripped her so that she would fall away from any furniture that might make a noise. Kaman landed heavily, the carpet in the quarters absorbing most of the sound. Astrid dropped on top of her, pulling the zip tie another couple of clicks tighter.

Kaman's face quickly turned purple, her eyes bulging and bloodshot, her fingernails gouging into her neck as she frantically tried to relieve the pressure. The position of the garrotte had forced her tongue out of her mouth. It was a grotesque way to kill her, but necessary and more importantly, silent. She needed Kaman's uniform and couldn't risk any blood on it. Also, she couldn't risk a fight with her, she was far stronger, and even now as she was dying, it took all of Astrid's strength to hold her still while she bucked and trashed her legs around.

It was all over in about fifteen seconds; her pupils dilated, her hands dropped, and her body went limp. She was dead. Astrid immediately pulled off the woman's skirt to avoid getting any unfortunate stains and dragged the woman to the side of the room behind the door.

She now needed a strategy to get rid of the male guard, Kobashi. He was tall, obviously very strong, and the tribe that he was drawn from is famous for their lightning-fast reactions, born of generations of catching charging deer by the antlers and wrestling them to the ground. She picked up the sidearm; it was a Nagler 12.5mm, a big brute of a pistol. She pulled the magazine and was not surprised to see the concave tips of the high cavitation rounds. These were devastating projectiles, made up of four individual lumps of lead held together within a thin copper cup.

On impact, the shape of the lead slugs would cause them to travel through the body at random angles, deforming and tumbling as they went. They cause massive damage, and it is a certainty that one or more vital organs would be hit. The copper cup would flatten into a ragged disc and slice through any soft tissue. One hit anywhere on the torso would be instantly fatal. This was a one shot, last resort, guaranteed kill weapon and although it had a theoretical killing range of seventy-five metres, it was hopelessly inaccurate at anything over five metres. This was largely due to its poor construction, its weight and the vicious recoil from the huge charge needed to push such a heavy round so far. Because of the size of the charge, the weapon had earned the justified nickname of 'the wrist breaker'. She pulled back the slide and saw the two rows of eight small holes in the top of the barrel either side of the fore sight, designed to direct some of the flash upwards and mitigate some of the recoil. The feature was only marginally effective and also made each shot incredibly loud.

The Nagler 12.5 was not a standard issue sidearm and had to be requested. It was more of a macho statement than a weapon, even just having fired one would imbue the owner with an elevated status. For a guard, it was a good choice as a last resort weapon when an assailant was too close for the standard issue carbine. But the noise it would make made it useless to her and she cast it aside, first pushing all the rounds from the magazine, ejecting the round in the breech and stamping on the magazine to deform it so that it couldn't be used. The knife was a different proposition though.

It was a beautifully crafted weapon designed for deep penetration in a traditional Correlan style, with a parallel blade that was just over thirty centimetres in length. The handle was fashioned from stacked oval layers of thick leather stuck together to form a perfect grip and absorb sweat so as to not get slippery. The hilt was brass and anodised to a fine matt black finish. The blade itself was about thirty-five millimetres across, heat-treated to harden the metal and form a dark grey coating.

Along each edge was a two-millimetre strip of exposed metal where the blade had been sharpened. Astrid tested the edge by running each side across her thumbnail; it had just the right amount of drag as it bit into the surface. It was sharp, extremely sharp. The end curved gracefully from the straight sides into a sixty-degree triangle, perfect for strength and penetration, again well sharpened. She looked along the length of the blade from tip to hilt. It was a shallow diamond shape that tapered out gracefully to the hilt giving it great strength and balance. Marks along the blade bore witness to its use, this had seen some combat and was probably an heirloom handed down through the generations, for it was of a quality impossible to obtain in Correla now.

She needed to get rid of Kobashi, but she would have to get him off guard and the garrotte would probably not work on him, he was clearly far too fast and far too strong; a plan formed quickly in her mind. The males from his tribe had another, much less impressive, reputation and she could use this against him.

Looking through Malaya's wardrobe, she found a dressing gown that was surprisingly sheer. In one the desk drawers, there was a roll of clear adhesive tape. She undressed, prepared herself then put on the dressing gown. She went into the main office and pressed the intercom button spoke as she had before.

"Kobashi, come into my office and leave your weapon on Krall's desk. Shut the doors behind you."

She moved into position in the middle of the room just as Kobashi entered. He was surprised, but not upset, to see Astrid standing there with her head bowed down submissively, wearing a completely see-through gown with nothing beneath it, her hands positioned over her breasts and crotch. As he approached, she trembled, feigning fear.

She opened the robe and let it drop to the floor.

"General Malaya wants to watch you fuck me," she said weakly, as she stood naked only a metre in front of him.

His slightly confused expression quickly turned into a leer as he unbuttoned his tunic. This was unusual, but not completely unexpected, and given who the prisoner was, the sexual violence towards women that the men in his tribe were famous for could be taken to the extreme. He was in no doubt that the general wanted to be the first to watch her suffer and he assumed Malaya was in her sleeping quarters and that they would move there.

He had the expression of a man who liked to dominate women during sex and arrogantly rolled his shoulders as such men do as he slipped the tunic down over his biceps. As it dropped down his arms, she struck with one hard kick between the legs. He instantly saw the move and reached forward with both hands to grab her leg, but the tunic pulled tight across his elbows and stopped him short. He doubled up in pain, and as he fell towards her, she reached around to her back, grabbed the knife that she had taped there earlier and thrust it up into his throat.

Holding the knife, she grabbed his hair and pulled him forward, kicking out his ankle to make him fall. With the tunic tangled around his elbows, he knew that he could not do anything to break his fall and, in that instant, knew he was about to die. She fell backwards parallel to him, still holding the knife in place.

The handle hit the floor first, Astrid's steely grip held it fast as the weight of his body drove the blade through his throat, through his spinal column and out through the back of his neck. She rolled his lifeless body over and pulled out the blade; there wasn't much blood, no major vessels had been severed.

From the corner of her eye, she saw a movement from the other room, one of Kaman's fingers twitched. Astrid went to her, this could be just residual nerve spasms and not any sort of conscious movement, but she had to be sure. On a shelf, there was a heavy brass candleholder, more ornamental than practical. It had a heavy square base, and three hard blows to the top of Kaman's head were enough. The finger stopped twitching.

There was now a lot to do before she could make her escape. She went to the computer on Malaya's desk.

Throughout the hours leading up to the death of Malaya, Astrid had kept an eye on the general's computer. It was still logged on, a staggering piece of complacency born of the arrogance of rank. The software was bespoke to the military, having been written by a professor at the prestigious university of mathematics and had been based loosely on more sophisticated western software. The main feature was a reduced folder set, designed to make navigation easier, with the added bonus that a military mind more used to brute force than finesse would be less likely to misplace important files. The whole directory set was viewable, and with the rank of major general, Malaya's access permissions meant she could look at anything across the whole network.

She opened the internal mail program, selected an off-base travel permit, entered Krall's name and sent it to the east gate. A couple of seconds later, a 'message read' notification came back from the east gate.

From this terminal, she could delete critical files or copy sensitive data, though this would take time and could be noticed. But this was not the mission, and she reminded herself that she had almost forgotten the mission once already.

One of the enemy's principal weaknesses was massive over centralisation, and where it applies to data, that means that all operational files have to be stored on the main server, with no copies anywhere else. Only private files were allowed to be stored on a local machine. Anyone found storing operational files anywhere other than the server would find themselves subject to military discipline.

The main server was actually a sophisticated network of sixteen mainframes spread over the whole country, all hard wired together with multiple redundant lines, and the whole network appears as one drive just labelled 'Server'. Once a file was saved, copies were made on all the machines, then when the file was accessed, it will come from the machine that had the lowest demand on its resources at that time, dramatically speeding up downloads. Each machine had two backup mainframes hard wired and hundreds of kilometres apart, the idea being that they couldn't all be hit, and the data would always be safe. Again, all thirty-two backup machines appeared as one backup drive.

For security, no Wi-Fi was allowed, so every single military computer was hard linked into this network and the resulting spider's web of fibre optic cable was simply huge. It was a closed network, and to prevent cyber-attack or any other form of intrusion, there was no connection to the global internet.

Astrid quickly found the two files she needed on the server and the duplicates on the backup drive. She used the search function to check whether the files were stored anywhere else – though she knew they wouldn't be, then with two clicks on each file she sent them to a file shredder. She clicked 'OK' on all four deletion warnings and activated the shredder. This would delete the files, then write 1010101010 etc. over the files, then 0101010101 etc. and would perform this action twenty times so that no file recovery software would ever be able to reconstruct the original data. In just a few minutes, her file and Captain Krall's were gone. There was an error in the programming that had never come to light, but Astrid's people had worked out from information from defectors and interrogation of prisoners, that as all the networked machines are configured to appear as one drive, not only was it simple to delete a file, deleting a file on one, deletes them on all. The reason it had never come to light was that no one had ever deleted a file; fear of military justice was enough of a deterrent.

Five hundred kilometres away, a message box flashed up on a screen at the network monitoring station below ground at the military intelligence headquarters. The corporal manning the station stared at the screen with his mouth open. "No, this can't happen," he muttered to himself.

The message simply said:

'Files deleted from Main Server: 2.'

'Files deleted from Backup: 2'

'File shredder activated for all deleted files.'

Deathly white, he reported to his supervisor, a notoriously grumpy captain who didn't really understand computers and felt that his subordinates knew this and ridiculed him behind his back, which they did. At this time in the morning, there was only the two of them on duty. The corporal didn't know if this was a good thing or not.

"Are you telling me that four files have been deleted by someone," said the captain, irritated.

"Yes, sir, and the file shredder has been run for all deleted files."

"Impossible, there must be a mistake, there is a strict rule, no one is allowed to delete a file, not even the Grand Field Marshal."

He lit a cigarette and leant back in his chair, trying, and failing, to give the impression that he knew how to handle the situation.

"Restore the file from backup, then run a diagnostic. No, first run a diagnostic on your machine, make sure there isn't a glitch there first."

The corporal sighed inside, he had studied computer science for five years at university and now he had to take instruction on what to do from a man he considered an idiot who had been transferred in from logistics and who's only answer for any given problem was "run a diagnostic" or "there must be a glitch".

"I can run a diagnostic on my computer, but I can't restore the files from backup, sir."

"Okay, I understand, when you are ready, I will come over and log in then you can use my access permissions," he said in a condescending tone of voice.

"It's nothing to do with permissions, sir, the files have been deleted from backup as well."

"What!" yelled the captain. "That's not possible, it's a court martial offence, minimum five years in prison. Find out what terminal was used, run a system wide diagnostic, that will tell us who did it, won't it?" A slight hint of desperation crept into the last part of the sentence.

"Yes, but I can't do that yet, sir."

"Why not?" snapped the captain, who was suddenly very aware that as officer in charge, he would have to explain this to the military police.

"It's 05.05, sir, the automatic system wide backup started at 05.00. Diagnostics can't be run during backup."

"How long is that going to take?"

"About another 20 minutes, sir."

"Well, run it in 20 minutes then," he said sarcastically.

"Can't do that either, sir."

"Why not, for fuck's sake?"

"At 5.30 am, all the heads of departments across all of the military services will be filing their logs for the previous 12 hours to the main server. Diagnostics can't be run while reports are being filed, sir."

"How long will that take?" The captain was getting exasperated.

"Usually two hours, sir."

"Oh, dear God, I'm in some pretty shit now." After a long pause, he glared up at the young man. "Rest assured, Corporal, if a ton of shit lands on my head over this, I'll make sure two tons of shit lands on yours. You had just better hope that it's a software glitch."

It's that glitch word again, thought the corporal, as he went back to his terminal. Funny thing, five years at university and they never told him what a glitch was, apart from being a word used by stupid people who want to look like they know what they are talking about. As he sat back at his console, the captain walked over to him.

"Look," he said with a slightly conciliatory tone. "We have data recovery software; can we use that?"

"I'm afraid not, sir, it won't work. The file shredder and the data recovery tool are the latest software packages that we have and are better than anything in

99

the world. When a file is deleted, it is actually still there, the file header just gets marked so that it doesn't appear in the file list, so to get rid of it completely, the shredder has to be run. If the shredder isn't run, then the data recovery tool just removes the 'deleted flag', and the file becomes visible again. Once the shredder has run, it automatically starts the data recovery tool. If even half of one byte is readable, it runs the shredder again. And one more thing, sir, the shredder will destroy any file relating to the original, which means that the log file is also gone. We won't be able to tell when the file was created, what type of file it was or anything about the file. It's just like it was never there."

"If files are never to be deleted, why is there a shredder in the first place?"

"The shredder is on the local machine and is only intended for use when deleting files on that local machine. But the way our folder set works when a file is accessed from the server, it will appear to the shredder as though it is a local file, sir."

The corporal was trying hard to show respect to the captain and only succeeded by respecting the rank and not the man. He dumbed down his answers just enough to get his point across without sounding condescending.

"The shredder is embedded so deep in the programming that a complete rewrite of the software would be needed, so instead of doing that, a total of four warning dialogues were written in. So, whoever deleted these, really wanted them gone, sir."

"Okay, let me think for a minute." The captain paced around for a few moments rubbing his temples. "But if it destroys the log file, will diagnostics help?" he said with more than a hint of desperation.

"Because nothing is ever deleted – or has never been deleted until now – the remaining files just stay where they are, and nothing gets shuffled around as more data is added, that data just tacks onto the end, sir. The diagnostic will just look for gaps, there should only be four, two in the main server and two in the backups. The only thing that the shredder won't remove is the data flag telling us which terminal was used to delete the file, sir."

The captain mused for a while. "Will anyone else have seen this message?" he said, deep in thought.

"No, sir, mine is the only terminal that monitors the server and backup."

"Good, let's keep it that way. Talk to no one about this, that's an order. Maybe the files were unimportant, we don't know, and maybe it won't matter."

"But a serious crime has been committed, sir," said the corporal firmly, emboldened by the captain's obvious weakness.

The captain stiffened. "*I* will tell the military police when *I* am good and ready, and when *I* have something to tell them – after *you* have got me something to tell them," his voice was stern, he had realised the corporal could get the better of him over this and had to turn it around.

"At the moment, all we have is that a person or persons unknown have deleted two unknown files and their backups using an unknown terminal somewhere in the country."

He sat down and lit another cigarette, but this just showed how much his hands were shaking. "So, diagnostics can't be run until 07.30, how long before we know whose terminal was used."

"About two hours, sir."

"Why will it take so long?" the captain gasped.

"There are tens of thousands of computers with many thousands of files on each one, sir. This diagnostic will open every file on every computer, log what sort of files they are, how big they are and when they were last opened then moves onto the next computer. It happens very fast and will not be visible to the user. Even so, it will take time. What we are looking for will be the file delete log on an individual computer; these have a flag to show the size of the deleted file. It is inconceivable that four other files registered in the deletion log would be exactly the same size as the gaps on the server. So, once we have that match, we have our culprit, sir."

"Well then, we could get lucky, it could be one of the first ones examined," muttered the captain hopefully.

"Even if it is, sir, we would still not know until all the computers on the network have been examined. Only then will it display the information, sir."

"Why is it so shit?" said the captain, increasingly exasperated.

"The diagnostic software is a bastardised version of software that was only ever intended for use on one machine. It was never intended for heavy-duty use like this. And there's something else you should know, sir. As I said, sir, every file on the computer will be opened and some of the senior officers really don't like their files being opened."

The captain pointed angrily at the corporal. "You said it would be invisible to the user," he snapped. This was going from bad to worse and he was getting irritable again.

"It will be invisible while it's running, sir, but if they happen to look at the file list, they will see that all the files on their computer were opened and closed over the course of a few seconds. There will also be a temp file saying that the log file has been accessed, sir."

"And I suppose that some of the files will be personally sensitive."

"Yes, sir." The corporal felt a little awkward, as if he was apologising for them.

"Love letters to the mistresses they're all fucking, I suppose."

"I can't comment on that, sir."

The captain got a strong cup of coffee, then sat at his desk and lit yet another cigarette; he rubbed his forehead and thought for a while. "Tell me about the access permissions, who could have done this?"

"Only the ranks of three-star generals and above have the permissions to look at level five, sir. It has all the tactical and strategic data. Battle plans etc. This is the only level that has unrestricted access to the backup system, sir."

"I simply cannot believe that a general would delete any files from backup, it's ridiculous to even think about it. Tell me about the passwords and codes that a general would have."

"For a general, there are two computer generated passwords, sir, only the general knows these and no record of them is kept. One is in the form of a user name and one in the form of a word, and there are two spellings of the word, if the second spelling is used it will let us know that the information has been given under duress and access will obviously be denied and the user is immediately locked out. Then to get to level five there are three eight-digit codes comprising numbers and letters, all case sensitive. The first code changes once a year, the second changes every four months. These are given to the user, and the third code is chosen by the user and they can change it at any time, sir."

"So pretty secure then, but I suppose they could have been stupid enough to write it all down or tell their girlfriends in the heat of passion," he said with heavy sarcasm.

"Or a terminal could have been left logged on, sir."

The captain leant on his desk with his head in his hands. "Unbelievable," he muttered.

****

Back in Malaya's office, Astrid noticed a USB stick in the computer, and a minimised folder with the file name 'Assassin' that was still open. She clicked on the folder; it opened to display a series of text files with the names of people that she had killed. She opened one and was shocked to see a fairly accurate description of one of her kills, Major Pell – a kill that had been recorded as an accident, but with enough detail to show that it wasn't.

The fact that these were on a USB stick meant that these were private and unlikely to be on the main server. She had to destroy the files to protect the assassination policy. She selected the entire folder and opened the shredder programme. In just under fifteen seconds, years of work by Malaya was gone forever.

Warrant Officer

Astrid needed to find a way of getting to the female shower room. She clicked an icon that brought up a schematic of the block she was in. The plan showed not only the layout of the corridors and positions on surveillance cameras, but also the staffing positions. Black circles indicated the number of staff due to be present in each office; all the staff had keys that they had to put in locks in their stations when they went on duty. This would make the black circles go red and the name and rank of the staff member would be displayed next to it. It was a reliable system, the rule ensuring that everyone used their keys was hardly ever broken as the penalty for non-compliance, like all punishments in the Correlan Army, was harsh.

She traced the route to the shower block; it was too far, and along the path, there were a lot of red circles. Many of the stations looked like they were open to the corridor; the female guard's uniform was a bad fit and she would have to walk past too many people and too many cameras. There had to be a better way.

All Correlan military buildings were single storey, so she would not necessarily have to use the main corridor, as she could easily climb out of a window. The building was a shallow 'H' shape, and there was a route around the outside of the building, but this had its own risks, though less so than the only other option. There was a strict rule that required people to use paths and the only staff allowed to walk on the grass were the groundkeepers. If she went this way, there was a danger of being spotted.

She studied the layout; there was an office directly opposite the female shower block, with a door on the inside of one of the 'H' legs that opened outwards, so it was likely to be an emergency exit, but this meant that there was, in all probability, no handle on the outside. A graphic indicated that there were a few steps up to the door. There was only one circle, and this was a red circle with 'WO' and a name next to it. The name was irrelevant, but the 'WO' meant Warrant Officer. These were usually ex-sergeant majors who had signed up for life but were either too old or too unfit for active duty. They were given trivial desk jobs to make them feel useful, but they were still fighting men who had seen a lot of combat and were not to be underestimated. This was the only way in.

She clicked another icon that showed the position, field of view and status of the exterior surveillance cameras. They appeared to be fixed on all the corners of the 'H'. Beside some camera positions were the letters 'CM' and other cameras had 'RBS'. A legend at the side of the screen showed 'CM' as 'Constant Monitoring' and 'RBS' as 'Recorded Backup Surveillance'. All the 'RBS' cameras were on the internal corners of the building. She clicked an icon that showed a grid view from all the cameras and a flashing icon confirmed to her that they were all on and working correctly. She thought for a moment, then clicked back to the building layout map and selected a side elevation rather than a plan. Triangles fanning out from the cameras showed the vertical field of view. All the cameras were looking out, and it appeared that their purpose was to spot an approaching threat in the distance, and there was a blind spot close to the walls. The only camera that covered the door to the warrant officer's station was labelled as 'RBS' and so would record to tape and would only be looked at after an incident. She could creep around, staying close to the walls and be out of sight of the crews that were watching the 'CM' cameras. The main risk was being seen by someone, but it was still relatively dark outside, and it could be done.

Looking through the draws in Malaya's desk, she found some money, eighty-five dhat in notes and a further forty in coins; one-hundred and twenty-five dhat, roughly the average day's pay and enough for a day or so. It was just before 5.10, and she had one more task to complete before leaving. That done, she put on Kaman's blouse, tunic and skirt; the fit was poor, but there was nothing else she could do. She grabbed her combat shirt and stuffed it in a plastic bag, picked up Malaya's dog tags, put them in her pocket and climbed out of the window. Pressing herself as close to the wall as possible, she shimmied around until she reached the five steps that led up to the door. Confident that she had not been observed, she went up the stairs, calmed herself and knocked. It was a gamble, if there happened to be another person in the room it would be trouble. There was no reply, and in itself, this was good, it meant that there was either no one else in the room, or one person that hadn't heard. She knocked again and heard the sound of a chair being pushed back and footsteps moving towards the door. It opened and an overweight man in his late-fifties filled the frame.

"What do you want and why are you out here?" he snapped.

Astrid glanced around him into the room, there was no one else. She said nothing but took a small step backward; he subconsciously took a step forward.

"I said, what do you want and why aren't you at your station?"

She fixed her eyes on his and took another pace backwards, this time down onto the first step. Again, he stepped forward. Again, she said nothing, but kept stepping backwards down the steps.

"What's wrong with your uniform, you look ridiculous." He matched her paces without realising it. "Answer me!" he growled.

By now she was at the bottom of the steps still staring into his eyes, he was halfway down.

He looked at the name on her tunic. "Wait a minute, you're not Kaman. Tell me who you are, or I'll beat it out of you."

She stood still and said nothing.

"Okay, you asked for this." He raised his hand to strike her, he exaggerated his gesture to intimidate her and he was irritated that it didn't.

He moved forward onto the last step and raised his hand again. He was now precisely where she wanted him, she dropped down and grabbed his ankles, then stood up sharply, pulling his legs forward and up, throwing him backwards. There were no railings to grab onto and nothing he could do to stop his head from slamming into the edge of the top step. His body fell limp, his eyes were open but looking in two different directions. He was unconscious; Astrid lifted his head and saw the crush injury across the back of his skull. She knew that blood would be already pooling in the area between the inner skull and brain and soon this pressure would push him into a coma that he would never wake up from. But she had to make sure, and so she lifted his head a little more, placed her hand on his forehead and slammed it back down onto the edge of the step; she heard the snap of the bones.

In the office, there was a box of matches, a packet of cigarettes and a plastic cup of coffee; she threw them down near the body. It would look like an accident – until the surveillance footage was viewed.

She entered the room and walked across to the door. The floor plan had shown the shower block to be directly across the corridor, just three metres. She listened closely for any sounds of activity, and satisfied that there were none, she opened the door, walked across the corridor and entered the shower block.

Krall

Timing was now critical; fortunately, there was a clock on the wall in the shower changing room. It looked like it was tied into a central system to enable all clocks on the base to be synchronised and accurate. It was 5.30am, and to make this work Astrid would have to be just stepping into the shower as Krall arrived. She hoped that Malaya had been right about her aide's punctilious timekeeping.

She turned on one of the showerheads and let it run until it got warm while she got undressed, then took a dry towel from a cupboard and wiped some sweat from her armpits and groin then stuffed it into the bag with her shirt – she would need these later.

It was quite cool in the changing room, but the clock told her that she didn't have long to wait. At 5.40, there was a noise outside in the corridor and she duly stepped into the shower as her target entered the room. Krall was wearing civilian clothes but carrying a standard issue uniform bag and a canvas holdall.

Startled, and looking a little awkward, she glared at Astrid.

"What are you doing here?" she snapped, curtly.

"I received orders late last night to report here. I was to leave straight away, been travelling all night, I thought I'd catch a shower. It's not a problem, is it?" Astrid kept her tone flat and matter of fact.

"It's not a problem," said Krall, whose body language said that it obviously was. "But why are you here?" Again, the abrupt manner.

"Don't know. I was just told to report to Major General Malaya's office, and that I would receive further orders when I got there."

"I am Major General Malaya's aide and if there were orders, I would have seen the paperwork," said Krall, somewhat pompously.

"It was a verbal order."

"From whom, may I ask?" Krall demanded, putting her hands on her hips.

"I received the order from General Valerian."

"Oh, I should have known," her voice softened a bit. "Look, it's nothing personal, but there will be nothing for you to do. Valerian does this all the time, he sends someone down, then calls to say that he thought that we might need a little help. You will wander around for a couple of weeks then you'll be sent back. He does it to wind up General Malaya."

"That's a bit odd for someone his rank, isn't it?"

Krall's voice turned a little gossipy. "They don't get on at all. It doesn't wind up General Malaya, she actually finds it a bit pathetic."

"A bit of needle is there?"

"Not from General Malaya, look, I've said more than I should."

Krall started to get undressed and despite her military training, was obviously self-conscious about getting naked in front of someone else. Astrid surmised that this was the real reason why she got in so early, so that she would have the shower block to herself. She entered the shower and with her back to Astrid, started to chat to cover her embarrassment. She talked about the weather, the cute guys in the local football team, what she watched on television the previous night and so on. All of it the sort of garrulous drivel that no one else would ever be interested in. Astrid was reminded of the old adage:

'The wise speak because they have something to say, fools speak because they have to say something'.

She was not listening to the stultifying content, but she was listening intently to Krall's voice because she needed to have that voice. Astrid's command of the Correlan language was second to none, but it was the high form, and not many people in the army would have such a refined tone. If she was going to impersonate this woman, she would need the accent, for she would undoubtedly meet people who would have been dealing with Krall on a daily basis.

She listened closely to the exaggerated intonation, the clipped consonants, and extended sibilants at the ends of sentences, and the slight raising of pitch at the end of every sentence. She had always found this last aspect irritating, as it made every statement sound like a question. She placed the accent at around one hundred-and-fifty kilometres northwest of the capital in the heart of the heavy industrial sector. Astrid had always thought of this as an ugly dialect, particularly so from a woman, but it was one of the easiest to impersonate.

Eventually the monologue turned to the obvious.

"Have you heard the news?"

"I heard something about a special prisoner, but no details."

"Yeah," said Krall turning around to face Astrid, forgetting her shyness in her excitement.

"I think we've finally got that bitch Peterman."

"Really?" said Astrid, feigning surprised interest.

"Yeah, and I hope the general's giving her a right hard time."

Krall was gabbling away, her eyes wide open. "I can't wait to see her, apparently she looks just like me, so much so that I've been arrested a couple of times and they were pretty rough on me, so just imagine what they are going to do to her. But whatever they do, it won't be enough, she deserves it."

Krall was prattling like an excited schoolgirl. She stopped and looked at Astrid curiously. "You know what, you look just like me, so you and me must look just like her." She let out a little laugh. "Imagine that, three people all looking exactly the same."

Astrid had heard enough. "There's a reason I look just like her," she said coldly.

"Really, what's that then?"

Suddenly Krall's face dropped in horror; she let out a gasp as she realised what Astrid meant. But before she could react, Astrid grabbed her by the throat and slammed her back against the wall hard enough for her head to crack one of the tiles. Stunned, her legs gave way and she crumpled down, as she did so, Astrid stepped over her, grabbed her head and wrenched it hard around to the right. Krall's slender neck snapped easily, killing her instantly. Her lifeless body slumped to the floor. Astrid stood back, letting the shower run for a while onto Krall's body while her muscles relaxed and her bladder emptied.

She dragged the body into the changing area and dumped it in a laundry hamper, rearranging damp towels and dirty clothes from the previous night to cover the corpse. She checked the time, she had just over five minutes to get dressed. While in the shower Krall really should have noticed and been suspicious that Astrid had been very careful not to get her hair wet, particularly as it obviously needed washing, and so she was able to dry herself quickly. She checked through the uniform bag, everything she needed was there, including clean underwear, which was a little luxury that she had not had for a while.

She dressed in Krall's uniform that was a good fit; she tucked her hair into her cap, put on the shoes, which were also a good fit, and then at exactly five minutes past six, with the civilian clothes in the uniform bag and her own combat shirt and the towel in the canvas bag, she stepped out of the changing room into the corridor and strode down towards the main entrance.

She met no one in the five minutes it took to get there, and grateful for that, she composed herself and walked briskly to the glass hatch beside the main door.

"My keys," she snapped, glaring at the guard slouching in a chair. The young man rose slowly to his feet.

"Hurry up," she said, tapping her fingers on the counter, he brought over a couple of keys on a key ring and handed her a sheet of paper, nodding to a pen.

"Fill out and sign the form, and I need to see your travel permit," he grunted.

She realised that not only did she have no idea what Krall's signature was like but, more importantly, she didn't know whether Krall was right- or left-handed. For years Correlan children that were left-handed were forced to learn to write with their right hand, but eventually nature would always reassert itself and as adults they always reverted to left-handedness. She would have to bluff this.

"I am General Malaya's aide, so I don't have to show you a travel permit, you fool. Now give me the keys, and I'm not going to fill out your stupid form, it's my car, and you know who I am, I gave the keys to you less than half an hour ago."

"You've got to fill it out and sign, it's the rules."

"I'm in a hurry, and I won't be long, so I'll do it when I get back," she snapped. "Now just give me the keys, I've got an urgent job to do and you are holding me up. Maybe you'll like me to mention your name to Major General Malaya."

With that, the guard tossed the keys on the counter, shrugged and walked away. Astrid took them and stepped out of the building. An ambulance had just arrived and was parked outside, a medical orderly stepped out of the back and ran up to her with a worried and expectant look on his face.

"Err, Captain," he said nervously.

"What!" she snapped, irritated.

"It's the warrant officer, ma'am."

"What about him?"

"He's dead, ma'am."

"And do you expect me to bring him back to life?" she sneered.

"No ma'am, it's just that his family will have to be informed, ma'am." He looked even more nervous now. "Protocol says that if it's a death on the base, they have to be informed as soon as possible."

"So, inform them then."

"But, ma'am, I…I…was t…told, erm…" he stammered. "Isn't that your job, ma'am?"

"I don't have time, you do it."

"What do I say, ma'am?"

Astrid sighed loudly. "How did he die?"

"Well, it seems that he stepped out of his office for a cigarette, ma'am, slipped and fell down some steps and banged his head. Looks like a brain haemorrhage killed him. He was found when someone went to collect some papers."

Astrid fixed a steely gaze on the man.

"Tell his family that he was neglecting his duties, left his post and his carelessness resulted in his death." The orderly looked terrified.

"Use those exact words and make sure a copy is on my desk by the time I return." She pushed past the man and strode towards the car park.

Car Park

The incident with the medical orderly could have been a problem, and she couldn't risk too many more face-to-face contacts while still on the base. Everyone has their own idiosyncratic habits and sooner or later she might run into someone who knew Krall well. She needed to find the car quickly. She called to mind the layout of the staff car park and walked quickly and purposefully, but also carefully so as not to make it look like she was rushing.

As she entered the car park she glanced down at the keys, there was no identification other than Krall's name on the fob, and she had no idea which one Krall's staff car was. All were the same make and model; large black, chunky road cars with four-wheel drive and raised suspension that gave them a limited off-road capability. They were unsophisticated vehicles with no remote lock/unlock facility, so she couldn't just press a button and see which sidelights flashed.

The whole of the car park area was overlooked by CCTV, and was certain to be monitored, so she couldn't try every car in turn, as this would undoubtedly draw attention. She thought quickly; it was six twenty am and overnight, cold air had come down from the mountains hitting the humid air and forming dew as it always did at this time of year. Within an hour or so the warming summer wind would dry everything.

Looking along the row of identical vehicles, she noticed that one car had no condensation. This had to be Krall's, she walked towards it. Each car had two 30 litre fuel cans on the back and as she passed behind, she surreptitiously tapped near the top of each fuel can with her knuckles, both responded with a dull thud of fuel instead of the clank of an empty metal container. This was good, because she may have to travel a fair distance in the car and didn't want to spend too much time at a fuel station.

With her heart in her mouth, she slipped the key into the lock and turned it. With a click, the lock button popped up, but instead of getting in, she opened the back door and put the case on the back seat. Then as nonchalantly as she could, she took the bag with the towel and the shirt and walked to a trash bin, dumping it as if clearing out some rubbish from the car. She slipped into the driver's seat, started the engine and drove out of the car park. This action would tally with the Email she sent from Malaya's terminal permitting Krall's travel off base, should any of the CCTV operators bother to check and should not arouse any suspicion.

Again, she recalled the car park and the road layout from it. She needed to head east. This would be the longest way off the base and the least likely route for her to make her escape, and she was counting on this. If the alarm was raised early, all efforts would be focussed on the route to the southwest gate, as it was the closest and the most obvious route out. A little bit of careful thought on the part of the Correlan military police would make them realise the bluff, but careful thinking was not high on the attribute list for the military police and they would go for whatever was obvious. She was counting on this too. She drove carefully, and by keeping the sun in front of her, she would inevitably arrive at the east gate.

The Kandalan Base was vast, and her journey to the east gate would take well over an hour, she desperately fought the urge to rush. Her instinct was to get off the base as soon as possible, but there would be too many eyes along the way, too many people wishing to ingratiate themselves with superiors by reporting a broken rule like speeding. She kept to the thirty-five kilometres per hour speed limit for a good twenty or so minutes until she was out of the main complex and onto one of the feeder roads where the speed limit was higher.

The time she had taken so far seemed like hours and she felt her stress levels rising as a result, she could feel her heart pounding in her chest and her breathing getting short. She reminded herself that stressed people make mistakes, so she opened a window to let in some cool air and breathed slowly and deeply until she felt her heart beat slow down.

At a junction, a long convoy of vehicles pulled out in front of her. The last two vehicles were troop transporters, open top lorries with rows of bench seats along each side and two rows back-to-back along the middle. They were full of soldiers, she estimated fifteen in each row, with at least two in the front, not including the driver. Over one hundred and twenty men, and if they were alerted to her, she would not stand a chance. She weighed up her options, there weren't any; this was a straight road with no turnings for another five kilometres, overtaking the whole convoy was out of the question and dropping back would look suspicious.

One of the soldiers at the back lit a cigarette, this was against the rules and he knew it. He looked straight at Astrid, fixing his gaze on her and arrogantly made no effort to hide his smoking. Her heart skipped a beat but settled down again as she realised that this was just the usual contempt that infantry had for staff officers who rarely, if ever, saw combat. He finished the smoke and flicked the butt at her which bounced off the windscreen dead level with her face. She glared up at him, but he just laughed then glowered at her and spat on the floor, a Correlan soldier's usual way of showing his disrespect to an officer.

She hoped that they would not be heading off base, and to her relief the convoy turned off at the next junction leaving a clear road ahead to the east gate. The ten minutes behind the convoy had been stressful and she knew that there would be one more challenge. The rest of the journey was uneventful, and she stayed just under the 65 Kilometres per hour limit. Thirty minutes later she was approaching the gate, she slowed to a halt and steeled herself for the inevitable confrontation with the guards.

East Gate

Just ten more metres and she would be off the base, just one checkpoint stood between her and the east gate. A surly oaf appeared at the side of the car, two others sat inside the small building watching out of the window, clearly amused by what they were anticipating. It was well known that the guards at the east gate were at best brusque, but most of the time they were just obnoxious. It was the least used of all the access points to the base and they all had a collective chip on their shoulders about it. He rapped his knuckles on the side window of the car; a disrespectful gesture in itself. Astrid wound it down.

"Give me your travel documents," he snapped.

The two in the building smirked; they would always try to outdo each other, winding up as many people as they could, and clearly enjoyed being difficult, a product of boredom.

Astrid scowled. "I don't need travel documents you fool, and remember I am an officer; you will address me as such."

She had expected a confrontation and had a pretty good idea of how it would go. The bounds of disrespect to senior ranks would be tested to the limit, but she knew that she had the upper hand, and that they knew that fact as well. This would be a tedious couple of minutes.

The guard sneered contemptuously. "May I see your travel documents…" He paused for a couple of seconds, then leant forward stopping just a few centimetres from her face. "…Ma'am."

"You have my off-base travel permit. It was sent to you by Major General Malaya earlier this morning." Time to play the ace card. "You do know who I am, don't you?"

"You are a captain attempting to leave the base without proper documentation, you do not have an off-base travel authorisation logged in the system and your destination is not specified. So, it is my duty to stop you leaving the base," he said with a supercilious tone. His colleagues sniggered.

"I am Captain Krall, Major General Malaya's personal aide," she said firmly, fixing her gaze on the man.

"I know that the exit permit was sent by General Malaya to this gatehouse this morning, and I also know it has been read. As you well know, the general does not need to specify a destination for my travel off base. Now, how do you think that General Malaya – the base commander, will react when I report to her that the guards on the east gate prevented me from carrying out her orders?"

The guard's expression dropped a little. Astrid pressed her advantage and made a point of reading the guard's name badge.

"I have your name, Latana, you will receive a visit later and you will be called to account for your actions, as will your idiotic friends in there."

Now it was her turn to lean forward; centimetres from his face. "Now open the gate," she hissed.

The guard's demeanour changed rapidly from gruff and arrogant to curt but a little nervous. He leant through the window of the checkpoint and slapped the button that opened the gate. It only actually took twenty seconds to open wide enough for her to drive through, but if felt like forever. Astrid eased forward and in no time was off the base.

"Fuckin' stuck up fuckin' bitch." Latana snarled as he sat back down with his two colleagues; his male pride bruised by having a woman get the better of him.

"You've got my name, have you? Well, I've got yours Captain fucking Krall," he shouted. "I'll have you one day, I'll find out where your quarters are then just when you're least expecting it, I'll grab you and I'll fuck you to death."

"What do you reckon she's got…" said one of the other men. "…a great big hairy muff, or neatly trimmed or all shaved off?"

"All off I reckon," said the other man, not bothering to look up from his porn mag. "I like it bald, makes them look a bit young. I like 'em young, like this." He held open the magazine showing a picture of a naked girl who looked, and probably was, under age.

"Oh, I like 'em hairy," said Latana, brightening up.

The crude humour raised Latana's mood and the three let their fantasy minds run free. But little did they realise, as they discussed the ever more perverted things that they would do to the woman, who they thought was Captain Krall, that in a few hours they would be arrested along with the guard who gave Astrid the car keys, and their lives would be over. All four would be charged with helping a prisoner to escape and this automatically included a charge of treason; within three days they would be tried, found guilty and publicly executed. As the charge included treason, the execution would be in the town or village of their birth.

The local population would be compelled to witness the hanging; there would be no choice in this matter – the army and military police would see to that. The prisoner would hold up a sign that he had been forced to write saying 'I am a traitor' along with their name. Then a rope would be placed around his neck, but no sharp drop to break his spine. Instead he would be hauled up to die of strangulation and his body left hanging for two days.

All of the local inhabitants would have to file past to take one last look at the wretched corpse; some would angrily hit the body with sticks or throw rocks. Some would spit at them or curse them and their family, maybe out of genuine anger, or maybe to put on a show in case they were being watched and feared denouncement. But most were just desperately sad.

But for the moment, the men were laughing and enjoying a cigarette.

****

Astrid was about a kilometre outside the base before her heart stopped hammering in her chest; the difficult part was over for the time being. She turned, heading south, driving for a few more kilometres until she saw the next thing she needed. She needed to be seen on the south road. She stopped at a service station, got out and purchased a couple of bottles of water and a sandwich to eat, making sure the cashier saw Krall's identity card.

She pulled out of the service station and continued heading south, if questioned, the cashier would confirm her identity. The garage surveillance camera would also reinforce in the mind of any pursuers the notion that she was heading south; it was after all, the logical way to go. They might guess that using the east gate had been a ruse, they might even think that it was a clever ruse. But a few kilometres along the road she would turn to head east, then northeast into and through the Phaal region, then head due north towards Balun. It was certainly the worst route home, and that was precisely why she had chosen it, it would get the least attention from whoever would be searching for her. But there was one more problem that she had to deal with, so she kept heading south.

She knew that all Correlan military staff vehicles at Kandalan had trackers, each encoded with the vehicles' registration and the name of the driver it was assigned to. They were supposed to be a big secret, and they were designed to spot officers who were deviating from a planned route and potentially defecting, but analysis of some captured vehicles soon identified the construction of the little boxes. Fortunately, they were all old analogue devices; simple, cheap but effective. The analogue bandwidth allocated to the trackers was very limited, so to avoid overloading the system and causing a whiteout from all the vehicles in a base, the trackers would only turn on once the vehicle was a certain distance from its home base, roughly 30 kilometres. To achieve this, the tracker would listen to a signal unique to its base, and once the signal strength had dropped below a set point, the tracker would switch on and broadcast its own code. Then simple triangulation from multiple receivers across the country would accurately locate it.

She stopped the car and took a pair of pliers from the vehicle's tool kit. The trackers were always fitted just underneath the dashboard in the wiring harness to the ignition switch. There were two wires in and two wires out. Assuming that the tracker hadn't been activated, she cut the wires, allowing as much cable length as possible on the tracker, then ripped down the headlining inside the car and pulled out the cables that led to the interior light; she would not need that. She cut a length of cable, stripped back the insulation, then twisted the bare wires together with the ones to the ignition switch to bridge the gap in the wiring harness before winding some medical tape around them to stop them from coming undone. She started the car and continued travelling south – not too fast, this was a sparsely populated area, but still, there was no need to draw attention to herself.

A bus depot caught her eye, and she stopped to survey the situation. All the drivers seemed to be in a cafe having a smoke and a coffee before starting their shifts for the day. She parked out of sight then moved quickly along the line of the vehicles, keeping out of sight of the drivers. She looked at the destination plates on the front of the buses, one indicated that its route would eventually take it southeast, but only after it had stayed well within thirty kilometres of the base until it was nearly due south.

This was perfect, and as Correlan bus drivers never lock the doors, she got in the vehicle and quickly installed the tracker in the bus ignition circuit, getting out just as the drivers emerged from the cafe. She slipped back to the car and watched as the bus driver started the engine and pulled out of the depot. Confident that she hadn't been seen, she started the car and eased out onto the road and finally turned to head east at the next junction.

Bodies

The military police walked through the door at eight fifty. With ten minutes to check-in, each showed their credentials and signed in, before moving on to the business of the day. A stern-faced military police captain, his rank equivalent to a chief inspector in the civilian force, a sergeant and three police troopers flashed their identification at the guard, and then signed the admission book. Astrid's arrest was not yet common knowledge, but the guard didn't question their presence, he had heard a rumour of a major development and this many MP's must mean something very big.

"Where are Major General Malaya's offices?" the captain demanded.

"All of the east wing is taken up by the general's staff. She has a separate office with just her and her aide at the—"

The guard was interrupted by a scream that rang out from the far end of the corridor. An old woman, part of the cleaning staff, backed out of the female shower block with one hand covering her mouth, the other trembling, pointing back into the room. The MP's glanced at the woman but thought little of it.

"A rat or something has spooked the old bat," grumbled one of the troopers. The captain snorted and finished signing the book; there was too much to do now to worry about rodent infestation, until she cried out again.

"D...dead, she's d...dead," was all the old woman could say. The captain nodded to the sergeant to go and have a look. Within seconds he called back.

"Sir, you have to see this."

The captain knew that the sergeant was professional and would not call him down unless it was important. He frowned with concern and strode towards the changing room. Inside, the large clothing hamper was in the middle of the room; some of the dirty clothes had been pulled out revealing Krall's discoloured face. He turned to the old lady.

"It was hard to move." The shock had given way to sobbing now. "I thought someone was playing a joke, so I looked inside and saw..."

The captain was ambivalent towards the crying woman and zoned out to the rest of what she had to say; he'd seen enough distraught old ladies in his time,

119

his only concern was the body. Who was she? It was a distraction that he didn't need, but this was clearly a murder and as a high-ranking military policeman it was his duty to investigate further. He had to start a basic preliminary examination, and then seal the room before calling in more military police to continue investigating. He pulled out a knife and slit the side of the hamper open. He reached in and dragged the cold body out.

The tell-tale signs of Rigor Mortis were starting to set in, the jaw was already fixed half open and at an odd angle, the neck was mobile but quite stiff, the arms and legs still had free movement, albeit with a little resistance. Her skin had started to darken with the reddish-brown hue of livor mortis from blood seeping from her capillaries, except for the left side of her body where pressure from her own weight had compressed the blood vessels and prevented the colour changes.

He was no pathologist but had observed enough death to give him a rudimentary grasp of a time line. He guessed that the clothes on top had kept the body warm, delaying the chemical changes in the muscle tissues. Given that fact, the warmth in the room and her physique, death had probably occurred no more than three hours ago.

Then he saw it. The cadaver had so absorbed him, he had not recognised the face. Was it Astrid Peterman, the prisoner he was due to take into custody? Of course not, he told himself, it would be absurd, ridiculous even, to kill her and dump her body here, and what possible motive would anyone have to do that. So who was she? When he heard of her capture the previous evening, he had printed off her picture and a bullet point dossier of her abilities – the full file would be far too large to print and read. He had studied the bullet points thoroughly, though unaware that her file had now been deleted and that these were now the only records available.

The dossier was in his car, but her picture was in his pocket. He took out a picture of Astrid and held it against the woman's face; they could have been twins. One of Krall's eyes was half-open, and ignoring the red stripe of Tache Noir that had formed across the white of her eye where it had not fully closed, he noted that even the colour of the iris was the same. He had re-read the dossier on Astrid before leaving that morning, he knew about her ruthless guile. He had never met Captain Krall, but a sudden cold feeling shot through him making him visibly shudder.

He stepped out of the shower room and shouted to the guard behind the desk. "You, come here, now."

The guard, realising that this was urgent, hurried down to the captain, well aware that he was leaving his station without permission from his commanding officer – a major breach of rules. As he stepped into the room he was taken aback by the sight of the naked female corpse, skin waxy and discoloured. Her head at an awkward, unnatural angle, the neck obviously broken. The captain stood over her, pointing at her face.

"Who is this?" he snapped.

"It looks like Captain Krall, Major General Malaya's aide," he said nervously.

"Does she look like this woman? The enemy woman Peterman?"

He shoved the picture of Astrid in the guard's face. The guard recognised the picture of Astrid.

"Yes, it does, it is well known on this base that Captain Krall is a look-alike for the enemy officer, General Malaya even gave her a special pass in case she ever got arrested. But it can't be Krall."

"Why not?"

"Because she had a travel permit issued by Major General Malaya, I gave Captain Krall the car keys at around six this morning, she was in a hurry and didn't even sign for them…" his voice tailed off as he realised the enormity of what he had just said.

"Where is Major General Malaya's office?" The captain demanded, the urgency in his voice tinged with a little fear; not fear for his own safety, but fear for the realisation of what might have happened.

"Back along the corridor and turn right. Her office and living quarters are at the end."

The captain turned to one of the troopers. "You, stay here with him, if he tries to leave…" He paused, anger taking his breath for a moment. "…hurt him."

"Yes, sir," snapped the trooper, then turned to glower at the guard. "Give me a reason," he hissed.

The guard slowly sank down into a bench and put his head in his hands as it all began to fully sink in.

The captain, sergeant and troopers ran to the other side of the building, arriving outside the general's door.

"Where are the guards?" one of the troopers muttered.

The captain stopped for a moment and composed himself. "Wait here, this could be unconnected," he said firmly, not really sure if he was reassuring his men or himself.

He knocked on the door. No reply from the intercom. He presses the 'Speak' button and listened to the light static from the 'com speaker to the side of the door, there were no sounds from inside the room. He grabbed the door handle and cautiously stepped into the anteroom. He was puzzled to see both the guards' carbines laying on a table and no sign of the guards themselves. It was unheard of – not to mention a court martial offence – for two guards to be missing from their station at the same time and to leave fully loaded weapons unattended. He felt uneasy as he crossed the room; a sense of foreboding came over him.

"This is most irregular," he said quietly to himself.

His anxiety rose as he approached the next door, this would lead directly into Major General Malaya's office. Entering a general's personal office without being invited was a very serious offence, particularly one as high ranking as her. But he suddenly felt very foolish as he remembered his rank and mission, and grasped the door handle firmly, he would not wait for her permission to enter. The arrest of Astrid Peterman vastly outweighed any protocol today.

Despite that, he let go of the handle, took a couple of deep breaths while he straightened his tunic, stiffened his back, and composed himself again. He opened the door and strode purposefully into the room, then clutched his stomach, doubled over and vomited.

On her desk sat Major General Malaya's severed head, dull eyes wide open staring at the door. Unable to believe what he had just seen, he looked up again and again heaved. The door to the left that led to the general's personal quarters was open. He looked in and saw walls and floor splattered with blood and the headless body of a naked woman on the bed. His stomach churned again bringing up bile. He took a tissue from his pocket and wiped his mouth, then looked at the desk again, this time controlling his revulsion. Malaya's head was propped up with books on one side and a combat knife jabbed into the desk on the other. Devoid of blood, the skin had a grey waxy, almost oily look. The mouth hung open, with a crescent of flesh gaping out over the severed jugular. Dry blood matted her hair.

Across the other side of the room was an eating area that doubled as an informal conference room. In there he saw the body of Kobashi and the incongruous sight of Kaman's body in just her underwear.

Ashen faced, he stepped out of the office. The sergeant and troopers were stunned at the sight of the captain's normally immaculate uniform covered in vomit.

"Seal the base and call for backup."

Valerian

Three-star General Lothar Valerian sat at his computer, his feelings conflicted as he looked at the report of Malaya's death and the other deaths. He was outraged that Astrid Peterman had escaped from the base commander's office, situated in the middle of the largest military base in the country. He was outraged that she had even spoken to at least three people while making her escape. He was outraged that she had killed five army staff, but at the same time in the dark place in his mind, the place where envy, jealousy, greed and all his other sinister feelings lived, a thought formed; he was glad that one of the dead was Major General Brigit Malaya – the woman he despised. The woman who had, in his eyes, stolen his promotion and then humiliated him. Few people knew the depth of his brooding animosity towards her, certainly no one in the high command knew. It started in training when they were both officer cadets and grew over the years into pure hatred. In public, he made sure that they were the epitome of army colleagues, in private it was a very different matter.

Malaya had always been one step ahead of Valerian when it came to promotion, and Valerian was an old-fashioned misogynist who was not able to comprehend that a woman could rise on her own merits and constantly told himself that she must have sucked and fucked her way to the top. He could not have known just how wrong he was about that. He didn't even know exactly how it had started in the first place, there were no rebuffed sexual advances, she was not his type, and he had no idea that he was absolutely not her type. They were in different classes, so there was no academic rivalry, it was just a simple clash of personalities, the sort of thing that training was supposed to eradicate, but for Valerian it had only enhanced it. For her part, the animosity didn't run as deep; Malaya just considered Valerian to be an over-ambitious, incompetent brute, fully capable of losing the war if he got promoted too high; she was determined to find a way of preventing it, and she did just that.

They had both risen to the rank of three-star General when Major General Kedara, the commander of the Kandalan Base, or Base Number One as it was often called, was killed in a car crash. They were both placed on the shortlist for promotion to the vacant position along with four other names. The army council interviewed all of them extensively, and all had their service record rigorously scrutinised. After a three-week process of elimination, all the other candidates were dismissed and only himself and Malaya were left. Promotion to commander of base number one was only one step away from a seat on the army council.

Then the day came for the announcement. In a flash, he remembered every detail of that day just over a year ago.

He sat, side by side with Malaya, to the left of the stage in the assembly hall of the army central headquarters. The five members of the army council sat to the right and a podium was positioned in the middle. Two hundred senior officers and their staff sat waiting for the announcement, over a thousand faces watching. All stood as Grand Field Marshall Hallenberg entered the stage and took a piece of paper from the Chief of the army council.

He remembered his thoughts.

She has seen many colleagues die in battle, but not as many as I have. In order to win a battle, she has ordered many troops to a certain death, but not as many as I have. She has viciously fought hand-to-hand and killed enemies in battle, but not as many times as I have. She has had many victories, but not as many as I have.

Bitterly he remembered.

But she has never been cut off with all her ammunition expended, then led a bayonet charge to fight her way to freedom. I have done that, I led from the front; this promotion is mine.

He remembered watching Hallenberg step up to the podium, unfold the paper, read it and smile ever so slightly.

The Grand Field Marshall stepped forward to the microphones, he gestured for the audience to sit then cleared his throat and spoke with unusual brevity. "The post of commander of base number one and now has the rank of major general has been awarded to General Brigit Malaya."

He remembered the cold flooding through his body, the sick feeling, the clenching of his fists and the faint red mist appearing in his vision. He remembered forcing a smile and joining in the clapping as Malaya stepped up and took her turn at the podium. He remembered her words – he would remember them to his dying day.

Her speech was not a long one, this was frowned on by the army council who thought that talking was the job of politicians, and that soldiers should do, not speak. She thought for a few seconds while the polite applause died down.

"My friends, I wish to thank Grand Field Marshall Hallenberg and the army council for bestowing this great honour upon me. I am confident that in my time as base commander, however long that may be, that I will do my duty to the utmost of my ability to hasten our victories."

Again, there was polite applause, and this was usually the que for the appointee to leave the podium, but she stayed and in a dramatic gesture waved her hand to silence the audience. The army council members frowned but saw that Hallenberg was intrigued and so stayed silent.

"As you are aware, the selection process was rigorous, and the army council made what must have been a very difficult decision, for my good friend General Lothar Valerian is an outstanding officer whose courage has always been an inspiration to me and should be an inspiration to us all."

She gestured to Valerian, who nodded in respectful appreciation. What is the bitch doing? *he thought to himself.*

"I believe that it is within my gift on this day – if I have read the army rules correctly – to offer General Valerian promotion, so that his talents, talents that I have admired for a long time, can be rewarded."

The army council conferred, nodding to each other then looked to Hallenberg for guidance, he was clearly appreciating Malaya's boldness and gestured for them to carry on.

"That is correct, please continue," said the chief of council. Valerian was confused; this was not what he had expected at all.

Malaya again cleared her throat and scanned the faces in the audience, then gestured towards Valerian in respectful admiration.

"General Lothar Valerian has vast combat experience and this needs to be put to the best use to ensure the total conquest of our enemies."

Delegates in the hall nodded and muttered to each other in approval. Valerian nodded to the audience to show his appreciation to them, but he was still confused, could it be that he had got her wrong all these years, and what did she have in mind for him? He couldn't be promoted any higher, there can only be one major general in the army, as this was the highest rank before joining the army council, and Malaya herself was now certain of that. So, what was it to be? Strategic planning? Weapons development?

"I hereby promote General Valerian to base commander of Training Camp North, where his skills can be passed on to the next generation of our fighters."

There was a brief moment of stunned silence, then, after seeing Hallenberg smile and start to clap, applause erupted in the hall and some even stood as a mark of respect for her.

"You utter, utter fucking bitch," whispered Valerian under his breath as his heart sank, Malaya had pulled off a clever, calculated humiliation. Training Camp North was for raw recruits, and everyone understood that it was the dead end of a general's career, no one had ever returned to active duty after being assigned to command a training camp. He would be teaching fifteen-year-old volunteers and sixteen-year-old conscripts the absolute basics of military life for six months before they moved to Training Camp East for actual combat training.

It was lose, lose. If the trainees were not up to scratch when they got to Training Camp East it would be his fault, if they did well when they got to active duty it would be seen as a result of their time at Training Camp East. Furthermore, a training division can have no campaign medals and, in an army where a regiment's status and thereby the standing of its commander is gained by the constant acquisition of medals, the lack of any would see Valerian's significance to the army inexorably reduce. Eventually, at a gathering such as the one he was now at, he would be at the back of the hall – if he was invited at all.

The motto of Training Camp North was: 'Per Institutionem Vistory' – victory through training, but a few years back a disillusioned commander had remarked that is should be 'Sine Honore Legioni' the legion without honours.

127

"General Valerian, would you like to say a few words?" said Hallenberg, gesturing to the microphone. It was more of an instruction than a question. The Grand Field Marshall seemed to be the only other person present who understood what was going on. He realised that there was friction between Malaya and Valerian, and he had a skill for spotting tension when others who should, didn't. And he liked winners, and Malaya had won decisively here, Valerian could not refuse this promotion.

"Of course, Grand Field Marshall," he said, bowing his head but seething inside. As he stepped up to the podium and leant in to the microphones, he fully realised that there was no way out now.

"I ask that you forgive me if I am a little bit hesitant," he paused for effect. "The generosity of my friend, General Malaya, now, Major General Malaya has taken me by surprise. I am truly honoured by this and wish to thank her from the bottom of my heart. I have followed her career and that career has been exceptional, she is truly deserving of the rank. I look forward to the time when she takes her rightful place on the army council."

A gentle ripple of applause rose from the audience and it took all of his composure to stop himself from cringing as he watched heads nod in approval of his words.

"I am also ready to do my duty to the full, so let me tell all those who will be joining the army, I will be hard on you, and my rigid discipline will turn you into unbreakable warriors. I am already planning a regime to ensure that we have the toughest, fiercest fighters the world has ever seen. Our enemies will fear us, and we will prevail."

His voice rose to a shout as he banged his fist on the podium to emphasise his point. He took a bit of comfort that the applause for him started while he was still speaking and was louder and lasted longer than it did for Malaya, but it was a pyrrhic victory, she had got the better of him and they both knew it.

He stepped towards her and held out the hand of friendship, she had no choice but to take it. They moved closer for the traditional kiss on both cheeks.

"How many cocks did you have to suck to get this one," he hissed into her ear as he squeezed her hand as tightly as he could. She winced a little at the pain, but gritted her teeth, smiled, then clasped her other hand on his. To the audience this was the two of them shaking hands in mutual appreciation. What they couldn't see was Malaya digging her fingernails into his skin, then dragging them across the back of his hand, peeling back four little ribbons of flesh.

"I got promoted, you got promoted, everyone's happy, I am, they are, why not you?" she said.

This was a game of chicken and fortunately for her, Valerian released his grip before breaking any of the bones in her hand.

"I won't forget this, you bitch," he whispered as menacingly as he could through a forced smile.

"I know, that's why I did it," she whispered triumphantly.

For the rest of his life, he never realised the simple fact that all those years ago, when he allowed the unit under his command to be cut off and run out of ammunition, then led a bayonet charge that cost the lives of so many of his men, was the reason he failed to get the promotion.

Over the year that he had been commander at Training Camp North, he stuck true to his word. His training was tough, harsh and brutal, as he took out his bitterness on the trainees. The death rate amongst the conscripts stood as stark testament. The philosophy was simple, make the training so hard and life in the camp so unpleasant that the trainees would be desperate to pass final exams to get out. The simple device of making recruits who failed the tests start the whole six months over again was usually enough to make them pass, such was the fear. The teaching staff at Training Camp East quickly found out that they had to rapidly improve the standard of their training, as the alumni of Training Camp North were hardened beyond anything they had seen before.

****

He read the report and clicked a link to take him to the pictures, he had read the descriptions, but nothing he had read prepared him for what he saw. He gasped at the first picture, the image making him visibly jump backwards in his seat. Malaya's severed head was sitting on her desk, dull eyes wide open staring towards the door, her skin having already taken on a blue tinge.

He had seen decapitations before in combat, and as vile as a decapitation is, a battlefield is full of vile sights. But there was something about the juxtaposition of the head being deliberately placed on the desk surrounded by banality of normal office things that took his breath away.

His hands trembled as he clicked through the other pictures. Malaya's naked headless body on the bed, the blood – there was so much blood. He had obviously seen blood before, but this was the blood of a colleague, albeit a hated one, and this disturbed him more than he expected. Kaman's partially clothed body was lying on the floor of the inner office with the garrotte still in place. Her face purple and bloated, eyes bulging out in a grotesque death stare, her tongue forced out of her mouth. Kobashi's body was face down on the floor, the exit wound at the back of his neck clearly visible. There were other pictures too, the military police photographer had done a good job. Pictures showed all the rooms in the suite, they showed detail of blood splatter on the wall behind the bed, the position of the bodies in relation to each other etc....

Krall's naked body shocked him, her head at an unnatural angle with the broken bone in her neck distorting her skin. He recognised the Warrant officer and was equally shocked at the damage to the back of his head. He opened a video file from the camera covering the warrant officer's door and watched with rising anger as Astrid killed the man. His anger was not just at the killing, but also watching as the experienced soldier allowed himself to be manoeuvred into what was obviously a trap.

"Dammit," shouted Valerian as he banged his fist on the desk. "He knew he was looking at an imposter, why didn't he stand his ground, why did he let himself be led?" He shook his head and knowing that his anger would distract him and cloud his judgement, calmed himself.

He got over his initial shock quickly and studied all the pictures dispassionately and in detail, then took a pencil and pad, talked himself through the sequence of events and wrote his ideas down.

"Malaya was obviously the first to be killed and Krall was the last, the only way to get to the shower block was through the warrant officer's room, so he had to be killed before Krall. Kaman had to have been killed before Kobashi, otherwise she would have seen his body. Only after they had been killed would she have decapitated Malaya and placed her head on the desk, otherwise they would have both seen it."

As dispassionate as he was trying to be, he couldn't suppress the shudder of revulsion that rippled through him. "Why did she cut Malaya's head off, what purpose did that serve?" he asked aloud.

He went back to Malaya's images, switching back and forth between them, and as he did so, he started to become perplexed. He tried to reason it out; there was no sign of struggle from Malaya, and nothing in the room was disturbed. She was naked and laying on her back on the bed; pictures from the bathroom showed her clothes were on the floor near the shower with no blood on them. So, was she naked when she was killed? Part of Astrid's combat uniform was also on the floor by the shower, along with several damp towels.

"Was she naked too? Were they both naked?" he said to himself in quiet incredulity.

He dismissed the thought as ridiculous, but it nagged at him, there was no sign of any other bloodstained clothing anywhere, and this was odd as there was a huge amount of blood on the bed and the walls. So, at the moment there was no other explanation. The more he studied the pictures, the more detached he became from the subject and the more interested he became in trying to work out the mechanics of it all.

He clicked back to the first image and zoomed in. Malaya's head filled the whole screen, he zoomed in further until the image was larger than life size. He scrolled down to her neck; this had been severed low down, level with the shoulders. He zoomed in again, this time to the irregular crescent incision around the torn jugular half way up the neck. This was not a knife wound. He remembered an incident with a World Council official who was remonstrating with him over alleged war crimes and being shown photos of civilian women who said that they had been raped by soldiers under his command. All of them had the same irregular crescent marks on their necks, they said that this was where the soldiers had bitten them during the rapes.

Why would both women be naked, and how did she get close enough for long enough to bite Malaya's throat? An unbelievable thought formed in his mind, but it was the only coherent explanation. The only rationalisation he could think of was that Astrid Peterman had ripped out Brigit Malaya's jugular while they were having, or about to have, sex.

He put his hands to the top his head and stared up at the ceiling in stunned disbelief. "How could I have been so blind?" he said aloud. "All that bullshit at her fiancé's funeral about never loving another man and now being married to the army; that was all crap! She was a lesbian. How did I not see that?" He laughed in incredulity. "And she had sex with a prisoner and the most dangerous woman in the country."

He thought quickly, *he* had to find Astrid and had to bring her in alive, and she would be made to say what had happened. Her confession was the only way, because his theory was so outrageous it would simply not be believed. After the confession, Malaya would be written out of the army record and the fools on the

131

army council who promoted her would be dismissed and discredited for failing to discover that she had a sexual orientation that was a serious criminal offence, particularly so in the military. He would assert that they had not been as diligent as they claimed, and he would finally get the promotion that he deserved. Then he would change the rules and appoint the other members of the army council to ensure that he would become Grand Field Marshal Valerian when Hallenberg eventually died.

He acted fast, the information about Malaya's death had only been sent to a few senior staff, and those lower ranks that had been involved in the discovery of the bodies had been ordered to keep silent or face severe military punishment. He felt lucky, he could put his name forward to lead the investigation, but this might take too long, so he would have to bypass the normal channels. This would be tricky and could easily backfire.

He opened his email program and in the 'To' box typed 'GFM Hallenberg'. It was the personal address of the Grand Field Marshal. He would have to pick his words very carefully, if he got it wrong it would be very bad for him.

"Sir, I have just learned the sad news of Major General Malaya's death at the hands of the criminal Peterman. You may not be aware, sir, but there was a special bond between myself and Major General Malaya – my Brigit – we were close, dare I say, intimate. I implore you, please let me be the one to lead the hunt and bring the perpetrator to justice so that she can pay for this heinous crime. I must do this to avenge my dearest friend."

Within ten seconds a reply pinged back from Hallenberg. Valerian opened the mail with a little trepidation. Just two words:

"Do it."

Valerian sat back in his chair, relieved, and started to ponder just how he would conduct his investigation and what sort of assistance he would get.

A couple of minutes later, the phone rang. It was Major Marek, Hallenberg's personal aide; a nasty, ratty and ruthlessly efficient man who used his unassailable position in the grand field marshal's office to say whatever he wanted with impunity, despite his relatively junior rank.

"You didn't follow procedure Valerian," he snapped in a clipped Midlands accent.

"General Valerian to you, remember your rank, I am a three-star general," said Valerian calmly.

"Don't interrupt me. I said you didn't follow procedure, Valerian," said Marek deliberately missing out the 'General' again. "You should have gone through me and I'll have you know I take a very dim view of people mailing the Grand Field Marshal directly and without consulting me first. But no matter, Grand Field Marshal Hallenberg has instructed me to inform you of the parameters that you will have to work to. They are quite simple, even you should understand. You will relocate to base number one and assume position of the temporary commander of Kandalan, your deputy will carry on at Training Camp North."

"We can't spare any troops for an external search, so if she gets off the base you will have to use the civilian police for your investigations, the commissioner for the Correlan police will be told that he has to report directly to you. Only when you are ready to make an arrest can you have any troops. Do it quick and you'll become the permanent Kandalan Base commander. Is that clear Valerian?"

"It is clear, and my rank is general, you would do well to remember that." Valerian struggled to keep his voice calm.

"I will remember you," Marek sneered.

"And I will remember you. Goodbye."

He put the phone down and dismissed his exasperation, one day he would take Marek down, but not today. He immediately started to study the map on his wall, looking for potential routes south, but all the time his ego made him keep looking back to the location of the Kandalan Base.

"I will be base commander and all I have to do is catch the bitch. Then my God, she will know the meaning of suffering," he whispered to himself.

He was deep in thought, pondering how to best use the civilian police – all of whom he considered to be idiots and too weak to join the military – when the phone rang.

"Valerian, Commissioner Ellet here." The voice of the police commissioner was stern. "I have been told that you are in charge of the hunt for an escaped prisoner. This should be my job, but rest assured that I will pass on any information that I consider relevant." The commissioner was obviously unhappy but kept just enough respect in his voice.

"No, Commissioner," said Valerian firmly. "You will pass on all information and I will be the judge of whether it is relevant or not. And in future you will address me as General Valerian."

"I don't have to state your rank; I am a civilian."

"A civilian under military command follows military protocol."

"So be it – General," snapped Ellet curtly.

"And if I suspect that you are holding anything back, I will extend my investigation to you personally. I will consider a charge of assisting the escape of a prisoner and that would be very bad for you."

"Are you threatening me? Because I'm not afraid of your big fat army boots."

"You would do well to remember that I will be keeping a log of anyone who I suspect is recalcitrant, and when this is over, there will be a reckoning and my castigation will be unpleasant."

"Huh, you'll get it all, goodbye," grunted the commissioner, putting the phone down and deliberately missing off the 'General'.

Valerian called his Lieutenant into his office.

"I have been given the task of finding the fugitive. Contact the head of military intelligence, tell them that this is my investigation and remind them that they now answer to me. Do the same for the military police."

"Very good, sir." The lieutenant turned to leave, but Valerian called him back.

Valerian had suddenly become aware of Astrid's reason for the decapitation and placement of Malaya's head on her desk. "Why do you think she did this?"

Valerian turned the monitor so that the lieutenant could see the image of Malaya's severed head. He had not seen any of the images and the colour momentarily drained from his face and he gasped, subconsciously putting his hand to his mouth.

"I don't know," said the lieutenant as he gathered his composure. "Was she...?"

"Yes," said Valerian, guessing the lieutenant's question, "the cut is clean, so I am certain that she was already dead."

"Why defile the body, why place it like that, it's disgusting. What purpose could it possibly serve?" the lieutenant asked rhetorically.

"She would have taken the dog tags, and without bolt cutters, decapitation would be the only way."

"But why did she have to place it on the desk like that?"

Valerian sat back in his chair and looked directly at his subordinate. "In combat, what is the worst state of mind for a soldier? What makes a bad soldier?"

"Fear?"

"No. Every soldier is afraid in combat, those who aren't are fools who get themselves killed. Fear is essential, it feeds the desire to stay alive. Have you ever been afraid in combat?"

"Yes, I have, sir, very afraid."

"So, have I. I have been so afraid I have even cried."

The lieutenant was taken aback at the general's candid admission but tried not to show it.

"Then I said to myself, no, I will not die today." Valerian sat up straight in his chair. "What does this image make you feel?"

"Sick, sir."

"Yes, that is natural. What else do you feel when you look upon this image of a defiled colleague. Do you desire revenge?"

"Very much so, sir," the aide snarled.

"I can see that it makes you angry, are you?"

"Yes, I am, sir."

"That is why she did it, a soldier meeting her will be angry, the desire for revenge will consume them. An angry soldier is a bad soldier, the heart rules the head, mistakes are made, and she will take full advantage of any mistake. Remember this when we meet her, and for this reason, no one else will see these images." He let these words sink in for a few moments. "Clear your mind of anger as I have done."

The lieutenant had no idea how easy it was for Valerian to clear his mind of the anger over Malaya's death.

Valerian then stood up and paced the room for a few moments, considering her likely routes back to Arralan. He tapped a map and muttered to himself. "She'll use the rivers," he grunted. "It's the quickest route southwest and she knows that there'll be no tracks to follow. She'll piss and shit in the water so the dogs won't be able to pick up a trail."

He studied the map closely, tracing various routes with his finger from Malaya's base at Kandalan southwest to the border. He stood back in silence stroking his beard, staring at the wall, pondering what he would do, trying to think as she would. He knew that she would have to avoid the main areas of population and all the main roads that led towards the border.

Eventually he spoke, "We will concentrate on these rivers." He jabbed at three points on the map. "They all lead to the D'Nar River, it flows south for almost a hundred kilometres, that's where she's heading."

But he was wrong.

At that very moment, Astrid was squatting down, relieving herself in the slow waters of a small river that flowed north, eventually leading to the mighty river T'har. Fifty metres downstream a pike detected a change in the chemistry of the water and moved his metre-long body out of the weeds to investigate. Twenty metres later the water chemistry reverted to normal and the Pike lost interest, sliding its grey green body back into the weeds to wait until prey came its way to be ambushed. A moment later, a small fish past by close enough, and with a flick of its tail, it darted out and sank its teeth into its victim.

****

Valerian and his aide arrived by helicopter at Kandalan and immediately started to organise the search. He studied the map of the huge encampment, thinking through the difficulties she would have in trying to get out.

"She's still on the base," Valerian announced from behind his desk in his temporary office. "She'll be hiding somewhere. This base is over one-hundred kilometres across, and there's no way she could have even got close to the perimeter by now. We have her uniform, get the tracking teams out."

"Yes, sir." The lieutenant saluted and left the room.

****

After a couple of hours, the lieutenant stood in front of Valerian's desk, the general had his head down reading a report. "What about the dogs?" he said without looking up.

"Sir, the dogs picked up the scent," the lieutenant said flatly.

"I am aware of that," said Valerian, still not looking up. "But from the tone of your voice I assume that this is not good news."

"No, sir, I am afraid it is not. An item of the fugitive's clothing was found in the back of a refuse cart, and that is what the dogs had been tracking."

Valerian made no comment, his silence intended to draw information from his subordinate.

"Captain Krall's clothing is missing, sir, as is her staff car—"

"She will head for the south gate," Valerian interrupted, still not looking up. "She'll try to impersonate Captain Krall. But she won't be able to get through the gate without a specific off-base travel permit; she is probably unaware of that."

"Actually, sir, I checked the backup video surveillance from the car park. Only one vehicle left in the right time frame. It headed out east. Before coming to see you, I checked the off-base travel permits. No official permits were granted, but an email was sent directly to the east gate very early this morning from Major General Malaya's office for Captain Krall to exit the base."

Valerian looked up, his face darkened. "How did she get the keys to Krall's car?"

"She was given them by the guard at the main entrance to Malaya's office block, sir," the lieutenant's voice was tinged with an uncharacteristic hint of anger.

"What!" bellowed Valerian. "Find out who gave her the keys and bring them in."

"The individual is already in custody, sir."

"He is a dead man."

****

"Fuck," said Latana, jumping up from his chair and looking out of the window, as three army police cars pulled up outside the east gate checkpoint and officers spilled out.

"She said we'd get a visit, but there's about ten of them."

The door kicked open and a huge army MP entered.

"Look, we didn't stop her, we were only having a bit of fun..." was all he could say before the cosh hit the side of his head.

File Deletion

The progress bar on the file delete diagnostic ground its way across the screen at a near glacial speed. The hours had dragged by as the diagnostic was running on the corporal's terminal. It showed that the message was genuine, and someone really had deleted the files. At eight in the morning other members of staff had arrived and sat at their terminals, they ignored the two men that they assumed to be working on a major problem. They could not have known just how major the problem was.

Both the captain and the corporal had been staring at the screen, both had been chain smoking and constantly drinking coffee. Both were visibly shaking as they willed the computer to work faster, though not through the excess of caffeine of nicotine now coursing through their veins, but through sheer nervousness. Then with an innocuous ping, it was all over, and they had the answer. Both men gasped when they saw the report, the captain visibly shook when he read it; he immediately hit 'Print'.

The message read:

Server files accessed and deleted: 2

Total Size: 81,036 MB

Time: 05.03

Backup files accessed and deleted: 2

Total Size: 81,036 MB

Time: 05.05

Shredder activated for 4 files.

Location: Office computer of Major General Brigit Malaya

"Oh my God, these files were huge," whispered the corporal.

"Oh no," was all the captain could say.

The Bus Driver

Danny loved being a bus driver, he loved his bus. Yes, it was old, yes, the leather seat was cracked, but it was comfortable and puffed out a pleasant smell of dry leather and old rubber whenever he sat on it. The steering was a little bit vague from time to time, and he referred to the gearbox as 'guess-o-matic' as he was never completely sure what gear he was selecting or even if it would engage at all. The paint on the dashboard had worn down to the metal where he always held on when getting in and out.

Some of the gauges didn't work, but they were not important; he didn't even need the fuel gauge. He always filled up the bus every morning and had been driving the route for so many years now that he knew he would have a quarter of a tank left at the end of the day.

Every couple of months, he had to replace the gaffa tape that held the instrument cluster together, but in the seven years that he had been driving her, the old girl, as he referred to it, had never broken down, had always started first time, and most importantly, the heater always worked in winter.

He liked his passengers too, for the most part they were regulars who he had hauled across the country through the hundred odd stops he would have to make every working day. He knew their names, and seemingly everything about their families. He had a smile for everyone and was affable; people liked to talk to him, and when they told him of any troubles they had, they said that his smile and occasional advice made their problems seem not so important. Though his days started early and finished late, all of this made him happy in his job.

It was nearly midday and about time to eat the sandwiches that his wife had prepared, they were his favourite, cheese and salami on his wife's homemade rye bread; the same thing every day. The sun had been playing on his lunchbox for the last few kilometres and had warmed the sandwiches a little. The cheese had started to sweat, and the butter had melted into the bread which had started to dry out and was curling at up at the crust a bit, but it still tasted good. He washed it down with a fizzy orange drink that too had got a little warm. There was the usual small apple pie which he always left until he was on his way home. He reached in the box for a chocolate covered biscuit, and on feeling the melted chocolate squish inside the wrapper, decided not to even try to eat it, he would save it and put it in his fridge when he got home.

He dropped off his passengers and was alone on the bus as he made the long journey along an underused road through the dry, near desert terrain, into the next town where he would collect another load of familiar faces. The road was mainly straight with a few gentle curves, and the absence of trees and hedges meant he could see far into the distance and would notice other vehicles in plenty of time. He would not have to worry about them – unlike when he had to drive in towns and cities, where he thought all the other drivers were unpredictable, erratic lunatics.

He didn't like having a radio on, he didn't like the mindless predictable music churned out by all the stations or the inane babble of the DJs. He was happy to be alone with his thoughts. He was daydreaming about changes he would like to make to his home, maybe some new furniture or some decorating and was unaware that he was crossing an invisible barrier.

Far away, in a room staffed by stern military men, an alarm beeped and a number appeared on a screen. The operator checked the number against a list and noted that it was assigned to Captain Krall. He looked up a list of authorised off-base movements for the day and could not find any relating to Captain Krall.

He followed protocol and triangulated the signal to get a fix on the location, marked it on a map, then triangulated again after thirty seconds to establish speed and heading. Unaware of the significance, he reported to his senior officer – who was aware of the significance. The officer immediately picked up a phone and called Valerian's Lieutenant.

****

"Sir, we have Krall's car," said the lieutenant.

"Where is it?" snapped Valerian.

"About thirty-five kilometres from the south gate, sir, heading south, but she's not on a main highway."

"How do we know it's her car and not any staff car, they are all the same."

"The tracker has just activated, sir, and there is no standard authorisation form issued for travel off-base for Captain Krall. All we know is that there was

140

an email sent from General Malaya's office directly to the east gate authorising an exit."

He paused, weighing up whether to elaborate. He decided to. "Sir, it is clear that the fugitive sent the email, General Malaya must have left her terminal logged on."

Valerian stood up sharply, a slight smile broke through his usual stony expression. "Hah, she doesn't know about the tracker," he gloated. "A helicopter will be the fastest way for us to get her. Get one organised immediately. We'll take two troopers with assault rifles and fixed bayonets, make sure they know just how dangerous she is. Get a full body restraint harness, we'll have to immobilise her, and take your sidearm as well."

"Yes, sir."

The lieutenant could not stop himself smiling as a curious emotion ran through him, the same emotion he used to get in combat when the point in the battle was reached where he knew they had won and were safe.

"One more thing, sir, she's not traveling fast, only about forty-five kilometres per hour."

"She's not drawing attention to herself, or so she thinks."

The lieutenant left, and Valerian subconsciously rubbed his hands together as he thought of how he would present the prisoner. He spoke quietly to himself.

"I'll have her within the hour, and then…" He looked at a map of the Kandalan Base. "…and then this base will be mine." He relished the thought of further destroying Malaya's reputation by informing the army council that she had broken critical rules by leaving her terminal active. He practiced a line in his head.

"Who knows what damage could have been done? Who knows what damage has been done?"

****

"There's only a bus," yelled the pilot over the din of the rotors as he scanned the road. "I can see for a couple of kilometres either side. There's nothing else."

The lieutenant selected the frequency used by the tracking station and jabbed the 'talk' button on the radio.

"Confirm target location," he yelled into the microphone, then listened intently to the reply, cross checking with a map.

"It's Krall's tracker," he shouted to Valerian.

"How accurate is the information."

"It's been detected by four different receivers, this will give us a fix to within five metres."

The mood sank in the helicopter as they realised that this might not be her.

"She found the tracker and put it in this bus," the lieutenant stated the obvious, he always felt that it was his job to do so, even though he often felt it made him look foolish.

"Yes," snapped Valerian.

"The driver might be an accomplice."

"Possible, but unlikely."

Valerian tapped the pilot on the shoulder. "Land in front of that bus, block the road."

A few minutes later the helicopter landed, the troopers got out and aimed their weapons at the bus driver. Danny slammed on the brakes.

"Get out," screamed a trooper. "Put your hands up."

Danny did what he was told and found himself inches from two bayonets while the lieutenant looked under the steering wheel of the bus.

"Found it, sir." The lieutenant emerged with a small box with wires attached. Valerian approached the driver, and to his surprise, Danny stood to attention.

"General Valerian," he said quickly, recognising the officer.

"How do you know who I am?" said Valerian, slightly confused.

"Sir, you were my commanding officer when I was in the army."

"You *were* in the army?" Valerian scowled. "You are young enough to still be in the army."

"I was injured out eight years ago, sir."

Danny stiffened and saluted, showing the stumps of his index and middle fingers, along with the mutilated thumb of his right hand. Medical teams had rebuilt his hand as best they could, giving him a thumb that was at best, perfunctory, but to be fair to the surgeons, they didn't have much to work with. Valerian noticed the burn scars on Danny's face and his ripped earlobe.

"My name is Daniel Thorin, I was a corporal."

Valerian relaxed. "Ah yes, I do remember signing your discharge papers. A shrapnel injury was it not?"

"Yes, sir, artillery shell fragment."

"It was a shame, and I recall that you had a bright future in the army."

"Leaving the army was the worst day of my life, sir, worse than the injury that caused it, sir," he said, standing straight and looking directly ahead. Valerian sensed the man's pride in his service to his country and acknowledged the injuries that he had received. Despite his brusque nature, he always felt sympathy and respect for injured servicemen, either in or out of service.

He gestured for the troopers to stand down.

"I understand your sadness, but the army must have troops that are fully fit. I remember that you would never be able to fire a weapon again. For that, I am sorry."

He put his hand on Danny's shoulder, reassuring him. "Now, we are looking for an escaped prisoner, very dangerous. It seems she put a tracking device in your bus."

Danny looked shocked. "She, sir?"

"Did you leave your vehicle unattended at any time?" Valerian continued, not wanting to give anything away to a civilian, even though this was a civilian who still showed a strong loyalty to the military.

"Yes, sir, this morning before my shift started."

"Was your vehicle unlocked?"

"Yes, sir, it was," said Danny with a heavy heart.

"It would seem that civilian life has caused you to lose some discipline."

"It won't happen again, sir."

"You are free to go."

The helicopter departed, Danny reattached the ignition wires and drove off. He was never the same again; his vehicle was always locked when he was not in it and he stayed within sight of it whenever he stopped. He viewed with deep suspicion every new passenger he picked up and seldom talked to his passengers other than to take their fare.

****

"She's still heading south," shouted Valerian to his Lieutenant over the roar of the helicopter as they returned to Kandalan.

"We know now that we can't track her, so get the word out to the police to be on the lookout for any staff car heading south. Stress to them that they are not to approach under any circumstances. They are to report a position only, we'll do the rest. And remind them that they are currently under military jurisdiction and any deviation from my orders will find them subject to military discipline."

"Yes, sir."

Valerian sat back and looked out of the window, seething inside that Astrid had got the better of him. He lit a Cavana cigarette, the pilot glanced over his shoulder when he smelled the cigarette smoke, it is illegal to smoke in a Correlan helicopter, but the pilot decided that it would be better for him if he said nothing. It was.

The Peasant Girl

The crucial part of Astrid's escape plan was to head for and travel through the Phaal region. To get there she would need to travel east of the base, then north. It would be an unlikely escape route, and most probably any search effort there would be cursory at best. The Phaal region was named after a religious sect that lived there. The land was poor, even by Correlan standards, and most Phaal were simple subsistence farmers; peasants, growing only what they needed and eschewing almost all modern technology.

Astrid had chosen this route as the religious doctrine of the area stated that people were born alone, and with the exception of their immediate family, they should live as individuals, and that they would die alone and only after death would they become part of a community. She would be able to move through the region freely, and any Phaal that she met would just ignore her.

For years, the Correlan military had tried to integrate Phaal into the armed forces, but their complete inability to take or even understand orders made them too hard to train. Those few that had somehow made it into a regiment became a huge problem in combat where they would often just stand up and walk away, oblivious to danger and get shot. Eventually the military gave up, realising that the dogma of their sect rendered them useless. The Phaal region was left to its own devices, with little contact from the army. She would be safe there.

The car was now a liability; a staff car this far from base would arouse interest, and she couldn't use the car to get through the Phaal region, as army helicopters routinely flew over the area and any passing helicopter would immediately report the sighting of a staff car. She needed to get rid of it, and soon. As she followed the course of a small river that was a tributary to the T'hah River, opportunity presented itself.

A young woman was standing in the river, the sleeves on her voluminous smock rolled up so that they didn't get too wet from tipping fish from a net into a bucket. Parked up on the bank was an old ex-military utility vehicle. To all intents and purposes, it was an agricultural tractor, the sort that would be recognisable anywhere in the world.

Though the Phaal shunned most technology, they had grudgingly embraced some types of vehicle. This one would have been obtained from a scrap dealer by bartering some goods after the army considered it beyond its useful life, so it would be many decades old. It was a testament to their latent engineering skills that the Phaal were able to keep these fifty-year-old wrecks running. Astrid stopped, got out and stood by her car.

"Come here," she ordered; the female did what she was told and stood a little way off with her head bowed down. Astrid could see that she was Phaal by the three horizontal burn scars, each about twenty millimetres apart across her left forearm near her elbow. The one furthest from her elbow looked newer than the others and fresh, this meant that the woman was between twenty and twenty-three but nearer twenty. Astrid knew what they were; they were called 'repentance scars' and just the sight of them sickened her.

"What is your family name?" Astrid said with an aggressive edge to her voice.

All civilians in Correla feared the military, even the Phaal, and despite her unease at talking harshly to a civilian, it was to be expected. The woman was outside of the Phaal region and if she was found by a search team she would inevitably be forced to talk, and Astrid couldn't risk her telling the interrogators about this nice military woman she met.

"Varna," the girl said timidly and with her head still bowed.

"And where are you from? – and look at me when you speak!"

The girl looked up fearfully. "Traline," she said nervously.

"Traline? You are a long way from your village, and you are out of Phaal territory. Why?" Astrid demanded.

"The fish are better here; the fish in the big river are small and taste bad. If you eat too many of them, you get sick and…"

"Shut up, I don't want a cookery lesson," Astrid snarled. "Do you have family in Traline?"

"Yes."

Astrid put on an air of menace. "Who?"

"My mother and father and my younger sister."

"Do exactly as I say, and I will not need to visit Traline; disobey me, and I might just make a special visit, I might stay for a couple of weeks."

She walked around behind the woman to intimidate her further. She had to make sure that this young woman would do exactly as she was told.

"I might bring a platoon with me, I am sure that my men would like to spend some time with your little sister and get to know her better. You see, my men have been away from their wives and girlfriends for a long time, I think they would like a nice young Phaal girl to keep them warm in bed. And maybe the older men might like to do the same with your mother."

Her voice turned dark and menacing. "While your father is made to watch." She paused for effect. "So, will you do as I order you?"

"Yes, I will," the woman said quietly, visibly trembling. "Please don't hurt them."

"Well, that is up to you, isn't it?"

The girl nodded in terrified acquiescence.

"Good, now can you drive that?" Astrid pointed at the staff car.

"I think so."

"Yes or no, can you drive it?" Astrid shouted.

"Yes, yes I can."

"Okay, good. Now take your clothes off."

"Huh?" was all the shocked woman could say.

"Do as I say," snapped Astrid.

The woman fumbled the buttons of her smock with trembling hands, nervously undressing and furtively glancing over her shoulders.

"There's no one watching," said Astrid. "Now hurry up."

The woman stood naked in front of her with one arm across her breasts and her hand over her crotch, tears forming in her eyes at the shame and humiliation. Strict Phaal religious dogma forbade any women to be seen nude in front of anyone except her husband, if this was ever found out, the priests would severely punish her. But she knew better than to disobey the military, particularly so right at this moment.

Astrid looked at her, she was slim, probably as a result of poor nutrition, with a young woman's figure, but it was clear that she would eventually get a more rounded womanly physique. She was also probably a virgin.

Astrid felt sorry for the girl and wanted to take her away and tell her about all the lies that her religion forced on her and how she didn't have to suffer the burns, and that her life held so much potential, a potential that would never be realised while the Phaal priests held such power. Part of the reason she felt sorry was that she was going to make the girl do something that at best would get her hurt and might even see her get killed.

It was an awful thing to do, and she knew it. This woman was a civilian; naive and uneducated, but Astrid had to think of the bigger picture and protect herself. If she allowed herself to be caught, she would inevitably be broken by the torturers and then thousands, maybe tens of thousands more people would get hurt or die. Using this girl as a diversion would buy the precious time that she needed.

"And the headscarf."

"No," cried the woman desperately.

"Yes," shouted Astrid angrily. "Think of your family."

With obvious reluctance and with an anguished look, the woman undid the knot and pulled the scarf off and handed it to Astrid, a bob of greasy black hair dropped just short of her shoulders. She was crying now, and Astrid knew why but on this particular matter she had no sympathy. Phaal women were told that they had to have their hair covered at all times and that showing their hair was a sin. This arcane religious law went back centuries and was simply just another means of control. The woman had her hands on her head trying to cover her hair, this being a greater humiliation than exposing her naked body. Sniffing back tears, she was startled to see Astrid taking off her uniform.

Astrid handed the uniform to the woman.

"Put this on," she ordered.

The woman did as she was told, then Astrid pulled on the woman's smock, it was dirty and musky with stale sweat; washing was clearly not high on Phaal women's priorities.

"Get in the car; drive due east until you see the south mountain road. Then head due south and do not stop for anything, I repeat, do not, under any circumstances, stop for anything. Get there as quickly as you can. When you get twenty kilometres from the border you will see a checkpoint, there you will stop, and you will be contacted and told what to do. Do you understand?"

The terrified woman just nodded.

"Good." Astrid tapped a compass on the car dashboard. "Now, what have I just told you?"

"I must head east, then take the south road to the mountains," she said timidly.

"And?"

"And I must not stop for anything until I am twenty kilometres from the border."

"Correct."

Astrid reached into the back of the vehicle and pulled out a large briefcase, the bag with Krall's clothes and a small tool kit. She tapped the briefcase.

"I have a device in here that will tell me if you have stopped and where you have stopped. So remember, what happens to your family is up to you and the sooner you reach the destination the better it will be for you and them. Now go."

There was no such device in the briefcase, just some tools, a basic medical kit and some bottles of water. There was no checkpoint either, but it was a convincing bluff. She knew that once on the south road it was only a matter of time before she was stopped. But as soon as they saw that they had a Phaal woman they would let her go, but she might get lucky, if she wasn't stopped, she would run out of fuel long before she got anywhere near the border.

Astrid wrapped the headscarf over her hair, and while tying the elaborate knot that Phaal women had to use, she wondered if she would get head lice, which would be a nuisance. But given that head lice don't live in greasy hair and the girl's hair looked as though it had never been washed, she realised that it was unlikely.

She climbed into the old vehicle, checked the fuel sight glass and was relieved to see the tank was about three quarters full. She pressed the starter, crashed the gearbox into first and lurched off down the road. Ten minutes later she had crossed the bridge and was in Phaal territory. All she had to do was turn left, head north, drive for about five hours, not look at anyone, and just stare at the road ahead of her. If anyone saw her, they would forget her even before she was out of sight. She was safe for the time being and for the first time in days, she let her mind wander.

Education was forbidden to the Phaal, except for Phaal priests who would be chosen at a very early age. The ones that were picked out were the ones who seemed to like to dominate other children, and in particular, those who showed a cruel streak. They would grow up hiding their true selves behind rituals and costume, preaching a relentless gospel of obedience to them and damnation of anyone who did not obey the rules they made.

Denial of even basic learning was the most powerful tool the priesthood had, and this made the domination of the ignorant easy. Only the priests were allowed to read and write, anyone even suspected of trying to learn was harshly punished, not by the priests, but by the ordinary Phaal, such was their fear of the supremacy of the religious leaders. These same leaders would open books with a flourish and held their audiences spellbound and in awe as they simply read the words from the pages.

She thought about the burns on the woman's arms, the 'Repentance scars', and a wave of anger flashed through her. Misogynist was too small a word to describe the Phaal priests, who for centuries had practised a particularly evil form of domination over women. All Phaal were taught that women were nothing more than sexual creatures that lured men from the path of godliness and decency – the simple fact societies have to breed to survive was ignored and instead was used as proof of the teachings. So ingrained was the doctrine, that all Phaal believed it, they also believed the priests when they were told that the sexual urges of females started at the age of fourteen and that these urges had to be kept in check.

Astrid found herself gripping the steering wheel hard enough for her knuckles to turn white as she thought about the mechanism by which the wholly natural sexual urges were 'kept in check'. On a girl's fourteenth birthday, she would be taken by her mother to the house of worship. In the centre of the room, there would be a metal fire basket full of glowing coals. She would kneel in front of this fire, and after a solemn lecture by the priest admonishing her for her immoral thoughts, the terrified girl would take a ceremonial item called 'The Object of Repentance', a sort of ornate knife with a blunt edge, from the brazier, and press the glowing red-hot edge onto her arm for as long as it took to say "I repent" or scream "I repent", as was always the case.

Often, if the girl did not have the courage to do this, her mother would perform the task, branding her own daughter. In this case, the daughters were frequently beaten by their mothers after the service for disobeying the priest and bringing shame on the family. If by chance the mother refused to carry out the branding, then the girl's arm would be tied to a block and the priest would carry out the task, though this time holding the glowing blade burning into her skin for as long as it took him to say "do you repent?" and for her to scream "I repent".

This sick ritual was carried out every three years throughout a woman's life, as it was said by the priesthood that it took three years for her lust to make her forget the pain. No exceptions were made for age either; old women who had somehow managed to live into their seventies still had to endure the ceremony.

If, as was often the case, the branding led to infection, the priest would simply state that it was her lust fighting the purifying effects of the burn and the weeping blisters would be clear evidence of the female's sexual desires. If it was

Pseudomonas or some other serious infection and the woman died, it would be taken as proof that she was not repentant, and that her death was a good thing. All Phaal believed it.

What angered Astrid most of all was that from a very young age, mothers told their daughters that this would happen and that it was their duty to endure it. So as terrified as they were, they all went willingly to the ceremony and suffer the hideous abuse and all to avoid upsetting the priest.

It was fortunate for the priests that it was still early in the day – they never left their dwellings until late afternoon – for if she saw one, she would have no hesitation in killing them. She was exceptionally good at making a murder she committed appear as an accident. She sighed and shook her head, there was so much wrong, and nothing she could do about it. She banished the thoughts from her mind and began to concentrate on the immediate tasks. The tractor was much slower that it should have been, and at this pace, she would not get through the Phaal region before nightfall and would need to find somewhere to sleep.

****

She had been driving for over three hours but had only covered about 40 kilometres and was deep in Phaal country. The low revving chug of the old diesel engine making the monotonous journey seem even slower than it actually was.

She heard them long before she saw them; the distinct rapid thump of the rotors, coupled with a high-pitched whine was a characteristic of the Falcon fast attack helicopter. It was not a particularly agile aircraft, but armed with a dual twenty-millimetre cannon, and with the option of four multiple unguided air to surface rocket pods or eight 200-kilo cluster bombs, the two-man Falcon was a powerful aircraft and the mainstay of the Correlan infantry air support wing. And there were two travelling towards her, fast, very fast.

She didn't raise her head to look up, no Phaal would be interested in them and the pilots would know that. She kept her head down and stayed facing directly ahead, avoiding the urge to glance up as the sound got louder. She would be in clear view of them by now, and her knuckles whitened as she gripped the steering wheel harder, waiting for the sound of them slowing to a hover either side of her and the rattle of twenty-millimetre cannon shells hitting the ground in front of her. But all that she got was the blast of the downdraught from the rotors as they both streaked overhead. Dust blew up all around, getting in her eyes and down her throat, but the sound was rapidly getting quieter. She didn't dare look around but trusted her ears instead.

The cannons in the Falcon track and pan in all directions and are controlled by the weapons officer who sat in a pod in front and just below the pilot. Powerful and accurate, the cannons are devastatingly effective and are 'always on', with the only safety interlock being a flip cover over the trigger. This gave the craft the ability for very quick target acquisition and fire.

However, the missile pods are fixed, requiring the craft to be lined up with the target. The rockets can be fired in a salvo of all 16, or, as the rockets are reasonably accurate, they could be fired individually. In this mode, the pilot would initially line up the helicopter, then a secondary set of controls are engaged so the weapons officer would have fine control over targeting. This was unpopular with pilots as suddenly they would not have full control of the craft, and a high degree of trust was required between the two men – trust which was seldom achieved.

While the cannons are able to be used virtually instantly, the rockets had to be armed. After a series of accidents with weapons discharges on the ground, a safety system was introduced.

****

The staff car had been reported heading southwest, and Valerian, ignoring the instruction to only use civilian police and no military units, had ordered the helicopters to intercept. The police were too far away and their vehicles too slow for the job. Besides, Valerian was quite sure that any civilian officers, all of whom were unaware of her abilities, would end up being slaughtered by her.

The pilots had been told who the driver was and had strict orders to bring her in alive, something that they relished. The kudos that they would receive would stand them in good stead for years. But they could not have known that it was not Astrid driving but the Phaal girl, desperately following Astrid's instructions to the letter in a misguided effort to save her family from punishment.

The helicopters had to reach, apprehend and detain her until land troops arrived. They had to stop her before she reached the road through the mountains. Once there, they would have no place to land the helicopters. Also, there were numerous tunnels through the mountains, some containing junctions, and once the car entered one of these, there could be no telling as to when or where it would emerge. Flying at top speed, they should just make it. Twenty minutes later they saw it in the distance; the staff car was driving fast along a road beside a river, heading towards a rise that led into the foothills.

"Once she's on that rise, there'll be nowhere for us to land and she's nearly there now," squawked the pilot in the lead helicopter who was the mission commander.

"I know this area well," came back the reply from the wingman. "After about five kilometres it flattens out again, we can take her there."

"She's on the rise now," said the weapons officer in the lead helicopter, peering through his targeting sight.

"We can catch up with her, and a few shots should make her slow down until we're through this first section. She doesn't know that we have orders to take her alive."

"Roger that," said the wingman.

The car was travelling along a single-track road cut into the side of a limestone hill. Going as fast as she dared, the girl had to dodge rocks and scree that had fallen onto the road, swerving to avoid the larger fragments. To the left was a vertical rock face about three metres high. The ground sloped away to the right of the road, gradually at first but getting a little steeper as she climbed the rise.

Thorny scrub bushes completing their annual life cycle dotted the ground, their leaves dry from the summer sun, and with desiccated seedpods open disgorging vast amounts of fluffy white seeds that were torn from the pods and carried on the wind as the car roared past. Both pilots scanned the lay of the land both sides of the road and judged that it was too steep to land safely.

By now, the two helicopters were closing fast and would soon be in a range where the guns would be accurate, using them now would risk hitting the car and killing the occupant. The wingman was behind and off to one side of the car but had a good view of the driver.

"It's a woman driving, she's in uniform, it has to be her," he reported.

"We'll give a few warning shots to get her to slow down, then I'll move on ahead, then you move in behind," the lead pilot ordered. "Once we're through this section, I'll land and detain the target, you remain airborne with your guns trained."

"Roger that," said the wingman.

The Phaal girl saw the helicopters in the rear-view mirror and was worried, and she was just bright enough to realise that they were much closer than they appeared in the mirror. She had no doubt that they were following her and might want her to stop. She thought about the woman army officer's odd behaviour and was puzzled as to why she was driving the car and why the woman had taken her clothes and her old tractor. But Astrid's words rang loudly in her ears and she thought about her little sister and what might happen to her if she didn't obey the instructions.

"...do not, under any circumstances, stop for anything..."

"Engage the target," ordered the lead pilot to his weapons officer, his tone flat and professional.

"Engaging the target now," said the weapons officer, his tone equally flat.

The weapons officer grabbed the joystick that controlled the cannons, then flipped open the safety cover on the arming toggle with his thumb and pulled the switch back to activate the armaments. Directly below him, the two cannon barrels instantly snapped up parallel to the body of the aircraft. He moved the joystick while watching a targeting display – little more than feed from a rudimentary camera with a zoom lens mounted in-line with the guns – on a screen in front on him. He pressed a small button that doubled the size of the image, then moved the joystick until the car was in line with the outer graticule on the sight.

"Target acquired, firing now."

He squeezed the trigger briefly, three rounds blasted from each of the barrels. Out of the corner of her eye, the Phaal girl saw the flash of the guns in the mirror and tensed. The rounds hit the road behind the car, each shot exploding on the ground, blasting gravel out in all directions. The girl flinched and automatically ducked down a fraction as she heard the clatter of debris against the rear of the vehicle.

The road ahead was much wider and smoother now and straight for as far as she could see. She gritted her teeth and pressed the accelerator to the floor. The helicopter crews were amazed to see the vehicle lurch forward and speed up with black smoke belching from both the exhausts as the engine revved to its top speed. Both pilots increased their speed to try and catch up.

The weapons officer moved the joystick so that the vehicle was on the lower edge of the screen graticule.

"I'll put some in the road in front of her; that should do it."

"Risky," said the pilot. "Do not hit the car, remember our orders."

"I won't," he said confidently as he squeezed the trigger again.

This time the burst was longer. Eight rounds from each barrel slammed into the rock face and road in front of the car. Sixteen small explosions threw gravel and shrapnel at the front of the car smashing the headlights, but still she kept her foot hard down, the car rocking violently as the wheels hit the small craters. With adrenaline pumping and sweat breaking out on her forehead, she glanced back and forth between the road and the mirror. In the distance, she could see a tunnel and knew that if she could make it to there, she would be safe.

He fired again, and again the rounds hit the ground but failed to make her slow down. The weapons officer frowned, then turned to a panel that controlled the rockets, turning a knob from 'Off' through 'Multi' to 'Single'. The targeting screen immediately changed to a forward-looking camera. The helicopter jerked sideways as he moved the joystick and pressed the fire button. A single unguided rocket streaked out of the pod towards the vehicle.

"What are you doing!" yelled the pilot, irate that command of the aircraft had been taken away from him without warning.

"We've got to stop her before she gets to that tunnel, the guns aren't working."

"By blowing her up?" shouted the pilot angrily.

"It's not armed, it'll just put a hole in the road, and then she'll have to stop and…" He glanced back at the panel, his eyes wide in shock. "Oh fuck, oh fuck," he gasped.

The pilot immediately saw the problem. "Oh no," he said fearfully.

The safety system that had been introduced after the ground fire accidents was simple. Each rocket now had a short cable fitted to carry an arming command signal, and when the rocket was fired, the cable would pull out and the weapon would arm itself as it left the launch tube. A switch in the cockpit controlled this. The idea was to prevent accidents on the ground as the weapons officers would only arm the warheads immediately prior to launch. However, after a few incidents where arming was forgotten in the heat of battle, it hadn't taken long for the weapons officers to get into the habit of arming the rockets as soon as they took off. This was unofficially considered safe practice and had become so routine that this officer had done it automatically as the craft left the ground and had simply forgotten that the rockets were now armed. The girl saw the flash of the rocket in the mirror and instinctively knew this was much more dangerous.

The rocket spiralled, veering off to the left at the last second and struck the rock face several metres to the left of the vehicle, its contact fuse detonating the high explosive warhead. The vehicle lurched up on one side and careened off the road, the girl unable to keep control. It ploughed through the scrubby bushes, hit a few bumps and ground to a halt with its front right wheel up on a rock and the bottom of the engine smashed. The lead helicopter overshot, its speed carrying it too fast and it carried on ahead turning in a broad arc.

Below in the car, the girl sat stunned; deafened by the pressure wave and with double vision that swam in front of her. The left side of her body was peppered with glass splinters from the window, and a rock the size of a man's fist had punched through the door and driven a shard of metal deep into her left knee. She felt no pain though as shock had numbed her. The driver's door had burst open, and she knew she had to get out. She stepped out of the vehicle and tried to stand but the damage to her knee caused her to collapse to the ground. With that, her pain sensation returned, she screamed, grabbing her leg with one hand and hauling herself away from the vehicle with the other.

The wingman had circled around by now and was hovering a short distance away.

"She's alive. Beaten up but alive," he said tersely.

The girl slowly dragged herself down away from the vehicle, her hearing was gradually returning, it sounded like she was deep under water but with a high-pitched whine that filled her head. She was only vaguely aware of the thump of the helicopter's rotor as she slumped down onto the damp ground. She laid still for a moment trying to catch her breath; wondering what would happen next and still not cognisant enough to figure out what the smell was and why she now felt wet in the driest month of the year.

The down draught from the helicopter blew around dry leaves, twigs and grass. A few blew under the vehicle and lodged up against the red-hot exhaust manifold. The constant blast of air from the rotor held the dry leaves up against the hot metal where they quickly began to char, with glowing red dots rapidly appearing. With the constant feed of oxygen, it only took a few seconds for the glowing spots to turn into flames which quickly spread downwards through the parched foliage.

Her vision was coming back to normal and the orange and yellow flickering suddenly snapped into focus. She abruptly realised what the odd smell was and why she felt wet, she was covered in fuel. Both of the spare tanks on the back of the vehicle had split open, fuel was flowing out and she was lying in a small stream of it. She looked at the flames, they were not near the fuel and the draught from the rotors was pushing the fire away, even so, a sense of panic gripped her. She struggled to her feet, trying to scramble away but the intense pain in her knee caused her to crash back down again. She grabbed at the scrubby bushes and tried to pull herself forward, ignoring the thorns as they punctured her skin, but she only succeeded in uprooting them.

Above, the helicopter moved position and the blast of air stopped. Almost at once a shrub under the vehicle burst into flames, the dry bark on its branches cracking and spitting out burning splinters that fizzled out in mid-air. She looked back at these while desperately grabbing for a purchase on anything to haul herself out with. Then with a loud bang, the superheated sap in the bush's trunk exploded into flame, blowing off a couple of the branches which landed near the fuel.

Screaming with the pain in her knee she got onto all fours and tried to move, but her left leg was too weak, and she fell back down again. She pulled herself up onto her hands and right knee and dragged herself forward; adrenaline coursed through her body giving her the strength to ignore the pain. She fell back down, and the uneven ground rolled her onto her back. She looked back at the flames just as one of the branches burned away enough to make it fall and start rolling. It rolled into the river of fuel.

Filled with terror, she watched as the shimmering blue light raced down along the stream of fuel towards her powerless body. She rolled back onto her front and tried to get away, dragging her injured leg. But it was too late, it only took a few seconds for the flames to reach her, and in an instant, she was engulfed.

"She's burning," said the wingman flatly as he watched the wretched figure thrash around in agony below him. "There's nothing we can do, she's toast." He watched, powerless as the shrubs nearby caught fire and burning bush fell on top of her. Somehow, she pushed that off and tried to crawl away, only to slump face down into a puddle of burning fuel. A large branch of a burning bush fell on her back, pinning her down.

"You stupid fucking arsehole," yelled the mission commander as he reached around the control column with his foot and kicked the weapons operator in the back of the head. "We're going to be in deep fucking shit for this. We'll probably get shot, you fucking idiot."

The girl's frantic movements slowed and as the shrub burned away, she rolled over onto her back. In this position, if she was still breathing, all that she would inhale would be flames. This would sear her lungs and she would lose consciousness and drown in the fluid that would fill them. Death would be mercifully quick now.

The mission leader heard his wingman's radio go quiet with the tell-tale click of the radio frequency changing. This meant he was reporting the fiasco back to base. A minute later the radio clicked back on.

"Got to escort you back to base," said the wingman.

"I've got to fly behind you and if you deviate from the route, I have orders to shoot you down. Sorry guys, it's nothing personal."

****

It was becoming harder for Astrid to ignore the hunger pangs and the dull headache over her eyes. She knew that her loss of clear thought was not only from lack of sleep, but also from the lack of food, and in particular, her sugar levels were getting low.

At various intervals along the side of the track were large round flat stones that were a geological feature, these could be useful. The vehicle that she was driving was notorious for having an inefficient engine that wasted a lot of energy as heat. This deficiency had been turned into an advantage of sorts with the fitting of a cowl over the exhaust manifold that could be adjusted to direct hot air into the cab allowing the vehicle to be used in the harsh winter conditions in the north.

Astrid stopped, picked up one of the stones, and after cleaning it with an alcohol wipe from the first aid kit, opened the cowl and wedged the stone onto the manifold. She took a knife from the tool kit and cut the drive belt to the fan at the front of the cowl then drove off once again. With the airflow reduced, the stone on the manifold would get extremely hot.

After several kilometres, she stopped as she drew level with a recently cropped wheat field. At the edge nearest the track there were some stalks that had been missed, and she was able to gather plenty of ears of wheat. She left the engine running while she sat with the smock over her knees, rubbing the ears of wheat between her palms, letting the grains fall into her lap while the light breeze blew away the chaff. She sorted carefully through the grains looking for any that were black and elongated.

These grains would be Ergot, the poisonous fungus that grows mainly on rye, but sometimes on wheat. Consuming that fungus would be very bad, as Ergot contains the precursor compounds that make up Lysergic Acid Diethylamide – LSD – and while it did not contain any actual LSD, it did contain powerful alkaloids that caused neurological and physiological problems. Hallucinations, seizures, convulsions, diarrhoea and vomiting would not be helpful right now.

There was no Ergot to be found, she didn't think there would be, as the previous year had been a touch drier than normal and Ergot usually formed after a wet summer. Even so, she did need to be careful. Satisfied that the wheat grains were clean, she put them onto a large flat stone nearby, she found another flat stone and started to grind the grains between the two. After a few minutes, she had an acceptable grist of wholemeal flour.

She took one of the bottles and added some water, then added a little salt by using part of a sachet of saline from the medical kit and mixed it all into a dough which she left to rest for a few moments while she picked some ripe berries which she then pressed into the dough. She stopped the engine and opened the cowl; heat radiated out from the stone, it was extremely hot. She divided the dough into three equal-sized balls then kneaded each one between her fingers, flattening them into thin rounds then placed them on the stone; they would not take long to cook.

After a couple of minutes, she flipped the unleavened bread over with a knife from the medical kit. When the bread puffed up and started to form blisters, she took them out and left them to cool a little. She had ended up with three circular flatbreads, each bigger than the palm of her hand and quite thick, she tore one open to check whether it was cooked through, it was.

The taste was so much better than she had expected; the carbohydrate was what she needed most, and the salt from the saline and sugar from the fruit were also important, but the three together tasted great. Maybe it was because she was so hungry, maybe not, but it seemed like the best flatbread she had ever tasted.

It was a filling meal and she didn't need to resist the urge to eat it all and was pleased that she could save the other two for the next morning.

Her hunger satisfied, she started the engine and continued the slow plod north. She knew that she would not get through the Phaal region in one day as she had originally planned. Now she needed to find somewhere to sleep, she may not be hungry anymore, but she was desperately tired, and the food had added to this. After about another two hours' driving, she came across a remote outbuilding, closer inspection showed it was a hay store. Perfect; the nearest building had been a couple of kilometres back and there had been no one in the fields, and none in sight. She found a couple of old sacks and shook them out, checking for evidence of rodents. There were probably a few mice around, but she still chose an area where there were no droppings evident. She spread the sacks out on a thick layer of hay, laid down and quickly fell asleep.

Helicopter Aftermath

Valerian sat quietly fuming as he listened to the police commissioner.

"If you had let a professional organisation search for the woman, she would still be alive, Valerian."

"I told you before; it's General Valerian to you," the general hissed into the phone.

"Not any more Valerian, she's dead and your amateur investigation is at an end, so I do not have to follow army protocol. Now why don't you go back to playing mother hen with those sixteen-year-old conscripts back in Training Camp North where you can't do any more harm?"

"Amateur?" he yelled.

"Well, maybe amateur is the wrong word; let's try incompetent, shall we? I reckon incompetence is the correct word here."

"How dare you; she would have sliced your flat foot cops into pieces the second she saw them."

"My 'flat foot cops', as you put it, would not have forgotten that they had armed the missile. I'd say what your weapons officer did can be classed as incompetence."

"That information was classified," yelled Valerian, suddenly aware that as he did so, he was confirming what was only a rumour. The official line was that the car had simply crashed, but the crater on the road told a different story.

"In my line of work, you find out really quickly that people like to talk, especially when others have fucked up as badly as your people."

Valerian slammed the phone back onto its cradle, but in his heart of hearts he knew the commissioner was right; Astrid Peterman was dead, her body was now burned beyond all recognition. His investigation was over, and with it all the chance of staying at base number one, becoming its commander and achieving his ambition of a seat on the army council and maybe even becoming Corella's leader one day.

The lieutenant placed a cup of strong black coffee on Valerian's desk.

"Permission to speak, sir," he said, standing to attention and looking straight ahead.

The general had learned over the years that this meant the man had a valid point to make and he had also come to respect the lieutenant's insights.

"Proceed."

"Thank you, sir." He looked at the general and nodded slightly; this was his usual preamble, but he would always have to get to the point quickly – anyone else would be bawled out immediately.

"Sir, I believe that it was not the fugitive Peterman who was driving the car."

Valerian's head snapped up, this was a suspicion that he had. "Sit down." He gestured to a chair. This was a rare event. "What is your reasoning?" he said, intrigued.

"It's too obvious, sir. Dashing towards the border by the shortest route in a highly visible stolen staff car? And across open terrain? Though I hate to say it, sir, she is smarter than that, sir."

The general steepled his fingers, tapped them against his chin and thought for a moment. "I think you are right." His anger at the phone conversation evaporated as his mind switched back to how to continue the investigation. "And whoever was driving paid a very heavy price."

"If we can find out who it was, that might give us a clue as to what direction she has been heading. Sir, I suspect that she has no intention of leaving the country for quite some time."

"I agree that she'll hide out and wait. But I've seen pictures of the body, and whoever it was, ended up laying in a pool of burning fuel for over ten minutes. I've never seen a body so badly burned. All we know is that it's female; we're not going to be able to identify her." Again, the general paused, thinking. "Do we have access to police reports?"

"Not at the moment, sir, but I can arrange it."

"Can it be done without the police knowing?"

"Yes, sir, we can intercept data as it is sent to the police central data servers. They will not be able to detect the intrusion; your security clearance can facilitate that."

"Good, do it." Valerian stood up and walked over to study the map. He jabbed a pin into the centre of the Kandalan Base. He turned back, a look of confidence returned. "My investigation will continue until I am told otherwise by Grand Field Marshall Hallenberg. I want to see crime reports from all police regions, but only things that are out of the ordinary. She'll have to change her clothes and she'll have to eat, so thefts of those things could be a pointer; let's see if we can find a pattern."

After the lieutenant had left, Valerian opened a drawer in his desk and took out a notebook, in it he wrote the name of the police commissioner, adding one more name to the list of people who had crossed him over the years. There was already a line through Malaya's name.

"Incompetence was what you reckoned was it, Ellet?" he muttered to himself. "Well, Mr Police Commissioner, there will be a reckoning. There will be a reckoning after I have caught the fugitive, after I have personally tortured her, after I have decided that she has suffered adequately for her crimes and after I have dragged her shattered body before the army council, so she can explain how she was able to get so close to Malaya. After I have executed her and after I have replaced those old fools in the army council and taken my place as the head of the army. Then there will be a reckoning and you will be first, I will second you to the army and put you in the front line in next year's spring offensive. You might even last a day," he said through clenched teeth as he put the book back in the drawer and slammed it shut, anger still seething in him.

Leaving the Phall Region

Astrid had been driving the decrepit machine since early morning, and it was early afternoon when she stopped, changed out of the Phaal smock, donned Krall's civilian clothes and strode purposefully across the footbridge over the river that marked the northern edge of the Phaal region. She was back in the land of normal people, and in spite of the fact she was a wanted person deep inside enemy territory, with all the danger that posed, she was relieved. There was something not right about the Phaal. She was not sure whether it was the total lack of education or the lack of any sort of empathy with their own kind, or the religious oppression with its attendant misuse of power that led to the inevitable abuse of the women.

No, it was something intangible, the place wasn't evil; it was just nothing. Thinking back, she realised that in all the time she had spent passing through the region, she had not heard birds sing, or seen rabbits, deer, or any wildlife. There must have been animals present, but they were invisible. She knew that some Phaal had seen her change her clothes and dump the smock at the side of the road, but she also knew that this obviously odd behaviour wouldn't even register with them and in minutes they would have forgotten all about it.

A walk of eight kilometres along a dirt track would get her to a main road, there she would catch a bus and make the one-hundred-and-ten-kilometre trip north to Balun. The town's full name was Balun Ahn T'hah, with 'Ahn' being an old Correlan word that literally meant 'Town beside the river of' but unfortunately the river T'hah, despite its size, was the most polluted in all of Correla. Thirty years ago, when the central planning committee was established, it was decided that Balun would no longer be a small provincial market town whose principal employment was agriculture and cereal farming. Instead, due to the river, it was to grow rapidly to become a major industrial town and would be the centre for all the small arms requirements of the Correlan military. Chief among the state-run companies was Nagler Small Arms, and all other businesses in the town existed to service the needs of Nagler.

The river's flow carried thousands of cubic metres of water every minute and was considered fast enough to carry the untreated effluent from the town and all the waste from the factories. Whilst this had been true when the town had a mere fifteen thousand people and no industry to speak of, no thought had been given as to what the effect would be when the population rose to its current level, over ten times as many. The dumping in it of thousands of litres of chemical, organic, human and heavy metal pollutants every day was not the concern of the planning committee.

There were no fish in the river downstream from the town for over 10 kilometres, until groundwater runoff, streams and tributaries had sufficiently diluted the flow. Even then the fish were small; mass die-offs in the hottest days of summer were common and the resultant swarms of flies were so dense they would darken the skies. Further downstream the river ran through the main agricultural region, where water abstraction to irrigate the fields was slowly poisoning the ground.

Farming skills handed down through the generations that would have recognised and prevented this had been lost forever as the young people had been conscripted into the armed forces or had been ordered to move to the towns to work in the arms factories. Yields of wheat were poor; in the past an acre would produce an average of fifty bushels a year, a ton and a half, now it was down to a third of that. Most years the grains were small and hard and were only suitable for cattle feed. Correla was gradually losing the ability to feed its people.

****

An hour after she had crossed the bridge, she was sitting by the side of a concrete road. She saw the bus when it was a couple of kilometres away, or at least she saw the conical plume of reddish grey dust that the bus dragged along behind itself. Eventually the battered grey blue vehicle, replete with rust patches, missing windows and swathes of gaffa tape holding body panels in place, ground to a halt beside her. The smell of dry dust and diesel evoking happy memories of childhood summers at her uncle's farm.

She got on, paid the fare and noticed that she was the only passenger. She sat halfway down the bus, trying to look as bored as possible to deter the driver from striking up a conversation. Fortunately for her he was so numbed from the monotony of his job that talking to her was never going to be an option for him.

The spongy suspension squeaked loudly but did a good job of mitigating the effects of the numerous potholes in the road and the drive was relatively smooth.

The road started to snake as it made its way through some rolling hills, the bald tyres crushing the smaller pieces of scree that had tumbled onto the road. The dust that this caused clung to the back of the bus, forming a red-grey cloud that billowed along behind the vehicle. The driver had to occasionally swerve to avoid the larger pieces of rock that would have damaged the suspension. The road had no barriers at the edges and a couple of sharp hairpin bends revealed sheer drops, off to the sides, and the slightest error by the driver here would have fatal consequences, but he was experienced and knew what line to take.

The bus struggled a bit on a steeper incline that took it to the top of the highest mound and when it got there, the view into a small valley was beautiful. Astrid looked wistfully at the vista; the countryside here was verdant and lush. Tall, thin conical trees poked up through a low cover of squat, spherical bushes that softened the hard lines of the rocky hills. A stream below babbled its way downhill. Astrid thought of all the prey animals that this would sustain – deer, rabbits, rodents big and small, and in turn the predators – foxes, wild cats, birds of prey, amongst others, that would keep the population in balance. And all of them oblivious to the chaos and turmoil of the human world.

An iron gate stood at the edge of a field by the road, though there was nothing either side of it. Even so, it was secured with a hefty chain and a rusty padlock, a faded sign said: 'No entry'. She smiled at the absurdity of it.

Walls and buildings made of dry stone, long since abandoned, marked out plots of land that had once been tended by farmers scratching a living from the soil. She imagined workers bringing in baskets of grapes and laying them out on huge mats to dry in the sun, while every day the farmers' wives and daughters would gently rake over the blackening fruit, turning it so it dried evenly. She thought about the farmers bumbling along on ancient tractors, returning from market having sold their produce. There always seemed to be a small child or two perched at the back of the trailer. Goats would be bleating in the background, the bells around their necks clanking softly, all blissfully unaware that one of them would soon be slaughtered to feed a family.

That was how she remembered the countryside from the hazy days of her youth. But now, roofs had caved in and animals had pushed over the walls. Weeds had taken over, with bramble, bindweed and ivy smothering the buildings as nature inexorably reasserted itself. In some places, Kudzu had spread, covering everything in its path with a green blanket. Its woody vines crushing and killing the trees and even pulling them over with the sheer weight of its foliage. Grazing animals could keep these invasive plants at bay, but all the grazing animals had gone when the farms were abandoned.

These rustic scenes would be a gift for a landscape artist, but there were few artists left in Correla; and this sort of art did not fit in with the plans of the central committee. If you could paint a propaganda poster you might get a job, otherwise you were drafted into the armed forces. She sighed to herself, sad at the fact that the simple life in this country had gone forever because of Hallenberg's drive to war.

The bus started the descent, this time it was steeper, and the road had several sharp hairpin bends, the driver crashing the gears to help slow the ancient vehicle. There was still a long way to go, so she ate the last piece of flatbread and drank half of the last bottle of water. Then placed the canvas bag against the window, leant her head on it and dozed.

****

At around eight in the evening the bus finally pulled off the road into a large lay-by on the outskirts of Balun. The driver grunted something incomprehensible which Astrid took to mean 'get off the bus; this is as far as I go'. She could see the buildings of the town and guessed a walk of around two kilometres would get her close to the centre.

The plan now was to hide in plain sight for a few days, and this meant walking freely around Balun, a town of nearly two hundred thousand people. Enough to be anonymous, but more than enough people to see her every day – including police. Fortunately, although the town's main industry was arms production, her research had told her that there didn't seem to be any military personnel stationed there.

Though she would need keep a reasonably low profile; she would do all the normal things, go shopping, buy food etc. She also needed to get some more money to buy new clothes as by now the description of Krall's civilian outfit must have been circulated. As she walked through the outlying streets, she checked out what other women her age were wearing, and it seemed that she could use the limited choice of styles available to work to her advantage. She would become just another generic woman in her early thirties, she would be just visible but at the same time fade into the background. She passed plenty of abandoned houses where she could break in without being seen and stay overnight.

The was a few dhat in Krall's purse, this, along with the money from Malaya's office, was a reasonable amount, but not enough to see her through the time that she needed to be here.

****

Astrid walked up to the counter of 'Mama Drodba's Cafe', ordered a coffee and a slice of cake. A thickset woman in her late fifties with grey hair and lines on her face from a lifetime of graft served her and gestured to a table at the end of the counter. She was clearly the owner.

"Help yourself," she said, smiling warmly and gesturing to a pile of magazines.

There were a few of the day's newspapers for patrons to read. She thanked the woman and flicked through the editions, discarding the local free ad papers before finding a copy of the early evening news which looked like it had national coverage. She went outside and sat at a table beside the front door nonchalantly reading.

She quickly scanned through the whole paper, making sure that she lingered on some articles so as not to draw any attention to herself. There was nothing about her; she had been on the run for almost two days now, but the news was clearly being withheld. She understood why, it would not be in the army's interest for it to be common knowledge that someone as dangerous as her could have escaped and made it so far, particularly with the manner of her escape.

She tensed a little when two men approached her table, she saw them out of the corner of her eye. They were clearly not police or army – too scruffy even by army standards, and the plain clothed police were anything but. They all wore the same outfit, heavy leather jacket, black trousers, black shoes and identical government-issue mirror sunglasses – even late into the evening. She held the newspaper up covering her face and thought about how to get away but became immediately aware that they had sat down opposite her on the same table. A finger appeared at the top of the paper and pulled it down.

"'Ello darlin'," said a swarthy man in his mid-thirties, clean-shaven but scruffy.

He smiled an unconvincing smile through uneven nicotine-stained teeth. He was wearing an old leather jacket, check shirt and faded jeans. A mop of dark, greasy hair flopped down partially covering one of his eyes, he brushed it back in a slow exaggerated gesture with his right hand while keeping his gaze on her. The other man was ratty, taller, even when sitting, and appeared to be much younger. His cheeks were hollow and the dark bags under his eyes, along with the purulent sores around his mouth indicated a bit of serious drug abuse, probably crystal meth. His hair was lank, shoulder length and mousey, he wore dirty jeans and a filthy T-shirt displaying the name of some obscure heavy metal band, along with an offensive profane statement.

"I'm Lenny and he's Ron. You lookin' for a bit of fun?" said the leather jacketed man.

"No," said Astrid firmly and put the paper up.

Again, Lenny pulled it down, this time he leaned forward.

"I've got some gear, it's pure, classy stuff. And I've got clean needles," he half whispered, but clearly loud enough for others to hear. "I can let you have a sample for free; well, when I say free, you'll obviously have to do something for it," he said as he stared at her breasts.

Ron laughed. "A pretty girl like her, she probably don't have to pay for nothing."

"Go away," said Astrid firmly.

Ron reached over to touch her; she slapped his hand away which took him by surprise. She could have easily grabbed his hand and broken his fingers if she wanted to. She briefly considered breaking his arm; it would be easy – lean forward at the last moment so that his hand slipped under her armpit, grab his wrist with her left hand and twist it so his palm faced upwards, while slipping her right arm under his, then just stand up. His weight would do the rest, the slightly thinner ulna would probably go first and if she was lucky the radius as well, but this was far too public. She needed someone else to intervene.

"Keep your fuckin' hair on," he snarled. "It's only a bit of fun."

"I said go away," she raised her voice, a couple inside the café looked up and seemed a bit concerned.

"No," said Lenny defiantly. "I think I'm going to sit right here, I can sit where I like, it's a free country." He leant back in the chair unaware of how inaccurate and stupid his last comment was. "In fact, I think I'll have a coffee." He stood up. "Oi, how's about a bit of fuckin' service," he shouted.

169

Ron slapped the tabletop a few times. "I want a fuckin' coffee an' all," he said looking around at the other customers. "What are you all fuckin' looking at?" he snarled.

The couple in the café got up and left.

Mama Drodba appeared in the doorway. "I ain't serving you two. Now clear off."

"Make us," sneered Lenny.

"Arni," she shouted over her shoulder.

"Arni Drodba?" said Ron. "That little runt, is he around? I ain't seen him since school." He turned to Lenny and spoke loudly for effect. "Weedy streak of piss he was. He was a pushover, used to get shit kicked out of him all the time." He looked the old lady straight in the face and sneered. "I heard he fucked off and joined the army when your old man took off with that other woman." But his face changed when Arni Drodba appeared.

Arni was a giant, with a shaved head, cauliflower ears, broken nose and thick eyebrows from too many rounds in a boxing ring. The trapezius muscles in his shoulders just seemed to blend into his head level with his ears. He was wearing a blood-splattered butcher's apron and a white vest that was stretched to breaking point across his huge chest, revealing an abundance of highly detailed tattoos that spread from his enormous biceps across his shoulders and down onto his pecs.

But on both of his forearms there were crude barrack room tattoos, the kind done by a fellow soldier with a sewing needle and ink; it was an incredibly painful procedure. Having just one small tattoo would take great courage; Arni's barrack room tattoos covered both his forearms from elbow to wrist.

"You got a problem, Mum?" he growled.

Ron sat back and gave Arni a contemptuous look. "Well, I see you get your looks from your mother," he jeered.

Astrid was worried, these two were far too arrogant, fearless even. To be so brazen suggested to her that they must have some sort of protection.

"These two are just leaving," she said.

"No, we ain't, we're staying right here," said Lenny.

Arni raised his hand, he was holding a half-metre long blood-covered butcher's knife. He took a step towards the two.

"You're leaving," he said, his voice deep and rumbling, his expression dark and menacing.

The two stood up and backed up a bit clearly weighing up their options.

Lenny turned to Ron. "Come on, let's go somewhere else, we're going to get nothing here."

"Yeah, this place is a fucking shit hole anyway," said Ron, kicking over a chair.

Arni glowered and took another step forward raising the knife menacingly, snorting like a bull. The two backed away then turned and started walking away towards the town centre, they had gone a few metres when Lenny turned around.

"You watch your back, Arni Drodba. I'm gonna have you. You ain't the only one with a knife." He pointed at Astrid. "And you can have that stuck up little bitch."

With that he turned back and the two of them carried on walking, although the pace was a little bit quicker than before. Astrid pretended to be frightened.

Arni took a step forward, Mama Drodba put her hand on Arni's chest to stop him going after them.

"Leave it, Arni," she said wearily. "I'm sorry about that love," she said to Astrid as she picked up the chair. "Those two have always been trouble, they're bad for business. That Ron, he's always been obnoxious, but Lenny, stay away from him, he's a nasty piece of work. Drug dealing scum that's what they are, everyone knows it."

She paused and thought about her words. "They take pretty girls like you and ruin them," she said bitterly.

"Why haven't the police dealt with them?" asked Astrid, though it was obvious why.

"Because they're informers," said the old lady resentfully. "Everyone knows that as well. They get pulled in, but are always released, then some other poor sod gets nicked." She shook her head in sad disbelief. "They think they're untouchable, that's why they're so cocky."

"Informing curtadas," said Arni, using the local slang for a vagina, still a harsh taboo word even in a working-class town like Balun.

"Language, Arni," snapped Mama Drodba. "You know I don't like it when you use that word, now go out back and finish preparing the meat for tomorrow."

"Sorry, Mum," he said as he turned and went back to the rear of the café. "But they're still informing curtadas," he said to himself just loud enough for Astrid to hear.

171

This was bad, the two men had enough time to get a good look at her; the café front was well lit, and they would easily be able to pick her out again. And if they were that cosy with the local police, it could be dangerous. They would have to be dealt with and this was a complication that she didn't need and didn't want. As loathsome as these two were, they were civilians, and what she would have to do would be a crime. But she had to deal with them and would have to wrestle with her conscious later.

She got up, grabbed her bag, thanked the old woman then set off in the direction that the men had taken. It didn't take her long to spot them, they were chatting to a girl in another café who seemed a lot more responsive. Astrid knew that some women were attracted to roguish men like them, it's a hormonal response that is the opposite of adrenaline, where sensing danger would draw women to the men rather than driving them away; she knew it, but she didn't understand it.

After a few minutes, all three got up and left. Astrid hung back in the shadows and tailed them. It was an easy tail, the girl knew nothing of her and the idea that Astrid would follow them could never occur to the men, so none of them looked back. They went down a long side road into a less than salubrious residential area. Incongruously, there was good street lighting that looked new. The straight road left nowhere to hide, so Astrid had to wait at the end of the road and watch to see where they went.

Towards the end of the road all three went up to a house that had its windows boarded up and went in. Astrid ran quickly and stealthily to the house, it was a large four floor detached property that had clearly once been the home of a well-to-do family when this was an area where wealthy grain merchants with delusions of grandeur would vie for social status with ostentatious additions to their already large houses and would have employed designers to create ever more ornate gardens.

That was a hundred years ago. It seemed that all the buildings in the road had been converted into apartments many decades later, then fallen into disrepair when the fortunes of the neighbourhood had declined. She listened hard for any sounds from the building; she heard the distant chat of the girl and the two men from somewhere above, and except for that, there were no other sounds. A dim light appeared through the gaps in a boarded-up window on the third floor. It had to be them.

She moved lightly on her feet as she entered the building, being careful to step where she saw the heads of nails in the floorboard to reduce the risk of squeaking that would give her away. She left her bag by the door and staying close to the wall, made her way up the stairs to the third floor. As she suspected, there were no other occupants in the property, and this looked like it was a regular haunt for the two men. They had chosen the third floor so that no one could look in, and the three flights of stairs meant that they would get a warning and have time to get out if someone approached. Not this time though, but she had no weapons, and there was nothing she could take. Everything would make a noise and give her away. This would have to be hand-to-hand.

She reached the landing on the third floor; a door was open, and a trapeze of dim light fell across the floor in front of her. She heard a nervous voice, it was Ron.

"She's breathing real slow Lenny, you've given her too much, I think you've OD'd her, it's just like the others."

Astrid stood out of sight beside the doorway and slowed her breathing to calm herself.

"Nah, it's okay, she'll be all right," said Lenny, even more nervously as he pulled the last of the clothes off the motionless girl.

"She's stopped breathing," said Ron unable to hide the alarm in his voice. "What have you done Lenny? I said you were giving her too much."

"You've killed her," said Astrid as she stepped into the room.

The girl was laying naked on a mattress on the floor with both men kneeling down looking over her. A rubber tube tourniquet around her upper left arm was slack and a syringe was still in the median cubital vein in the crook of her elbow. Beside her there was all the paraphernalia for the use of intravenous heroin – foil wraps, a candle, a spoon, another syringe and a pack of new needles. Her head had rolled to one side, she was facing Astrid, her pupils fully dilated and her eyes wide open in a ghastly death stare.

"Well, what have we got here?" said Lenny as he jumped to his feet, hoping that bravado would cover his shock at being discovered. "The stuck-up bitch wants a bit of fun after all."

"It won't be fun for you," she said coldly.

"She's seen too much Lenny, you'll have to do her as well," said Ron, standing up, panicking as his arrogance dissolved. He backed up to the far wall and made fists with his hands as people do when they don't know what else to do.

"Oh yeah, I'll do her all right, but first I'm going to have some fun," said Lenny, ignoring Ron and focusing on Astrid as he pulled a large single sided hunting knife from its sheath on his belt. He sneered at Astrid. "I'm going to have fun slicing you up a bit before fucking you and cutting you into little pieces."

He liked women to be afraid of him, but this woman clearly wasn't. He held the knife between his thumb and forefinger at its hilt and waved it up and down so the blade flopped around. "This is razor sharp, it'll hurt like fuck when I cut you. Are you scared little girl huh? Is big bad Lenny scaring you, huh, are you frightened, huh?"

"You're holding it all wrong," she said calmly as she moved slowly towards him. Without realising it, he took a small step backwards.

"Do fuckin' what?" he said, irritated that she was not scared of him and puzzled by her comment.

"I said, you're holding it wrong, I will take it from you, and I will kill you with it."

Lenny half laughed and glanced back over his shoulder at Ron. "Did you hear that Ron, she reckons she's gonna kill me. She don't know me, does she?"

This was the moment Astrid was waiting for; the movement she knew he would make. He would take his eyes off her for a split second and she would make her move. As he turned to look back at Ron, she stepped quickly forward, snatched the knife from his hand and slammed it diagonally into the left side of his chest between the third and fourth ribs. Lenny let out a startled grunt as she grabbed him and pulled him to her, forcing the blade in further. She twisted the handle in a circle, levering the blade against his ribs, lacerating the heart before wrenching the knife out sideways.

She pushed him to one side where he slumped to the floor and died. It had all happened so fast that Ron in his panicked state hadn't really taken in what he had just seen. All he knew was that his friend had been attacked and he acted on instinct. His instinct was to fight; if his instinct had been to run, he might just have survived.

He stepped forward and threw a punch aimed at her face, but she had already flipped the knife around in her hand, so the tip was pointing towards her elbow and the safe edge was against the skin of her forearm. She put her arm up to block the punch and instead of hitting her, he punched the blade, slitting his fist open between the index and middle finger. He yelped in pain and in a reflex reaction, pulled his hand away and down towards his abdomen, holding the cut together with his other hand trying to stem the flow of blood. He looked up at Astrid and froze, only then did he actually see Lenny's knife in her hand.

She quickly threw a punch at his head, but she was aiming just below the chin and at the last moment flicked her wrist to push the blade out. She struck a few centimetres below Ron's left ear, the force of her thrust carrying the blade through the jugular vein, carotid artery and trachea. Blood immediately foamed in his mouth; he clutched his throat as he dropped to his knees. As he fell, she kicked him in the chest to make him fall away from her, so she would not get covered in the blood that was now erupting from his neck. He landed on his back and died without making another sound.

There was a fair bit of blood on the clothes she was wearing; this could be washed out but would take too long to dry. There was nothing she could do for the girl, but she could use her clothes. The dead girl was similar height and body size so the fit should be okay. She looked through the girl's clutch bag, there was the usual detritus; key ring with car, house and random other keys, along with a deformed piece of plastic that had once been a caricature of a cat. There was a purse with a few dhat in it, a pack of tissues, a couple of tampons which she felt would soon be needed, some out of date pain killer tablets, some make-up, a tube of mosquito repellent and a small torch.

But most important was an ID card, the address showed she was from out of town. The ID was old and due for renewal within a year; she could use this, but the picture would not fool anyone. The laminate had started to come apart and she would be able to separate the two halves easily; she still had Krall's military ID and if she could use the picture from that, she could make a passable forgery. It would not stand up to anything other than cursory inspection, but these would be bridges that she would have to cross when she came to them.

Across the hall there was a bathroom that would have once been the height of elegance. She checked the washbasin, there was no hot water, but the cold water still ran and was clean enough for her to wash with. She blew dust off the mirror and checked herself; there was no blood on her face, but her hands were covered. She rinsed them for a few minutes, rubbing her hands repeatedly to get the last of the blood off and was struck, as she always was, by how long it took to get rid of the last traces. She looked around for a towel, but the only one in the room was filthy, so she flicked the water from her hands and they dried quickly in the warm evening air.

She cleaned Lenny's knife and used it to separate the two halves of the ID card, they came apart cleanly without tearing. She was able to pick out the picture, which came out in one piece. Then, using just the tip of the blade, she cut out Krall's picture from her ID card and placed it into the dead girl's. She heated up the knife blade using the candle, then, using some of the foil to protect the surface of the card, pressed the flat of the blade down onto the ID card, the heat reactivating the glue and sealing the picture in. The result was okay, just okay, but better than nothing.

She dropped Krall's ID card and the girl's picture down through a gap in the floorboards, then put on the girl's clothes. The fit was acceptable, but the shoes were a little tight and she would probably get blisters, so she took a couple of plasters and put them on her heels. She wiped her fingerprints off the knife, then placed it in Lenny's hand, curling his still warm fingers around the handle. She packed Krall's clothes into the canvas bag, kicked over some of the rudimentary furniture so as to make it look as if a struggle had taken place, then slipped out of the building and headed towards the town centre. It was time to get some money.

Astrid was now dressed in what appeared to be the de rigueur night fashion for a woman in Balun, the clothes' style was the same the only difference was the colour combinations. She was wearing red shoes with heels a little higher than any she had worn before, black three-quarter leggings and red bolero top. The ensemble was finished off with a pair of large, round, blue tinted glasses that had no corrective effect and were for show only.

This had quickly become known as 'whore chic' and had been made popular by the popular singer Shana, a girl from the town who had shot to national fame after she claimed in a newspaper interview that she had been a prostitute and that it 'had been fun'. These were the clothes that she had worn for the interview and the style had immediately been picked up by the clothing stores once the pictures were published. Most of the girls who wore this particular uniform were not prostitutes and only wanted the look. The girls who worked as prostitutes probably would not be able to afford the clothes anyway.

There were more than enough female sex workers in Balun, and the reason for this was quite simple, all men between the ages of sixteen and forty-seven were conscripted into the armed forces and most of these men had families. The social welfare system in Correla was poor and inefficient, with meagre handouts for those who qualified there was only just enough to live on. So when the men died in battle or were so injured that they could not work, there was not enough money to feed a family. The wives and mothers would reluctantly turn to prostitution; they convinced themselves that as it had never been illegal, they assumed that it would only be a bit of sex and they could hang on to their dignity. But they were wrong, so very, very wrong.

For the most part, Correlan women are subservient, and the men can have all the sex they want with their wives or girlfriends; the men would go to prostitutes for the kind of sex that their partners refused to do. And in dreary towns like this, that usually meant violent, sadistic sex. Deaths were common, but the police had no interest in investigating these, the view was taken that death for these girls was an occupational hazard.

Sometimes if a girl had more than one client at a time, there would be fights, and if any of the men died, this too was not investigated. In both cases, they would just be recorded as accidents. The police commissioner was even on record as saying that 'he would rather investigate the death of a dog hit by a car than the death of a whore, because the dog was an innocent victim, but the whore had chosen the lifestyle'.

Once a woman had made the decision to prostitute herself, any notion of retaining her dignity quickly evaporated as she slowly sank deeper into the client's desire for perversion. Drinking would start very quickly, to numb the aches of previous encounters and dull the pain of the coming day. The preferred drink was a local spirit distilled from a brew made from hazelnuts, it was cheap, strong and readily available. Some manufacturers would flavour the spirit by dropping in a couple of leaves of a particular bush. A fungus that grew naturally on the leaves would give the drink a slightly hallucinogenic and anaesthetic quality.

When the alcohol stopped working, the slide into drug abuse was inevitable. At first these were cheap cannabis derivatives, but as the emotional addictions took hold, the price went up along with the strength, crystal meth was often next, followed swiftly by heroin. And then she had another mouth to feed, her children and now her drug habit.

But with so many girls available the only way to get more money was to be willing to accept more depravity, to be willing to suffer more for longer, and as the last vestige of self-esteem drained away, the need for the drugs grew inexorably. Soon she will have forgotten about her children, her only preoccupation would be getting through the next day, putting up with another bruise on her face or broken rib, just to get enough money to chase the dragon one more time.

Astrid looked at the other girls; all seemed to be wearing slightly different versions of the 'whore chic', and she wondered that if they really knew the truth, would they still wear the costume. And it was debateable whether Shana had actually ever been a sex worker; Astrid wondered if Shana knew, or even cared, how many women she had condemned to a short life of wretchedness. But she knew that she would have to be careful, because by being dressed the way she was, she could attract unwanted attention, but it was a risk she was prepared to take.

****

A little way out of the main built-up area she saw an opportunity to stash Krall's clothes and possibly return there for the night. The obviously abandoned single story building sat back from the road, with a concrete path leading from the gate to a gravelled apron that circled the building. The ground to the front was knee deep in dry weeds but showed no signs of having been walked through.

Certain that she was not being observed, she eased through the gate and stepped only on the concrete slabs so as to not leave a track through the foliage. She did a careful circuit of the building, listening for activity from inside. There was none. The back door was not fully closed and using the torch, she could see that there were no footprints in the dust on the floor inside. She pushed gently on the door, wincing as the hinges creaked, and let herself into the building; it was dry inside and she noted a couch that was reasonably clean and that there were a few other items of furniture.

The building seemed to have been vacated fairly recently and decay had not yet set in. From her knowledge of Correlan society she knew that abandoned buildings were just left to slowly rot, and squatting was unheard of, so she should be safe enough here.

She stashed the clothes behind the couch and slipped back out onto the road and headed into town. After about forty minutes she was well into the built-up area. It was getting late and had the bustling activity of every town this size at this time of night. People around her were going about their business, more

178

focussed on getting to where they were going, than taking any notice of her, which was perfect. Couples walked arm in arm, groups of people chatted loudly outside restaurants.

Groups of young men stood outside bars, beers in hand, talking loudly and laughing. One man saw her and wolf-whistled, she turned and blew him a kiss but kept on walking. The wolf-whistle was good-natured and hers was the kind of reaction that would be expected; the men laughed even louder as they teased their friend. Music, bright lights and the smell of street food could have been an easy distraction, but she had to stay alert, but not make it look like she was staying alert.

As she walked through the town, she suddenly became aware of a car slowly following her, she glanced across the street at the reflection in a shop window. As she feared, it was a police car. Usually there would be an older officer and a rookie straight out of what passed for a police training college. The younger man would do all the police work with the older man showing the tricks of the trade and giving backup when needed.

They would almost certainly stop and ask for her papers, but the ID she had made was not going to be good enough to fool even the thickest of Correlan policemen. A plan formed quickly in her mind, it was a big gamble, but she had no other options; she couldn't kill her way out of this one.

She had heard of a blackmail scam aimed at the police in industrial towns like Balun, she hoped the older man knew of it too. She heard the car stop behind her and a man get out, slamming the door. She heard the distinctive clack and click of a police standard issue sidearm being cocked and its safety catch released.

A youngish, slightly hesitant, male voice came from a couple of metres behind her. "Identification papers – now!"

It was a voice that tried but failed to sound authoritative; she guessed he must have been around twenty or twenty-one. Approaching from behind was the usual ploy, it was designed to intimidate. She had two choices, she could turn, or she could run, and if she ran, she would make an easy target and would get hit in the back by a couple of heavy calibre bullets before she'd taken five paces from the weapon that was now trained on her.

For all their faults, the Correlan police were all excellent shots, as time on the shooting range comprised the bulk of their training; running was not an option. He could check her papers, or he could shoot her, either way this would be good training for the rookie officer.

She steadied her nerves, turned around, smiled, made the big innocent eyes that men seemed to like, raised her voice a few semitones and affected an immature tone and said, "My name is Zena and I don't have no papers, but…"

She unzipped the bolero top and held it open exposing her breasts, making sure that the older man could see what she was doing. She glanced over her shoulder as if she was acknowledging someone. "Most guys can recognise me by these, now if you have a good feel, you'll be able to identify me in the dark."

"Must be my lucky day," said the young officer, smirking as he flicked on the safety, holstered his gun and rubbed his hands together in anticipation.

"No, it ain't," growled the older man in the car. "Get in, and you, you fuckin' slag," he jabbed his finger at Astrid. "You can just fuck off out of here and don't ever let me see you again."

He knew that there would be someone in the distance with a long lens taking pictures, making sure that they got shots of the officers fondling the girl, shots of their faces and shots of their name badges, police numbers and the car registration. A couple of days later an envelope would land on their desks with big prints of all the pictures and a note just saying: 'Leave my girls alone'.

There was never a demand for money, but it was still a crime – technically it was blackmail, but so trivial it would not be worth pursuing, particularly as they would still have to explain why they were groping a woman. This is what he knew, because he had been caught by it when he was young. But he was wrong; this time it had been a bluff and it had worked.

Astrid zipped up her top, pouted petulantly at the older man, then turned and walked confidently on into the town. But she was not happy, this had been a very big gamble and she had got lucky, and luck has a habit of running out. She cleared her thoughts and focussed on the next pressing task; to get the money she needed, and now she knew just where to get it.

Ahead of her was a nightclub with a gaudy neon sign above the door that said 'The G Spot'. The pink glowing tubes were shaped like a woman's body with the outline of a cocktail glass where the crotch would be.

"Perfect," she said to herself, already aware of the sort of clientele that would inhabit the club. Pickings would be easy there.

Night Club in Balun

"Well, you can't come in then can you," sneered the girl in the ticket booth of 'The G Spot' nightclub.

Astrid pouted. "But it's fifteen dhat to get in, and I've only got fifteen, so I won't be able to by any drinks," she whined, like a spoiled girl.

"Well, oh fucking dear," said the girl without looking up from her magazine.

"Can't you do me a favour, huh?"

"No, now piss off, you're annoying me."

An enormous blob of a doorman noticed a commotion brewing and waddled over.

"What's up?" he wheezed as he took a tissue from his pocket and wiped away beads of sweat that had formed on his forehead from this tiny bit of exertion. Astrid wondered just how effective he could be at his job; probably not very.

"She ain't got enough money, so she can't come in," again, the girl didn't look up from her read. Astrid turned to the man and looked up at him with helpless little girl eyes. She stepped towards him, put her hand between his legs and stroked his penis, which immediately started to stiffen.

"If you do me a favour and let me in, I'll do you a favour later, because..." She paused and looked him up and down. "...I like big men." She held his erection and stood on tiptoe to whisper slowly in his ear. "And you feel like a really, really big man to me." She looked him straight in the eye, opened her mouth and poked her tongue into her cheek a few times, suggesting fellatio.

An inane grin broke onto his face; it was unlikely that any woman had ever spoken to him like that before. He was big, he was fat and he was stupid, and naïve enough to think that Astrid meant it. She did not.

"Go on," he said, pushing the door open.

"Later then," said Astrid. She smiled and ran her tongue around her lips then blew a kiss to him as she entered the club. The doorman stared at her backside as she walked through the door, the girl behind the grille glared at him, snorted contemptuously and went back to her trashy gossip mag.

The nightclub was perfect, not because it was a place where she would normally want to spend any time, but because it was heaving with people and it was dark, it was tacky but perfect for her. The first thing that hit her when she walked in was the heat and humidity; hot, damp, smelly air that was a mixture of smoke, stale beer, cheap perfume and sweat. Patrons at the bar yelled their orders to the overworked bar staff, who strained to hear above the din from the sound system.

On the crowded dance floor groups of men and women gyrated around loosely in time with the deafening music; one hundred and twenty beats per minute of generic dance tunes. The speakers crackled with every beat. The DJ, who bobbed around in his booth like a demented jack-in-the-box, holding his headphones tight to his ears, was pushing the system far too hard as all DJs do, and the amplifiers were distorting as they strained under the workload. It sounded like some of the speakers had already failed, so to maintain the volume, the system had to be pushed even harder. Sooner or later the place would suddenly go very quiet; Astrid hoped it wouldn't be tonight.

Astrid glanced at the floor, there were no tell-tale squares of silver foil, no discarded plastic bags, no torn strips of cardboard, or any of the other requisite trappings of narcotics. There were no drugs here, this meant that somewhere else, probably a building nearby, drug deals were done, and this place was kept clean to not draw any attention from the police. She looked around – carefully – there didn't seem to be any cameras either. But what there was were several large, modern flat screen TVs bolted to the walls playing porn movies on loops. The women in the club either didn't notice or didn't care or didn't mind.

In a far corner, some girls were on their knees eagerly giving blowjobs to a group of men, switching back and forwards between them. The men were happy, and the women seemed more than willing. The girls appeared to be in some sort of competition to see who could please the men the most; smiling at each other and laughing as they swapped partners, hitting high fives as they did so. Satisfied men sat with their flaccid penises on display, others sat in anticipation with erections in their hands, while a few couples stood by watching while they fondled each other.

Getting drunk and having casual sex night after night was the only escape from the mind destroying drudgery of these people's lives. Once the central planning committee had assigned someone a job, then that was it. If that job was at the Nagler small arms factory in Balun, you were there for the rest of your life. You couldn't leave.

Most of the dancers looked completely drunk, lost in their own little worlds, and most of them seemed oblivious to each other. Off to one side, a group of three obviously very drunk girls were tottering around on ridiculously high heels, each with a drink in one hand and a cigarette in the other, whooping and yelling at the tops of their voices. Their short dresses and low-cut tops left nothing to the imagination, particularly the fact that they had no underwear on at all. With consummate bad timing one of the girls put her hand in the air and yelled. "I've got to have a piss," just at the only point in the evening where the music stopped.

All three burst out laughing; the unembarrassed girl tottered off towards the toilets, staggered sideways then fell over, ending up sitting against the wall. Her friends seemed to think that this was the funniest thing that had ever happened and were pointing at her and crying with laughter. The girl also burst out laughing, then vomited all over herself. This made the other girls laugh even more, to the point that they were unaware that they were actually urinating.

Avoiding this, Astrid made her way around the edge of the dance floor towards a cigarette machine, dodging the flailing arms, most of which seemed to be holding a glass of beer, also dodging the broken glass on the floor. She fed a few coins into the machine and pulled a knob to release a packet of Cavana Mild filtered, the brand she had noticed that most of the women were smoking. She didn't need the cigarettes – she didn't smoke but needed a convincing excuse in case anyone was watching.

Now she had a diagonal line across the floor to the bar. She pushed her way through the dancers, expertly picking their pockets as she went, using the techniques that the Special Forces commandos had taught her; bumping into guys, pulling their wallets, then saying sorry so they look into your eyes as you take the money and put the wallet back. Pretending to trip over a handbag, then taking money out as you smile and say sorry to the owner and hand it back. Don't take too much, she remembered, twenty or thirty dhat at a time and don't dip everyone.

She bought a beer that she had no intention of drinking, it was just for show, and then made her way up the edge of the dancers to the far corner where it was relatively quiet to plan her next move. She had about 500 dhat, just over a week's wages, a quick calculation flashed through her mind, was any more worth the risk?

She took a cigarette from the packet, put it in her mouth and casually lit it in a way that she had practised so that she didn't have to inhale any smoke and then stood for a few moments casually observing the crowd with the nonchalant mannerisms of a smoker; bringing the cigarette up to her mouth and appearing to take a drag, but not actually doing so. Every now and then she took a drag, so she could be seen blowing out smoke, she didn't inhale, she knew that if she did, she would have uncontrollable coughing that would give the game away. She also had to suppress her gag reflex as the disgusting smoke filled her mouth. Occasionally, she knocked off some ash by flicking the filter tip with her thumbnail, ignoring the ashtray and flicking the ash straight onto the floor as everybody did.

Every now and then she picked up her glass and pretended to take a drink, but the last thing she needed was to consume any alcohol; she was satisfied that she was blending in.

"You're very good," said a man's voice behind her. "I've been watching you; you see it takes one to know one."

Astrid was expecting a few crappy chat-up lines throughout the evening, but this was no chat up line. She hid the fear inside her and turned around. A gaunt man stood looking her straight in the eye.

"What?" she shouted, sneering and gesturing to the speakers, then pointing to her ears.

"You heard, you've been dipping." He smiled, recognising the play dumb routine. "The name's Asher. Don't worry, I'm not the law."

She sneered suspiciously at him.

"You're good, I'll give you that, but I'm better, work for me and you'll get double, but you'd have to pay me a percentage."

He looked hard at her for a few seconds and frowned. "Don't I know you?" he asked rhetorically. As he studied her face, she put on a look of indifference and turned her head. "I know all the girls in this town, but that's not where I know you from."

"Only just got in town," said Astrid with the common accent of the region, pronouncing 'town' as 'tan', bringing herself down to his level. "Let's go outside and talk about money, I can't hear a fuckin' fing in here," she said coarsely, dropping the cigarette on the floor and stamping it out.

With a sideways nod of his head, he gestured towards the back of the room. "This way then."

As he led her towards a back door, she noticed that he walked with a heavy limp on his left side and that his left arm seemed stiff. They emerged into an alleyway that led down to a back road. The light above the door was bright and illuminated a couple of smelly garbage dumpsters and about a third of the alley. High brick walls on either side tapered out along its length. A couple of moths fluttered around the light creating disproportionally large shadows and giving the impression of movement that extended into the darkness.

She noticed that there was a camera but could also see the cable to it was broken and even if it did work there was too much dirt on the lens for it to be of any use, and to be this neglected, it may well have been a dummy anyway. Towards the end of the path, she could see old, half-finished building work, just foundations really, long abandoned, then a small step up to the path that ran along a road. Brick rubble lay randomly along the path, if she ran this would be a problem as she could easily trip once she got into the darkness. Another plan was needed.

"Okay, what's the deal," she said.

"I tell you where to go for the best pickings. You'll make a thousand a night, you give me three hundred." He paused and looked hard at her. "You know. I ain't seen you in person, but I have seen your picture before." He scratched his chin deep in thought. "No, it can't be," he said quietly to himself. "Anyway, any less than three hundred a night and I'll slit your throat," he said half laughing. Then tried to sound menacing. "You wouldn't be the first little girl I've cut up."

"If you can catch me...peg leg," she said curtly, then pointed to his leg. "Where did you get that limp? And your arm looks like it's fucked. Good job it's your left arm."

"What do you mean by that?" he growled.

"It that means you can carry on being a wanker, don't it?" she sneered back.

He scowled at her for a moment then laughed, she knew how to play the game, he would try to intimidate her; she would show a whole load of attitude back. "This is going to work out nicely," he said.

"Maybe," she said with half a smile, letting him know she fully understood why he was trying to bully her – that it was an act, and that her bravado was also an act. "So, you didn't answer my question, where did you get the limp?"

"Injured out of the army two years ago. I was in the third infantry, guy next to me stepped on a land mine, and it blew him to pieces. I was hit by his rifle, nearly took my leg off. It smashed the bones and took some of the muscle off my arm. I'm lucky to be alive." Suddenly his expression changed to one of shock. "It is you, we were shown a picture, we all had to memorise your face and…"

She stepped forward and slammed her fist into his stomach a few centimetres below his solar plexus, putting all her weight behind the blow. As he doubled over, she slipped her right arm under his head and closed it around his throat, locking it in place with her left arm, closing off the blood vessels in his neck. In a futile move, he grabbed her around her waist and pushed forward hoping to make her fall back or loosen her grip. She had anticipated this and took a deep step backwards, making him stumble and loose his footing, and as she held his head, his falling body weight crushed his thorax. She could feel him quickly losing his strength; with the blood supply to his brain cut off and his diaphragm in spasm he would be unconscious in seconds and dead very soon afterwards. A few moments later she let his lifeless body fall to the ground.

After rolling him into a shadowy area behind the bins, she took his wallet, removed all the money and dropped the wallet beside him so that it would look like a mugging gone wrong. She left him and picked her way carefully along the path and was nearly at the road when the lumbering figure of the doorman appeared at the end of the alley.

"Oh, it's you," he wheezed. "The door alarm went off, I thought someone might be trying to get in without paying."

"Oh, hi honey, I was just coming to get you, follow me," she said sweetly, quickly glancing up and down the road, there was no one in sight except the doorman.

"You got something special planned for me then?"

"Oh yeah, something really special, but we've got to go this way."

She turned and pointed down the alley knowing that he would follow her, as he was dumb enough to do whatever she said, particularly as he thought he was going to get some oral sex. She knew that most men do what they are told in that situation.

As the man stepped down from the pavement she turned and kicked his knee hard. With his heel jammed against the kerb, his leg broke easily. He cried out and fell forward. Off balance, he slumped down and to the right with both hands on his broken leg. At the edge of the concrete there was part of the unfinished building work and a rusty piece of reinforcing steel bar stood up out of a concrete block by several centimetres. As he fell, Astrid grabbed his head and forced it down onto the block. The reinforcing rod punched through his skull just behind his right ear. He died almost immediately. She didn't take any money this time, she wanted this to look like an accident, but quickly raided his pockets and found nothing that could be useful. It was time to go, find something to eat, then back to get some sleep in the building she found earlier.

A little way further down the road, some drunken revellers were leaving another club and seemed to be heading back the way Astrid had come into the town. She crossed over and tagged along behind them, just far enough behind so they would not take any notice of her, but close enough for a casual observer to think she was part of the group. She mimicked the rolling inebriated gait of the girls in the group to enhance the illusion, occasionally staggering to one side and holding on to a wall in order to make it appear that she was trying to regain her balance.

A couple of the men in the group were discussing loudly whether or not to go to the red-light district and were gesturing off to the left. The women were discussing equally loudly about the fact that the men didn't need to as they had them for a good time if they wanted. Eventually the men got their way; the girls agreed on a visit and they all wheeled around the next left-hand junction. Astrid stopped and rubbed her heels as if checking for blisters, this gave her a chance to surreptitiously look around to see if she was being watched, she was not. People leaving the clubs all seemed to be going the other way and no one was looking towards her. Ignoring the junction, she carried on walking straight towards the outskirts of the town; she took a right, then a left and was now on the road that she had come into town on, and towards the house where she had dumped Krall's clothes.

Walking quickly, but casually, she made her way out of the town away from the commercial area and into a part of the town that was undeveloped with open plots of land fenced off with chain link, most of which had fallen, or had been pushed over. As in the alleyway, some of the plots were just slabs of concrete foundations for buildings that had been started and abandoned for some reason. The advantage for her was that this gave her a good view ahead for some distance and gave her early warning of three youths up ahead. The young men had obviously spotted her, and one stepped into the middle of the path while the other two leant back against a fence. She quickly weighed her options; turning around was not one of them and crossing the road would only invite trouble. As she drew closer, she guessed that they were in their mid-teens, all macho and spotty with nowhere near enough experience with women.

"Oi, oi, what have we got here?" said the one in the path as she approached. "Show us your tits love."

Astrid kept walking towards him, which seemed to unsettle him a bit. "Do you want to come back to our place?" he said weakly.

She said nothing and walked straight past him while he stepped aside without thinking. Embarrassed and completely at a loss of what to do next, eventually he shouted. "Well, fuck you then," more to impress his mates than anything else. Knowing that in order to act like a local, some sort of response was needed; without looking back at him, she stuck her middle finger up.

"Don't that mean she wants it," said the youth, looking at his mates for support. "Maybe we should follow her."

"Nah, she's telling us to fuck off," said one of the other boys, amused at his friend's embarrassment.

Killing these three fools was never an option and she carried on walking as the young man gave vent to his bruised pride.

"I wouldn't waste my jizz on you anyway, you fucking slag," he shouted, but his voice was not yet fully broken and jumped an octave. His two mates sniggered at his humiliation as they skulked away, leaving him standing on his own. Any pretence at a threat in his voice had vanished and been replaced with this pathetic display of juvenile bluster. She listened hard for their footsteps following her, but as she expected, there were none.

A street food vendor was starting to pack up for the night when Astrid approached. Wary of the food hygiene standards, and generally distrusting of the street food, none the less she needed something to eat and drink. She asked for two bottles of water then pointed to an overcooked beef burger and asked for it to be put in a fresh bun, but as she did not know how it had been washed, refused the salad.

She also got a large cup of potato fries that would be completely safe. She paid and carried on her way. The beef was probably the safest bet and overcooked was better than undercooked and the fresh bun shouldn't have any mould. Even so, she took the first bite with a bit of trepidation. The seals on the water bottles were good and that made her eat the rest of the meal with a little more confidence.

As she continued out of the town's commercial area towards the more residential part, she passed a few shops, the sort that have a limited variety of goods and only exist to service local needs. One sold clothes, another food and there was one that seemed to do a bit of everything. She noticed a 'Help Wanted' card in the window. This would be her first call in the morning.

It was late by the time she reached the residential area and she quickly found the vacant house set back from the road where she had hidden the clothes. The housing was sparse with large gaps filled with bushes and trees between the various dwellings. Some were occupied, but the open space linking them was adequate for the level of privacy that she needed. This would do for tonight, but no longer.

Certain that she had not been seen, she again checked around the outside of the building, all windows were shut and showed no sign of having been opened for some time. She made her way around to the back door and could see by the light of the torch that the twigs she had placed in the doorjamb a few centimetres from the ground were still in place. It was safe to go in.

The building had not been abandoned for too long and the roof was still intact. Inside, the rooms smelled dry and dusty, with no odours from animals either living or dead. She stood quite still, listening for any scuttling, fluttering, scratching or scraping sounds, there were none. Scanning quickly with the torch she located the bag of clothes and the couch. There were curtains at all of the windows, but even so, she used her torch sparingly.

Towards the rear of the building was a kitchen, there was only one window that looked out over some fields and this had thick slatted blinds fitted, so she was able to use the torch a bit more here. Looking under the sink, she saw a mains water stop cock. The water in the pipe made a brief rushing sound as she cracked this open half a turn and the pressures equalised. She listened for the sound of running water elsewhere in the building, there was silence.

She took Krall's T-shirt from the bag, which she had folded in on itself to stop it from drying out too quickly. This was the only item of clothing with blood on it from the fight and the quick wash with plain water she had given it had not got rid of all the blood. She gently turned on a squeaky tap and stood back while it spluttered out brown smelly water, but after a few moments the water ran clear and smelled fresh. To one side of the sink was the remains of a bar of soap, not much, but enough. She soaked the T-shirt and rubbed the soap over the remains of the bloodstain. After rubbing the cloth against itself for a few minutes, she checked it against the light of the torch. The T-shirt was as clean as it was ever going to get. She wrung out as much water as she could then hung it over the back of a chair, hoping that the warm summer night air would dry it sufficiently by morning.

She made her way back gingerly to the room with the couch; there was no sound of mosquitoes, but it's the females, the silent ones that bite, not the male buzzing ones, so she smeared some of the insect repellent on the exposed parts of her arms and legs, then using the bag of clothes as a pillow, laid down to sleep.

Getting a Job

Astrid woke with a start and had to shake her head a few times to get her vision into focus. Her dreamless sleep had not been long enough and as she sat up, she had to resist the desperate urge to lie back down and sleep for a little longer. The angle of the sun told her that it was between six and seven and she would soon have to make a move as there would be people around making their way to work. She had saved half of the burger and some of the chips from the previous night for a breakfast of sorts. The fat in the cold burger had congealed and moisture from it had condensed inside the paper wrapper and soaked into the bun making it slimy. As gross as it was, there was sufficient nutrition for her needs, but despite that, she was glad to wash it all down with some clean water from the second bottle. This would be enough to keep her going for a few hours.

She took off the party clothes from the previous night and immediately became aware that by sleeping in them during a warm summer night she had not done herself any favours with regard to body odour. A wash down with cold water helped a little but the effect was mainly psychological, and she knew it. She stood for a bit waving her arms outstretched to dry off, then got dressed in Krall's civilian clothes and despite the precarious situation she was still in, found herself dwelling on the idea of some clean underwear. Rubbing her teeth with her finger wetted with the bottled water – she would not risk the tap water – did little to remove the taste of the cold burger.

She noticed an itching on both her ankles, and on closer inspection, discovered a ring of small red bumps that seemed to itch even more now she was aware of them.

"Great," she said quietly to herself, "flea bites."

She must have got these outside before putting on the insect repellent. Fortunately, inoculation for insect borne diseases was mandatory and she was up to date with all her jabs, even so, fleas were one of the few things that made her cringe. Irrational as she knew her disgust was, given the vast numbers of equally bad, and many worse biting insects, she would always associate fleas as carriers of the plague that wiped out nearly a third of the world's population in the Middle Ages.

Cautiously, she pulled a curtain open a fraction to allow light in so that she could check her appearance, and as she expected, she was scruffy. The bloodstain on the T-shirt was faint but still clearly visible, her hair was a mess and all the clothes were creased, but she could use her dishevelled form to her advantage. Today she would need all her acting skills, chief among which is her uncanny ability, by simply changing her demeanour and gestures, to make herself appear to be much younger than she really is.

She dampened her hand and smoothed her hair as much as she could, then cracked open the back door a fraction and looked out. Convincing herself that there was no one to see her leave the building, she slipped out and walked down the path to the road and began to head back into town towards the shops. There were some people in the distance, but far enough away that if they saw her, they would not be able to identify her, even if they took any notice. At this time in the morning people are only concerned with getting to work and grumbling about it; her presence probably didn't even register with them.

The 'Help Wanted' card in the window of the general store was sun bleached; Astrid guessed that it had been there for quite a while. She could see a woman setting up some boxes in the store, it was early and there was no one else in the shop. This looked hopeful; she entered and walked to the counter. The woman stood on a small box with her back to the counter while she arranged tins and jars. She was in her late middle age, with a tress of Auburn hair that was shot through with wiry grey strands that refused to be tamed into a ponytail and curled out with a mind of their own. Astrid stood quietly and waited while the woman rearranged some tins on a shelf behind the counter.

"I'm not actually open yet."

"I need a job," Astrid said quietly.

"You're the first one that's asked," said the woman, without turning around. "I can't pay much."

"I don't need much, just enough to pay for food and somewhere to live." Again, Astrid spoke quietly and put a slight sad inflection into her voice.

"You'll be lucky to find somewhere to live," said the woman as she finished writing price tags.

She turned to face Astrid and her frown deepened. The woman was a bit over weight with a chubby round face; her eyebrows seemed set in a permanent frown and she looked fed up with the world. Astrid suspected that the woman had been good looking in her youth, but her deportment and the lack of a wedding ring told a story.

Standing before the shopkeeper was a young woman out of character with her usual customers; her clothes had seen a few days wear and were creased and slightly dirty, but the young woman didn't look like some of the scruffy girls from the town. She dismissed her speculation and got to the point.

"The work's hard, the hours are long, and the pay is rubbish."

"I don't mind what I do," said Astrid, not looking up.

"Well, the first thing you can do is look me in the eye."

Astrid lifted her head, and as the woman studied her, she sensed some sadness, but this wasn't her concern right now. "I need someone to stack the stock out back and keep tally of orders. I'm going to be stocking up for the autumn soon so there will be a lot of work to do. Are you any good with numbers?"

"I studied accountancy at university," lied Astrid, avoiding eye contact, her voice feeble and slightly tremulous. "I am qualified."

The woman crossed her arms across her chest, cocked her head to one side and studied Astrid for a while. "So, what's a well-spoken, pretty southern girl with a qualification in accountancy doing asking for a job in a general store in a dump of a northern town like this then, huh?" she said, with more than a degree of suspicion in her voice.

She sighed. "I just need a job."

"Are you in trouble with the law?"

"I've not committed any crime," Astrid said timidly and looked away.

"But you are in trouble and you've run away from home haven't you."

Astrid looked down and nodded ever so slightly.

"Is it a man?"

Again, she nodded, this time sniffing back a tear.

"Are you pregnant?" the woman said, sounding slightly cross.

"No…" She gave a humourless half laugh. "…surprisingly."

"So then, what's the problem?" said the woman, firmly.

"Please, I don't want to talk about it, I just need a job."

"Look, my name's Daria and I need help here, I can't do it all on my own anymore, I'm not as young as I used to be. You are the only person who has shown any interest in a job. So, if I am going to give you a job, I need to know what the problem is." Daria softened her tone of voice. "What's your name, love?"

"Vitria."

Daria looked askance at Astrid. "That's not your real name, is it?"

Astrid shook her head ever so slightly. Daria shrugged. "Well, I suppose it is best that I don't know, so Vitria it is then." She looked a bit serious again. "You haven't told me what the problem is."

Astrid sighed and again avoided eye contact. "There is this man, a powerful man, he's rich and he's a politician, he was much older than me; he was a friend of the family. He bought me presents when I was a child – even then I thought he was a bit creepy. It carried on after I got married; my husband didn't like it and as a result the marriage didn't last very long. After that, the man kept pestering me, saying that I could be his now, but I didn't want to. Then…" Tears welled in Astrid's eyes. Daria put her hand to her mouth, her eyes wide with horror, because she knew what was coming next. "He raped you, didn't he," she whispered.

Tears rolled down Astrid's face. "Many times."

"Oh, you poor girl."

Astrid wiped her eyes with her sleeve. "I said I would run away, he said if I did, he would send someone to find me and take me back to him, and he would kill me."

"Why didn't you tell your family?"

"There was no point, they wouldn't have believed me. He'd been a friend of my father's for years. My dad was always saying what a good man he was, his standing in the community and all that rubbish. If only he knew the truth…" Astrid let her voice tail off, implying greater detail.

Daria sighed and shook her head wearily, it was the kind of story she had heard too many times before in her life. "When can you start?"

"Right now?" said Astrid cheerfully, acting as if in appreciation but in reality, relieved that her ruse had worked.

"No, you're not going to start right now, because to be perfectly honest my love, you stink and you need some new clothes, and just look at your hair."

"I have some money, there's a clothes shop down the road. I won't be long."

"No," said Daria firmly. "Give me some money, I'll go and get you some clothes and you can stay here and have a shower. Given what you have told me, I think it's best if you stay out of sight."

"Won't it look a bit odd, you know, you will be buying clothes that clearly wouldn't be for you?"

"No, I'll just say I'm buying them for my daughter, she's about your age."

Astrid's heart fluttered. "Where is she then?"

"Oh, she lives a long way away – the other side of the country, I don't see her from one month to the next; her work keeps her away for weeks at a time. And she never calls me."

Daria was clearly in her element now, taking charge, organising things, doing what mother's do. "You are going to need to stay pretty much out of sight and I know that it's not going to be easy, but it's for the best. You can go out of the back door when you need a bit of fresh air and sun, there's a bit of a garden and I'm not overlooked, so you should be safe."

"But I've still got to find somewhere to stay."

Daria sighed. "Look, love, there's a room out back, it's clean and dry, and there's a pull-out bed. You can sleep there for now and we'll see how it goes, okay?"

"Oh, thank you, thank you so much, you have no idea how much that means to me."

Astrid handed over some money, and then, remembering her craving from earlier in the day, paused and said sheepishly. "Can you get me some underwear as well?"

Given all the combat situations she had been in; sleeping rough, scavenging for food, living in foxholes for days at a time, she was slightly embarrassed with herself for wanting this creature comfort.

"Is there a pharmacy nearby? I've got some insect bites and they itch like mad." She put her hand on her crotch. "And I think I've got a bit of thrush."

At least these parts of her story were true, she had noticed the yeast infection first thing in the morning and attributed it to the clothes that she had appropriated the previous night. This had to be dealt with, because thrush, though not dangerous, would be unpleasant and a distraction.

"Of course," smiled Daria knowingly as she winked her eye. "Girls know what girls want. But shoes might be a problem, I'll get a pair of trainers in your size and you'll just have to take a chance. I'll get you some toiletries as well." She looked at the stain on the T-shirt and frowned. "That's not your blood, is it? Are you hurt?"

"No, it's not mine. Clumsy me, I tripped in the dark and fell on some fresh road kill, I tried to wash it out but—"

"Ooh, animal blood," interrupted Daria. "Dirty, no point trying to wash it out, better burn it. You can get nasty diseases from animal blood."

Astrid nodded, even though she knew that a good hot wash was all that was needed but burning the clothes would be a good idea anyway.

"I think there might be a bit of blood on the jeans," she said, looking down at herself and pandering to Daria's obvious germ fixation.

"Just leave all your clothes out and we'll have a fire tonight, then you can start afresh, that should make you feel better."

Daria directed the woman she knew as Vitria through to a bathroom that had clearly been added to the building fairly recently and was effectively a separate room. As she left, Astrid heard her lock the cash register and the doors to the main building. The shower was new and was powerful without any alternate hot and cold pulsing. Shower gel served as both a body wash and a shampoo, with a fragrance that wasn't overpowering. It was the first proper wash she had had since she was in Malaya's quarters, and it left her feeling far more refreshed than she expected.

With any luck, getting a good night's sleep and some decent food would bring her mind back into focus, a mind that had started to drift. Most of all now she needed to be sharp, it was critical that in the next few days that she kept up the pretence of a young female needing sanctuary. She rubbed her hair dry and sat wrapped in a huge soft towel, eyes shut, centring her thoughts.

After about an hour Daria returned with some bulging bags that in addition to clothes, seemed to contain everything a woman would need. Astrid opened them with an enthusiasm that wasn't hard to fake. Right now, the toothbrush, toothpaste, anti-histamine ointment and the tube of Clotrimazole cream were her number one objects of desire. After a few minutes, she emerged back out of the bathroom, then took the clothes.

She quickly dressed herself with the baggy T-shirt and jeans that Daria had bought. The clothes were neutral – nothing outlandish, Daria had chosen well and even if she was seen, she would not stand out. The trainers were a good fit and another little luxury that was very welcome. Astrid made a mental note to herself to not get too comfortable.

"I took a guess on the bra size, is it okay?"

"Yeah, a good fit, thanks."

"Right, some ground rules," said Daria firmly.

"I set up shop at seven thirty in the morning. I open at eight and close at ten thirty at night. I'll need you out back all the time. Deliveries are every day between seven thirty and eight thirty, and they just dump the stuff in the drive; I'll sign for it, but you'll have to move it into the store once they've gone. Once you've done that, you'll tally up what's been sent and check that against my orders. I don't want you in the house just yet, and for your own sake, not in the shop during opening hours. We'll take it in turns to buy food, but obviously I'll have to go and get it and I'll cook. No offence love, but I doubt you've spent too much time in a kitchen. Okay?"

"That's all fine with me. I'll give you some money for food today."

Though there was no hint of a threat, both women knew that Daria had the upper hand. At any moment, she could speak to the police and it would be all over.

****

Next morning Astrid scanned through the papers, one national tabloid and one local rag which both seemed to be about eighty-five percent adverts. Daria noticed her intensity as she read every column of every page, starting with the national.

"You're looking for a piece about you, aren't you?"

"Yes, and there's nothing…at least not yet."

"Well, anyway, that's good for the time being. Can you pass me the local?"

Daria only bothered reading the first four pages, the next ten were either adverts or sport.

"Another girl has copped it," she said, cross at what she had just read.

Astrid affected a shocked tone to her voice. "I saw that, they say she was a prostitute who died of a drug overdose and that there were two guys with her who died in a fight. Is that sort of thing common here?"

Daria snorted angrily. "One is enough, isn't it? Poor girl, she probably had to take the drugs so she wouldn't know what the bastards were doing to her. The men around here, they're pigs, they're bad enough with their wives and girlfriends, but when they get a…" – Daria shuffled awkwardly in her chair, embarrassed at discussing prostitution – "…you know, a working girl, they think they can treat her like a piece of meat – do whatever they want – slap her around, and so what if she ends up seriously hurt or worse. The police don't give a shit."

"It says that there was a guy killed in a mugging as well."

Daria sneered. "Well, at least that one will be investigated," she said sarcastically, but then noticing Astrid flinch, calmed down.

"Oh, I'm sorry love, I didn't mean to rant at you, but it's just that it happens too often around here. I've seen too many pretty young girls like you get their lives destroyed."

****

After a few days Daria invited Vitria into the house for meals, Astrid never felt like a surrogate daughter, more of simple company for Daria. The work pattern had quickly established itself; when deliveries were due, Daria would open the gates to the yard, and these were tall, solid double doors with a sturdy lock on the inside. Eventually a delivery van would turn up and deposit cardboard boxes of various sizes. Daria would sign for them; the van would leave, and she would shut and lock the gates. Then Astrid – Vitria – would carry the boxes into the store and check them against the orders. Any shortages would be delivered the next day.

One day after a particularly large order, Astrid checked the delivery and found one complete box was missing from the delivery, this was unusual, normally the number of boxes was correct, but the contents were not. What was also unusual was the van returning after half an hour. A skinny teenager jumped out of the driver's seat and went around to the back of the van and took out a large cardboard box. Daria opened one of the gates.

"You sure shifted them quick," he said looking at the empty yard. "I thought you said you ran this place on your own."

"I'm stronger than I look you know," she said, trying to look confident.

"Nah, I reckon you've got a toy boy out back helping you." He nudged her elbow and winked. "I bet he helps you in more ways than one eh? And I bet you show him a trick or two in the bedroom, you naughty little thing."

"None of your business," she said, trying to sound mysterious, but inside she was cringing at the barefaced cheek of the boy who was young enough to be her grandson.

"Well, I'll leave you two love birds alone then." He winked again, then got back into the van and drove off. Daria didn't know that Astrid had heard everything. It was time to go.

Early the next morning, before Daria was up, and with genuine sadness, Astrid wrote a note and left it on the counter.

Dear Daria, I want to thank you for everything you have done for me, but I have to go now. You were right when you said that it was for the best that you didn't know my real name. The men who are looking for me are dangerous and if I were to stay any longer it would become dangerous for you. You didn't have to help me but you did, and your care and kindness has touched me deeply. If you do ever discover my real identity, please don't think harshly of me.

Vitria

Daria knew this would happen eventually, but still shed a little tear for the girl she had come to feel so close to, though she was puzzled by the last part of the note; why would she ever think harshly of her?

It was time for the penultimate part of her plan. She needed to head west to the farm once owned by her uncle, the farm he left years ago when he took his family and defected. His family link to the enemy, as the Correlan military saw it, was starting to become a problem. The Correlans had finally worked out that he was Astrid's uncle, and despite the fact that he and all his immediate family were true Correlan citizens, he had started to receive very thinly veiled threats and suggestions that he was a spy.

Though what there was to spy on was difficult to see. There was nothing but farmland in any direction for many tens of kilometres, and there had not been any military activity in the area throughout the course of the war so far. This was the last purely rural part of Correla left, though the relentless march of Kudzu was fast destroying all the arable land.

Walking briskly in the clear morning air, Astrid headed south towards the southern rail station, calling to mind the timetable that she had memorised before starting the mission. The southern station was small and had little use which would help her keep a low profile, and mainly had trains heading north and east. She needed to head out southwest and there was only one train service a day from this station that headed west. It was the seven-fifteen train. She arrived at the station just before seven o'clock and scanned the timetable again.

To her horror, she saw that the times had recently changed and that no trains from this station headed southwest any more, the only train to do so was from the northwest station and that was due to leave today at seven fifty-five and also there was now only one train every four days that headed southwest. She looked at the times of the bus shuttle service between the two and realised that she had missed the only connection. There was no way she could walk the distance and the regular bus service would not get her there in time.

She quickly assessed her two options; she either had to get to the northwest station to catch the westbound train now, or hang around Balun for another four days and catch the next train west. The northwest station was much busier with a far greater chance of being spotted, but she could lose herself in a crowd. She couldn't go back to Daria, and now that she had nowhere to stay, remaining in Balun could draw unwanted attention. There was only one choice, she had to go north, and she now had less than an hour to get there, which meant she needed a car.

Walking back away from the station she saw an opportunity; it would be unpleasant, but necessary. A little way off, a middle-aged woman was in the process of parking her car in a side road. Astrid looked around and confirmed to herself that there was no one else about. In amongst the junk at the side of the road was a piece of shiny metal, about thirty centimetres long and about five wide, with soft rounded edges; it looked like a bit of trim off a domestic appliance. She picked it up and walked briskly towards the woman, who was now out of the car, locking it.

In one swift movement, she grabbed the woman, pushed her back onto the car and raised the metal, touching it against her throat. The metal was far too blunt to do any harm, but Astrid new that the shock of seeing the apparent blade and the coldness of the metal on her skin would convince the woman that it was a knife. Her imagination would fill in any gaps.

"Give me your keys and your phone, or I'll kill you and take them anyway," she snarled.

"Please don't hurt me," the woman pleaded, as she fumbled in her bag pulling out the keys and her mobile phone.

"That's up to you, now chuck them down there on the ground." Astrid pointed down towards the front wheel of the car.

The woman did what she was told. Astrid turned the terrified woman around and faced her towards the back of the vehicle.

"Now start walking and don't turn around or I'll cut your throat."

She shoved the woman forward and waited until she was a good distance away before getting into the car and driving off.

Later, the woman, distraught and becoming hysterical, would tell the police that she clearly saw that the knife held to her throat was a domestic carving knife with an ornate ivory handle. She would also say that the young woman was obviously a heroin addict, as she could see needle marks on her arms, but later stated that her attacker had been wearing a long sleeve shirt. The police officers made all the right noises, but quickly realised that the woman's contradictory description was useless, and as she was not physically hurt the case would just be recorded and did not warrant any further investigation. Once again Astrid had been uncomfortable treating a civilian so harshly, but she needed the car.

She arrived at the station with only minutes to spare, bought a ticket, boarded the train and settled into an empty carriage. The train into the remote west of the country didn't get many passengers and with any luck no one else would get into her carriage; even so it was a long journey and she picked up a discarded newspaper to hide her face as the train pulled into stations along the way. No one got on, and the paper even had an article about the westbound service being further scaled back to a once-a-week service.

It was mid-afternoon before the train finally reached its destination; the end of the line. The station was deserted, and the only other passenger had got off many stations before. Astrid got out and recalled the map she had memorised. It had been many years since she had been here and little, if anything, had changed. The driver immediately started the return journey – there was no point in waiting any longer. She watched as the train pulled out; she had a long walk ahead of her now, four hours minimum at a brisk pace. She had built up her stamina during her time with Daria, regular meals and good sleep had seen to that, so she was confident of reaching the farm by nightfall.

Special Forces

Despite the huge resources of the Correlan military, they were not able to monitor the border with complete continuity. Several of the monitoring stations had old systems that were of poor quality and unable to detect very low flying aircraft. Arralan planners had identified several areas that the Correlan military considered to be unlikely points for any medium to large-scale actions and that had patchy radar cover. With care, a small force could get through and travel some distance into Correla undetected. This could only be done a few times at the weak spots, after that, the Correlan military might become aware of this shortcoming, and they would take steps to introduce greater monitoring. The time had come to use these oversights once more.

It was through two of these gaps that two helicopters streaked through, one in the southwest, another one hundred-and-eighty kilometres east. Each carried a four-man special operations team, each team with a small box of electronics.

"We do need to actually arrive at our destination," said the leader of alpha squad to the pilot with the usual sardonic tone of a military voice, as the helicopter skids brushed the top of some trees.

"We have to fly this low, any higher and the radar will pick us up," said the co-pilot not taking his eyes off the radiation detector, looking for any indication that radar emissions were tracking the helicopter. "The route is complex. If I see anything we'll have to abort."

"We're not going to abort," said the squad leader firmly.

"So don't worry, we'll get you there," said the pilot.

At that moment, the skids hit the top of a tree, twitching the aircraft sideways for a moment.

"Oops," said the pilot as he turned and grinned at the squad leader.

The squad leader grunted and sat back in his seat. Twenty minutes later the helicopter landed next to a deserted building. Unused for decades, it was a small, rough stone hut with a domed roof that had stood for over a century and had been used by farm workers to shelter from bad weather. This had been identified as the best place, as it was the only man-made structure of its type for miles around and in an area abandoned by the farmers.

The team jumped out of the helicopter, three of the squad formed a defensive perimeter, their weapons cocked and ready, while the squad leader took the box into the hut. He opened the lid exposing a keypad, he typed in a code, then inserted a key and turned it. An LED flashed once showing that the device was active.

"You have thirty days," he said quietly as he removed the key, then covered the box with some ragged sacks and detritus from the floor of the hut.

After thirty days, a small explosive charge within the box would detonate, destroying the box and everything in it. The same would happen if the box was tampered with or the wrong code was entered.

One hundred and eighty kilometres to the east, the same thing was being done by Omega squad, though the box they carried was hidden randomly with no special attention paid to its location.

An hour later both helicopters arrived back at their base. The whole operation had taken just over two hours and now radio operators were listening intently to Correlan radio intercepts, listening for any mentions of the operation. There were none, Correlan airspace had been successfully penetrated without detection, no weapons had been discharged, the packages had been delivered and everyone returned safely. This part of the mission was a success by any measure, and only time would tell if the second part would be as successful.

Crime Reports to Valerian

"You asked for crime reports from regional police forces, sir," said the lieutenant as he stood in front of the general's desk holding a large sheaf of papers. As usual, he would have to wait silently until the general had finished whatever it was that he was doing before even acknowledging the lieutenant's presence in the room.

Eventually, without looking up, he spoke. "Specifically, I asked for reports of crimes out of the ordinary, theft of clothing or food. These things would appear trivial to the local plods in the police but are the things that she would need. And we do need to know these things, so I sincerely hope those reports you are holding have some relevance."

The lieutenant placed a stack of reports from towns within a hundred kilometres of the Kandalan Base on the desk.

"Good grief," moaned the general. "These are just crime levels out of the ordinary?"

"Yes, sir, I have read through all of them before bringing them to you. They are from the weekend starting on Friday night and I'm afraid that they don't contain any information about clothing or food thefts. It seems that most of them have just reported higher than normal levels of drunkenness and fighting."

The general scoffed with contempt. "Higher than normal levels of drunkenness and fighting? Are these out of the ordinary? Of course they're not. These are no doubt a result of the start of the football season. These are not of any use to me."

"It would appear that way, sir, though there is one report that is a little out of the ordinary. It's from Balun. A spate of pick pocketing in a nightclub—"

"Pick pocketing! Why is that relevant?" the general interrupted gruffly, frowning at the insignificance he perceived.

"She may need money, sir," tentatively ventured the lieutenant.

"No, she won't risk urban areas, this is not important," said Valerian dismissively. "Not to mention the fact that Balun is two hundred and fifty kilometres on the wrong direction; she will be heading southwest, not northeast."

"...and there were four non-accidental civilian deaths," the lieutenant continued, pressing his point as hard as he dared.

"Four civilian deaths!" exploded Valerian angrily. "This is not our concern. Why are you bothering me with this?" he shouted.

"One was ex-military, sir, ex-army and to be precise, the third infantry. He was at the nightclub where the pick-pocketing took place; I just thought you should know."

The lieutenant still thought that the pickpocket reports were significant and knew very well that the general was always concerned for the welfare of ex-service men, particularly so from the infantry – his old unit – and this would mitigate his current iracund state of mind.

Valerian frowned with concern and softened his tone a fraction. "Is it connected to the other three?"

"It is unlikely, sir; the others are a dead prostitute and two of her clients; he was at a nightclub on the other side of the town."

"How out of the ordinary are four non-accidental deaths in Balun?" said Valerian, suddenly interested.

"I did some research before coming to see you, sir; Balun is known as a hard, working-class industrial town with frequent bouts of violent crime. Reported statistics show that they would expect to see a murder every two or three weeks on average. And about three in every four would be related to domestic incidents. Four non-domestic murders so close together is out of the ordinary, but not unprecedented, sir."

"So, they'll have their work cut out investigating all four at once."

"No, not really, sir. The police chief doesn't care about the deaths of prostitutes or their clients; he is on record as considering it an occupational hazard. They are concentrating on the nightclub murder."

"Good. So, who was our man?"

"His name was Asher, sir, there was an incident about two years ago where he got badly injured. He got an honourable discharge out the service. He'd moved around quite a bit and seemed to have been making a living as a pickpocket. The police were aware of his activities but could never catch him red handed, sir."

"That's why he moved around a lot. How did he die?"

"He appears to have been strangled after a short scuffle, sir. His body was found in an alleyway behind the nightclub where the pickpocket activity has been reported. He probably picked the wrong pocket and they went for him to get their money back; his wallet was found nearby, empty, sir."

"Allowing himself to be strangled," Valerian mused aloud in an irritated voice. "Sloppy, very sloppy, why didn't he fight back. We train our men for this." His voice a strange mixture of frustration and concern.

"He wasn't in good shape, sir; he was hardly able to walk. He was injured out of the army after being caught in a land mine blast. It did a lot of damage to his left leg and arm and the hospital couldn't fix him enough for him to return to active service. He was lucky to survive at all, that's probably why he got away with being a pick-pocket, sir; no one would suspect a cripple."

"But he was still agile enough to pick pockets and get away with it."

"Yes, sir, and initial reports said that he was seen chatting with a young woman before leaving the premises through a door that led into the alley and the woman was with him, sir."

"So, she was the honey trap to get him to go outside where others were waiting." He paused, thinking. "And nobody heard anything?"

"No, sir, by all accounts the music is played very loud in the club."

Valerian snorted derisively. "He probably thought he was going to get his cock sucked."

"Also, sir, there was an accidental death nearby. It seems that the club doorman might have heard something and gone to take a look, slipped and fell on some masonry and died from a head injury."

"So, the imbecile doorman could have intervened and saved our man if he hadn't been so stupid and clumsy," Valerian snapped angrily. He paused for a moment. "A man risks his life for his country only to get killed by one of the fucking arseholes that he fought for."

There was a long pause, he stood up, snatched up a packet of cigarettes and took an unfiltered Cavana cigarette from it then held it unlit, staring at it deep in thought while he paced back and forth behind his desk. Finally, he turned to the lieutenant.

"Find out if he had any family and see that they are looked after. I don't care that he had become a petty criminal, he was one of ours. Dismissed."

The lieutenant had shuffled the Balun report to the top of the stack and was about to open it.

"Shall I leave this report with you, sir?"

"No," snapped Valerian crossly, not even checking to see which report it was. The tone was set for the rest of the day. The general despised civilians and was always aggravated when he heard of an ex-serviceman's death at the hands of one. Irascible at the best of times, today there would be more shouting than usual.

The lieutenant left the room and shut the door behind him. The general lit the cigarette and took a drag so long that it burned away almost a quarter of the cigarette's length. The draw was deep, and he had taken in a lot of smoke. The lack of a filter resulted in much higher levels of tar and nicotine, this coupled with carbon monoxide now entering his bloodstream made his head swim for a moment. Lost in thought, he absentmindedly chewed and swallowed the odd bits of tobacco that always ended up in his mouth when he smoked the unfiltered version of Cavana. He looked at the map, there had been no sightings.

"Where the fuck are you, you fucking bitch," he muttered.

The Car and the Oil Worker

"The heroin death in Balun, sir," said the lieutenant as he stood at the desk waiting for the general to finish reading a report.

"What about it?" he said not even looking up.

"It seems the female was not a sex worker, sir; she was from a relatively well-off family from outside of the town. They reported her missing a few days ago and identified the body this morning."

"Why would that stop her from being a whore?" Valerian snorted derisively.

"It is unlikely, sir, she was a regular at restaurants in one of the better parts of town, far away from the red-light district."

"So, the police may investigate it properly now," the general grunted with more than a hint of contempt in his voice.

"They have started, sir; they have looked again at the two men who died at the scene. As you are no doubt aware, sir, the police in Balun do not bother to investigate the deaths of sex workers or their clients, so it was originally just reported as two male dead, one female dead. The assumption was that after she died of an overdose, and the two men then had a fight and died from their injuries. Now they are taking it more seriously."

The general looked up, his interest piqued. "How did they die?"

"One had a stab wound to the heart and the other had his throat cut. A hunting, or combat style knife was found with one of the bodies."

The lieutenant placed the medical examiner's file on the general's desk.

The general sat back in his chair, put his hands together as if he was praying and tapped his index fingers together a few times.

"Have you ever stabbed a man in the heart?"

"Yes, sir, in combat."

"And what was the effect?"

"The man instantly slumped to the ground and was dead in seconds."

"Yes, that's because of the sudden loss in blood pressure. And have you ever cut a man's throat?" He took the pathologist's report and read a passage from it.

"…both the jugular vein and the carotid artery were cut in a single pass with a very sharp bladed instrument…"

"No, sir, I have not."

"The effect is the same, and for the same reason." He read a passage further down the report.

"…a single stab wound to the heart had penetrated the pulmonary artery, then it appears that the blade was twisted in a circular motion which lacerated the Aorta and the Superior Vena Cava…"

"So, do you think that a man stabbed in the heart would be able to cut another man's throat, or a man with his throat cut would be able to stab another in the heart?"

"No, sir I do not."

"Someone else, someone very skilled with a knife killed them." He banged his fist angrily on the table. "She did it, she was there."

"There is something else, sir, the dead female had a car—"

"And it is missing?" interrupted the general.

"Yes, sir."

"Find it," he snapped. "If she's taken it, she would need to get fuel and it should be easy to track. Let's hope it was low on fuel. We'll have to use civilian police now. Tell all the police divisions that this is top priority, everything else can wait. And stress to the police that this is find and observe only, do not apprehend unless I say so. If she is with the car, the last thing we need is a couple of flat-footed local cops being strangled with their own intestines. Dismissed."

As the lieutenant left the room, the general walked over to the map and stood staring at it for several minutes, stroking his beard.

"Ten days," he muttered. "Ten days and she could be anywhere."

Less than three hours later, the lieutenant was back in front of the desk.

"They've found it, sir."

"So soon? How can they be sure it is the right car?"

"They are sure, sir, it is a rare imported western model, bright red colour, very distinctive."

"Where is it?" demanded Valerian.

"In Lashan, sir."

"Lashan!" he said incredulously. "That's 200 kilometres northeast of Balun, that's completely the wrong direction."

He got up from his desk and walked over to the wall map. He studied the route the car would have travelled, there was pretty much only one road. After a couple of moments, he turned to the lieutenant.

"Do we still have eyes on the vehicle?"

"Yes, sir, the police are tailing it."

"Well, it seems that finally we have a bit of luck. Is she driving the car?"

"No, sir, the car is being driven by a man. He may be an accomplice."

"Unlikely, she knows what we would do to get information from anyone who helps her. She will avoid interactions with anyone."

The general sat back at his desk and thought for a while in silence, thinking through the options. Lashan is a town that only exists because it is the point where two main roads through the region cross. It has an oil field, this brings in a bit of money, but the oil is poor quality and the reserves are so small that the major international oil companies aren't interested. It has a small amount of farming, largely subsistence, but with a bit left over to ship out to also bring some money into the town.

But other than that, Lashan sits inside a vast open plain; to the west, north and east there are thousands of square kilometres of flat featureless ground. No cover, hardly any trees, a virtual desert. Any vehicle moving on one of the dead straight roads would easily be spotted. But this was the first break so far, and he needed to act.

"Have him arrested and bring him here, I will question him. Have the guards soften him up a bit, nothing too heavy, just enough so that he knows just how deep the shit is that he is standing in."

****

There were two subterranean levels below the military police building. Level one was the holding area with four huge cages, each capable of holding fifty prisoners. This level was for processing, taking details, photographing, fingerprinting and all the other formalities of arrest before the prisoner was taken to the second level down, which was simply known as 'The special room'. Prisoners could wait days in the squalid cages, often asking if the process could be hurried up, assuming that they would be moved to a proper prison where they would at least have a bed of sorts. They soon regretted their request when they saw the horrors of 'The special room'.

The second level down had a long dimly lit corridor with ten cells on either side and was for interrogation. The whole place was designed to induce misery. Built from cast concrete, the walls, floor and ceiling were painted gloss grey. This made all the flat surfaces sonically reflective and with no soft furnishings of any kind, the effect was to amplify any sound. The damp air stank of fear; even the guards hated it down here, and they took this out on the prisoners. Each cell was three metres high and six by six metres square to allow free movement of several people in the room at any one time, even though there was only ever one prisoner. Rows of hooks were set into the ceilings and studs were set into the floor to allow chairs or tables to be firmly fixed in place.

The cells were lit by a row of bulkhead lights high up on every wall, with a couple of electrical sockets on the wall near the door. The floor sloped gently to one corner where a stinking drain was the only direct contact with the outside world. Heavy steel doors had openings in them with thick metal grilles across so that hands could not be pushed through. There were sliding covers over the grilles, but the guards always left these open, this was so that the occupants of the other cells could clearly hear the suffering of other inmates. Out in the corridor there was a water outlet to allow the cells to be hosed down after an interrogation had ended.

Six hours after he had given the order to bring in the car driver, the general strode down the steps and through the thick double doors into the special room under the guardhouse. He was unmoved by a long, agonised scream that came from a cell as he passed. The prolonged scream was high pitched, and it was hard to tell whether it came from a man or a woman. If he had looked through the grilles on any of the cell doors as he passed, he would have seen the terrified occupant huddled in the far corners of the cells trying to get as far from the door as possible, each one either nursing some appalling injury, or beside themselves in panic as to what awaited them.

Most had no idea why they were even there; it was routine for the political police to visit towns and encourage denouncements, which were almost always untrue. The prisoners would probably have been denounced by a neighbour as a way of getting back at them over some petty squabble. Or had been reported to the police for breaking a law that they didn't even know existed.

Valerian admired this place. With the twisted logic of Correlan politics, this was a place of true equality, a perverted utopia where no exceptions or special account was ever made. Young or old, male or female, rich or poor, social standing or skin colour; none of it made a difference. All were treated to exactly the same level of brutality.

The general entered cell number eight. A man was hanging by his wrists in the middle of the room from ropes attached to two of the ceiling hooks. His heels were just off the floor, so he could only support his weight by pulling on the ropes around his wrists, or by standing on tiptoe. He was stripped to the waist and there were several red wheals on his back and chest where the guards had whipped him with their belts, and there was redness on his face where he had been punched and slapped. Three other men were in the cell; a sergeant by the door was overseeing two guards. One guard was taunting the man by waving a set of thumbscrews in his face. The mediaeval instrument of torture was popular with a lot of the guards; thumbscrews were simple, portable and very effective. Just the sight of them would instil abject fear into a prisoner, as was being ably demonstrated.

"Cut him down," ordered the general.

The guards cut the ropes around his wrists; as he slumped down, they grabbed him under the arms and hauled him upright, then stood back so the man was in the middle of the room. He stood fearful and shaking, rubbing his wrists and wincing at the pain in his shoulders, desperately trying to avoid eye contact with anyone in the room. The general stood in front of him, stern faced, looking deep into the man's eyes. He stayed silent for two, maybe three minutes. He knew the power of silence, it gave the victim time to worry about what was coming next and assume the worst. To a victim, every minute of silence would feel like an hour.

Eventually the man broke the silence. "I don't know what you want, I don't know anything, please don't hurt me," desperation in his voice.

"Shut up," hissed the general. "You may only speak when I ask you a question."

"But I don't know what you want."

The guard sergeant stepped forward and slammed his fist into the man's abdomen. He doubled over and dropped to the floor in agony and rolled onto his side, clutching his stomach. As he gasped for breath the sergeant leant over him.

"Are you fucking deaf or are you fucking stupid, you little piece of Lashani shit," he yelled.

"You were told that you could only speak to answer the general's questions. Now if you speak again without permission, I'll cut off your cock, so you won't be able to fuck your pig of a mother ever again."

It was a common belief that the Lashani were all inbred, and that incest, and in particular intergenerational incest, was common. Given the high number of birth defects, the low average intelligence and the remoteness of the place, it may have been true.

"Stand up, take your time," said the general calmly. "Take all the time that you need. We have plenty of time."

The pain had subsided a bit, but the man was starting to panic; his diaphragm had gone into spasm and he couldn't breathe. The room started to swim, and he felt he would never breathe again, but at that moment the muscles relaxed a little and he gasped a breath. Slowly he rolled onto all fours; gasping for breath and moaning from the pain in his stomach, he pushed himself up to a half crouch then slowly straightened up until he could start to pull himself upright. It was a full four minutes before he was standing anywhere near fully upright.

"Do you know who I am?" said the general.

Not knowing whether he should speak or not, the man just shook his head.

"I am General Lothar Valerian of the army of the People's Republic of Corella and I am here to help you. I am hunting a dangerous escaped prisoner of war. The prisoner killed five people during the escape, five army people, my people." He stressed the 'my'.

"The fugitive is also wanted for questioning regarding the murder of four civilians in Balun and the manslaughter of another along the south mountain highway. As you can imagine, this is a very serious investigation, so the sooner you help me, the sooner you will be out of here."

The man went to speak, to protest his innocence and his ignorance of the escapee but changed his mind when he saw the sergeant making a fist.

After a long pause, the general smiled and relaxed his shoulders a bit. "Do you like to drive?" he said, with an avuncular, friendly tone to his voice.

This took the man by surprise, he hesitated, confused by the sudden change in the general's attitude. The sergeant had moved around behind him, and the man felt a sharp jab to his kidneys. He gasped and arched his back as the pain shot through his body.

"Answer the general," the sergeant snarled.

"Yes, I like to drive," he said, cringing, reaching around to rub his back and baffled by the question.

"Yes, it is very unusual to find a man who does not like to drive; the freedom and the sense of power one gets from controlling a vehicle can be very pleasant. Particularly if one is driving, say, with the family on holiday, taking in the views and so on. Do you agree?"

"Yes." The man didn't know if all this was a good thing or not, he suspected that it wasn't good.

"Now tell me, do you need to drive for your work?" again, the affable tone.

Immediately he replied. "Yes, I do have to drive for my work."

"And what is it that you do?"

"I am a maintenance inspector, I have to check the well heads every day and decide if any work needs doing." He glanced back warily at the sergeant, hoping not to get another punch.

"I see, so you have to drive to the wells to check them."

"Yes, driving is the only way I can get to all of them."

The man was nervous; he didn't understand the line of questioning and was anxious as to whether he was saying too much or too little.

"And I assume that you have to write reports to be distributed to the maintenance engineers."

"Yes, I do."

"And then you have to drive to the wells to check that the work has been carried out to an acceptable standard. Am I correct?"

"Yes, that is correct."

"And write another report to sign off the work."

"Yes."

"So, you have an important job that has a high level of responsibility. Am I correct?"

"Yes, that is…err…you are correct." The man was confused by Valerian's friendly attitude and stammered, if this was about his work, why had he been treated so harshly, and why he was being questioned by the army. Again, he glanced back at the sergeant.

"Don't look at him, look at me," said Valerian as he leant forward a bit, cocking his head to one side a little, his face once again stern and serious. "Do you agree with me that if you were blind, you would not only lose your job, but you wouldn't have the enjoyment of driving?" his voice was now harsh and menacing.

Fear rose in the man with intensity that he had never experienced before, the fear took his voice. The sergeant raised his fist and the man blurted out his answer just in time.

"I agree," was all that he could say.

"Hold him," said the general. Two guards grabbed him by the wrists, pressing against the backs of his elbows locking his arms straight against his body. His trembling legs buckled but the guards held him firmly. Valerian reached into his pocket and pulled out an ornately carved piece of animal bone. He pressed a button on it and a blade as long as his middle finger sprang out, the bright steel glinted and seemed to reflect more light than was available in the room. He pressed the edge against the man's cheek and slowly drew it across. The man whimpered as the skin pared open easily; blood flowed down to his chin and onto his chest. Valerian withdrew the knife, the sergeant handed him a cloth and Valerian calmly wiped the blood from the blade and handed the cloth back.

"That is so you fully understand that I am not at all squeamish. The pain, suffering and misery I bring to people does not bother me."

He nodded to the sergeant. "Hold his head still."

The sergeant grabbed the man by the hair. Valerian pressed the tip of the blade into the man's lower left eyelid, not too hard, just enough to break the skin a fraction. What little colour the man had drained away in an instant.

"I am going to ask you one question," he said, slowly and quietly, then paused for a few seconds.

"And if I am not satisfied with your answer, I will slowly push this blade into your eyes and blind you."

Again, he paused, allowing his words to sink in and the fear to build in the already terrified man.

"Where did you get the car?"

"I stole it, I'm sorry." The man gasped immediately. "I was in Balun, it was easy, the window was open and the keys were in the ignition; it was easy, it was easy," his words half speech, half crying. "I'm sorry. I'm sorry I stole it, I'm telling the truth I swear, please don't blind me, please," he cried out, panicking.

Valerian withdrew the knife, folded the blade away and put it back in his pocket.

"Release him."

The guards let go and the man slumped to the floor and immediately curled into the foetal position, repeating, "I'm sorry," over and over, his voice slowly descending into howling sobs. Fear finally got the better of his dignity and he lost control of his bowels and bladder.

"He's free to go," said the general. "Get him out of here."

A scream from a cell further along the corridor abruptly stopped. The sergeant nodded to one of the guards to go and find out why. If the victim had just passed out, that was not an issue, they could start again in an hour or so. But if the guards had used too much force and the victim had died, that would be inconvenient, if only for the fact that living victims can walk out of the cells and go home; a corpse would have to be dealt with. Then he would have to – as he always put it – 'explain in practical terms' to the guards that the object was to keep the prisoner alive. In other words, beat up the guards.

****

Valerian sat at his desk and pondered the events of the past days. He lit another one of his disgusting Cavana cigarettes and drew in the smoke deeply; it was his third in a row. He got up and paced the room, the smoke hung heavily in the still air of the office and little vortices formed behind him that appeared as if his very thoughts were escaping from his body.

The Cava tobacco plant had been crossbred with wild tobacco and had twice the nicotine and tar content of the next strongest variety. He also liked to smoke the unfiltered version of the cigarettes. He knew that these would eventually kill him, but in amongst his thoughts about Astrid he also pondered the possibility that one day they would meet, and she might kill him and cheat the cigarettes of their chance.

He turned to the lieutenant who had been sitting in silence at his own desk in the office.

"She made the heroin death look like a prostitute doing a trick to score some drugs, knowing that the police wouldn't investigate and wouldn't bother to look for a car. Then she set up the car so that it would be stolen and throw us off when we eventually found it. That, and the tracker switched into the bus; they were all set up by her. Add to that the poor girl who she must have made drive the staff car; all of these were distractions that she knew we would find."

The lieutenant frowned and was genuinely puzzled. "If she knew we would find them, why did she do them? They are all traces; she's showing us that she is still in the country."

"The reason she's doing it is that now when we get a genuine sighting, we won't believe it. She is clever, and she is going to pay very dearly for it."

He walked over to the map and studied it for a while, tapping Balun, Lashan, the mountain road where the staff car had crashed, and the road where Danny's bus had been stopped. "These incidents are hundreds of kilometres apart; they are not random improvised tactics. She planned this, all of it, and her plan will fail. Nobody is that good."

But he was wrong.

The Farm

Though overgrown, the entrance to the farm was exactly as she remembered it. The farmhouse was set back nearly a kilometre from the road, and the farm track curved around a copse so that the road was not visible from the farm. As she approached the front door of the farmhouse, Astrid wondered if her uncle had left the keys in the usual place. Reaching down behind a window box to the side of the door, she found them. It was a silly place to leave door keys, as it would be the first place a thief would look. But this region was so remote and sparsely populated that crime was unheard of, and they were only really there in case someone locked themselves out.

One key was steel, the other brass, and both had surface corrosion, but to her relief, worked. The door was stiff and opened with a creak. A fusty smell of dust greeted her, but not the acrid air of damp and decay. She moved from room to room, opening windows as she passed through to let fresh air in. All the furniture was covered with dustsheets; it seemed that both her uncle and aunt were convinced that they would return one day. 'Plan ahead' was her uncle's motto. She remembered him talking to her when she was very young.

"A farmer's life is all about planning for the future, and what I do now will make things easier in the future. You see, you just don't know if you will have time later, you don't know what problems will come up. Who knows what will happen in the future eh? So, plan ahead."

It was good advice, advice that she had followed all her life since. And knowing this she knew exactly what she would find.

Off to one side of the kitchen was a metal lined walk-in store cupboard, inside she found tins of meat, beans and all manner of preserved vegetables. There were packets of dried goods; beans, vegetables, dried milk and fruit, all still sealed. There were tins of tea and coffee and glass jars of sugar. All the provisions were in good condition with no sign of mould; she checked the 'best before' dates, and as she expected, all had plenty of life left. The metal lining had done its job and kept out rodents.

There was also a water filter machine with boxes full of bio filters that would make the well water safe to drink. There were more advanced filters that fitted in a small, hand-held pump system that her uncle used to use when he was away from the farm all day. There were fast moving streams all over the farm and he could just fill the pump with this water, pull the handle to pressurise the device and within seconds have water that was perfectly safe to drink, thus removing the need to carry heavy containers with him all the time.

This larder was well stocked – very well stocked indeed, with a lot of preserved food, in fact the shelves had a huge variety. She was curious, if her uncle and aunt had expected to return, then they would have soon been able to feed themselves with fresh food.

"So why is there so much preserved food?" she asked herself.

She closed the door and went to the back door of the kitchen and made her way outside. At the other side of the kitchen garden there was a brick building that housed a gas-powered electricity generator. There was no mains power supply in this region, so all farms had to have generators. Her uncle had built his onto a shock-mounted frame with stout springs that acted as dampers to prevent vibrations from transmitting into the floor of the solid double lined brick building. No one wanted to put up with the drone of the generator all day long and she remembered that there was hardly any sound when it was running, just a quiet hum that was not unpleasant.

Around the back of the generator house was a metal cage that sat on the north face and was always in shadow, in it were twenty or so large gas bottles and a few smaller ones, all of which still had their outlet plugs in place, meaning that they were likely to still be full; enough for many months, though she doubted whether she would be staying too long.

She dragged a gas cylinder into the generator room and hooked it up, she opened the valve and watched the gas pressure gauge twitch and settle on 'Full'. Then she turned on the ignition switches in the correct order and cranked the starting handle. In a tribute to her uncle's policy of forward planning and fastidious maintenance, the generator started immediately, and she saw that a couple of lights had come on in the house. She stepped out of the generator room, shut the heavy double doors and listened; the generator was barely audible.

She smiled to herself, pleased that she had remembered the start sequence that her uncle had shown her all those years back. She would allow herself to reminisce later, but it would be dark soon and there was still important work to do. She reminded herself that by now, they should have worked out where she was heading, and it was not if they came for her, but when they came for her. She thought that given the passage of time since her escape, it was unlikely that any helicopter forces would be assigned to a search this far out west, they would almost certainly use a standard troop transport vehicle. This was yet another gamble, but a pretty safe one.

The only way into the farm by land was down the track, and the entrance off the road was not visible as the small copse on the bend in the track close to the road blocked the view. Her uncle had set up a simple electrical circuit that would warn of any vehicles approaching. A few metres from the road, before the bend in the track and off to one side, there was a small box mounted to a post; in it was a microphone. There was a cable in the ground that ran all the way back to an amplifier and speaker in the kitchen.

When she was a little girl, she would delight in speaking into this to announce her arrival whenever she came to stay. She had noticed that the box was now overgrown with brambles, but there was no apparent damage and there was no reason to expect it not to work. She was confident that the system was not broken, and now that she had power, she switched the amplifier on and turned up the volume. A few crackles later, she could clearly hear the rustling of leaves and the chirps of birds. This would give her about six minutes warning of anything travelling down the track.

The sun was low in the sky, she closed the shutters on the windows and as she did so, she noticed that the heart shaped hole in the centre of every shutter had been hastily covered with a piece of plywood, meaning that come the morning, no light would come in, but then again, at night no light would go out either. With all the shutters closed, she could have all the lights on, and no one would know she was there. This aroused her curiosity again.

She turned on a tap and water spluttered out, it was cloudy and slightly discoloured, but quickly ran clear as the filters in the system did their job, but though it was running clear, the water came from a ground source close to the farm, and her uncle had told her that to be certain of being safe, never to drink this water unless it had been boiled, even though it had passed through a bio filter, as these didn't have the finer secondary filter of the field units.

An electrical board on the wall housed a current output meter from the generator and circuit breakers that controlled power to various parts of the building. She flicked on 'kitchen', 'hall way', 'bedroom' and 'bathroom', and each time noted that the metre needle dipped slightly before returning to its original position. Then she turned on the hot tap, not surprisingly the water was cold and very dirty from sludge that always builds up at the bottom of a hot water tank when it's not used for a while, and it was several minutes before the water ran clear. She turned off the tap and flicked the breaker marked 'Immersion heater'. The current meter needle dropped by four amps and stayed there. The contact breaker stayed on which meant the heater element in the hot water tank was working correctly.

Next to the electrical board were two large rechargeable flashlights. Red LEDs flashed to show that they were both charging. She removed each one from its cradle and switched them both on, they glowed dimly, but at least this proved that they worked. She replaced them; the LEDs would turn green when they were fully charged.

In no time at all, the green LED flashed on one of the torches. The light outside was fading fast, so she took the torch and went outside to get a gas bottle. She dragged one of the smaller gas canisters up to the back door and connected it into the supply for the kitchen then made herself a cup of black tea and fixed herself a meal of rice and beans with some tinned ham. While she ate, she pondered over the unusual things she had seen here, the shutters and the amount of preserved food. While looking in the store cupboard she had noticed that along with some generic pain killers, anti-inflammatory drugs, anti-histamines, antiseptic creams, plasters and all the other contents of a basic first aid kit, there was a packet of multivitamins, which she thought was a bit odd, considering her uncle's family would have had a perfectly balanced diet. However, she knew that despite her time with Daria, her diet had been poor for a while, so they would come in useful and she took a couple.

It was completely dark now and she needed to sleep. She felt drawn to her old room and at first glance was not surprised to find it exactly as she had left it. But the more she looked, the more curious it was. The furniture was all in the same place, as were the pictures on the wall. The carpet was the same and the room had not been redecorated. The bed was unmade, but with sheets and blankets in one vacuum bag and a pillow in another to keep them fresh.

On the dresser was a washbag with toothpaste, a toothbrush, a flannel, soap, some sanitary products, shampoo, deodorant and a large pack of toilet rolls. In fact, everything that she needed and all new and still unwrapped. Pulling open a drawer she found towels, also in vacuum bags. She opened the wardrobe, in it were several sets of very practical clothing – military style cargo jeans, shirts, jackets – all suitable for prolonged periods outdoors and in all weathers. There was underwear, again all new and in storage bags, there was even a few pairs of new boots, the kind needed for walking over rough ground. There were several sets of identical clothes and boots that were in different sizes and it would not be hard to find a combination that fitted her.

"Oh uncle," she said softly. "You were always talking about planning ahead, but when you left, you weren't planning to come back, but you knew that I would."

A warm feeling flooded through her; the thought of her uncle and aunt's foresight in preparing everything for her despite the stress that they were under as they prepared to flee the country.

The speaker in the kitchen had a long extension cable and she was able to move it to her room. She doubted that they would come at night, but it was better to be safe. She made the bed, then selected some of the clothes that she would wear the next day. She had a shower and settled down into bed. The sounds of the night coming from the speaker didn't bother her, she found it calming; and the thought of all the creatures out there living their lives oblivious to the chaos and destruction of the human world, put things into perspective. Sleep came easily.

****

"Police in Balun have reported a carjacking, sir," said the lieutenant.

"So what, they must have hundreds of car jackings every year, why are you telling me about it? It's a matter for the Balun police," grumbled Valerian.

"It happened near the south railway station, sir. A witness – the ticket officer – said that a woman read the timetable and appeared to be concerned about the lack of a westbound train, the woman's description is similar to the one who committed the carjacking, sir."

"Again, so what?" snapped Valerian.

"The woman's description matches our fugitive, sir."

"You mean a woman with dark hair, brown eyes in her late twenties / early thirties, average height, average build. Like thousands of other women in Balun," said Valerian sarcastically.

"The car was later found abandoned at the northwest station, sir, and a woman of the same description bought a westbound ticket. The ticket officer there remembers her clearly as she was the only person heading west. That was two days ago, sir," the lieutenant persisted patiently.

Valerian sighed. "I assume that there is a point to all of this, so get to it," he said gruffly.

"Sir, Peterman's file had two parts, one had military details, and one a bullet point information sheet. Before the files were deleted, the arresting officer who discovered Malaya's body, had downloaded the bullet point version of the file which had tactical information along with a photograph. We thought that this was the only information we have, but there was another file which had detailed personal information. This was also deleted."

"So how do you know about it then?" Valerian's usual irritation subsided as he reminded himself of his Lieutenant's efficiency.

"I took the liberty of looking through Malaya's computer. It appears that she had downloaded and saved the personal file, sir."

"Did she now? That is a clear breach of regulations," said Valerian, fighting hard to control the sudden smug feeling and not let it show. 'Indiscipline' he thought, this was something else to damage Malaya's reputation when the time came to confront the army council. "But how does it help us?"

"It tells us that Peterman had relatives that lived on a farm in the remote west of the country and that in her youth, she regularly stayed with them. They abandoned the farm some years back, leaving the country and defecting to the enemy, sir."

Valerian thought for a minute. "Farms out west were at best few and far between, and all were abandoned years ago. There's been no military activity in the west from either side, so there's a good chance that buildings will be intact and there may even be clean water. No one lives there anymore, so my guess is that if she was the carjacker and did get on the westbound train, then she will be hoping to hole up for a few weeks somewhere familiar before making her move southwest."

The lieutenant nodded in agreement. "Sir, she must have had somewhere to stay in Balun, do you want me to find out if anyone had harboured her?"

"No, it will take too long, and we would undermine the army if it became public knowledge that she had been allowed to escape, and more importantly, how she had escaped. There are still elements within the civilian population that oppose the army and are against the war. And there are also far too many journalists sympathetic to their view that we haven't dealt with yet – but their time will come," said Valerian with an air of menace, then he paused and thought for a few more moments.

"We need to keep this low key. Find out where the farm is, and then we'll go there. We'll take a couple of squads of recruits from Training Camp North, and they'll need to be armed, don't tell them what they need to be armed for, say that it's a training exercise." Valerian smiled as he thought about capturing Astrid. "Arrange the troop transport from Training Camp North to bring the recruits here along with their training sergeant. We'll travel with them."

"Very good, sir."

Valerian stood up and studied the map of Correla, tracing an arc from the east gate of the Kandalan Base out and northeast through the Phaal region, on up to Balun then out west.

"I underestimated her," he whispered to himself. "She had me looking in completely the wrong direction."

The lieutenant pretended not to hear this rare admission of fallibility.

"One more thing, sir. I found an encrypted USB stick in Malaya's office, and I used the decryption tool on my computer and was able to break the encoding. You should also know that I discovered that General Malaya had a file of her own on Peterman. There are various documents speculating on Peterman's private life etc. General Malaya seemed very concerned with the woman's sexuality for some reason. There were several image files with the pictures of Peterman enlarged and enhanced. The file log showed that it had been viewed many times. It seems that she had a fixation with the enemy officer."

Valerian had not shared with his Lieutenant his discovery that Malaya was a lesbian and decided not to do so now. His one fear was that Peterman's confession of a sapphic relationship with Malaya would be dismissed as just another story she will invent during her interrogation to end her torture, and Malaya's reputation would remain intact. Now he will have documentary evidence to back it up.

After the lieutenant left, he lit a cigarette and sat back in his chair feeling self-satisfied that things were finally going his way. He blew a large cloud of smoke up into the air and stared deeply into it.

"Soon, very soon, I will have destroyed both of you," he said quietly to himself.

****

She woke at first light; there were no clocks to tell her the time, but she knew that at around this time of year that if the shadow of the edge of the farmhouse was parallel to the driveway, then it was about six thirty. She remembered being told by her aunt how to tell the time throughout the day by using the shadows of the buildings. She washed and got dressed, then went to the kitchen and made herself a breakfast of tinned potatoes, sweetcorn and the rest of the tinned ham. As she ate, she pondered her options; just how long could she afford to stay here.

Throughout her time in Balun, she had kept a close eye on the newspapers, looking for any mention or picture of her, there had been none. It had been nearly three weeks since her escape from the Kandalan Base and she was hopeful that her apparent escape route through the east gate then southeast through the country had been enough of a misdirection. By now searches would have been called off there. Before she got on the train, she had taken one last look and a couple of newspapers, there was nothing, but she had been seen in public, stolen a car allegedly at knifepoint, with the victim having a clear view of her face and spoken to two different ticket clerks at railway stations.

As a child, she often accompanied her uncle and aunt to farmer's markets in the region, she was known to many of the other farmers and their families, but even though that was years ago and almost all of the farms were now abandoned, someone might still remember her – the Correlan Army had a special way of making people remember things. She had to consider the possibility that if had she been recognised by anyone in Balun on that last day, a pursuer might be able to work out where she was heading.

If by chance a pursuer had been at Balun North Station and got an ID from the ticket clerk even on the day she left, it would take time to work out where she had headed. They would then need to get a squad together and arrange transport. Railway would be out of the question, so a troop transport truck would be needed. The road west was notoriously poor and if, as she suspected, the squad was drawn from the Kandalan Base, the truck journey would take at least two days. She would allow herself three days before moving on.

Despite this, she needed to have a plan to deal with any hostiles should they suddenly appear. There was the ubiquitous farmers' favourite, handy for pheasants and rabbits, a double-barrel shotgun and about fifty rounds of 12-gauge ammunition, this was hard-hitting at close range, but loading and unloading was cumbersome and way too slow; they would have fully automatic Nagler assault rifles and she wouldn't stand a chance against these. There was a point two-two calibre hunting rifle with a box of one hundred rounds that her uncle had shown her how to use and kill rats with. This was an old bolt action rifle that used long round ammunition and was in itself quite hard hitting; a well-aimed shot to the throat where there was no armour would be effective. But again, reloading a bolt-action rifle would be slow and no match for the trooper's weapons, though it would be better than nothing.

She cleaned and oiled the rifle and checked that the barrel was clear, then loaded one round, went outside and found an old rusty bucket and set it on a fence post. She walked back about twenty-five metres and fired a test shot, the bullet hitting the bucket and passing through both sides. She loaded another round and fired along the track towards to road and saw dust kick up about two hundred and fifty metres away. If she could shoot and move, then she would have a slim chance, providing that a small squad would come for her, but only if the squad was small. There were no other weapons, a bomb would be a better choice. But she didn't have a bomb – yet.

A little way from the farmhouse was the main barn that was used to store grain; her uncle had designed this himself and it was unusual in that it had what was effectively a basement. The original idea had been to have the grain stored in one-ton tote bags rather than piled up on the floor, and once the harvest was in, they would be emptied one-at-a-time through a hatch in the floor where equipment could screen and process the grain into a packaged premium product which would emerge on a conveyor belt ready to go straight onto a lorry.

He did his sums and reckoned that even while his investment was being paid off, he could turn a profit of an extra forty dhat per ton. So rather than have to pay for another building he combined the storage and processing.

And he would have turned a profit if the central planning committee hadn't reduced then frozen the price of wheat. Fortunately, he hadn't committed to the purchase of the screening equipment, so all that was left now was a big barn with a hole in the middle of the floor and what looked like catacombs underneath.

Astrid looked at the barn and its relationship to the farm track. Her uncle had bricked up the hole where the product was to have emerged, and it was impossible to tell from the outside that there was a basement. The main roller shutter was padlocked shut so the access door to one side of it would be the only way in. She grabbed a torch then went to the barn, took the lock off the side door and went inside. It was empty and almost completely dark, with the only light coming from some translucent panels in the roof, most of which were completely covered with moss.

The stillness of the air and the shafts of light gave the place an eerie feel. It took a few moments for her eyes to adjust to the low light and even then, it was hard to see into the corners of the barn, despite the brightness of the torch beam. Gingerly, she moved forward to locate the hole in the floor, and as she suspected, it was almost impossible to see. She could make this work. She lifted the planks of wood that made up the hatch and dropped them into the underfloor area, leaving a hole just over a metre square, then went back to the house.

In the kitchen storeroom were two, twenty kilo bags of flour, she slit open the tops and felt inside, the flour was still fine and free flowing. In the farm workshop, she found some oxy-acetylene welding equipment with two full cylinders of oxygen, a workshop inspection lamp with a large, old-fashioned incandescent bulb, a long mains extension lead, a can of kerosene, some rag and some hose. She dragged all these components into the warehouse, and working by the light of a torch, positioned them in the far corners of the barn, furthest from the door, one set on each side. A set being one oxygen cylinder and one bag slit open with a hose from the cylinder pushed into the flour. She hung the lamp on a hook on the far side of the barn, with its cord running down to the basement, she smashed the bulb and wrapped a cloth around the exposed filament, then soaked it in fuel. She now had a bomb, and if they came for her, all she would have to do was get them all inside. She left a torch by the side door and went back to the farmhouse.

She found a map in her uncle's office and spread it out on the kitchen table and quickly located the three hill peaks that she needed to head for. There was over two hundred kilometres to go, and after thirty or so kilometres, the road petered out to a rough track and soon after that the track disappeared into rough scrubland, leaving only the paths trodden by the cattle that used to be farmed there, where the land was too rough for arable farming.

Getting to the rendezvous point would be too difficult on foot. Her uncle's four by four was parked in one of the barns, though even in a sturdy off-road vehicle like his, it would be hard going and slow. But then again, her uncle used to have a motorbike.

She found it at the back of the farm workshop. It was a three-fifty, four-stroke, air-cooled two-cylinder trail bike with thick knobbly tyres, a narrow frame and high, wide handlebars; perfect for off-road use. The air intake and exhaust were mounted high to enable the bike to be safely ridden through waterways, and her uncle had fitted a large box on the back to carry provisions for when he travelled the perimeter of the farm. The keys were still in the ignition, she turned them, and not surprisingly, nothing happened. A few minutes of tinkering later had the battery out, on the bench, and hooked up to a charger.

She removed the spark plugs and cleaned them, then put a small amount of oil in each cylinder and gently cranked the engine to lubricate the pistons before replacing the plugs. The access panel to the air filter popped off easily, exposing the corrugated paper which looked new and unused – something that didn't surprise her. At the bottom of each carburettor was a fuel drain plug; she turned the tap on the fuel tank then opened the plugs to flush out any water that may have condensed over time. Some sludge dribbled out and soon the fuel ran cleanly.

There was a can of fuel, along with a bottle of additive that stopped fuel from deteriorating, this was nearly empty, and she guessed that it had already been added to the can of fuel. She emptied the can into the bike's fuel tank, filling it about half way – though she had no idea how far this would take her. She checked, adjusted and lubricated the drive chain, injected some oil into the clutch and brake cables, pumped up the tyres and checked the gearbox oil then went inside to prepare a pack for when she needed to leave.

After about two hours, the needle on the charger dropped a little, indicating that the battery was nearly full. She placed it back in the bike and got on. She turned the ignition key; a red light came on. She turned on the fuel and kicked the starter. It took four heavy kicks before the engine spluttered into life; the engine ran for a few seconds belching out thick blue-grey smoke then cut out. One more heavy kick and the engine started, and this time kept running with the exhaust smoke quickly clearing. The exhaust was efficient, and the bike was much quieter than she expected. She got on, pulled the clutch lever, kicked the bike into first and did a practice loop of the farmyard, running halfway up the drive and back to check that the brakes and gear change were working properly.

"You never forget how to ride," she said to herself as she parked the bike in the workshop.

It was too late in the day to leave now, even on the motorbike she would not get far before it was dark. She would stay one more night then leave in the morning.

The Barn

The truck turned off the road and stopped just short of the bend, with the occupants unaware that they had passed the microphone. Astrid heard them immediately, it was just gone quarter to ten in the morning, and to get here this early they must have been traveling through most of the night. They would be tired and edgy, and this was dangerous. She ran upstairs, grabbed her uncle's binoculars, and standing well back in a dark corner of the bedroom, trained them on the bend in the track. She kept the windows closed so that reflections from the window would hide the glint from her lenses. She saw a flash in the undergrowth in the copse; it was from the lieutenant's field glasses.

She ran downstairs then out of the front door, and walked slowly and nonchalantly towards the barn, stopping a couple of times, pretending to check something. She was certain that she had been seen, and certain that they would not be aware that she knew they were there. Once inside the barn she grabbed the torch, but even with this she had to pause for a few seconds to allow her eyes to adjust to the light, then she quickly moved to one far corner and turned on the valve to one of the oxygen cylinders, then ran to the other side and turned on the second cylinder. The hoses in the bags of flour were soon blasting out jets of the fine dust unseen in the darkness. She doused more fuel on the rag over the lamp, then moved into position and waited.

"She's gone into the barn; she hasn't seen us," said the lieutenant as he got back into the truck.

"Good," said Valerian. "Move on down, and keep the engine quiet," he said to the driver.

The atmosphere in the cab suddenly got very serious; the lieutenant checked his sidearm, pulling the magazine on his Nagler nine-millimetre pistol, checking that the rounds were correctly loaded, then slid it back into the weapon, cocked it to chamber a round, flicked the safety on and put it pack into its holster. The sergeant checked his pump action shotgun, then opened the hatch to the troop compartment.

"Load up and get ready for combat, and if any of you little shits open fire before I give the order, I'll personally blow your stupid fucking brains out of your stupid fucking heads, got that?" he snapped to the troopers who were raw recruits with only a couple of month's training.

Nerves were getting the better of some of them and he was worried. He briefed them on what they had to do and how they had to form up once inside and hoped that one of them wouldn't get trigger-happy. Experience had shown him that once one fires, they would all open up.

The truck driver killed the engine and let the vehicle coast silently to a halt a hundred or so metres from the barn. Valerian was impressed but said nothing. The sergeant gestured to the troopers to get out and put his finger to his mouth to make sure they understood to keep quiet. They jumped down and quickly and quietly moved towards the door. Again, Valerian was impressed at just how well trained and professional they already were, this time he nodded his approval to the sergeant.

Astrid had prepared her ground well. The only direct light came from a single roof panel that had been kept clean by rainwater running over a copper fitting then flowing down over the glass. The minute amount of copper ions in the water acted as a bleaching agent keeping the glass clean. All the other panels were covered with moss and dirt, giving the whole warehouse a dingy feel with just one shaft of bright light cutting to the floor through the fine airborne dust motes. The shutter was locked down with a couple of padlocks, so the only way in was through a door on the other end of the warehouse next to the main shutter. The Correlan Army was not known for its subtle tactics in missions such as this. They would come through the access door.

She had heard them coming and positioned herself behind the shaft of light, just far enough in the beam so that she could be seen, but not fully illuminated. She heard voices, then the door burst open and the men poured in, fanning out to form a broad arc, some kneeling, some standing, all with their weapons aimed and ready, she heard the clatter of safety catches being released. There were fifteen troopers, a driver, a staff sergeant and a lieutenant, all wearing full combat uniforms with the crude but effective heavy steel and canvas body armour and helmets with visors that covered their eyes.

The troopers had the standard issue Nagler nine-millimetre automatic assault rifles; powerful and destructive with their hollow point ammunition that could tear bodies apart. Fragmentation grenades hung in pouches on their vests. The sergeant had a combat shotgun, no doubt loaded with flechette cartridges, each of which was loaded with sixteen hardened steel darts designed primarily to penetrate body armour and devastating on an unprotected body. The lieutenant levelled a 9mm Nagler automatic pistol, in all certainty also loaded with its usual hollow point ammunition, far more accurate than the 12.5mm and every bit as effective.

Astrid eyed them all carefully, fixing her gaze on each man in turn, they were armed for combat, not an arrest mission. They were all clearly nervous despite their superior numbers and firepower, and she would have to be careful not to spook any one of them into opening fire. Once that happened, they would all loose off. There was an eerie silence, then finally, as she expected, Valerian walked through the door into the barn. He stood at the centre of the arc of men wearing just his staff officer's uniform. No combat clothing, no body armour and only his holstered sidearm. Astrid stepped into the shaft of light.

"Oh my, how very dramatic," said Valerian sarcastically as he straightened his tunic.

"Captain Astrid Peterman—"

"Colonel Astrid Peterman – Major Colonel to be precise." She deliberately interrupted Valerian to irritate him, knowing that he would not have known that this wasn't her real rank. It was intended to confuse him and he would have questioned what else he didn't know about her. It worked.

"Major Colonel Astrid Peterman," he sneered. "I am General Valerian of the Correlan people's army, and you are under arrest, come peacefully and you will not be harmed, resist and my men will hurt you." He emphasised the '*will hurt you*' and clearly enjoyed the menace in the understatement.

She knew who he was; intelligence had created a substantial report on him which used words such as 'narcissistic', 'egotist', 'ambitious' and 'self-centred' in his personality profile and it also defined him as a risk taker. She had correctly surmised that he would want to be the one to track her down. This was good, and it was highly unlikely that he would have informed anyone else of his mission, thereby ensuring that the prestige associated with her capture would be his and his alone.

"I thought that there was a rigid order that I am to be taken prisoner alive and unharmed and that no one was to break that rule."

Valerian resisted the urge to tell her that he wanted her alive, so she could tell the army council the dirty little secret of how she was able to get so close to

Major General Malaya. But she might say something, then one of the men might repeat it and steal his thunder. No, it was better that she didn't suspect that he knew.

"That was true, but Major General Malaya gave that order to protect her aide, Captain Krall and you know all too well that she does not need protecting any more. And Malaya is no longer 'active' in the army since you killed her," he said, raising his voice to near shout.

"So, I give the orders now and I am free to modify existing orders as I see fit. I will take you alive and relatively unharmed because I want to hear your screams as you suffer days of excruciating torture. I want to see your face as they flay the skin off your back and pull out your fingernails. I want to watch cigarettes being stubbed out on your chest. I want to see your body stiffen as electricity burns its way through you. I want to be present when your shattered body is finally dragged into the great square of the people and you are forced to confess your sins for all to hear before your public execution. I want to see the look on my people's faces as you finally die in agony, hanging from the great execution frame by a wire around your neck. But make no mistake I will take your head back in a box if need be."

Astrid straightened her body and ignored the boorish bluster intended to cow her, it failed. It failed because it was what she wanted him to say. She wanted him to massage his own ego by trying to intimidate her and thereby lull himself and his men into a false sense of superiority.

She looked at each man in turn. "If you leave now, I will not pursue you, you have my word on that." She paused briefly. "But if you stay, I will kill you all. You have my word on that."

A couple of the young troopers laughed and scoffed contemptuously.

"She's having a fuckin' laugh. Eighteen guns pointed at her, she don't stand a chance," one of them said quietly.

The staff sergeant looked nervous, he gestured to the men to fan out a little more. A cold shiver ran down the lieutenant's back, beads of sweat formed on his brow. He had done his research, he had read the bullet point report printed by the arresting officer back at the Kandalan Base and he knew how resourceful she was, and he just couldn't see how she would be able to defeat them all. But there was something about the barn that he didn't like, something was wrong.

For a moment Valerian was incredulous, but soon regained his composure. "Your arrogance will be the death of you."

232

"And your stupidity will be the death of you and your men," she replied forcefully.

He turned to the sergeant. "Aim at her feet."

The barrel of the combat shotgun dropped a few degrees. Valerian turned back to face Astrid.

"This weapon has a new charge; we call it sickle shot. Loads of little razor-sharp crescents that were designed to cut through and destroy electrical wiring harnesses, but we found that they are very good at ripping flesh away and leaving just the exposed bone, as some of the prisoners of war found out during testing. Oh, they seemed to find it most unpleasant."

He was provoking her, he wanted her to react. She resisted. He raised his voice to a shout. "So, I say surrender or face the consequences."

"Okay," said Astrid, as she raised her hands and took a couple of paces forward. The men visibly relaxed. A couple even lowered their weapons, Valerian didn't notice, he was too taken aback with the sudden change.

"It is a bit too dusty in here for my liking anyway," she said, matter of fact.

At that point, Astrid placed her arms across her chest and hopped forwards with both feet. Standing in the beam of light had been partly for theatrical effect, but the real reason was that the men would focus on her, and the hard contrast between her illumination and the dark surroundings was such that they would have been unable to see the slight change in floor level.

The lieutenant immediately realised what she meant and why the room felt wrong.

"Don't shoot," he yelled. "There's dust in the air, look."

He gestured up towards the shaft of light where there were now enough flour particles to make swirling patterns that were clearly visible.

Astrid crashed through a layer of cardboard that covered an open access hatch and fell three metres onto the pile of sacks that she had positioned earlier.

"Get her you fools," screamed Valerian. The troopers rushed forward.

With her feet together and knees bent, she rolled to the side just the way that the parachute instructors had taught her. In one clean movement, she rolled up onto her feet and dashed for the alcove, flicking a switch as she ran past. She grabbed a large sack from a large tub of water she had prepared and crouched down inside the cast concrete arch, covering herself with the wet sack, then put her fingers in her ears opened her mouth and breathed out.

Above her, the men were nearly at the hatch when a flash caught Valerian's eye. On the far side of the room there was a bright glow just beneath the paraffin-soaked rag. He couldn't see the rag, only the glow and instantly realised the danger.

"Get out…" he shouted, but too late. The glow from the twisted filaments of the broken light bulb became brilliant white and ignited the rag which in turn detonated the dust in the air. And in that instant, the whole warehouse became an enormously powerful bomb. The elevated levels of oxygen created a blast that was bigger, with the over-pressure sustained for longer and was much hotter than an ordinary dust explosion.

The lucky ones died instantly as their bodies were picked up by the shock wave and smashed against the concrete pillars, the unlucky ones died slowly as they were blasted though the wooden walls out of the building, every internal organ ruptured and their uniforms on fire. The blast wave picked up Valerian and slammed him against a horizontal bar that broke his back. The staff uniform he was wearing had no armour with its associated belts and buckles and the force of the explosion ripped off all of his clothes, breaking his arms in the process. He slumped to the ground unable to move, screaming as all the hair on his body burned in the oxygen rich atmosphere.

A few minutes passed, during which time she heard the shrieks of the men as they burned. A couple of grenades exploded in the heat putting those troopers out of their misery, and slowly the pitiful cries of the dying men faded. The wet sack had protected her from the flash that burst down through the open access hatch and ripped through the basement area, but the shockwave had hit her hard, knocking her down onto her hands and knees.

Dazed and winded, she looked around; small flames flickered from what little there was to burn. She found the old wooden ladder she had used earlier; this too had been protected by wet sacks. With it propped against the hatch, she climbed up to the devastated floor of the warehouse. The thin walls had all gone along with most of the roof, and the concrete uprights and steel roof bars gave the appearance of being in some kind of huge mechanical ribcage.

Several charred bodies lay around the edge of the building, twisted and contorted from the impacts. A couple were laying on their backs, the heat from their burning uniforms had made their bicep muscles contract pulling their forearms up and turning their hands into blackened claws. It was unpleasant to go around and check all the bodies, but she has seen things like this before and

234

had to make sure they were all dead. If they knew they were about to die, Correlan soldiers were trained to play dead and wait until an enemy approached then pull a pin on a grenade with their last bit of strength.

There was a low moan from one body; someone was still alive. She walked over to the charred naked body. It was Valerian, he was laying on his back. The body armour that the other men had been wearing had crushed their chests when the blast hit them, then had gone on to hold the flames as their bodies burned, the thick canvas acting as a wick as their body fats melted in the heat. The light clothes that valerian had been wearing had been ripped off and prevented him from being burned alive, this had saved him – for now.

"Help me," he gasped, wincing as the blackened skin around his mouth cracked open and clear fluid seeped out.

"No."

He let out a guttural groan, straining to form words and flinching from the pain as he did so.

She looked down at him. "You will die from these wounds, but not quickly. Even if you lived…" She kicked one of his legs; a layer of skin the size of a man's hand slid off his thigh. Watery pink fluid flowed freely from the wound. This should have been unbearably painful, but Valerian didn't react. "Even if you lived, your back is broken; you are paralysed from the waist down and your arms are smashed. You have one hundred percent burns to your body. Even if I wanted to help you, infection would kill you in a couple of days, there'd be nothing I could do to prevent that."

She bopped down beside him. "Now I could leave you for the animals tonight, an easy meal for the wolves maybe, but I must go, and you have something that I need."

She tugged at his still warm dog tags. He gasped at the pain that it caused and glared up at her. One of his eyelids had burned away and the eye was opaque from the heat and useless, but the piercing blue of his iris and clear white of his other eye was in stark contrast to the charred blackened skin of his face.

She let go of the dog tags and stood up. "I don't have a pair of wire cutters, so you know what that means, don't you!"

He grunted, the pain of the burns preventing him from speaking anymore.

Laying against a wall a few metres away in a pile of ash was a leather holster. Valerian was narcissistic, like most of the army top brass, and the standard issue plastic holster for his sidearm was never going to be good enough for him, he preferred a five-millimetre-thick hand tooled leather one instead. She opened it and pulled out the pistol. The outside of the holster was burned and still quite hot, but the weapon inside had been insulated by the leather and although warm, was safe to handle. With no great surprise, the pistol was a Nagler twelve-point five millimetre automatic, an egotist like him would not have anything less. She pulled the magazine and checked that it had the usual high cavitation rounds.

She slid the magazine back in and looked Valerian in the eye. "I gave you a chance, but you didn't listen. You know my reputation, you could have left and taken your men to safety. I gave you my word that I wouldn't pursue you, but instead you stayed, so you are responsible for the deaths of your men."

She pulled back the weapon's slide, chambering a round then stood back a couple of metres training the weapon at his head, both hands on the stock, arms slightly bent, one leg out behind her. She flicked off the safety as Valerian lifted his head and turned to face her, summoning all his strength and defying the agony. "Do it, you fucking bitch," he gasped, "do it." She squeezed the trigger.

Despite being braced for the recoil, the kick of the gun knocked her back on her heels. When she regained her balance and looked back at Valerian, she saw that the round had done its job; his head had disappeared. A red triangle fanned out away from his body, dotted with pieces of skull and grey matter, blood was flowing freely from his neck. A pink mist hung in the air, making her breath taste metallic, she tried not to breathe until the light wind carried the haze out of the building. The gun was far and away the loudest she had ever handled and with her ears still ringing, she bent down to ease the dog tags out from the tattered ribbons of skin and tendons that was all that was left of his neck.

She pulled the magazine, pushed the rounds out and trod on them all, deforming them. She removed the gun slide and used it to bend the firing hammer, jamming it against the body of the gun then tossed the now useless weapon to one side, no one who found it could use it. She walked out of the building and rinsed the blood off the dog tags and put them in her pocket alongside Malaya's.

Astrid checked all the bodies and saw that most had died instantly. A few that had been blown out of the building were laying amongst the shattered wood from the barn. She took their weapons, pulled the magazines, ejected the ammunition and crushed the magazines, then removed and bent the firing pins, again, rendering the weapons useless to anyone who might come across them.

Some of the bodies had been torn apart when the grenades they carried detonated in the heat, but there were still a few live grenades. She gathered these, put a couple to one side then unscrewed the fuses on the others and dropped the grenade bodies and rounds of ammunition into a deep unused well. She pulled the pins on the fuses and chucked them away letting the small detonation fuses explode harmlessly. Her mission was over, it was time to go home.

Going Home

She went back to the farmhouse and changed into the clothes and gathered together the items that she had selected the previous night. Some of the terrain she would be travelling through would be thick, thorny scrubland and she had chosen boots that came high over the ankles, combat style trousers, a tough shirt, combat jacket and a cap that had a flap of cloth that would cover the back of her neck. She grabbed the bag she had prepared and put the two grenades in the side pocket, just in case. She had heard stories of bears further south but had never seen any. She took a map from her uncle's office and put it in her thigh pocket.

With the generator turned off and the gas cylinder disconnected from the kitchen pipe, she locked the house door and placed the key in its usual place. There would probably be smaller predators to deal with along the way; she had already rendered the troopers' Nagler weapons useless, but they would have been no use to her anyway as they were too bulky. She took her uncle's rifle, slid it into the plastic pipe that was fixed to the motorbike and snapped on a cap to prevent it getting wet if she had to cross any waterways. She picked up a box of ammunition and put that in her bag.

She dropped the bag into the carry box on the motorbike and kicked it into life. She pulled on a pair of leather gloves and rode off along the drive, she stopped as she got level with the truck and took its keys, then roared down the drive and turned right onto the road to head south. The road's lack of use beyond the farm was immediately apparent; plants had pushed their way through cracks in the concrete and some small shrubs had lifted the surface. Even so, she found that the thick tread on the tyres gave the bike excellent grip and she could maintain a high speed.

Fifteen minutes after she left, the ants found the first body, thirty minutes later the scavenging birds appeared. An hour later the foxes were ripping apart Valerian's corpse.

After an hour or so, she passed a farm that had long been abandoned. The land here was not suitable for cereal farming and all farms in the hinterland south of her uncle's had been cattle farms. Years before, and soon after Hallenberg had seized power, discontent had grown in the general population over the increasingly restrictive laws that were being passed. Hallenberg sensed this, and in a move that negated the discontent and consolidated his power, he ordered the freezing and then reduction of the price of meat.

Suddenly Correlans had all the beef, lamb, pork, chicken and any other meat that they wanted at unheard of low prices and without a thought given to the farmers who were producing the meat. The central planning committee had already assumed control of animal feed supplies, and the price of this to the farmers continued to rise. Eventually the cost of raising livestock outstripped the price that the farmers could get for the animals, and the farms inevitably closed. The Correlan public was blissfully unaware that now, all the meat they ate was imported by the government, bought at market rate and massively subsidised to allow it to be sold at Hallenberg's declared price. Such was his cult of personality that no one ever questioned the prices and believed that the low cost was due to his market reforms.

Beyond this farm, the road had seen far more years of neglect and got dramatically worse, with small trees having broken through the surface and the pressure from their roots breaking and lifting the concrete. She slowed but was still making a good speed. An hour later, the road, what was left of it, just ended. She stopped for a moment to get her bearings. To one side there was another abandoned farm, its barns collapsing in on themselves with rotten timbers exposed like the fingers of a giant hand. This had obviously been the last farm in the region so there had been no point in the road continuing. It would now be just fields and rough tracks.

Checking the map, she saw that she would soon reach a range of hills. She should be able to navigate these on the bike by following the tracks made by wild deer and she estimated that there was about fifty kilometres to go. With luck, she could reach the rendezvous point before it got dark.

A little way off there was as small stream, the weather was still quite warm, and dehydration was a distinct possibility. She took a biscuit bar from the bag along with the water filter device and the rifle – just in case. The water was slow moving and cloudy; she put the filter nozzle in the water and drew the plunger back, noting that the filter certainly took dirt out of the water as the body of the device filled up with clear water, and she had to assume that any harmful biological agents would have also been removed. She would find out soon enough on that point, she mused as she drank the water and ate the biscuit bar.

She kicked the bike into gear and moved onto the rough field, dodging the thorn bushes and was grateful for the thick combat jacket that protected her from the bramble barbs that caught in the fabric as she rode past. The plastic guards on the handlebars were also welcome, as they covered her hands and stopped them from being torn to shreds, the leather gloves were quite thin and would not have stopped the thorns. She got through the scrubland into an area that was more open but had rough terrain. She stopped for a moment to pick off the spines that had lodged in her sleeves, thorns that would have ripped her skin, were it not for the clothing she had chosen. She started out again and carefully picked her way around rocks until she found a track. She was able to increase the speed a little and stopped every fifteen minutes or so to check her map.

Four hours later she arrived at her destination; she saw the stone hut in a flat area between three distinct high hills. She took the rifle and her bag, then dumped the motorbike and walked cautiously towards the hut. Once inside, she located the box that had been placed there by Alpha squad, she opened it and entered her code. She hesitated before pressing the 'Enter' button, she was positive that the code was correct, but was also aware of the effect that the explosive would have if it was wrong. She hit the button and a light flashed once, confirming that a data burst had been transmitted.

One hundred and eighty kilometres away, the box left by Omega squad detected the transmission and started to broadcast an Arralan distress code at ten-minute intervals. Far away at their base in Arralan, Alpha team scrambled to their helicopter and were airborne within five minutes.

Deep inside Correla, a monitoring station also picked up the transmission, and an operator called over his superior. He was an intelligence officer who had come to his own conclusion that Astrid was still in the country. Without waiting for approval, he ordered two helicopter squads to the location of the beacon, with orders to apprehend anyone they found there.

Astrid sat in the hut, took the grenades and placed them on the floor, then pulled the magazine from the rifle and loaded it with the ammunition and slid it back in, pulled back the bolt and chambered a round. She checked that the safety was on, then put the weapon to one side.

The data burst that had triggered the decoy beacon had been just under a second long; these units were robust and had never failed before, so she was confident that the decoy would have been activated, but she worried that the transmission was by necessity, powerful, and however brief, it may have been detected and triangulated her position. Only time would tell, and if she had been detected by the Correlans, she would not go down without a fight.

An hour later, she heard the thump of a helicopter rotor and crouched down in the hut with her rifle at the ready. It soon became apparent that the helicopter was Arralan. She heard it set down and the sound of men forming a perimeter. She cautiously looked out. The squad leader ran to her and waved her in, signalling that the area was secure, once she was aboard, he went into the hut and activated a second code on the box. Two minutes after the helicopter took off, the box exploded, destroying the technology that could have been useful to the enemy. After an hour's flight, she was back in Arralan territory.

Half an hour later, one of the Correlan squads carefully approached the decoy transmitter that had been placed under a pile of rocks. A sergeant looked at it and saw a button marked 'Stop Transmission'. Without thinking he pressed it. The resulting explosion killed him and critically wounded two others.

****

"Mission accomplished, sir," said Astrid to Colonel DeSalva. "Here is my report." She placed a document file on the desk. "And here is the required proof."

She couldn't hide the triumphant feeling as she placed Malaya's and Valerian's dog tags on top of the file.

"Well done and thank you. The Correlans are not happy, it seems now that Malaya was one of Hallenberg's favourites. We intercepted a lot of radio traffic relating to her while you were away. As for Valerian, it seems they are not so worried about him."

"It was not an easy mission, sir."

DeSalva looked at her with a strange expression on his face. "Sending you on that mission was the hardest decision that I have ever had to make. The risk was too great, and you are too valuable to us."

She knew that it is often hard for the commanding officer to order someone on high-risk missions, where the probability of survival is slim, but this is the burden of duty for a commanding officer. She thought back to her training, when an instructor had told her,

"Always remember, that no matter how much respect you have for your commanding officer or how much respect they have for you, the commander is

not your friend, and you are not theirs. You are just a tool, just another weapon for them to use. This is how it has to be, because one day they may have to send you on a mission that they know will end in your death."

Still, DeSalva had visited her just before she left and had shaken her hand. She knew then that he didn't expect her to return, he couldn't hide the look in his eyes.

"Sir, my desire to kill Malaya was strong, and I know now that this was revenge and not the justice that I have always claimed, but my desire to stay alive was stronger. However, I do accept that in the past, my need for revenge had caused difficulties between us, sir, and I apologise for that and I…"

DeSalva waved his hand to stop her. "I know how much this mission meant to you personally, and for myself for that matter. Riedel had not only been a member of my team but had been a friend. Commanding officers are not supposed to have friends, but—"

"We are only human," she interrupted. "You said that to me ten years ago, sir. I've never forgotten it, because it makes us who we are."

DeSalva smiled, and there was a brief moment between them where the division between commander and commanded ceased to exist. "Yes, we are only human."

Astrid frowned. "There is something else, sir."

DeSalva noted the change in her expression, a serious look had come into her eyes.

"What is it?"

"I would like the army psychiatrist to give me an in-depth analysis of my sexuality, sir."

"Why?" said DeSalva, unfazed by Astrid's comment.

"The mission nearly failed, sir. It's all in the report."

"As you wish, but your mission did not fail. Whatever happened, happened for a reason. Your mission was a success."

****

Back in her quarters she was struck with a strange but pleasant feeling; she had a calmness that she couldn't quite place. She looked at her desk, the same desk that she had sat at for so many years, meticulously planning her missions, studying the targets and channelling her creativity. The corner on the right-hand side was worn away and rounded from her constant picking at it. The top layer of wood veneer was missing, exposing the fibres of the particleboard. She hadn't really noticed just how bad the damage was before. She hadn't even noticed the splinters on the floor below it and had certainly been oblivious to her actions that led to this while she was focussing on planning a mission.

"I better go and get another desk," she said, as a smile broke on her face.

Riedel

Ten Years Earlier

It had been two years since the attack at Brandon. For the first few months she did have the nightmares that the doctor had warned her of. Burying herself in studies had helped her focus on the present, but the memories of that day still loomed large in her mind.

She didn't feel mentally scarred, but there was something deep inside her, a feeling that went beyond indignation, a feeling that wouldn't go away. She wasn't angry, because she knew that holding on to anger could affect her work. Nevertheless, there was an ire simmering, she wanted to somehow strike back, but couldn't see how.

Nurse Peterman had been on shift for a couple of hours in the huge civilian hospital. She had finished her training and was now fully qualified and working in the trauma section, and so far, the day had been relatively quiet. A loud buzzer sounded, signalling that an emergency was coming in. Her team rushed to meet the air ambulance and they were surprised to see a military medevac helicopter on the pad. Two army paramedics got out and wheeled out a stretcher with a young man, about Astrid's age, in civilian clothes. She was puzzled, it was very unusual to have a military helicopter used for civilians.

His thigh was heavily bandaged, but blood had started to seep through the cloth, and he was clearly in a lot of pain.

"His name's Riedel. Gunshot wound to the femur, bone shattered by the looks of things, we did our best to patch him up on the way. We gave him as much morphine as we could, but that wore off and we couldn't give him any more," yelled the medic over the noise of the helicopter.

"You've got to take it from here, we can't wait, we have orders to leave immediately," shouted the pilot as he started to increase the speed of the rotor.

She held out her hand for documents. The medic shook his head. "There's no paperwork, sorry."

The team pushed the gurney into the hospital, turning their faces away from the blast of the helicopter. Astrid shielded Riedel's face with a blanket to protect him from the dust and grit thrown up as it took off. He grimaced with the pain at every slight bump as they wheeled him into the emergency ward but said nothing.

X-rays showed that the bullet had struck the femur but had only chipped off a piece of bone, surgery fixed this. What was of greater concern was the infection; Correlan soldiers were in the habit of pushing the tips of their bullets into the ground to pick up bacteria. The round had gone straight through, and though the entry and exit holes were relatively small with not much tissue damage, both wounds were already swollen and weeping cloudy pink fluid. Antibiotics took their time, but he was young and fit, and after a couple of weeks the wound was clean, and both flesh and bone were well into the healing process.

Astrid had been assigned as Riedel's primary care nurse and her tasks included coordinating all the aspects of treatment and recovery. She would assist him into a wheelchair to take him to physiotherapy and noted that he didn't refuse her help or try to struggle into the chair by himself. He was intelligent enough to let her do her job without any male pride getting in the way.

Physio treatments were twice a day and the second was always late in the evening. She took to sitting with him after the second session, as it was usually the end of her shift. They talked a lot, she talked about her life as a child, first in Correla and then Arralan; the tragedy of the war and the incident at Brandon that had made her want to become a nurse. He spoke quietly and calmly with an educated voice that carried authority and maturity way beyond his years. She found his voice mesmerising as he spoke of loyalty, the sense of duty that had put him in harm's way and the fact that this same sense of duty took away any fear.

Once he spoke in Correlan to tease her and was surprised that Astrid was also fluent in the language. His eloquence inspired her; more and more she looked forward to hearing him speak. At first, she kidded herself that spending time with him was just part of a therapy to aid his recovery, but deep down she knew that ever so slowly, she had fallen in love with him.

Four months passed, and the physio's work was done, he was able to walk unaided and without a limp. Then the day came for him to leave hospital, and Astrid was conflicted, she was happy that he was fit and healthy, but deeply sad as she realised that she would probably never see him again. He had said that there was nobody waiting for him at home and this was just as well as his work was dangerous. She didn't ask what he did, and he didn't tell her, though it was obvious to her that he was a spy.

A doctor signed his notes and shook his hand. "You can go home now, any problems, just come back. But you shouldn't have any."

He turned to Astrid who had come in early to see him before he went. He shook her hand, holding it for a bit longer than was really necessary. She wanted so badly to put her arms around him and hold him forever, but instead, stoically shook his hand and said goodbye. When he released his grip, he drew a small circle in the palm of her hand with the tip of his finger, giving a feeling that she felt in her heart. He looked deep into her eyes and smiled.

"Thank you for everything," he said softly. "I hope we meet again sometime."

Astrid was speechless, all she could do was nod. The tingling sensation in her hand had not subsided when he turned and left.

****

Nine months passed slowly without Riedel, but life had moved on for Astrid, though there was still no one for her to go home to and she still thought of him every day.

The alarm sounded for an incoming emergency, her heart fluttered when she saw the military helicopter on the pad.

"Shot just above the hip a couple of days ago, flesh wound, but not good. The round went all the way through but it's infected. Hollow point round, big exit wound, he's in a bad way," shouted the pilot as the stretcher was taken out.

Astrid gasped as she saw Riedel's unconscious body and the bloody bandage around his waist. She was shocked when she looked at his face, his skin was grey, cheeks hollow, dark patches surrounded his eyes. His breathing was laboured even though he was unconscious. It was bad, really bad.

In the trauma room, she cut off the bandage to reveal an inflamed and swollen entry wound. She eased him onto his side and saw the large exit wound, also swollen and fiery red. She felt a little relieved as the position of the wounds meant that no vital organs or major blood vessels had been hit. Even so, her hands shook as she cleaned both wounds, dressed them with fresh bandages then gave him an intravenous injection of a powerful antibiotic before taking him up to the ward. She stood looking down at him, fighting the tears and biting her lip as her anxiety failed to go away.

He slowly opened his eyes and reached out to hold her hand. "It was worth getting shot so that I could see your face again," he whispered.

Emotion hit her like a freight train, and for a moment, she just stood with her mouth open. "I'm not worth that pain," she said, barely able to speak.

"Yes, you are, you are beautiful, and I look like shit."

She realised that she was shaking; it was hard to stay professional. "You are very ill; we have to make sure your body can heal itself. I will be here when you wake up."

A doctor appeared; Riedel didn't flinch as a cannula was inserted in the back of his hand; his eyes slowly began to close as the doctor pressed the plunger on the syringe.

"I think about you all the time," he managed to whisper just before his eyes closed and he slipped into unconsciousness. Soon his heart rate and breathing slowed and stabilised.

"I can't stop thinking about you," she whispered as she bent down and kissed his forehead. The doctor pretended not to see.

****

He waited in the shadows, behind trees and hedges where he knew the CCTV didn't cover, he had waited there all day, hidden, unseen by all. At the back of the staff car park was an area with a big sign saying, 'Locum Doctors Only'. There was only one car. He had seen the car arrive early that afternoon and a youngish male doctor get out. The doctor had seemed to be unfamiliar with the surroundings, so he was probably new to the hospital. It was now getting late in the evening and a shift change was due.

Doctor Imran Chandra looked happy, if not a little tired, as he walked back to his car. There had been much to do today, but no major dramas. Patients seemed to like him, and although he was not supposed to react to this, it was a nice feeling to have. Staff that he had worked with so far also seemed to like him and he felt that this was a hospital that he would enjoy working at, if and when a permanent position should arise.

He was debating his future; as a locum, so far, he had been on general medical duties, but he saw himself as a consultant one day, this was his ambition.

Kidney function fascinated him, so, should he be a renal specialist, or urology specialist, though right now all he was looking forward to was a glass of Pinot Noir with his meal when he got home, then indulging his guilty pleasure of a trashy TV reality show where contestants would go on blind dates, then criticise each other live on the show a few weeks later.

He knew it was all faked and that most of the contestants were actors, but the trivial premise of the show and the clunky script that the contestants had to read helped take his mind off his work. The last thing he felt was the hammer blow to the back of his head. He didn't feel the hand on his throat choking his life away.

The assailant hid Chandra's body then took his bag with the white coat and all the other paraphernalia that a doctor needs and strode purposefully back into the hospital, signing in on the register with the usual illegible scrawl of a doctor and mumbled something about being late and the terrible traffic. The receptionist was hanging up her coat, having also just come on duty and took no real notice of him. He slipped into a rest room, changed into the white coat and exited into the main corridor, nodding acknowledgement and smiling at the staff as he made his way towards a map of the hospital. Those staff that he met, or who saw him at the map, just assumed that this handsome young doctor was very new and every bit the perplexed newcomer, bewildered by the complexity of the hospital layout as all the fresh intake of staff were.

A young female nurse noticed his confusion and approached him.

"It's easy to get lost here. What ward are you looking for?"

"Oh, I feel so very foolish, it's my first day here, and this is by far the biggest hospital I've ever been to," he said in his best upper class Arralan accent. "Six years at medical college and they teach you everything except how to read a map." He laughed, pretending to be embarrassed. "So, gunshot trauma, where will I find that?"

"They are usually put on the third floor, ward C20. Lifts are at the end of this corridor. Turn left by that coffee machine."

"Thank you, thank you very much, have a nice day." He smiled and gave her a respectful nod as he turned and left.

"And you." She was aware that she was blushing as she watched him walk away. "He's cute," she said quietly to herself.

Within minutes he was in the ward. He approached the reception desk and squirted some hand sanitiser into his palm. He rubbed the gel over his hands in the manner approved by the hospital, so as to appear to be a genuine member of staff.

"Where can I find Riedel? I just need to ask him a couple of questions," he asked the receptionist, who was still in the process of logging on to the system and was scanning through forms from the previous shift, and only paying cursory attention to him.

"He's in a side room at the end of the corridor on the left. But you won't be able to speak to him, he's in a medically induced coma," she said, not looking up at him.

"Oh, I didn't know that. Has he been able to talk to anyone?"

"No, they put him out pretty much as soon as he got here. He's been under for a couple of days now."

"Oh, okay, but I'd better just go and check his notes anyway."

A few moments after he had left, Astrid arrived at the reception. The girl behind the desk looked up at her cheerily.

"Dr Chandra has just gone to see your 'special' patient," she said, aware of Astrid's affection for Riedel.

"What for? He was checked by Dr Moreton less than half an hour ago. He was the last patient to see before he went off shift."

Just at that moment a buzzer sounded and the relay monitor from Riedel's room flat lined.

"Oh, his heart monitor must have come off again, you'd better go and sort it out," said the receptionist.

Astrid sensed that there was something very wrong. She turned and ran to the room and was just about to get there as the doctor came out.

"You're not Chandra," she shouted, then noticed some blood on his sleeve, she glanced into the room; there was blood on Riedel's chest.

He pulled out a knife and swung it at her; she had seen enough defensive wounds to know not to grab the blade and instead grabbed his wrist just below the thumb so that he could not bring the knife to bear on her arm. Instinctively she knew he would throw a punch with his left hand and grabbed that with her right hand, then, instead of the natural reaction of pushing him away, she pulled him forward and head butted him hard on the bridge of his nose, splitting it open and spraying blood onto her face, he gasped and cried out. She brought her knee sharply up between his legs; he doubled up in pain and as he did so, she let go of his hands, stepped back and kicked his feet out from under him, making him fall heavily to the ground, hitting his head on the floor. She was just about to dive onto him, when a pair of hands from a burley hospital porter grabbed her and pulled her away.

"He's killed Riedel, he's killed him. That's not doctor Chandra," she screamed.

****

Astrid sat in silence in a side room of the hospital administration section. The shaking had subsided as the last of the adrenaline had left her body. The red mark on her forehead was turning from pink to a pale yellowy blue bruise. She hadn't wiped off all of the blood from her nose, and some was still visible where it had mixed with her tears and ran down her face. Alone with her thoughts, she knew that this had changed her, she felt different inside, though she couldn't place the feeling. She wasn't angry, but at the same time she felt a deep desire for revenge.

The deaths of Bernie and Davida and all the other people at Brandon had changed her before, but despite her love for Bernie, Riedel's murder was so much harder to take, and she knew that everything about her life was now different. Her crying had stopped, that time had passed, and she now knew that she would never feel the same way about anyone ever again.

The door opened, and a military man walked in.

"My name is Captain DeSalva, I am with military intelligence." His tone was friendly and with a hint of concern. He frowned slightly. "You should know that we found Dr Chandra's body in the boot of his car."

Astrid sighed, looked down and shook her head slightly. She had already assumed that Chandra was dead, but the confirmation still hurt her.

DeSalva sat down opposite her. "I want to talk to you about tonight."

"Am I under arrest?"

"No, far from it, you are a witness, not a suspect, so you are free to walk out any time you wish, and no charges will be brought against you. I hope you don't mind, but I asked that you be kept here so that I can go over a few things with you while they are still fresh. I realise that this a hard time for you, but please hear me out; if it gets too stressful just say stop, and I will respect your wishes."

"Thank you, but I think I'll be okay."

"Firstly, is there anything you would like? A cigarette maybe?"

"No thank you, I don't smoke."

250

"I see you have water, would you like anything else, coffee, tea. Though I'm guessing you're not hungry right now."

She shook her head slightly. "I'm fine with water but thank you anyway."

He opened a folder and was ready to take notes.

"Okay. You are Astrid Peterman, a nurse at this hospital where Riedel was killed, you confronted and overpowered the assailant. Am I correct?"

Astrid closed her eyes. "Yes," she said weakly as she recalled seeing the blood on Riedel's body.

"I am sorry for the formal language, but we must establish what exactly happened from your point of view."

He noted that Astrid was sitting with her hands by her side, and usually people in this situation would have their arms crossed in front of them, it is a classic, though often subconscious, defensive position. It told him that she would be completely honest and also showed that she was not intimidated by him – something that he was hoping for.

"It's okay, I understand."

"Your shift had finished, but you stayed on to be with Riedel, because you were close to him, weren't you?" he said softly, treading a fine line between fact and compassion.

"Yes." She was surprised at how the mention of his name affected her and she sniffed back a tear. "We get assigned to a patient and some of us like to spend extra time with them. Everyone knows it goes on; it's not encouraged, but it's not discouraged either. We're not supposed to have feelings for our patients, but…" Her voice trailed away.

"We are only human," DeSalva finished her sentence. "It's long been understood that injured soldiers recover quicker and with better results when nursed by females and it is not surprising that some nurses and patients can become emotionally attached." He paused, weighing up how much to tell her. "Riedel was not his real name, and I can't tell you what his real name was. He worked for me as an undercover agent in Correla. And I think you have a right to know that he spoke of you often, his feelings for you were strong."

Astrid looked away, swallowing hard to try to clear the lump in her throat, this time unable to stop the tears; she had never experienced this depth of feeling before. DeSalva took a packet of tissues from his pocket and placed it in her trembling hand.

"I am so very sorry," he said. He waited for a few moments and avoided eye contact while Astrid calmed herself.

"Riedel had vital information about the enemy's ultimate plan, information that we are never going to know now. All that we do know is that they are prepared for a long haul, a war of attrition. We are vastly superior, both tactically and technically but are massively outnumbered. The Correlans are a fecund race, twins are common, triplets aren't out of the ordinary and they have a higher-than-normal percentage of males. In short, they can afford to lose huge numbers of men, whereas we can't. They will try to grind us down, though our intelligence-led tactics will prevent that. But as I said, there is a final plan, but we don't know what that is now."

Astrid wiped the last tears from her face and looked directly at him. "What do you want from me?" she asked.

DeSalva avoided the question, he needed her to have the background first and he wanted to wait for the right time before answering her. "The assassin refused to answer any questions until I told him that as he was not in the Correlan Army uniform and had no Correlan identification papers, that he would be tried as a spy and as he had murdered two people he would be shot. He became quite cooperative after that. Major Brigit Malaya sent him once Riedel's cover was blown. She's a hard-arsed bitch, and she's rising quickly through the ranks and—"

"I'll kill her," interrupted Astrid with a determination in her voice that went beyond bravado.

DeSalva was not surprised by this, in fact he had expected it. He nodded slightly, acknowledging her resolve. "You may get the chance, but not without some training."

"What do I need to do?" she said firmly.

Again, DeSalva delayed answering, sensing her desire, but not wishing to jump ahead too soon. "I reviewed the CCTV of your altercation; your tactics were perfect, who taught you to fight like that?"

"Nobody, I've never had a fight before."

DeSalva studied her for a moment. "Are you saying that it was all done on instinct?"

"Yes, I didn't think about what I was doing, it just seemed obvious what to do."

"The whole episode took just seven seconds. CCTV captured it from two different angles, one showed your face. I saw no fear in your eyes."

"I was not afraid."

DeSalva paused again, reading some notes and weighing up his options. "Could you kill someone in cold blood?"

"Yes." She answered firmly and without hesitation. "Yes, if the justification was there."

DeSalva read some more of his notes then looked back at her. "Since the enemy has used an assassin to kill outside of normal combat, we can do the same and it would be allowed under international law – as absurd as it is to have laws governing the organised murder of people. I am putting together a small unit and I'd like you to join it. We will be operating outside of the regular military forces and all will be answerable to me and no one else. Field Marshal D'Frey has sanctioned it within the last hour."

"Who is he?"

"D'Frey is head of the joint chiefs of staff, in other words, the most senior military officer in the country and has ultimate authority over all branches of the military. Now, back to the most pressing issue for us. Their troops are poor, little more than cattle with weapons, but some of their commanders are reasonably talented; intelligence will identify them and gather data, then we will target them and take them out, and you must realise that this means killing them. Is that something you'd be prepared to do?"

"Yes, I'll do it."

"You will get your chance with Malaya, I promise you that, but she's relatively low ranking at the moment, and there are other more senior targets that will have to be dealt with first."

"I understand."

"Okay then. You will be sent to a training camp for a few weeks, there you will learn the basics of military life. But I don't want you to be too indoctrinated into military thinking. It has a command structure that can be a bit rigid and what you will need is flexibility and be able to work independently."

He opened a file on his computer and started drafting an order. "You will be fast-tracked through basic training and then spend some time on the front line with combat troops, because that really is the only way that you and I will know if you can take the pressure of warfare. It will be hard; do not underestimate just how hard combat can be. Then you'll come back and do advanced training with special forces, where you'll learn a whole lot more, and that will be harder, much harder."

He looked at her and frowned slightly. "Combat is vile, and by its very nature, it brings out the worst in people. You will see horrible things and you will be expected to do horrible things; ghastly things that will challenge your humanity. And I need to know if you really are prepared to do all these things."

"I am," she said, then looked him straight in the eye. "...sir."

He took a document from his briefcase and placed it in front of her.

"Once you have filled out and signed this form, you will be in the military and subject to military law. For obvious reasons, you are forbidden to talk about Riedel to anyone other than me. Is that clear?"

"Yes, sir, very clear."

Training Camp

Astrid stood in line with five other recruits at the training base; all the other recruits were male. A stern sergeant marched up to them.

"I am Regimental Sergeant Major Thackery," he shouted. "I am in overall charge of your training, and at all times, you will address me as 'Regimental Sergeant Major'. How do you address me?"

"Regimental Sergeant Major," came the response in unison.

"For the purposes of training, over the next couple of weeks, the six of you have been put into a team and being in a team means that when one of you succeeds, you all succeed, when one of you fails, you all fail." He looked directly at Astrid. "And when one of you fucks up, you all fuck up."

Astrid showed no emotion at the comment. Thackery stared at her for a moment, studying her face, looking for a sign of weakness; he saw none. He turned to address them all. "As you are a team, you will all be billeted in the same quarters."

He looked at Astrid again. "Recruit Peterman, stand over there."

She moved and stood where he was pointing. He turned to the male recruits.

He slowly paced along the line of men. "This is a combat training unit and for the first time ever we have a female who will be going into front line action. All six of you will be training together, you will be eating together, you will be sleeping in the same quarters and you will be treated exactly the same. You will respect recruit Peterman's privacy. There will be no sexual contact, there will be no sexist comments or actions. Do I make myself absolutely clear?"

"Yes, Regimental Sergeant Major."

He left and a training sergeant marched them to their quarters.

****

Astrid had just finished unpacking her bag when Thackery appeared at the door.

"Recruit Peterman get into my office now," he yelled.

"Yes, Regimental Sergeant Major."

Astrid stood to attention as Thackery took a USB stick and plugged it into his computer, he selected a file called 'Body Cam Combat Compilation' then turned his monitor so she could see it. He looked at her with barely concealed irritation.

"You're not actually a recruit, are you Peterman?"

"No, Regimental Sergeant Major."

"What are you then?" he snapped.

"A volunteer, Regimental Sergeant Major."

Thackery grunted. "You have been sent here by Captain DeSalva and I have been told that I am to report your progress back to him. I have also been told that field Marshal D'Frey has personally approved it and I am not to question why I have to do this. I have no information on your background, so you can imagine, I am not very happy about this situation, but DeSalva must have his reasons and I have to respect that."

He picked up a dossier and flicked through it, reading DeSalva's request. "You are to receive training for front line operations."

"Yes, Regimental Sergeant Major."

"And spend some time with front line troops. Are you sure you want to do this?"

"Yes, Regimental Sergeant Major."

Thackery sat back in his chair. "There are plenty of women who serve in the Arralan armed forces, and some are at the front line as medics, but none are in front line combat roles." He pointed to the screen. "This is the sort of thing that you will be expected to do."

He pressed play. The video showed a furious firefight, men were yelling instructions, others were screaming in pain. A jerky image showed a Correlan soldier a few metres away, there was a flash and a bullet tore the side of his face off. The video stopped and another started; a Correlan military vehicle had crashed and the fuel tank had exploded. Men were trapped inside, and she heard their screams as they slowly burned to death.

Thackery hit 'pause', sat back in his chair and studied her for a moment, frowning deeply. "We were low on ammunition, I got a report that more Correlans were heading towards us, so I gave the order to let them burn rather than waste ammunition by putting them out of their misery.' He paused. "I will let the video run, so you can see and hear what we had to see and hear." He pressed 'Play' then sat back, studying her, waiting for her reaction.

The driver's side window smashed, and a screaming man tried to crawl out, his entire back was on fire. He got half way out then seemed to get stuck. He looked directly at Thackery and screamed the same words over and over in an obscure Correlan dialect.

"Have you any idea what he is saying, recruit Peterman?"

"Yes, Regimental Sergeant Major."

"Well, what is he saying?" he asked, slightly taken aback.

"He is saying, 'Kill me, I'm begging you, please kill me,' Regimental Sergeant Major."

Thackery was surprised, not only at Astrid's knowledge of the dialect from such a remote part of Correla but at her demeanour as she watched the video. She showed concern and a little disgust but did look not shocked.

"We had been in the field for a couple of days and had been cut off. Our mission had been to locate an Arralan reconnaissance squad. We found them, and they were all dead; all had been brutally tortured. But my decision to let these men burn was not revenge for that. Some of my men were completely out of ammunition. I had one full magazine left and we had a few grenades with us. There was open ground between us and them, if we had gone over, we could have killed that man with a blow to the head and not wasted any ammunition, but then the Correlans would have picked us off, or captured us. I couldn't let my men be tortured. Hence my decision."

He stopped the video. "It took five minutes, but no more Correlan soldiers turned up so I could have shot him." He paused to let his words sink in. "These are the kind of decisions that have to be made during a battle."

He started another video. "This is what grenades do to bodies."

It was the aftermath of a battle, the helmet cam was looking down; there were bodies without arms, without legs – some of the men were still alive. There were eviscerated bodies with all the internal organs laying on the ground. He stopped the video and glared up at her. "Do you really want to do this?" he snapped. "Do you really want to be the one who takes these men away from their loved ones forever?"

"Yes, Regimental Sergeant Major," she replied without hesitation.

He pointed angrily at her. "The Correlans use barometric bombs. Do you know what they are?"

"No, Regimental Sergeant Major, I do not."

"Just before the bomb detonates, it releases a huge cloud of an atomised high explosive. A charge ignites it and the explosive combines with the oxygen in the air and creates a massive pressure wave, far greater than a normal explosive. The general public are told that it kills by burning up all the oxygen in the air so that the victims die by suffocation. That is partly true, but they leave out the bit where a soldier caught in the blast has his body compressed, and as this affects the abdomen, the internal organs are forced out through the nearest opening. Soldiers are often found staggering around with their bowels hanging out of their arse."

He studied her again, looking for a reaction, but again, seeing none. "Some of them live for hours like that, but there's nothing that can be done for them, the damage is too great and they die. No prizes for guessing what would happen to you if you were caught in a barometric blast." He saw her stiffen and noted the look of resolve on her face. "When you stick a bayonet in someone you feel their death, you hear them crying out for their mothers. You smell their death," he hissed through clenched teeth. He leant forward and jabbed an angry finger at her. "If you have any doubts, then I want you out of this training camp now. Do you have any doubts recruit Peterman? Do you?" he shouted.

"No, Regimental Sergeant Major, I do not have any doubts."

"We shall see," Thackery grunted.

He selected another video file from a helmet camera.

"During this operation, we were ambushed by a large force and had to fall back. One of my men got separated and was hit in both legs, he was stuck and couldn't move, we were pinned down and couldn't get to him. It was late summer and there was a lot of dry grass and leaves."

He scowled and seemed to seethe with barely suppressed rage. "The Correlans fired a flare into the grass a little way off from him. The dry material caught fire straight away and started spreading towards him. We could all see what was going to happen." Anger flashed across his face. "They did it to draw us out, they knew we would try to rescue him. A couple of my men tried to reach him but were cut down."

The video image showed the ground as the helmet got turned away, but still recorded sound.

"Can you imagine what it is like to be there and watch a person burn to death and to not be able to do anything about it? Can you imagine what you would feel as you hear their screams?"

"I don't have to imagine, Regimental Sergeant Major. I have witnessed people burning to death with nothing I could do to help them. I heard their screams."

Thackery was shocked. "Where?"

"I was at Brandon during the first Correlan attack, Regimental Sergeant Major. A fuel bowser was hit, many people were burned to death."

Thackery's attitude changed abruptly. "You were the civilian girl at Brandon?"

"Yes, Regimental Sergeant Major."

"And you were the one that helped Colonel Collard's men."

"Yes, Regimental Sergeant Major."

Thackery sat silent for a few moments. "Colonel Collard had been my commanding officer. I went to see him in hospital; he told me about you."

Thackery gestured to a chair. "Please, sit down," his tone of voice now much less aggressive.

"Thank you, Regimental Sergeant Major."

He smiled and half laughed; even he was finding it tedious.

"For the time being, just call me 'Sergeant'."

"I will, Sergeant."

"Colonel Collard said that you became a nurse."

"That is correct, Sergeant, I was with the film crew, I was an actress. We were filming when the Correlans attacked." She paused and sighed. "People died right in front of me, Sergeant, they died horribly, I was the only one of the entire crew that survived. I lost two very good friends."

She swallowed hard as she recalled that day. "One of those two had her body ripped open, but she was still alive…" Her voice descended to a whisper as she fought her emotions. "An army medic found me, he said that there was nothing that could be done to save her and that she was in agony. I administered a lethal dose of anaesthetic that killed her. It doesn't matter that the law allows a mercy killing; I killed my friend."

Thackery's jaw dropped open a fraction.

She sat up straight and looked him in the eye. "After that, I went with the medic and did what I could to help the soldiers wounded in the attack. I saw how brave those soldiers were, even those who knew that they were going to die. Captain Tavares told me how the Correlans had waited until all our artillery had been removed before starting their bombardment so we couldn't fire back and that sickened me. I changed on that day and suddenly realised that all my dreams of fame as an actress were so petty and that I had to do something for my country."

"And so you became a nurse."

"Yes, Sergeant."

"So why are you here now?"

"There was another incident, Sergeant, it was instigated by the Correlans. It has changed me forever."

"What was the incident?"

"I am forbidden by law to say what it was, Sergeant, and to be frank with you, even if I could, I wouldn't want to."

Thackery sat thinking for a few minutes, digesting all that she had said and trying not to show how shocked he was.

"I don't sense anger in you, but you are clearly a driven individual. You need to keep that in check and channel it into your training. Don't let your heart rule your head."

"I won't, Sergeant."

"Dismissed."

****

"The assault course," yelled the training officer. "Welcome to two kilometres of hell. This is a test of courage, teamwork and stamina."

He pointed to a map of the horseshoe-shaped course. "There are numerous tasks to overcome, you must complete all of the obstacles, those who don't will have to keep trying until they succeed. You must all complete the course, or you will all have to do it again tomorrow. Training officers will be at each piece of apparatus and will take notes."

The first tasks were simple enough; low, narrow beams to run along without falling off. There were rope swings over muddy pits, low barbed wire to crawl under without getting snagged, and monkey bars to hang from to cross over pools of water.

"This is going to get harder guys," Astrid said to the group, as they approached a three-metre-high wall.

Jansen stood with his back against the wall, his hands cupped in front of him. Astrid took a run and jumped at him, placing her foot in his hands. She jumped up and positioned herself across the top of the wall, grabbing the guys as they came up and helping them over. Matthias was second to last and stayed on top to help Astrid pull up Jansen.

Off to one side a training officer made notes.

Next was a rope ladder up to a small platform ten metres above the ground. There was then a one-metre jump onto an even smaller platform, with no safety line or net. It was a simple task, but Mueller looked down and froze; Astrid shouted encouragement to him and eventually he made the jump. Then all that was left was the tunnel. This was the most feared of all the obstacles in the assault course.

Two, three-metre wide and two-metre-deep pools of muddy water were connected by a submerged tunnel, five metres long and just under a metre wide. Recruits would have to dive into the pool one at a time, find the entrance in the pitch black, then haul themselves through to the other pool. As one emerged, the next recruit had to enter the tunnel and would be pulled out once they reached the end. Everyone got disorientated in the murky water; panic attacks were common once a recruit was in the tunnel, and there had been one death from drowning in the past.

****

"There was an incident in the tunnel today, a panic attack. It involved recruit Peterman," said the training officer to Thackery.

"Hmm, I thought that would get her."

"No, it's not what you think, it wasn't her that had the panic attack. Haas went first then Mueller went in, he struggled a bit but was okay. She was third in, she got through okay, and Recruit Matthias was next. She waited for him to emerge, but he didn't."

"Is Recruit Matthias okay?"

"Yes, he is…" – the training officer raised his eyebrows – "…after Recruit Peterman dived back in, crawled into the tunnel and pulled him out."

Thackery's eyes opened wide.

"Matthias said afterwards that he panicked as soon as he got in the tunnel. She went into the tunnel, grabbed him and hauled him out. She was crawling backwards for over four metres, dragging a panicking man."

Thackery sat in stunned silence.

"She checked his vital signs, and once she was sure he was okay, stayed to pull out Olsen and Jansen, checked whether all the guys were okay, then got Matthias to his feet and continued on with the exercise, practically carrying Matthias until he got his strength back."

The officer left, and Thackery opened an email program, typed DeSalva's email address and wrote a report.

Tricks and Survival

It was two in the morning when the six members of Astrid's exhausted troop trudged back into the barracks, dumping their backpacks on the floor. Some of the recruits slumped down beside them, unable to keep standing. Once their eyes closed, their mud-covered faces became featureless. They had completed twenty-six hours of a non-stop cross-country route back to base, with numerous difficult obstacles to negotiate.

Thackery was there to meet them and smiled. "Well done, everyone. I know that was tough, so you'll now get a break from training. You will not need to be on parade at six am, instead just go to your next class at ten. The canteen will stay open for your breakfast."

Some of the recruits sighed with relief as they picked up their kit and trudged back to their quarters. Some got in their beds fully clothed, too tired to take their clothes off. None took any real notice as Astrid got undressed and put on fresh clothes.

"Why are you putting on fresh combat fatigues?" said Haas through a yawn.

She turned to address all of them. "I know we're all tired, but this is a trick, they're not going to let us sleep," she said, trying to instil a sense of the deception in them.

"I don't think they will be able to stop us," said Matthias as he closed his eyes and immediately started snoring.

"We've got to sleep, I dunno about the rest of you, but I'm fucked," said Muller.

She watched as they all got in bed, and though she was desperately tired, she knew that this apparent relief was just another test. She had some caffeine pills and had been reluctant to take them as she didn't want anything to assist her training, she wanted it to be all her own stamina. Once on a mission she might not be able to call on stimulants, so it was vital that she should fully test herself and to know just what she was capable of. However, the fatigue of this day and the hangover tiredness from the previous day's training meant that she would not be able to stop herself falling asleep.

She tipped a couple of pills into her hand and looked at them, these little balls of sugar each had the caffeine equivalent of ten cups of strong coffee. She hesitated, then took a glass of water put the tablets in her mouth and swallowed. Five minutes later she was wide-awake and fully alert.

"I'm going to pay for this later," she muttered to herself.

Astrid broke a glass bottle and left some of the shards on a table, placed a pillow under the blankets on her bunk then stood behind a door and waited. At four am the door quietly opened and Thackery entered. Astrid's bunk was nearest the door and he went straight to it.

"Wakey, wakey. Time for some more training," he said as he pulled back the covers, then stopped short when he saw that there was no one in the bed.

She moved towards him, he heard her and turned, she thrust her left hand towards his groin. He grabbed her hand and twisted it away from him, and as he did so she thrust her right hand up to his neck, stopping a centimetre before she touched him. He froze, realising what she had just done.

"That could have been a shard of broken glass in my left hand. I would have aimed for your femoral artery."

She looked down and saw that both of his hands were holding her left wrist.

"If I had a shard in my right hand, I would have now severed your carotid artery. In the time it has taken me to say this, you would have bled out and died."

He saw the broken bottle and a smile broke out across his face.

"Very good." He released his grip and turned to face her. "How did you know?"

"We had already done two route marches, each with assault course obstacles, a third would be pointless unless there was something else to test us at the end of it." She looked at him and smirked. "And it's not like you to be nice to us is it? Regimental Sergeant Major."

He roared with laughter, at which point the others started to wake up, scratching their heads and looking gormless.

"You still need to be on the parade ground at six."

"I'm sorry, Regimental Sergeant Major, I can't hear you, because you're dead. And the last instruction you gave us was to go to our class at ten."

He squinted at her for a few moments, then raised one finger and frowned. "Okay, just this once I'll let you have it, but never again. Do you understand me Peterman?"

"Yes, Regimental Sergeant Major."

He turned and left the room, trying hard not to show how much she had impressed him.

****

DeSalva read the report on the night's activities and nodded with satisfaction. "Anticipation, improvisation and execution. Exactly what I had hoped for."

****

Sergeant Thackery stood at the head of the classroom, then gestured for them to sit. "You will soon be put into the field for survival training. It will take two days and you will not be allowed to take any provisions with you. You will have to forage for food and find water. This lecture will show you what you can and cannot eat."

He paused and looked at the recruits.

"If you are surviving behind enemy lines, what will cause you the biggest problem?"

Olsen put his hand up.

"Search parties?" he suggested nervously.

"They will be a problem, but there is a more important issue."

He looked around the classroom at the blank faces. Then Astrid put her hand up. "Dehydration?"

"Correct. Finding clean, safe drinking water is crucial, you can go for a couple weeks without food, but only around three days without water and shorter than that if its hot. Once you start to get dehydrated, you will become fatigued, weak and dizzy. You will have a headache and chills and will not be able to concentrate. You may put this down to illness, but it is vital that you recognise the early signs. At around five percent of fluid loss, fatigue becomes extreme, you will become nauseous and very weak. Beyond this you may have seizures. It goes without saying that your ability to evade capture will be severely compromised."

Thackery placed a standard issue canteen on his desk.

"You will always have one of these, it is your friend so look after it. When you find clean water, you will naturally fill it. Do not be tempted to find other containers for water; there is a limit to how much water you can carry. Each one-litre canteen weighs just over a kilogram when full. If you carry too much water in hot weather, you will sweat more and expend more energy carrying the extra weight and this will negate any advantage. You will need to find a fast-flowing source of water – high up if possible. Look for where the animal tracks stop, then it shouldn't have too much excrement in it. You will be given sterilisation tablets, they make the water taste disgusting but safe."

Olsen put his hand up again. "What if there isn't a ready source of water."

"Drink your urine," said Thackery flatly.

A shocked groan rose from the recruits.

"If it's cloudy and thereby indicating and infection, it is not safe to drink. Clear, fresh urine has no living organisms in it, so it is sterile and safe to drink."

He looked at his class and noted the disgusted sneers. "I understand your reluctance, but at some time it may become something that you have to do to save your life. So, how do you do it?" he asked rhetorically. He shrugged his shoulders. "Simple enough. Pee into a container, tip it into your mouth and swallow."

Again, the appalled faces.

"Don't wait until you have run out of water, you want your urine to be as clear and light coloured as possible. Some of you will have seen science programs and will know that most of what you taste is actually what you smell. So, hold your nose and then all you will taste is a warm liquid that is slightly salty."

He pulled a packet of strong mints from his pocket and smiled.

"I always carry a packet of these. They help a lot! And also reduce the chance of you throwing up at the thought of what you've just done." He smirked. "After the first couple of times you get used to it."

****

After a full day's lecture on what plants, bugs, grubs and insects were edible and how to prepare them, the class went outside. The survival training area was set away from the main camp and situated in an area of woodland. It was late in the evening and there had been no meal breaks, only the occasional glass of water. Thackery called them into a group.

"I guess you're all hungry."

"Starving," said Olsen.

266

"Okay, we'll have something to eat soon, but first you need to know how to start a fire with a fire stick. Gather dry wood."

Muller put his hand up.

"Are we going to have to eat bugs? Regimental Sergeant Major."

"Wait and see."

The group set off and quickly found a large amount of brush, ranging from small twigs to large dried out branches.

"Good," said Thackery as he arranged a pile of leaves and twigs then the larger pieces to form a cone above that. He took a box from his bag and took out some fine wood shavings. "This is a fire starter, the wood shavings are impregnated with an oxidiser, it will catch fire easily, but you have to keep it dry."

He placed a small amount beneath the twigs then took what looked like a metal rod and scraped his knife along it. Bright sparks shot out towards the twigs and immediately the wood shavings caught fire. In no time the rest of the wood had caught and created a substantial fire.

"Now we just need something to eat. Wait here."

Thackery left the group and went to the back of the training hut, emerging later with a sheep on a lead.

"This is dinner." He looked at the blank faces of the recruits. "Who's going to kill it?"

The guys in the group looked more shocked than when he told them that they may have to drink their own urine at some point. Some of them took a small step backwards, Astrid stayed put and Thackery noticed.

"Come on, who's going to kill it?"

He was getting the same reaction that he always got. "What's wrong?" he said firmly. "I thought you lot were hungry." He frowned at them. "You will be expected to stick bayonets in humans, shoot humans in the face, blow up humans. This is an animal."

"We are all hungry, Regimental Sergeant Major," said Matthias. "But the sheep's done nothing to us, it's not trying to kill us, so it doesn't seem right to kill it."

"So out in the field you'd rather starve to death than kill a cutesy little Baa Lamb?" Thackery said sarcastically, his voice designed to humiliate them, then he took out his combat knife, placed it on a table and pointed to it.

Before anyone could answer, Astrid stepped forward, took the knife then stood astride the sheep. She reached forward and grabbed the sheep's muzzle, pulled its head up and slit its throat, holding the gash open to let the blood spray away from her.

"For fuck's sake, Astrid," gasped Matthias. "Of all of us, you were the last person I thought would do it."

She ignored his unintentional sexist inference as she lowered the sheep to the ground, she knew it was just shock talking. The animal's legs thrashed in a running motion, then slowed to a few twitches and stopped.

She wiped blood from the knife blade, placed it back on the table and looked down at the dying animal.

"It's not dead yet. You'll know when it is because it'll piss itself and maybe shit itself as well. So, you have to make sure you don't get any of that on the bit you wanna eat. Drinking your own urine is one thing, and I don't know about you lot, but I don't want to drink sheep's piss."

Thackery looked at her with a questioning expression on his face.

"My uncle had a farm; I stayed there many times when I was a kid; he used to take me with him on field trips that would take a couple of days. He showed me how to shoot rats, how to snare a rabbit, wring its neck to kill it, gut it and then cook it on a fire. Although his farm was arable, just growing wheat and barley, he would buy a sheep at the market and would show me how to kill it like that."

She pointed to the now dead sheep. "And he showed me how to butcher it."

Thackery gave her an almost imperceptible nod, an appreciation of his growing respect for her. He took the knife and handed it back to her.

"Recruit Peterman, please show the team how to butcher the carcass."

"Yes, Regimental Sergeant Major."

Minutes later, strips of mutton were hanging from sticks, cooking quickly from the intense heat of the flames, fat bubbling and boiling then sizzling as it dripped into the fire. The aroma of the charring meat filled the air and made stomachs rumble.

"I'll be mum, shall I?" she said with a wry smile on her face as she cut up the cooked meat and handed it around to the group. Thackery couldn't stop a smile as he took his piece.

DeSalva's going to love my report on this one, he thought to himself.

268

Weapons

The range instructor placed targets on Thackery's desk.

"Look at this grouping. Ten rounds on the 25 metre range this morning; first session."

Thackery examined the scattering of the ten holes on the half-metre square of cardboard.

"I wouldn't call that a grouping."

"But they are all on the target."

The instructor placed a second target on the desk.

"Now look at this, it's from the second session."

Thackery took a ruler and measured the cluster of holes.

"All within 100 millimetres, not bad, but all are down and to the right a little."

"Yep. Now look at this one. Third session."

All ten holes were in the centre, all within 60 millimetres and five were in the bullseye.

"This one is very impressive," said Thackery as he handed the target back. "Clearly these are from three different recruits, one of which has the makings of a marksman."

"No, they are all from the same person."

"What?" said Thackery, shocked. "Who?"

"Recruit Peterman."

Thackery's jaw dropped open. "You're kidding me."

"No, I'm not. And get this, she's only ever fired a fifty-year-old bolt-action point two-two. A farmer's gun, something with a kick so light I could fart harder. This was a nine-millimetre assault rifle. And there's something else, she was quick."

"So, it could be beginner's luck. Put her on the urban warfare range tomorrow, let's see how she gets on."

****

Astrid stood at the start of the urban warfare set, a mock-up of a town with streets, homes and shops of all shapes and sizes. Her weapon was ready, cocked, loaded and with the safety off.

The training officer opened a notepad and wrote some details down.

"This is a live firing exercise. As you make your way through the course, various targets will appear, some are enemy combatants, some will be civilians. It goes without saying that you only shoot the enemy, shooting a civilian will result in a failure of the exercise. Regardless of how they appear, once hit, the target will fall backwards. Failure to neutralise the correct target within four seconds will also result in failure of the exercise. The object of the test is for you to make it from one end of the town to the other having scored hits on all the enemy targets."

She breathed deeply to calm her nerves then entered the course. Immediately an enemy target popped up in front of her, she fired twice, and the target fell back. Two more appeared in quick succession; both fell rapidly. There was movement in her peripheral vision, she turned quickly, ready to shoot but stopped when she saw the target was of a small child. She carried on walking, crouched down and with her weapon at her shoulder, a target appeared in an upper window at the same time as one appeared on the ground on the opposite side of the road. Four shots in under three seconds dropped both the targets.

A target appeared from a side road, but it was of a woman walking a dog, but Astrid noticed that directly behind it there was a target of an enemy soldier. She dived to her left and fired, missing the civilian and knocking down the enemy. A target of an enemy soldier appeared but with a civilian target immediately behind. If this was a real enemy soldier a shot would go straight through the body and hit the civilian. Astrid ducked to her right and fired, hitting the enemy and again, missing the civilian.

Ten minutes later and after three magazine changes, she had used all her rifle ammunition; she slung the weapon across her back and pulled her side arm. Two magazine changes later she was out. Another target popped up, she drew her combat knife and ran towards the target. The instructor blew a whistle.

"The exercise is over, but if that one hadn't killed you the next five would have. Well done, Peterman, that was very good." He checked his notes. "You should have fired three shots at the targets. Your training was for three shots to the body, yet you only fired twice."

"I knew I had a good chest-area body shot and saw the target start to fall. I decided not to waste further ammunition or time."

The instructor wrote something on a clipboard, then frowned at her. "The target in the upstairs window appeared before the one on the ground across the street, yet you wasted precious time when you deliberately moved and took the ground target first. Why was that?"

"The upstairs window was closed, and the enemy would have had to either open the window which would have taken time, or fire through it and compromise accuracy, plus he was further away. The target on the ground was the greater threat."

The instructor didn't say anything, just made a note.

****

"What was her hit score?"

"Two shots per target. All targets were hit with at least one chest shot – one hundred percent hit rate. Ninety-two percent hit with two shots."

"Were any civilian targets hit?"

"No. That woman is a machine."

Combat

After a month she left the training camp and joined a front-line regiment.

Here, fighting with regular forces, her leadership skills emerged, adapting quickly to changing situations and retaining a clarity of thought when circumstances became confusing for others. She gained the nickname 'sponge' for her ability to absorb and process huge amounts of information while under pressure, and more importantly, apply it with intelligence.

This, and her ability to innovate in difficult situations, was channelled back to Captain DeSalva, who had no regrets about offering her a place on his team. At first, he had worried about her, she was driven, and he had wondered if her experience with Riedel would cloud her judgement, but it was soon obvious that it didn't.

A year after serving on the front line, and after distinguishing herself during many operations, it was time to leave the regular forces and join DeSalva's unit.

****

The mission had been rated as low risk, but her squad had been ambushed and a vicious firefight had ensued. They were all low on ammunition and her assault rifle was out, the tension of the situation and the adrenaline coursing through her, had made her lose track of the number of shots she had fired. This was a bad mistake, one that she knew she must never make again. The Correlan squad had been small and most had been taken out, but she knew that there were still two unaccounted for in the area.

Her squad leader was dead and two others wounded; the medic was the next in line and ordered her to go forward while he tended to the injuries. She slung her rifle across her back and drew her pistol. She entered a wrecked building and inched her way forward, listening intently for any sign of the Correlan soldiers.

One appeared through a doorway in front of her, he was side on. He turned his head, saw her and turned his body to bring his weapon to bear. She raised her pistol and squeezed the trigger. She saw the flash of her weapon and the cloud of smoke ballooning out from the muzzle and watched as the bullet headed towards the man. He leant back in a reflex action, twisting his head as he tried to avoid the shot.

She saw the around strike just below his right eye and watched as the skin ripped open and the bullet drill into him. Everything seemed to be happening in slow motion, then a moment later the back of his head erupted, with blood and brain matter blasting out onto the wall behind him.

For a moment she froze and stood staring at the body. She walked slowly towards it, her breathing short and her heart in her mouth.

She heard a Correlan voice, then a grenade rolled in through the doorway, it stopped less than a metre from her. These were powerful weapons, and she instinctively knew that she would not be able to get out of its kill radius in time; in a reflex reaction, she dived forward, grabbed it and threw it back. She heard a panicked cry, then the blast of the grenade detonating. There was brief scream then silence. She felt compelled to go and check the body; she told herself that she was checking that the soldier was no longer a threat, but knew that in reality, she needed to see what she had done.

There was a low moaning from around a corner as she approached, she turned to see a young Correlan soldier badly injured but still alive. A fragment had ripped his abdomen open, and his hands were on his stomach as he tried to hold in his intestines. Her mind flashed back to the injured soldiers at Brandon as she performed triage on them. She remembered the anguished looks on their faces as they realised that she could do nothing for them and that they would soon die from their injuries. Some sat stoically accepting their fate, some were gripped with fear and some cried; all were in pain and she had no way of alleviating that. This young soldier had the same look in his eyes.

He turned his head to face her, then raised his hand and pointed to his forehead.

"Please," he whispered.

The image of Davida came to her; she remembered what she did to her friend, and she realised what the young man wanted. She levelled her gun at his head; he closed his eyes and nodded slightly. She shot him, and as she pulled the trigger, she thought she saw a faint smile on his face.

She sat up in bed, the recurring dream wasn't a nightmare, it was her mind replaying her first two kills over and over. There had been many other kills since, but only these two came back to her. She looked at her right hand, the hand that had held the knife that she had thrust into a man's heart. She remembered the details of that encounter but had no dreams about it. She sighed as she thought of what she was doing.

"Less than a year ago, I was a nurse, now look at me," she muttered to herself.

****

DeSalva opened a dossier.

"General Lashay is your first mission. He has a holiday home in the northeast and intelligence has discovered that he will be travelling there with his wife in a couple of weeks. No other family members are expected to be present. Study this file and come up with a plan; it must look like an accident."

He passed the folder to her then looked at her and frowned. "You have killed enemy soldiers in combat, but this will be different, and sometimes collateral damage cannot be avoided."

"I understand, sir," she said, knowing full well that he meant that Lashay's wife, a civilian, may also get killed when she carries out the mission.

"The area where you will be going is fairly remote; we'll book you into a small hotel that we have identified. Your cover will be that you are an amateur wildlife photographer capturing the autumn migration of birds. You will be given all the kit that would be expected, binoculars, cameras, different lenses etc....practice using these, so if you are seen you will appear to be experienced. The cameras will have images preloaded and with the metadata adjusted so the date stamp is correct for the time you are there. Make sure you are familiar with all of those images. You will have Correlan identification papers, but we'll fly you in from a third country to one of the regional north-eastern airports, they have quite lax security and you won't have any problems. You'll be there for a week and you'll fly back out of the same airport."

DeSalva handed her the file. "Any questions?"

"No, sir."

"Dismissed."

Astrid saluted and left. Combat with the ordinary Correlan soldiers was meaningless in the overall war, they were pawns in the game; expendable and easily replaced. Now she felt a buzz of adrenaline as she realised that she could finally start to do serious damage to the enemy's war effort.

Colonel Grover

Present Day, Five Weeks After Astrid's Return from Her Mission to Assassinate Malaya

Astrid was once again sitting in Colonel DeSalva's office. He frowned and looked stern; Astrid knew that this meant he had some bad news.

"As you may already know, we have had some setbacks recently. Several units have been ambushed, the Correlans were ready for us and seemed to know everything about the missions. All of the missions were planned by Colonel Grover's staff." DeSalva took a deep breath, his expression changed to one of barely concealed anger. It took Astrid by surprise; she had never seen him like this before. "And Colonel Grover is missing."

"What!" A flood of cold shot through her veins as the reality of this hit her.

He frowned deeply. "We checked the printer in his office, the log showed that hundreds of documents – all highly sensitive – were printed out the day before he disappeared. Thousands of pieces of tactical and strategic data. If he had saved the files to a data stick this would have flagged up immediately, but the printer in his office is not monitored."

"And you think that he had been passing genuine tactical information to the Correlans to gain their trust and show that he was not a double agent, sir."

"Yes, bits and pieces at first, it seems to have started about two months ago, now this."

"Sir," her voice was anxious. "Did any of our people die?"

"Yes, twelve, all the rest have been taken prisoner."

She visibly shuddered at the thought of treason from a colleague. "I feel sick."

"You are not the only one." DeSalva shuffled some papers on his desk, then pulled out a document relating to Grover's wife. "What did you think of Sabine, his wife?"

"I didn't like her, sir, but more to the point, I didn't trust her. There was just something sly about her, but I could never put my finger on quite what it was, there was nothing specific, but I just got an uneasy feeling whenever I met her.

She was a social climber and avaricious. I noticed that at social events, she would always ingratiate herself to the wives of officers senior to her husband and would pointedly ignore the wives of other ranks."

"Yes, that had been noticed, and over the past couple of months, she has been spending money well beyond the salary of a colonel; she likes expensive things."

"Am I right in thinking that she is the daughter of Correlan dissidents, sir?"

"That is correct. They were royalists and left the country after the fall of the monarchy and became Arralan citizens. She was born here, so was automatically an Arralan citizen and no questions were raised when she married Colonel Grover a couple of years back, apart from the fact that he was significantly older than her, he was actually older than her father."

"And you think that she may have persuaded him to defect, sir."

"Yes. We took an interest after her spending habits were noticed. Her parents were killed in a car crash a year before she married Grover and she always claimed, well, boasted, that she had been left a large inheritance, but when we checked, her parents had nothing. She always paid with cash; no money came out of the bank, so the balance always looked right and tallied with Grover's pay. The question is, where was she getting the money from?" he asked rhetorically.

"Correla, sir."

"Correct, some of the money was traced back to a foreign embassy that acts on Corella's behalf. Spending coincided with the ambushes. No doubt a sort of sick 'thank you'."

DeSalva pulled another document file, took a picture from it and showed it to her. "This diplomat was seen with Sabine several times, and he was photographed giving her a package, it's possible that it was completely innocent, but highly unlikely given the circumstances. He has diplomatic immunity, so we can't take any action against him, but we have increased the level of surveillance on him in light of his recent activities."

Astrid swallowed her anger so she could concentrate and not let her emotions cloud her judgement. "As I recall, sir, Grover was badly injured and given a desk job."

"That's right, he was no longer fit for front line duties and was given the task of liaison between active units and logistic supply. About six months ago, he started talking incessantly about finding a way to end the war. He kept saying that there had to be a simple way and was distressed when he heard about casualties. He had a notebook with the names and family details of all the soldiers under his command that had died in combat. He became very agitated and was ordered to see the army psychiatrist; it was when he didn't show up for his appointment that we knew something had happened." DeSalva picked up the notebook. "He must have accidentally left this behind. In it are a number of thoughts that he had written down that are increasingly desperate and rambling about the length of the war and the number of deaths. The last entry was a one-line sentence – underlined."

He slid Grover's notebook over to Astrid; she gasped as she read the words, 'Would life under Correlan rule be so bad?'

Astrid felt herself becoming angry as she read the words again, but quickly calmed herself.

"Where is Sabine, sir?"

"Sabine is also missing, presumed to be with him."

"They must have contacted her first, sir."

"There is no doubt that they did, we found letters that she had been receiving for months. They purported to be from relatives in Correla, presumably these made their way to her via the same embassy that was passing money to her. They were very well written – presumably by the Correlan intelligence, and they painted a very different picture of the Correla that we know. The letters were very subtle, very convincing and all designed to tug at her heartstrings. There was never a return address, as it was explained in the first letter that she should not attempt to reply as this would draw attention to her."

"This was a clever ploy; the one-sided communication increased her sense of isolation, and although convincing her husband to commit treason was never directly mentioned, it was strongly hinted at, along with a carefully worded promise of money should there be a way to make the war end. We believe that in the time leading up to their disappearance, she was using the embassy to send messages and negotiate with the Correlans."

"Have we any idea where they are, sir?"

"Not specifically, but we have had some intercepts, one message has just come in. There is a remote farmhouse in the southeast and coded radio traffic has referred to 'the assets' having just arrived there." He paused and seemed slightly nervous. "It is vital that the Correlans don't get those papers, you must find them and immediately destroy them; you can't risk bringing them back."

He hesitated and then looked Astrid straight in the eye. "You should know that this is not just a mission to locate the documents and destroy them." He

277

maintained unblinking eye contact. "It is also a mission to kill Grover, as he would still be able to give them critical information. Are you okay with that?"

"Yes, sir," she answered without hesitation.

"Grover knows we will send you, and you can't risk him or Sabine seeing you, so it will be a sniper mission. You'll go alone; there's no time to get you a spotter, obviously you'll need to get close to ensure a hit. You will need to move quickly on this, intelligence suggests that they have been told to stay put for a few days, we don't know why, but what we do know is that we don't have much time. This is urgent, if the Correlans get those documents, it could be all over for us."

"What do I do with Sabine, sir?"

"That is your call, I am not interested in what you decide to do with her, but I know what I would do."

Astrid had already decided what to do with Sabine Grover.

DeSalva handed her a requisition form, some maps and a document file. "The armoury is preparing a weapon for you as we speak. Study the information; helicopter in two hours."

"Yes, sir." Astrid stood, saluted and left the room.

****

She lay motionless on the ground, her rifle beside her, loaded and ready. She trained her binoculars on the farmhouse kitchen windows, as it would be the most likely place to see them. After about an hour, she saw Sabine get a large glass of red wine, then moments later Colonel Grover appeared, he looked tired and drawn. It is one thing to think about treason and another thing to actually do it, and the weight of his decision visibly bore down on him. Sabine said something to him, and he seemed to cheer up a little, but his gloomy expression returned as soon as she left the room.

A few moments later she returned, and he held her by the shoulders and started talking to her. Astrid could see the expression of anguish on his face, and he appeared to be saying over and over, "What have I done, what did you make me do?" She could only see the back of Sabine's head and had no idea what she was saying, only that it seemed to make Grover even more desperate. He said something else to her, then they turned, and Astrid could see Sabine's face.

Sabine's eyes opened wide and she smiled broadly, then clearly said, "But we'll be rich," before turning and leaving to room again.

Astrid moved into position, readied her weapon and flicked off the safety catch, she could see him clearly through the scope. Grover was pacing back and forth, his head down and shaking slightly. Then he abruptly stopped right in front of the window and took a deep breath. She had a clear head shot, and she could also see Sabine had come back into the room and had started talking excitedly to him, but he was ignoring her. He just stared out of the window directly towards where Astrid was laying.

Even though he couldn't see her, he knew she was out there and understood what she had to do; he moved closer to the window and opened it. He closed his eyes, nodded ever so slightly then relaxed his shoulders and smiled, as if a great weight had been lifted from him. Her finger tightened on the trigger.

Through the scope, she saw blood splatter against the wall behind him as he dropped to the ground, dead before he even started to fall. She saw Sabine screaming, with Grover's blood on her face, she was panicking and staring down at him. Astrid put down the weapon, drew her sidearm and ran to the farmhouse. She kicked open the door and saw Sabine bent over Grover's body, sobbing.

"Oh Astrid, thank God it's you; you've got to help me."

Astrid didn't reply, she raised her pistol and shot Sabine twice in the head.

She moved quickly from room to room, and finally she discovered an attaché case, she opened it and found the documents and spread them out over the floor. Outside, there were some fuel cans in the back of the vehicle that Grover and Sabine had used, she opened them and poured the contents over the floors in each room, then emptied the last can of fuel onto the bodies of Grover and Sabine. She stepped outside and raised her sidearm again. A single shot was all it took to ignite the fuel. In seconds, the whole building was ablaze.

She stepped back to watch, then suddenly became perturbed. This had been far too easy, sensing danger she turned to run, but before she could move she felt something thump into her thigh, it was a Correlan tranquiliser dart. It had been a trap.

They could have easily killed her, but the dart meant they wanted her alive. She was mentally prepared for interrogation and knew she would be brutally tortured and that everyone eventually cracked; she would be no exception. But she also knew that they would use powerful psychotropic drugs that would destroy her will, and she would not be able to resist answering any of their questions. The drugs would eventually destroy the neurotransmitters in her brain that controlled conscious movement, this would leave her fully conscious but imprisoned in a body unable to move or speak ever again, but seeing, hearing and feeling everything; she would be utterly helpless as her body was inevitably abused.

It was better that she ended it now by her own hand. She drew her sidearm and tried to raise it to her head, but it suddenly felt very heavy and dropped to the ground. She pulled her combat knife and tried to press it into her wrist, but the dart was working faster than she could react and that too slipped from her grasp. Her head began to swim, and her vision doubled. She fell to the ground just barely aware of her surroundings.

The last thing she saw before falling unconscious was a blurry image of a nervous looking Correlan soldier standing over her. The last thing she felt was a kick to the ribs, and the last thing she heard was him shouting, "We've got her."

Hallenberg

Astrid sat on the floor in a windowless cell; she guessed it was the morning after her capture and she was still a little groggy from the tranquiliser. Handcuffs around her wrists and manacles around her ankles allowed some movement but tied her to the floor. Her ribs hurt from the kick she had received and the swelling on her thigh ached where the dart had struck. No attempt had been made to dress the wound where the dart had been removed; it's barb had torn her skin when it was yanked out and blood had soaked into her combat trousers. Apart from that, she was unharmed.

Major Marek appeared and opened the cell door, he placed a chair in front of her, glared at her, then spat on the floor before turning to leave. An old man dressed in an elaborate uniform appeared and sat in front of her.

"I presume you know who I am." His abrasive voice seemed to carry an air of threat in every word.

"Grand Field Marshal Godin Hallenberg, supreme ruler of the republic, saviour of the nation and protector of the people," she replied, with a slight air of disdain.

"That is my full official title," he said pompously.

"I think it's a bit grandiose. It makes me wonder what is missing in your life."

Hallenberg laughed, then leant forward and sneered. "Do not, for even one-minute, think that you can goad me, woman," he snarled.

She realised that it would be pointless trying to provoke him, despite the ego that accompanied his megalomania.

"I presume that you will threaten me with various forms of torture if I do."

"Oh no, far from it. You are no doubt wondering why you haven't been raped yet."

Astrid was wondering why she had not been mistreated in any way. She had been handled roughly but not ill-treated, and there had been none of the sexual violence that Correlan soldiers were known for, even though this would have been easy for them. She decided to say nothing.

"I gave an order that after your capture, you were not to be harmed in any way. I want you to be unsullied when I personally put a bullet in your head tomorrow and not tainted by my soldiers' animal desires to take turns on you – to satisfy their lust while you suffer a woman's most feared of violations – understandable though their desires are."

He smirked as he noticed the slight shudder run through her as she thought of how she would cope if she was raped. "They could have debased you to the point where you would welcome death, and if you were broken there would be no satisfaction for me."

She had tried not to let her revulsion show, but despite the horrors of war and the constant threat of a painful death, the thought of being helpless while being sexually abused struck at her very core. She steeled herself, stiffening her back, determined not to let any other feelings show. She kept quiet and fixed her gaze on him, her mind racing through escape options and dismissing them one by one as futile.

Hallenberg took out a cigarette, lit it and blew smoke into the air, he had an expression of conceit as he relaxed back into the chair, placing one foot on the opposite knee in the classic figure-of-four display of arrogance. "You know, you shouldn't think too harshly of Grover, he only wanted what we all want."

"And what is that, exactly?"

"An end to the war, obviously."

"He was a traitor, because of him, some of our people died."

"That is true, but we don't now have the information he was going to give us; it was lost in the fire you started. That information would have significantly shortened the war. No matter, it just means the war will last longer. We will win eventually." Hallenberg smirked and jabbed a finger at her. "And more of your people will die because of your actions."

He sat back, smug in the knowledge that he had scored a good point. "In any case, you were the real target all along, the data was just a bonus."

This had been a clever move by Hallenberg, he had correctly guessed that the anger over Grover's treason would mask the real purpose and she had fallen for it.

Hallenberg waved his hand dismissively. "I am not so bothered about Valerian going missing, he was a decidedly average officer who had only risen to his position by virtue of still being alive; I simply assumed that you had killed him."

Astrid nodded; Hallenberg grunted, then sat back in his chair. "However, I was well aware of Brigit Malaya's sexual orientation; she was an outstanding officer, truly gifted. She came to my attention while she was still in officer training. She was fearless and driven; she had a total command of the four 'R's, she was resourceful, she was ruthless, she was relentless, and above all, she was remorseless, she was everything I want in my officers.

"It was obvious to me that she had killed Aster and it would have taken a lot of courage to murder a fellow officer, so she must have had her reasons, and this level of ruthlessness only enhanced her reputation in my eyes. As for the woman he was with, I knew that that there had been leaks by someone, so after she was killed, I planted some fake information; details of an operation that DeSalva would fall for." He leant forward and sneered at Astrid. "He fell for everything else, didn't he!" He sat back; his smug expression returned. "DeSalva took no action, so I knew that the information hadn't been passed on and that she had been the source of the leaks."

He sat looking at her for a few moments, though he seemed be looking through her, deep in thought. "Brigit Malaya was a brilliant officer, and once she was on the army council, I was going to change the rules so that none of the others would be replaced when they died. Eventually she would be the only member, and I would then appoint her as my chosen successor. She was the only one with the abilities to rule Correla and maintain the law and order that I have achieved."

"By law and order, you mean the brutal oppression and murder of anyone who disagrees with you!"

He waved his hand dismissively and tutted. There was another period of silence as he sat thinking. "Kedara was the only other one that came close to her level of cold-blooded efficiency. I encouraged their friendship so that they could learn from each other." He abruptly stopped. "Did you have a hand in his death?"

She shook her head indifferently. "No. He was on my list though; I hadn't found a way to get close to him, but I would have done," she said blithely, then it was her turn to lean forward and sneer. "I was glad when he died, it saved me a job!"

Hallenberg seemed a little shocked, then smiled arrogantly as he understood her desire to try to unsettle him.

"As for Malaya's personal life, I'd known all along that she was a lesbian, and I didn't care. Her eulogy at Davat's funeral was very moving." He scoffed and half-laughed. "Even though I knew it to be a pack of lies. I even knew about her episode with Anna Pradova at Don Bahlia, and I also know that there are many other good people in the army with similar sexual orientations. You see, I don't care who they fuck, so long as it doesn't stop them killing. So after she had been elevated to her rightful place on the army council, I was going to use her as a reason to decriminalise homosexuality in Correla and now, without her example, that is something else that is not going to happen now" He jabbed his finger at her "because of you."

He sat for a moment and let the impact of this sink in, once again self-satisfied in the knowledge of how much it would irritate Astrid. "I'd had my eye on Grover for a while and when I found out about Sabine's weakness, I started feeding her the money. But after you killed Malaya, I had to do something about you. I brought my plans forward and everything fell into place nicely."

He sat looking at her with a conceited smile on his face. "So, whatever the outcome, I would either get you, or the data, or ideally, both. I knew that DeSalva would send you, he's so fucking predictable."

He sat studying her for a while, arrogant in the knowledge that she now realised just how clever his plan had been.

"Why then didn't you take me before I burned the place?"

"You got there quicker than I expected, and I commend you on your swift action. Grover's defection happened sooner than I expected, and my team was not ready. Had you been an hour earlier, the team would not have been in place and would have missed you. And if you were an hour later, I would have both you and the data," he said breezily.

"Grover was a good man; how did you corrupt him?" she said tersely.

"I was always going to get to him through his wife; you probably know about the diplomat and the letters. She didn't write back, but she told the diplomat what she wanted. Oh Sabine, that stupid, greedy little bitch. Grover just wanted peace, she just wanted a big house and lots of money. I gave instructions that she was to be shown pictures of one of the northern chateau's, two thousand acres of land, a private lake with speedboats, she would get luxury cars, horses, a wine cellar, all the usual stately home stuff. I had her told her that she would be given that and have a staff of ten servants – she said she wanted twenty, which I agreed to. I also had her told that she would receive five million dhat a year and all she would have to do was persuade her husband to give me the information I wanted. She said she wanted ten million a year, which I also agreed to."

He took a deep drag on the cigarette and blew smoke into the air again. "She wouldn't have got it though; they'd have both been shot before they even got there." He scowled and sat forward in the chair to emphasise the next point. "I don't like traitors either."

He sat back in his chair and there was a period of silence as they both looked at each other, his eyes full of smug conceit, her eyes full of contempt. He took a final drag of his cigarette, threw the butt into a corner of the cell then slowly and deliberately blew smoke at her. She resisted the urge to cough as she breathed in, or blink as the smoke stung her eyes. He noticed it and smiled.

"As for my final plan, Riedel had a fairly good idea, but Malaya saw to it that you didn't get the information from him. She didn't actually have the authority to order his killing but did so anyway, and her initiative impressed me greatly; I wish all my officers had that same streak in them." He smirked. "I was so pleased when I heard of his death, and the manner of his death; again, it was another streak of brilliance by Malaya." His expression changed to one of contempt and he sneered at Astrid. "I didn't know, or care for that matter, about his family, but to be killed when so close to home, and in a hospital where he was supposed to be getting better; well, that must have hurt them." He sat back, revelling in his cruelty. He couldn't have known about her feelings for Riedel, and she seethed inside but was determined not to let it show.

Astrid steeled herself and looked his straight in the eye. "What is your final plan?" she demanded, not really expecting an answer.

Hallenberg shrugged. "Well, since you are going to die tomorrow, I'll tell you how I am going to eradicate your people, it will give you something to think about during these last few hours of your life; you can take that time to dwell on your failure to stop me."

He looked deep into her eyes and saw the hatred in them, and her discomfort pleased him.

"All your triumphs and victories – I allowed them to happen. All our secret weapons programs that your wonderful intelligence agency discovered – I let them discover. I did that, so you'd think they were so good and that your spies were so clever. And you fell for it, you fell for it over and over again, and you never discovered the one I was really working on. A bioweapon working at the genetic level that will render all Arralan males sterile. I am almost there, but I need an antidote for my own men, that is proving harder, though I suspect that some of the scientists are dragging their feet, some mumbo-jumbo about ethics, but I'm sure I can find ways to motivate them. I have postponed the spring offensive; this will now happen in summer next year. This will give me time to fully develop the weapon and harden all my fighting vehicles against your new anti-tank armaments that you have rather foolishly set so much store by."

Astrid's heart skipped a beat, Hallenberg had no reason to lie. If the Arralan rockets failed to stop the advance, then the war would be lost and Hallenberg would be free to unleash his bioweapon. Cold fear flooded through her as never before, he noticed it and smiled.

"I will introduce the weapon into the water supply, so even males in the womb will be born sterile. It doesn't make women sterile, and in time Arralan females will breed with Correlan males. After three generations, there will be no true Arralan blood left, and the country will be reunited as it was before the split."

"Genocide!" she shouted.

"Yes, genocide, but in a kind way," he said condescendingly. "No industrial scale slaughter, no extermination camps. The Arralan people will just die out naturally."

"The world won't let you."

"Oh, don't be so naïve, do you really think the world gives two fucks about you? You have no oil, and you have no precious metals or mineral deposits. You have nothing, so don't flatter yourself," he said dismissively.

"Then what do you want?" snapped Astrid.

"Your food," Hallenberg snapped back. "Your wheat fields, I need them to feed my soldiers. A reunited country will be able to feed everyone."

"Arralan and Correla have always been separate countries, they've never been united, you know that."

"But the world believes that they were once united, and that all I am doing is reuniting them, which is why they won't help you."

"They believe it because of your lies," she shouted, unable to contain her anger.

Hallenberg stood up and walked out of the cell, then stopped and turned to face her.

"Make the most of the coming hours, they are your last," he said as he left.

Marek returned, took the chair and locked the cell door, again spitting on the floor at her feet as he left.

****

286

Hands grabbed her arms and dragged her up three steps, she was outside on a platform of sorts; the cool air told her that it was early in the morning. She felt the grip of many hands on her arms and legs holding her still as the manacles were released from her wrists and ankles. She had received nothing to eat or drink for over twenty-four hours and was weak and dehydrated. She struggled but realised that she was not strong enough to break free as she was shoved back on to the trunk of a tree. Her arms and legs were pulled back and the shackles attached again.

The bag was pulled off her head and she immediately recognised the surroundings.

"Do you know where you are," came the unmistakeable rasp of Hallenberg's voice. He stepped out in front of her. He was wearing a ceremonial robe covered with strange, almost mediaeval designs.

"Of course, I do; this is the forest of Rek."

This was a clearing in the north-eastern forest that she had seen pictures of. After Hallenberg came to power, he ordered that this place would be the killing ground for all the members of the Correlan royal family. Many hundreds had died here as family trees were scoured for anyone that could claim the throne. There were a couple of guard towers and sentry boxes, but apart from that, it was just a clearing where one large tree had been left. This is what the condemned had been chained to; the gouges in the tree trunk bearing witness to the volume of shots fired. This was the tree that she was now shackled to.

"And you are no doubt aware of this particular site's significance in my country's history."

"This is the place where all the members of the Correlan royal family were murdered."

"I prefer to say that they were eliminated. It was a glorious day when Correla was freed from oppression and the people could live freely."

"Glorious?" she gasped in exasperation. "You tortured them."

"Nobody was tortured," he quipped facetiously.

"You had them lined up to watch as one by one they were tied here and took a bullet to the head. That is torture."

"They had to know the price that they were paying for their reign of tyranny, and the attendant suffering they imposed of the Correlan people."

"One of them was a child, you murdered a child," said Astrid angrily.

Hallenberg scoffed dismissively.

"Princess Alethea was eight years old," she shouted.

Hallenberg sneered. "Look, nobody likes shooting little girls in the head, but it had to be done. She would have grown up and had children, and they would have been able to claim the royal bloodline, even if they were bastards. Then we would have had the pathetic spectacle of the public fawning over some little brat who would grow up believing that just being born in the right bed somehow entitled them to a lifetime of privilege and mass adulation."

The contempt rose in Hallenberg's voice as he spoke. "And what did they do – these royals? Did they lead troops into battle to defend their realm? No. Did they come up with scientific breakthroughs that would benefit their 'subjects'? No. They just absorbed resources and gave nothing back. They sickened me, so I prevented that wretched future scenario."

"By shooting an eight-year-old girl in the head," she said, unable to control her disgust.

"Yes," he snarled. "By shooting an eight-year-old girl in the head, the dynasty of leeches was exterminated."

"You shot her yourself, you are a monster."

Hallenberg seethed. "Remember where you are and what is going to happen to you in a few minutes' time," he said through clenched teeth. "The law – because we do have laws – only allows me one shot and it would be a shame if I were to miss and just wound you. The law then states that you would have to be left here until you died, for however long that might take."

"I am not afraid to die, and I am not afraid of you and your ceremonies, you're pathetic," Astrid spat out the words, contempt in every one.

Hallenberg lashed out, striking her face with the back of his hand. She spat some blood onto the ground then slowly turned to face him.

"Assaulting a prisoner just prior to execution is against the law in Corella. Be careful Hallenberg, you wouldn't want to be arrested for breaking one of your precious laws now, would you?"

"Well, maybe tomorrow you can call a lawyer," he said sarcastically. "Oh no, you won't be able to because you'll be dead."

She watched in silence as the leaders of the Correlan machine took their places in the chairs that were lined up in front of her. The uppermost echelons of politics and military were present, all wearing the same robes as Hallenberg. There was the puppet government, theoretically they were elected politicians chosen by the public, but who were, in reality, simply appointed by Hallenberg.

Next were the twenty men that made up the central planning committee. Then there was the pitiful sight of the five octogenarians of the army council shuffling into the front row, with all the generals from all the branches of the Correlan military sitting behind them. Five hundred of them, all the powerful men in the country were gathered to witness Astrid's execution, some glaring at her, some laughing and pointing. She scanned the faces and recognised several that were on her kill list.

She instinctively tugged at the restraints, but knew it was hopeless and Hallenberg noticed it. He sneered at her. "What is it that you say to your comrades? 'Never give up hope, there is always hope', so where is your hope now?" he jeered.

He turned to face the audience who fell silent immediately. "My friends, we are gathered here today, our ceremonial robes showing that we are all equal in the presence of our enemies, and this is a great day for Correla. The scourge that has taken so many of our dearest friends will soon be herself dead."

He turned and pointed at Astrid, and with this gesture, the ritual had started. Major Marek stepped up holding a box, which he opened and presented to Hallenberg. Hallenberg took an old revolver and one round from the silk lined box. Marek sneered a contemptuous smile at Astrid then stepped down to take his seat. Hallenberg held the gun up so that all could see it.

"In keeping with tradition, this gun is only used for the vilest of our enemies, and as always, only one shot will be fired so as to make the prisoner aware that they are only worth one bullet."

He made a show of loading the weapon, then paced back and forth holding it aloft as if it was a precious religious artefact. A ripple of applause ran through the assembled crowd. He turned to face her, grabbed her chin and pushed her head up. "I say again, where is your hope now?" he sneered as he shoved her head away.

She looked down at the ground, anxiety rising in her. "There has to be hope, there is always hope," she whispered, but she knew her death was only minutes away. Soon the muzzle would be pressed into her forehead and it would be all over. She hung her head as Hallenberg grandstanded before his sycophantic audience.

A movement on the ground caught her eye and a flood of adrenaline surged through her. A red dot was tracking across the platform in front of her. Hallenberg was standing still, next to her, ready to carry out the execution. The red dot stopped at his foot then slowly tracked up his body. He turned to her, his expression a mix of arrogance and triumphalism.

"Lift your head up woman, take it like a soldier," he snarled, and with an arrogant smile on his face, turned to the crowd, looking back and forth to either side to accept their approval.

She looked up at him and smiled. "Goodbye Hallenberg," she said cheerfully.

He looked at her and sneered with incredulity.

"What?" was all he could say before his expression turned to fear as he realised what was about to happen. The red light of the laser sight registered briefly in his sight, as did the muzzle flash. Before he had time to react, a bullet entered his head through his right eye, the exploding charge blowing the back of his head off.

Two mini guns opened up on the crowd, scything through them; they fell like dominos. Sentries jumped out of their boxes to return fire but were blown up in air like burning rag dolls as rockets streaked out from the undergrowth and exploded. The guard towers exploded in balls of flame before the soldiers in them had time to react, as rockets hit these and detonated the ammunition stored there.

Marek had the presence of mind to drop to the ground and pull the body of one of the army council on top of him for protection during the first salvo; there was a brief lull in the shooting, he assumed that weapons were being reloaded and saw his chance. He got up and ran towards the forest to try to hide in the dense bushes, but a minigun operator saw him and trained his weapon. Marek's body disappeared in a red haze as a hail of fragmentation rounds struck.

Arralan Special Forces poured out of the undergrowth, picking off the last of the Correlans as they went. It had taken seconds.

"I'm sorry that we cut it so fine," said the force commander as bolt cutters broke the manacle chains.

"We only received confirmation of your location three hours ago, and to be honest, we didn't think we'd make it in time, but we were unopposed as we flew in. With all the top brass here, no one gave to order to intercept us."

Peace

With Hallenberg, the army council, the central planning committee, and the senior generals all dead, the war was, to all intents and purposes, over. Within days, the remaining senior army staff officers approached Arralan for peace talks, and in a gesture of good faith, unilaterally ordered their troops to cease all combat operations and return to their bases.

In return for ceasing arms production, Correla would get food aid. Farming advisors would be supplied by Arralan and the former arms factories would be refitted to make the agricultural equipment that was sorely lacking, with the intention of returning Correlan farming to the level it was before Hallenberg imposed his dictatorship and put the central planning committee in place. The Correlan troops were retrained in agriculture and given land, and the vast majority welcomed this, sick as they were of the harsh military life and the dreadful standard of living that they and their families had been reduced to.

Some regiments were quickly reorganised into civilian teams to fight the spread of Kudzu, slashing back and burning huge swathes of the plant and returning the land to food production. Many of the former soldiers relishing the job of cutting and burning, so that they could return to their former homes; farms that had been destroyed by Kudzu. Agricultural specialists in Arralan started working with scientists in Correla to find a biological way to control the weed.

Contraception was made freely available with education programs established to teach birth control. This was welcomed by the Correlan woman, weary from the constant demands of childbirth.

There were the three scientists from the bioweapons facility that had been working on the sterility weapon and all confirmed that they had indeed been dragging their feet. Not only did they consider it completely immoral, but they had found that the weapon caused aggressive cancer in women. All documentation and records relating to the weapon were destroyed and the facility razed to the ground. The scientists even offered to allow themselves to have hypnotherapy to make them forget the work they had already done.

****

A little over two weeks after the effective surrender, Astrid received an order late one evening to visit Field Marshal D'Frey. She had never met him before and wondered why he needed to see her now. He was alone in his office, with no members of his staff on duty. She was shocked at his appearance; he looked much older than in the pictures she had seen of him. He was tired and had a desperate sadness in his bloodshot eyes, a far cry from the pictures she had seen of him during the war. Then, he was a confident and intelligent leader when directing troops, his personality making the troops carry out his orders not because they had to, but because they wanted to – regardless of the danger. In social situations, he had been every bit the raconteur, known for his lengthy and hilarious after-dinner speeches that frequently had the audience roaring with laughter. He was inspirational and loved by all under his command. But not anymore, he was a broken man.

He gestured for her to sit, even this seemed an effort. On his desk was a set of Correlan dog tags, he slowly moved them around with his finger. There was silence for half a minute, then she noticed the tears in his eyes.

Shaking and hesitant, he finally spoke. "My wife died two weeks ago."

"I'm sorry to hear that, sir."

He nodded appreciatively and sighed. "It was unexpected."

He tried to regain his composure but failed and made no effort to hide his tears as he stared into the distance, deep in thought. There was another long silence while he breathed deeply to try to regain his self-control. He dabbed his eyes with a tissue and swallowed hard before looking at Astrid. "Her maiden name was Riedel."

She immediately realised the significance of the statement.

"The man whose murder set you on your path, was my son, my only child. No one, not even DeSalva knew that." Again a long pause while he breathed deeply. "There were complications during the birth, and she was not able to conceive anymore." He slid the dog tags to her, they were Malaya's. "My only regret is that I was not able to get these for myself. You can keep them as a memento of a job well done."

"Thank you, sir." Astrid sat for a moment unsure of what to say, he was clearly deeply distressed, and she decided not to enquire about his family.

"What will happen to the assassin, sir, will he be released from prison now?"

"No, that is not possible." D'Frey sighed. "I went into his cell last week and killed him with my bare hands, the post-mortem will record his death as a heart attack."

She felt a twinge of guilt in the knowledge that the assassin had died in this manner – illegally – and only days away from being freed. Grief had driven him to do this, but for so long she had wanted to do the same.

D'Frey nodded to the door, it was time for her to leave. She stood, saluted and left. As she got to the door he spoke again. "The war is over, and the part you played was exemplary; now go and live your life, find someone to love and cherish every second with them. For when they are taken from you..."

His voice trailed off as emotion got to him. He swallowed hard and regained his composure.

"...When they are taken from you, the pain is unbearable."

She saluted again and left the room.

The next morning, he was found dead in his office, an open picture frame with a photo of his wife holding his baby son was on his desk. His service pistol was on the floor beside him.

****

Astrid sat in a coffee house in the centre of a Correlan town; a woman sat down opposite her, she stared at Astrid, her face stern, her eyebrows set in a permanent frown.

"Can I help you?" said Astrid, guessing what was coming next.

"I know who you are. You killed my son," said the woman. "No civilians were supposed to know about you, but my cousin was his commanding officer, he told me about you and showed me your picture."

"I'm sorry." Astrid braced herself for abuse.

"Don't be," the woman said flatly, Astrid was shocked, it was not the reaction she expected. "You were doing your duty and my son was doing his."

Her face softened as she remembered her child, then turned to sadness. She sighed, and her shoulders dropped a little. "He only wanted to be a dentist, it was all he ever wanted to be, not a footballer or a fighter pilot – just a dentist. When he was drafted into the army, I wrote to Hallenberg to at least let him be an army dentist."

She paused and sighed again. "I got a message back from his aide, Marek, saying that I should not have written to Hallenberg, it basically said how dare I presume to influence the great leader and my son would now be sent to the front…" her voice trailed off.

The two women sat in silence for a few moments, then, to Astrid's astonishment, the woman reached over and took her hand, the hand that she must have known held the combat knife that killed her son. She squeezed gently as if in doing so she would somehow release herself from pain of the loss of her child.

"I don't hate you, I hate what you did, but I hated Hallenberg more. I hated him with every fibre of my being. He was the reason my son died, you were just the mechanism. I just wanted you to know that."

Tears welled in Astrid's eyes partly through the sadness she had caused and partly in admiration of the strength of this woman's courage. The woman got up and left without looking back.

****

A reconciliation commission was set up to heal old wounds from the war. There were to be no show trials, no grandstanding or reparations. Both sides had open access to war reports, as it had been recognised that both sides had broken rules, and an unprecedented level of contrition spread across military and political leaders on both sides. Leaders of the Northern Alliance were invited to take part in the commission, and after agreeing to give up their weapons, were granted semi-autonomous status, funding for their children's education, health care and recognition of their unique ethnicity.

Astrid had open access to the Correlan military archive and spent many hours there. One short report detailed the disappearance of General Lothar Valerian and his Lieutenant. The document correctly associated this with the ordering of a troop transport with a staff sergeant and fifteen armed recruits to be sent from Training Camp North to base number one at Kandalan and surmised that Valerian and his aide had then travelled in the vehicle. He was still the commander of Training Camp North and was free to use the recruits for training purposes, as he saw fit. The report made a special note of the fact that the recruits were armed, despite having not completed their firearms training.

If he had used regular troops, he would have had to deal with army administration and there would have been too many questions asked. It was further surmised that this was why the general was going to use trainees in her apprehension. No details of where the truck was heading were logged and as a result the occupants of the truck had not been found. The report also noted that these unusual steps were due to Valerian's desire to bring her in and not have to share any glory – military code for a maverick.

She immediately contacted army headquarters to request a team to be directed to visit her uncle's farm and recover whatever remains they could find.

Astrid was particularly interested in the reports around her assassination of Malaya. There was one particular folder marked 'Top secret. Eyes of GFM Hallenberg and army council only'. This was a paper folder, which had not been stored electronically. Most of the files it contained told her that they had guessed most of the details correctly, then she came across the report from the helicopter mission that flew over her as she passed through the Phaal region. It was unusually detailed and chronicled the chase of the staff car through the flat lands into the mountain region, how the driver seemed skilled and refused to stop even after being fired upon.

It had been assumed by the pilots that this meant she was at the wheel such was the urgency of the driving. Astrid began to get an uneasy feeling as she read about the chase entering the rise that led to the mountain tunnels and the firing of a missile that was accidentally armed and the resulting explosion near the car that sent it off the road. The report detailed how the driver survived the crash and although badly injured, managed to get out of the vehicle only to the collapse in a stream of fuel that ignited and burned her to death.

Astrid cried out in anguish and slumped forward on the desk, sobbing. What had the war done to her? She had seen people die in fires, some from napalm strikes that she had called in to save her own fighters from being killed; it was the worst way to die. But that was war and those had been enemy soldiers; this girl was a civilian that had done nothing to her and had paid a horrific price.

The next day she resigned from the army and then applied for and was given the position of special envoy. Her command of the Correlan language and knowledge of the country, its regions and customs made her the perfect candidate, and she was determined to bring about a lasting peace. She was respected by the Correlan military, even by those who knew they were certain to have been on her kill list and as such was able to move freely throughout the country.

Censorship during the war meant that few civilians knew who she was or what role she had played. Her role now was to rebuild Correla; co-ordinating reconstruction, with Arralan technicians training demobilised soldiers in skills needed for the rebuilding and modernisation of the cities that had seen no development for decades. Many army officers became managers in construction companies, and in time, some senior officers even set up their own businesses – private firms; a concept that was unthinkable only six months previously.

Astrid had been instrumental in securing finance for most of these nascent companies and had close contact with the owners. One of them, a former one-star General, took her to one side one day.

"You know, I joined the army to serve my country and my people. The people are the country, but under Hallenberg, the people were an inconvenience, we turned our guns on them, we put them in prison. How is that serving the people? Hallenberg gave the orders and we had all sworn an oath to carry out his orders, but we despised him. Many of us felt that way; it is good that he is gone."

So much was changing in Correla and changing fast. She was determined to keep up the momentum.

****

Astrid sat opposite Commissioner Ellet in his office at the Correlan police headquarters. He had just finished reading her statement on the deaths in Balun. He took off his glasses and fixed his gaze on her.

"You freely admit to murdering these civilians. Yes?"

"Yes."

"In court, how will you plead to these crimes?"

"Guilty as charged."

Ellet frowned. "As you will have confessed, you won't be executed, but the judge will have no other choice than to sentence you to life in prison without the possibility of parole, no other sentence is allowed for murder. And in confessing, under Correlan law, you forgo your right to an appeal. Do you fully understand the implications of that?"

"I understand."

The commissioner sat back in his chair and thought for a few moments. "You know, I don't think Hallenberg wanted the war to end. He didn't see the young men on the street in wheelchairs, or blind, or with empty sleeves, or hideously burned and disfigured. He once told me that the more that died, the better, for it reflected 'the greatness of the struggle' – apparently. You would have seen the same sort of thing in Arralan, of that I have no doubt."

Astrid was confused by his statement, though it was no secret that there was a great deal of animosity in Correla between the civilian police and the military. "Our hospitals are full of young men and women," she replied.

"And with grieving families at their bedside."

She nodded.

"You are a civilian now, aren't you?"

Again, she nodded.

"I understand that you have been directly helping with the rebuilding of Correla. I have spoken to some former senior military figures, who all say that you display no triumphalism. They say that you are the only person who can bring about lasting change and that you are working tirelessly to achieve it. They say that you are pushing hard to get funds released to aid the families of former Correlan soldiers."

This was true, but she didn't acknowledge it, she felt that in doing so she would be self-serving. "There has to be peace, both sides have lost far too much."

He leant forward. "So, tell me, how can you do that if you are rotting in a stinking, fetid cell in one of our wretched prisons for the rest of your life, a life span that would be considerably curtailed?"

"I committed crimes. I knowingly and deliberately killed civilians. I have to pay for that."

Ellet picked up the statement and read some passages again. He sat back in his chair and thought for a while. "I joined the police force to do what is right for my people; that is what I have done for all of my career and that is what I intend to keep doing. A judge is bound by the law, and a legal system that is inflexible. As the police commissioner, I am not so restrained."

He put his glasses on and read a paragraph then looked back at her. "As for the Phaal girl, that was not your doing."

Astrid frowned. "I knowingly put her in harm's way. I am responsible for her death."

"It wasn't you that fired the missile," he said, dismissively.

He read the account of Asher and the doorman.

297

"I'd say that Asher's death was self-defence, and the doorman…well, he could have stopped you getting away, so that could be construed as self-defence, but it seems more like an accident to me."

Astrid frowned, she knew what she had done, Lenny, Ron and Asher were self-defence in her mind, but the doorman was no accident, so why was he making excuses for her actions. Ellet acknowledged her concern at his flimsy reasoning.

"The other two," he said firmly and with a hint of disgust. "These two were contemptable scum – low life – and were indeed informers, but never gave us any meaningful information, no big fish for us to get our hooks into, no major crimes were solved or indeed prevented. It was just title-tattle, the kind of information we could have easily got through other means. But for some reason, the police chief in Balun had faith in them, he was convinced that they were always about to give us some vital information. He has recently been removed from office on corruption charges."

Ellet frowned deeply. "Lenny and Ron were the main suspects in the deaths of three other girls; deaths by heroin overdose, just like the poor girl you saw, but they were never charged. It appears now that the police chief destroyed evidence that confirmed their involvement and suppressed any further investigation. There is the obvious suspicion that these two were paying him, but we have no proof of that…yet."

Astrid recalled the old house in Balun. "I heard Ron warn Lenny that he had given the girl too much; his exact words were: 'I think you've OD'd her, it's just like you did to the others'."

Ellet smiled. "Well, that's as good as a confession in my eyes, but the question is, did these two deserve to die? The answer is yes. Should they have died by your hand? The answer is most definitely no. They should have swung from the end of a rope in a prison courtyard."

He leant forward again. "I appreciate your honesty, and you are obviously a woman of great courage and integrity to come here and confess to me in such a candid way, knowing what the outcome would be, but I have to do what is right for my people, and what is right is for you to continue to help restructure Correla."

He held up her statement. "This is hand written, are there any copies?"

"No," she replied, then watched, astonished, as Ellet dropped the sheaf of paper into a high security shredder, its mechanism grinding the paper into dust, impossible to reconstruct.

"There will be no charges; your conscience will be your prison."

"Thank you," said Astrid as she turned and left.

She knew he was right, and of all the killings she had committed, she would bear the guilt of these murders for the rest of her life.

****

One evening, at the ambassador's house in Correla, Astrid met and was stricken with a colonel in the Correlan air force, a fighter pilot in the newly reformed air force that she had helped restructure. They met subsequently, both through their work and a few times socially. They quickly began a relationship, meeting up as often as their work schedules would allow. The lovemaking was always passionate, often intense, frequently torrid and sometimes bordering on animalistic. Both admitted that they simply could not contain their desires. But after a few months, despite finding the piece of her life that had been missing for so long, Astrid grew restless. She grew tired of the infrequent liaisons, snatched weekends or quick one-night stands at hotels. This had to change.

As they sat one evening in their favourite restaurant, the colonel noticed that Astrid hadn't eaten anything.

"Are you going to push that food around your plate all night or are you going to eat it?"

"I'm not really hungry," Astrid said, putting down the cutlery.

"And you are avoiding eye contact with me, if you have something to say, then say it."

"I do have something to say."

The colonel stiffened and frowned. "Out with it then."

Astrid looked up and this time made eye contact.

"These past months since I met you have been the best of my life—"

"I sense a 'but'," the colonel interrupted.

Astrid took a deep breath. "Yes, there is a 'but'," she said nervously, her voice tremulous. She went to start speaking but fumbled for words as emotion froze her brain; though this time it was genuine, unlike the faking she had done with Malaya. The colonel's face grew stony and stern, the frown deepened.

Astrid had never seen the colonel like this before and was nervous. Finally, she sighed and reached down into her pocket.

"We can't go on meeting like this – oh God, that's so corny, isn't it?" She shook her head slightly at her use of such a hideous cliché; she was far more eloquent than that, but anxiety was getting the better of her.

"What I want to say and what I am failing miserably at, is that…Well, it's just that I want, no, I need, more, I need so much more. So, will…" She held out her shaking hand and opened it. In her palm was a small box about thirty millimetres square. She opened it to reveal a gold ring with a single diamond.

"Colonel Tzarev, will you marry me?"

The colonel opened her eyes wide and her jaw dropped open in disbelief. Suddenly her expression changed, the cold stare replaced by the vivacious, playful eyes that Astrid found so alluring.

"Yes," she said in a half whisper. She sat stunned and for a few seconds forgetting to blink. "Ask me again, so I know I'm not dreaming."

Astrid smiled, she had desperately feared rejection, but now her tension evaporated.

"Colonel Lena Tzarev, will you do me the honour of marring me?" she said confidently.

Lena said nothing, she just held out her hand. Astrid slipped the ring on her finger and Lena sat looking at it. "It's beautiful, but why were you so nervous, you must have known I'd say yes."

"I know, I know," said Astrid, suddenly feeling a little foolish for worrying so much. "You are the most beautiful thing in my life, and the best thing that has ever happened to me. I want you as my wife and I want to hold you forever." I can't find the words to express how much I love you.

Nervous tension was scrambling her brain and letting her emotions take control. Feelings that she had suppressed for so many years were finally released, and a hint of desperation crept into her voice.

"You might have said no, and I don't know what I would have done, I can't imagine life without you. I love you so much, I fell in love with you and I am still falling, I'll never hit the bottom, I never want it to end. I love…"

Lena leant forward and put her finger on Astrid's lips. "Shush," she said gently. "I feel exactly the same way. But you're babbling now and welling up, you'll smudge your makeup if you start crying."

Astrid smiled, she was glad that Lena had stopped her because she was about to cry. They held hands across the table for a few moments.

Lena squeezed Astrid's hand tightly. "You know, I never believed in love at first sight until I met you. I love you with all my heart and you have no idea how much it means to me that you have asked me to marry you."

"You are everything to me, you are my world now," said Astrid, her voice disappearing into a whisper as emotion caught her throat. She fought back the tears that were welling up again. "Why do I want to cry when I am just so happy?"

Lena thought about Astrid's words for a few moments then stood up and banged a spoon on the table to get the attention of everyone in the restaurant. The general hubbub died down and everyone turned to face the two of them. Lena pointed to Astrid. "This is the woman I love."

She gestured to Astrid to stand up.

"Oh God," Astrid whispered to herself as she stood up, suddenly feeling very self-conscious and very well aware that she was blushing.

"This wonderful woman has just asked me to marry her and I have said yes. I will spend the rest of my life with her."

Somebody at the back started clapping, then others joined in, someone whistled in approval. Lena put her arms around Astrid and kissed her on the lips. The applause got louder, and a few people cheered. After it died down, Lena thanked everyone and they both sat down and spent a few moments looking deep into each other's eyes. The maître d appeared with a bottle of champagne.

"The meal is on the house along with this bottle of champagne. The manager likes to do this for any couple that announce their intent to marry in his restaurant. He has also asked me to say that should you need catering services for your wedding, our staff are highly experienced, and our rates are very competitive."

Astrid smiled to herself, the champagne was clearly not the best on the wine list, but it was a great sales pitch. Free enterprise had returned to Correla.

She looked at Lena for what seemed an age, she was radiant, beautiful, her every move full of grace; incongruous as this was to her role as a fighter pilot. Time seemed to slow down, and she relished every second of it. She felt a tug on her arm that brought her back to the world and turned to see a jolly faced, rather large lady, easily in her seventies and missing all her front teeth.

"Back in the day love, I'd have married you– not that they'd have allowed it though, we had to keep quiet about that sort of thing back then. I married this daft old sod instead." She nodded to an old man asleep at the table, arms crossed with his head down, snoring softly. She reached over and put her finger under his chin, gently closing his mouth to shut him up. "I do love him, but I fancied a little bit tonight and he isn't going to be any good to me now, is he? So why don't us girls go back to your place and have a threesome?"

Lena and Astrid sat, mouths open in amused shock. Then the old woman laughed and slapped Astrid gently with the back of her hand.

"Only joking love, but why don't you two go home and give each other a good old seeing to. You know you want to I can see it in your eyes."

Lena looked at Astrid. "That's a bloody good idea, shall we?"

As they left the restaurant, a ripple of applause followed them, and aware that they were being watched by everyone, Lena stroked Astrid's bottom. A cheer went up, and again, someone whistled.

"You know your panties are coming off as soon as we're home," whispered Astrid.

"Difficult," said Lena.

"Why?"

"I'm not wearing any."

****

Shortly after they married, Lena resigned her commission and took a job as a flight instructor with a civilian airline. Tourism was burgeoning, and the airlines had a desperate need for pilots; Lena found she had a talent for teaching. Astrid still had her position as an envoy for the Arralan government but reduced the number of hours she worked. They bought a house not far from the former Kandalan military complex; the bulk of the site having been redeveloped for civilian use. The air wing at the base had also been decommissioned but the runway had been retained and this part of the former base had been rebuilt into a major civilian airport and was where the airline that Lena worked for was based.

After a few years, they both realised that they needed something else and adopted two orphaned girls, one from Correla and one from Arralan. This family unit had all the usual ups and downs, but one day a nervous trainee pilot panicked during a landing and crashed. Both the pilot and the instructor survived, but the trainee had both legs broken, and Lena suffered head injuries. She was in a coma for three weeks, Astrid never left her side and was holding her hand the day she came around.

At first, she seemed to have made a full recovery, but a week later, she blacked out for a couple of seconds. It happened a few more times and showed that the damage to her brain was enough for her pilot's licence to be withdrawn and although she was sad that she could never pilot an aircraft again, she knew it was for the best.

Both the girls met boys and eventually both got married and started families. Watching the children grow was the greatest joy of Astrid's life and gave her a whole new perspective. More than ever now she was determined to find a way to prevent another war. Trade between the two countries had been flowing ever more freely and there was a growing sense on both sides that this should be made formal. She had been the first to officially mention unification and was promoted to the role of senior Arralan negotiator in talks. The discussions were deliberately slow; no one wanted a rushed settlement. Everyone wanted the devils in the details to be properly dealt with. But as the talks progressed, Astrid noticed that Lena's health was deteriorating. Lena died of a stroke at the age of sixty-one.

Astrid was bereft and despite all the efforts and support of her daughters, she was inconsolable. The unification committee agreed unanimously for an adjournment until such time as she could return, but she never did. She died in her sleep four months later, the doctors could find no medical reason. Her daughters said that she simply died of a broken heart.

Eighteen months later the countries were formally united and became one. What could never have been achieved in war had been achieved in peace.

Two years later, and after a unanimous vote in the unified senate, a statue to Astrid was erected on the old border.